MUST LOVE

Famine

A SISTERS OF THE APOCALYPSE NOVEL

SHELLY CHALMERS

www.scchalmers.com   www.shellychalmers.com

Cover design by Paper & Sage Designs

ISBN 978-1-7750206-4-6

For all the dreamers: dream big, fight hard, and never lose hope. I believe in you. When we follow our dreams, we create the magic in this world.

For Matt and our girls. You mean the world to me. Lots of love!

ACKNOWLEDGMENTS

First, thank you to all of you who read *Must Love Plague*, and generously wrote reviews and / or told me how much you enjoyed the read. These books are written for you, and knowing they've found their audience is incredible.

Thank you as always to my 2014 Dreamweaver sisters, and all the things I've learned from you before and since book one. You continue to amaze and educate me, and I am honored to be one of you.

A big thanks to my editor, Tera Cuskaden, for your help polishing this book to a shine and for your kind words. And to Christa Holland with Paper & Sage Design for the beautiful cover – even if it did take a bit to find just the right pig. ☺

Thank you to my critique partner, Shelly Alexander, for always forcing me to do better, and for your continued patience. You're probably due sainthood soon.

Thank you to my family and friends, who bought and read my first book, and have asked about this book. I couldn't be me without you, and I am touched and honored with your support.

Neelam, thank you for being my best friend, and for always being there for me, especially when I most need you. You'll always be my first reader, my first fan, and a big reason why I never gave up. I can't wait to spoil Little Peanut as much as you've spoiled my girls.

Thank you especially to my husband and my girls, for all your patience and support. I hope someday I can encourage you to follow your dreams as you've allowed me to follow mine.

Shelly Chalmers

CHAPTER 1

Ginny Lack's life could be described as a really bad reality show. Tomorrow's episode would be titled *Marrying the Man of Her Parents' Dreams*. Which was much less scary then the second episode: *Don't Screw Up and End the World*. Because right about now, she was balancing on the tightrope of insanity, keeping secrets from everyone, and there'd be no one willing to catch her if she fell.

Which was why, instead of getting a manicure or something relaxing the night before her wedding, she was jogging across the gravel of her parents' backyard as subtly as one could while carrying a two-foot stepladder. The wind rustling through the autumn leaves and plastic wedding bells strewn around the yard in no way concealed the crunch of her footsteps from the back door of her parents' place to the guesthouse.

"I don't see how this is necessary." Roger the grasshopper communicated telepathically from her hair, his back-alley Cockney accent rattled and high-pitched. The little green guy clutched several strands and held on

1

for dear life because of the wind and said running. It was a bit more of a lope at this point.

Her slipper came loose and skidded off. No time to go back. She might be spotted. That new yard light Dad had installed was far too bright. *Frosting!*

With the amount of sins she'd racked up all her life, swearing had to go, and the pseudo-swear almost had as much bite as the real thing.

But not nearly as much bite as the gravel on her bare feet. Of course, she couldn't have been born into one of the other horsemen clans, one that didn't shrivel every blade of grass within shouting distance. Nope, she'd been born into the Famine clan, who made weed killer look plant-friendly. Because sneaking across a soft and plushy lawn would have been waaayyy too easy.

She grit her teeth and loped on, the light of the guesthouse a warm beacon.

Yes, she was getting hitched tomorrow, and this time she'd get it right. That whole messing-everything-up phase? Done with. Ruining this marriage like she had her first? Not going to happen. Hopefully. As soon as she got through tomorrow's ceremony. And married a man she'd never actually met.

Oh dear lord, she was starting to hyperventilate again. Cue the boob sweat and flashy lights before her eyes. She leaned on the ladder a moment, wheezing.

"You humans. So overdramatic about the whole sex-thing," Roger suggested unhelpfully. Thank gods she was the only one who could hear him. *"Let's go back to your room. Get some rest. See the bloke tomorrow. He's cute? Marry him, shag, it's all good. You have more important things to worry about."* He—or rather it—was another problem. Her symbolic horse, and a sign she was really becoming the horsewoman of Famine.

Long story.

One she couldn't focus on at the moment if she didn't

want to be seen.

Back to running across the extra-sharp gravel. And hopefully not passing out. She squeezed the stepladder and considered the bright windows, trying to keep the crunch of her footsteps to a minimum.

Front window would be too obvious. She'd try the kitchen window and see if she could get a peek, just one tiny peek, of her fiancé. Who, like her, had agreed to the marriage sight-unseen. Well, kind of not. There had been photos in the dossier, but because this time she was determined to let her brain be in charge rather than her foolish heart, she'd made Mom throw his out. Besides, originally, they were supposed to have gotten to know each other before the wedding. But then the League of Extraordinary Assholes had tried to take over Beckwell in their bid to end the world and no one had been able to travel in or out of the town limits.

Then a magical plague had crashed her bachelorette party earlier tonight. It'd been a rough week. Suddenly, it was too late to back out of the wedding. The whole romance of the arranged-marriage thing dried up the minute she'd watched her best friend, Piper, and the man of Piper's dreams valiantly battle for their love and lives before pledging their hearts to each other.

While she was off to marry a stranger. *Voluntarily.*

Sometimes, it was like she had the intellect of a half-baked muffin under her unruly red curls.

She slowed her step for a sneakier, quieter walk around the side of the guesthouse. Hopefully the windows weren't open so her fiancé and his family didn't hear her panting from the run.

Oh yeah. That was the trouble with this side of the house. Some idiot had planted rose bushes all along the side, and by some miracle, her family's combined Famine powers hadn't killed them. Not these vindictive things. They didn't bloom, but boy were they efficient in thorn production.

Ginny swallowed a sigh and opened her step stool. Ugh. There was no way to avoid all those thorns. Still, braving a few scratches was a small price if it meant she caught a glimpse of her husband-to-be. The lights were still on in the guesthouse, so he must still be awake too, right? Yeah, okay, she could have just knocked on the door like a normal person, but the whole magical plague thing had taken all intelligible conversation right out of her. Tonight's plague drama and general grossness had ruined any chance of charm. Better to see if she could sneak a peek.

All the screw-ups in the past twenty-eight years had led to this moment. Modern women in this society didn't let their parents choose their husbands. But the way she seemed to choose men? Better anyone *but* her. She'd tried to choose her new Famine partner so objectively, she'd even refused to look at his photo or name, in case it biased her.

So what was so wrong with him that he'd agreed to an arranged marriage?

The stepladder and the rose bushes did not make friends. In fact, the rose bushes seemed determined to knock over and possibly devour the ladder as she stuffed it in among the plants, the faint light glowing from the kitchen window still well above her head. Five feet eleven came in handy—not that she usually snooped through windows—but this wasn't one of those times.

The ladder roughly propped in the rose bushes, Ginny eyed the dimly lit climb, then sucked in a breath and stepped on. The little ladder wobbled, thorns clawed at her legs, and she grabbed at the guesthouse wall for support. Up one step. Two. *Cupcakes!* Even on the second step, her nose was barely above the bottom of the sill. She'd have to climb to the top step—which wasn't safe on level ground, let alone when the ladder was throwing down with rose bushes.

Soft footsteps crunched in the gravel.

Ginny froze.

The footsteps had been pretty quiet. Inhumanly quiet. She didn't feel her brother's characteristic chill, yet reached out to him telepathically anyway. *"This one's for us, Thomas. Leave me alone right now."* He had a tendency to materialize at the most inconvenient times.

She blew out a shaky breath, braced herself on the house, and climbed up onto the top step. The ladder trembled, but held. Her plan was simple. Woo her husband. Get him to help her learn about her Famine abilities. And absolutely, under no circumstance, get tripped up by love. She needed to gain her abilities and help save the world. Love couldn't get in the way of that.

Now, if she could just get a peek at him...

More soft footsteps, too quiet for a normal person. But not too quiet for a ghost.

"Not now, Thomas," she said telepathically again.

"Um, Ginny..." the grasshopper tried, the politest he'd been yet.

"Please, bug—" she communicated back.

"It's Roger."

Sugarplums. She clenched her teeth. *"Please, Roger. Some horse of the apocalypse you are. You have to ride ME. I will deal with the whole becoming Famine weirdness later. Right now, I just want to see what my fiancé looks like and would appreciate one minute without anyone asking any questions, offering any commentary, or otherwise presuming to know what I want. Please."*

The insect settled down in her hair with a "humph."

Ginny peered into the window.

The guesthouse was an open floor plan, with the kitchen connecting into the modest living room. A lamp burned bright in the corner.

An older man stood near the far window wearing a

navy sports coat over his broad shoulders and cravat—seriously, a *cravat?* Ginny flushed at the feel of her yoga pants and tank top but focused back on the gentleman. Cravat-man stood near the sideboard pouring amber liquid over ice in three tumblers. His sun-bronzed skin highlighted the silver in his blond hair, and, squinting, she could just make out the faint creases around his eyes. Nope, he was too old. He wasn't her groom. Probably the father.

Everything about him said just how much higher his family stood in the Famine clan ranks, which meant they should have had more paranormal ability, too.

Ginny bit her lip. Surely that meant her fiancé would understand how it felt, growing up with all that pressure like she had. He could be the ally she was hoping for. The one who could help her gain and control the rest of her abilities.

Of course, that didn't mean he'd take it well if she confessed her ability to assess a person's character through touch and the associated taste they evoked. Telling anyone you tasted people and that everyone had a distinct flavor just sounded wrong.

Cravat-man said something as he carried two drinks back toward the sofa and his companion, but Ginny couldn't hear the words. Probably something very cultured in that British voice. He handed one of the drinks to the woman who had her back to Ginny. Also blonde, though more of a washed-out ash blonde. Pearls, dressed in something pale green and probably expensive.

Holy cupcakes. These people could have been James Bond's parents. If, you know, their tragic dying hadn't turned him into, well, James Bond. They were so. Darned. Perfect. Could she possibly become part of this family?

The grasshopper stood and tugged on a few of her hairs, then circled the top of her head. Those little feet in her damp hair gave her the heebie-jeebies. Still, it kept its mouth shut. Which, from the near nonstop litany of observations, droll repartee, and general criticism of everything since the moment she'd met the thing four hours and thirty-three minutes ago, was something of a miracle.

The father took a seat beside the mother.

Then someone interesting stepped into the picture.

Ginny's breath shuddered, and she leaned closer, the ladder creaking.

Almost as tall as the father. Fairly broad across the shoulders. Blond, too, though slightly less tanned—that was good, less chance of skin cancer and all. His jaw was strong, and he said something undoubtedly witty as he crossed the room, his lips twisting slightly in an almost-smile before he reached the sideboard and his drink. He threw that one back, and then the boy poured himself another.

Er, not boy. Man. Quite possibly her fiancé.

Ginny's knees and feet hurt from standing on the narrow stepladder, and she shifted slightly. The ladder rocked. She froze, hands braced against the house again.

The faintest sound of disturbed gravel, so light, maybe she'd imagined it.

She searched the window again for a glimpse at the boy-man.

He wore a crisp pullover suitable for afternoon polo and stood chatting with his parents, one hand casually in his pocket while he held the drink with the other. He could have been at some event with the British Royals.

He was good-looking. Very handsome. Just...quite possibly not old enough to legally drink in some countries. Twenty maybe. Perhaps a few years older if he was cursed with one of those baby faces.

Ginny made a face, and lifted her foot to ease the ache in her right knee. That made her practically a cradle—

The stepladder lunged left.

The roses and the ground gave out from under her. The ladder toppled.

Oh frost—

She didn't have time to complete the almost-swear. Ginny went down in a messy tangle of yoga pants, stepladder, and rose bush.

Someone caught her before she hit the ground.

She bit back a muffled scream.

Someone muscular and tall, who triggered her ability. The mouth-watering taste of dark chocolate, toasted coconut, and just a kiss of sea salt burst on her tongue.

Someone who most definitely was not her dead brother Thomas.

Someone who had witnessed her spying on her fiancé's family.

Oh, *cupcake*. If that was James Bond's family inside, looked like she'd just found 007 himself.

Right about now, she probably shouldn't wish she'd just been captured by a homicidal stalker. Hoping someone else had planned to spy through the windows and she'd just gotten there first was not what she should have wanted. Then again, she'd never wanted what she was supposed to.

He let her down slowly, and her body slid against his, evidence that he might trigger the taste of chocolate, but he'd clearly never imbibed in his life. Nope, not in the past two lives. He was lean, rock-hard muscle. Broad in the shoulders, narrow in the waist.

Her toes found the gravel. He still stood at least four inches taller than her, maybe more since anything more than two seemed like quite a bit. She patted his forearms in some bemusement, muscle and vein twitching beneath her touch, the skin lightly haired.

She couldn't find her tongue. Really didn't want to

look up and find his face. Because if he wasn't as attractive as the rest of him, well, that would be disappointing. If he was as attractive as the rest of him…far better to dissolve in a pile of shame into the gravel.

"You all right?" he said, his voice deep. And, *holy gingerbread*, with an accent like that, it was clear why James Bond always got the girl. Or at least into her panties.

Besides mortified beyond belief? "I'm fine." Because that's the kind of thing you're supposed to say. "Thank you for saving me." Good manners were a must for any daughter of Famine. At least, Mom always said so.

"Do you always peer through windows at night?"

Only when I'm about to marry the stranger inside. "No. This, uh, this is a first for me." She tried to sound breezy and humorous, but instead she probably sounded more like a strangled duck.

"Um hmm." There was an edge of amusement tickling the sound. "Likely to become a habit, do you think?"

"No. I, uh, think I'm cured of it. Especially when rosebushes are involved."

His chuckle wrapped around her in the darkness, caressed her in places it had no business being, and made her want to make him laugh again.

She hadn't felt that way in…she didn't know when. If ever. Even her first husband had never made her ache so much that she wanted an excuse to press herself against him, feel the chuckle ripple through his body and through her.

And so, she made the mistake of looking. At a narrow face with killer bone structure evident even in the dim light, the shadows and his stubble further highlighting the sharpness of his cheekbones, a lean nose, and intense eyes.

Nope. Not a disappointment. That face perfectly matched the super-body. If he hadn't acted or modeled, he'd made one or two women swoon in his lifetime.

"Are you here for the wedding tomorrow?" he asked.

"Uh, yes?" If he wasn't her groom, she had no business thinking about aches and ripples and swooning.

More amusement again. "You're not sure if you're here for the wedding?"

"I'm not quite sure how to answer," she said truthfully. Was he or wasn't he? He could have been part of the groom's family. Ugh. After meeting him, any idea of arranged marriage seemed even worse. Good reason why she couldn't admit she was the bride.

Yet…what if it was him? What if the man-boy in the guesthouse wasn't her fiancé?

Not so great that he'd caught her spying on his family.

There went those tingles chasing up and down her, circling in her middle like sugar-drunk butterflies.

What if she got to marry James Bond?

"Eye on the prize, little sister. We want to ascend as Famine. Not get your heart broken again." Thomas's voice whispered through her, and a chill chased over her skin, startling goose bumps up and down her arms.

Well, frosting. Trust her dead twin to kill the mood.

CHAPTER 2

Who the hell was she, this would-be spy who made him think of spring freshness and the bright sound of laughter on rainy days? Laughter in bed, before they turned the rain to steam. Her curves had been lush and inviting against him for those few moments, and that little scrap of cloth she wore as a shirt only served to emphasize her natural assets.

James Derth watched the woman beneath hooded lids as her gaze ran over him in similar fashion and she bit her lip. Always a good sign.

Except, suddenly, she stiffened and twisted away from him. "I'm sorry. I-I need to go," his sweet-little spy said, her face pale in the moonlight, a riot of curls spilling down her back. He'd have bet his last pound she was blushing.

"Did I say something wrong?" He followed her, his quick footsteps crunching in the gravel.

"No, it's not your fault," she said, wincing with each step.

A quick peek at her feet found them bare, the toenails a dark color indistinct in the dim, but for her? Pink. No...cherry red. A color to hint at the depths of her passions. Desire flared deep within him. Along with loud internal flashing lights and alarms.

He was getting married tomorrow. To someone else. And gods help him, he would never turn into his father, chasing tail and cheating on his wife. Tomorrow he'd marry a woman whose dossier showed a flighty personality as she flitted from one failed career attempt to another, a first failed marriage, and no clear goals in life. The photo her family had included was blurred, probably retouched, of a woman looking up into the sun, her features appearing sharp and angular, no smile, hair somewhere between brown and red. Everything screamed she was a spoiled Famine princess now back living off of her parents' charity, corrupted by Famine bloodlines. When it became obvious to seers around the world that she'd rise to become *the* Famine and one of the four about six months ago, her parents had seized the opportunity to be rid of her. They'd contacted the most influential Famine clansmen and bought their spoiled princess a rich husband.

His lips thinned. That husband being him. He might not like her, but he wouldn't cheat on her, either, for so long as the marriage lasted.

He just had to keep reminding himself that this marriage would give him the opportunity to stop Famine and one of the horsemen for good. Save millions of lives. In ten days from tomorrow's wedding, if he didn't turn her over, convince her to give up her abilities, or swear an oath of non-harm, the gods' enforcement agency, USELESS, would more than prove they didn't fit their name. They'd hunt he and his new wife to the ground and execute on sight.

The mystery woman bit back a soft moan and took

another tentative step.

He ignored all the alarms and strode after her. The worn soles of his favorite shoes still provided more protection against the gravel than she had. "You're not going to take your ladder?"

She shot him a swift glance over her shoulder, and picked her way through the gravel faster. Another soft hiss of pain. "Nope. I'm good. Not very sturdy anyway."

His lips twitched toward a completely inappropriate smile. "Your entire spying career, over just like that?"

She shot him another look, one he couldn't decipher through the shadows. "I'm not cut out for subterfuge." Another step and she gasped, her ankle going out from under her.

He had the pleasure of catching her in his arms for the second time that night. But this time he scooped his arm beneath her legs and curled her against his chest. Enough of watching her make painful progress across the gravel.

"This is becoming a habit," he said, his voice unexpectedly husky.

Picking her up like this may have been a mistake. A real clanger. Because it brought her scent whirling around him, something sweet and mouth-wateringly delicious he couldn't put a name to. It brought her curves against him, those full, soft breasts bumping against his forearm. And making a few parts of his body a good deal less soft.

For a moment, it felt as though the very earth trembled beneath his feet.

He needed to get her safely to the paved patio before he did something else barmy. He might not be entering into a loving marriage, but he'd remain a gentleman. His footsteps crunched over the gravel quickly. Her breast rubbed against his arm more, making it obvious how chilly it was outside, her nipple hard. Her body slid against his chest. Those trousers of hers seemed to be made of an entirely too-thin fabric. Was the ground shaking, or were those his knees?

Her eyes had widened and her hands had gone up to his shoulders when he'd caught her, and they rested there still.

"I'm sorry," she said, her voice a breathy whisper.

He smiled at her, the words to some witty response dying a brutal death as realization hit him. He couldn't read her. Not a sound, not a hint.

His ability, one of his few Famine abilities, was that the moment he touched someone, their deepest needs and desires floated up to him like words on a pond. He knew what they lacked in their lives, what they'd ached for all their days. A gift he'd exploited many times in the past—to both their benefits. The usually wealthy, lonely widows at the charity events he hosted always left happy.

A gift that, until today, until this woman, had never failed him before.

He stopped dead middle of the graveled back garden.

The only ones immune to his ability were other Famine clansmen…or members of the other horsemen clans, like Pestilence, Death, or War. Even then, he usually picked up some whisper of want.

Not with this woman.

"Who are you?" he said, her skin silken and hot beneath his fingertips.

She caught her juicy lower lip between her teeth.

He tried not to groan.

"We probably should have started with that," she said softly, her voice breathy.

The moonlight caught the edges of her bright hair and lent a red halo to frame her sweet face. Her gaze glinted in the dim, and he wished absurdly he could see what color her eyes were.

She sighed. "I'm your fiancée."

Oh, coconut macaroons. Well, wasn't this just fantastic. She seemed to have put Double-O into a catatonic state with her words. He stared at her, unblinking. When was the last time he'd taken a breath, anyway?

Although…no big complaints on the being pressed against him, against all those firm muscles. His arms were steel bands around her. And yeah, fine, that was probably a cliché from one of her favorite books, but if it worked, it worked. He'd picked her up and carried her like she was petite and fragile—neither of which, sadly, had been an accurate description since before her first birthday. Of course, if he passed out, he'd either drop her, or drop her and then fall on her.

"If a man's going to fall on you, better it's a good looking one," Roger piped up. He was helpful that way.

He didn't seem especially helpful in any other way so far. Her best friend, Piper, who was now the embodiment of Pestilence, had started with a magical toad, who'd turned into a skunk, who'd turned into a Porta Potty truck, vehicles being the modern version of a horse-like conveyance. But lucky Piper, since Pestilence had empathic abilities, her skunk communicated in images and emotion.

Not Roger. Famine had telepathic ability, evidently meaning Ginny received a constant litany of comments in her head since the moment they'd met. Considering he'd started out as a grasshopper, the most disgusting insect there was next to beetles, it was a bit worrying to consider what he'd turn into next. Hoping he somehow became mute was probably too much to hope for. Gods knew what kind of vehicle he'd turn into, if she ever achieved her full abilities.

James wheezed out a breath. Oh, good. Much less sexy if he passed out.

"I heard that, you know." Roger sounded testy,

providing further evidence that he was privy to her thoughts whether she wanted him in there or not. *"And I was just about to tell you the best move to get you two shagging tonight, ahead of schedule."*

Dirty-minded grasshopper? Check. Too-hot-for-her-good Double-O fiancé? Figured. *Sugar cookies*. The one time she'd stood up to Mom and told her to burn the photo that was included in the dossier—the one time Mom had actually listened—and of course it came back to bite Ginny.

On paper, her fiancé had looked like the perfect ally for her plan. Upper-class Famine family with more abilities than hers, knew more about their clan's history, worked in famine-stricken areas throughout the world—so surely he'd caused some of it, intentionally or not. Mom and Dad were in love after their arranged marriage, so it wasn't hard to pretend she was marrying him because they wanted her to. Someone who might be able to appreciate that just because she wanted ultimate power didn't mean she wanted to end the world or anything. With his help, hopefully she wouldn't do it accidentally, either. Maybe she could even help save the world.

Of course, then he had to go and turn out to be hot. Someone who'd rescued her—twice! Then scooped her up and carried her across the yard just to protect her feet. So much for wooing him to her side. Fortunately, Thomas had faded back into wherever he went when he wasn't with her, leaving her just with one unexpectedly hot fiancé and the bug.

"Um, could we talk about this?" she said.

He took a breath and calm slid over his face like a chilly mask. Too bad. That smile of his had been gorgeous.

No. Better he was calm and all business. Not hotness. No meltiness in her midsection. No falling in love.

"Let's get you safely to that patio first, shall we?" he

16

said, that delicious accent curling around her like the taste of him. His spicy scent enfolded her, and then there was the whole carrying-her-in-his-arms thing. He didn't even seem winded.

Well, *strawberry shortcake*, there went the meltiness in her core again. She was curled against his chest, cradled in his arms and able to appreciate his aroma fully. That delicious taste of dark chocolate and toasted coconut burst over her tongue again, while his spicy masculine scent enfolded her.

Her pulse sped and teenage girly-fantasies seemed alive and well. The very earth seemed to tremble beneath him. Which was ridiculous.

She blocked Roger out by inhaling the scent of her fiancé. And here she'd thought it might be hard getting physical with him, someone she barely knew. Her brother Thomas thought she could seduce her new husband to her side if necessary, to cement their relationship and guarantee his assistance in gaining her abilities.

"You're going to take relationship advice from a dead guy?" Roger said.

Sadly, the yard was not that big, and Double-O slowly lowered her to her feet when they reached the edge of the generous patio near the back garden door. She slid down him until her bare feet found icy concrete. Not that she noticed the cold much, with all that hard heat in front of her.

"Er, thank you." She stuck out a hand like a ninny, her face on fire. What were you supposed to do after a man carried you around in his arms? Curtsy?

"James Derth." He took her limp fingers and squeezed. His palms, callused with work, sent a shiver of a different kind skittering through her. His delicious accent curled around his words like warm chocolate.

Dratted hot men anyway. Hot men and chocolate: her two greatest weaknesses. Though only one of them had ever been a big part of her life.

Then his name registered. Well, *frosting*. She massaged her forehead. "James? Your name is really James?" The questioning of which was probably not helping her look saner. She should have listened more closely when Mom spit out details like an online dating ap. Ginny had been more concerned with his Famine name and history than she had about his first name. He'd become just J. Derth, fiancé, in her head.

"Do you suppose the more times you ask it's likely to change?" Roger quipped.

Why couldn't the ground open up and eat her whole? *"My first husband's name was James."* Though that James had always gone by Jimmy.

Meanwhile, current James cleared his throat. "I'm sorry, is there something wrong with the name?"

"Oh, of course not!" she said. Nope, not sounding saner yet.

"Could save some embarrassment in the end. No screaming out the wrong name when you two shag. He does look like he'd be talented in the sack," Roger said.

"I'm sorry. That was too forward of me. It just appeared as though the gravel pained you." James's polite smile faded.

"Roger, please shut up. It's really hard to have two conversations at the same time." Besides, with Jimmy there'd never been much need for name-screaming. Not the good kind, anyway.

Aloud to James she said, "Oh, no, that was…" Inspired? Impossibly romantic? "Nice. I, um, must be tired, and it'll be an early day tomorrow. We should get to bed. Separate beds! I mean, if you still want to marry me tomorrow." She snapped her lips shut and squeezed her eyes closed.

Maybe if she didn't look him… She took a deep breath and, eyes still closed, spoke again. "I'm sorry. This must look strange. And it's beyond awkward. I...I didn't look at the photo your family sent because we were originally supposed to meet before the wedding, but then with the ceremony tomorrow...I just wanted a peek at you."

Maybe he'd call the whole thing off. Which didn't seem fair, but if that was the kind of person he was, it would be better they didn't marry. Besides, not getting married would mean one less person to keep secrets from.

A break would be nice after the craziness she and her friends had just gone through as one of them gained their power. It was possible this man wasn't the ally she'd hoped for. Plus, there was the secret organization they'd named the League of Assholes who wanted to use the four women to end the world. Maybe he'd agree with them and want to end the world.

"Don't give up on him so soon," Roger said, making appreciative sounds. He shifted forward in her hair. *"As your horse, I'm supposed to encourage you, right? Give you good advice, moral support? Well, my advice is to do the beast with two backs with this pretty boy pronto."*

"Not helpful, Roger," she directed telepathically.

The only one who hadn't said anything was James. Wait, had he taken the opportunity to run?

She peeked open one eye.

James stood there, his expression considering. He offered an encouraging half-smile.

Ginny opened her eyes fully. Gulp. Maybe he was the kind who needed to look her in the eye when he dumped her. There'd been a few boyfriends like that. Most of them preferred texts and emails though. And that one who liked permanent marker across her windshield.

"Are you trying to give me the brush-off, Ginny?" His voice made her name sound sexy and spirited, and then he stepped forward and took her hands loosely in his.

Sparks shot through the connection, straight to her

girl-parts, who voted on a parade with fireworks, and she tried to shush them, her face hot enough as it was. "I, um…" This was her chance to pull out gracefully. Maybe even find a way to lessen the shame for Mom and Dad. She cringed. Ugh. But there were still all those guests coming tomorrow, the caterer, the decorations, all the details. Never mind her plan. If she wooed James to her side, he could help her rise as Famine…and keep everyone from asking too many questions while she did so.

She looked up into James's eyes. In the dark it was hard to say whether they were gray or blue, but probably blue, dark lashes framing the eyes, the lines of his face hard and completely masculine.

Could this man be her ally, the partner she'd always dreamed of? He could be someone she could trust. Maybe he wouldn't fall in love with her, maybe they'd just have a marriage of convenience, but she'd been keeping secrets from everyone else so long it was hard to say anything without fear the truth could slip out.

"You don't actually believe this much hotness comes along every day, do you? He's dreamy." Roger's voice had gone wistful. *"At the very least, take him out for a test ride. I'm betting he handles all the curves very skillfully."*

Ginny ignored the insect, instead focusing on the electricity sparking through the small connection to James. "I wish I knew you better."

He took a small step closer.

Her breath grew rough.

"You're not at all what I expected," he said, a hint of puzzlement in his words. Then he seemed to give himself a shake, and the mask came back up along with a smooth smile. He stepped closer again, his hands sliding farther up her arms, sending shivers tingling through her. "The decision is up to you. But for my part, meeting you tonight has been an unexpected pleasure. I believe we could be good together."

"Say yes!" Roger practically screeched.

James waited, his fingers gently caressing her arms.

She wanted reassurances. But what could she ask? She was marrying him for her own reasons, and he certainly was doing the same, especially seeing now how hot he was. Surely he didn't have any problem getting women. He could have had any bride he wanted. Why her?

"Please, please, please!" Roger begged.

"I…well…"

Bright light abruptly spilled across the graveled yard, and the patio door slid open.

"Ginny, is that you outside? Who's with you?" Mom called from the patio door. "Gracious, what are you doing up this late?"

James was left in shadow, Ginny's back to the light.

Footsteps padded across the patio. "Is this your slipper?" Mom said. "Why are you out in your slippers? It's October, and it's freezing. Come inside before you catch cold."

James stepped back, his fingertips sliding slowly down her arms, catching at her hands.

Sparks cascaded through her. Marrying a stranger was insane. Wanting to marry him after she'd known him all of ten minutes was even crazier. She had to remain objective, focused on her goals…not the muscles, and the tastiness, and her growing litany of fantasies.

He let the shadows engulf him almost entirely, only the glint of his eyes and a faint silhouette visible.

Maybe he secretly was a spy, or a ninja, because he vanished into the dark really well. He was gone by the time Mom reached Ginny's side.

She slid her aching feet into her slippers but couldn't resist a tiny look back, hoping to catch some glimpse of James.

CHAPTER 3

Morning sun streamed through the windows of the Lack guesthouse. James scowled at himself in the mirror while he adjusted his tie and tried to decide whether he was ruthless enough to go through with this sham of a marriage. Millions of lives depended on him doing what was necessary, but could he really stop her at all cost? Of course, if he didn't turn her over or prove her harmless, USELESS would execute him in ten days, too.

Despite their name, USELESS was anything but, as the much-feared enforcement agency of the gods. The gods never had paid attention to what the acronyms for their administrative and legal branches sounded like, only that they implied self-importance. The United Supernatural Exalted Law Enforcement Secret Service made the CIA and the KGB seem like kittens. USELESS agents worked for USED, the UN for the gods, and by the time USELESS started investigating any unfortunate paranormal who caught their attention, the gods had probably already decided they were guilty, or a threat to their power. Some of the senior agents were little better than assassins.

James tugged harder on his tie, but it refused to lay flat.

Sweet Ginny was in more trouble than she could imagine. Because of him.

When Mom had sent the betrothal offer, he'd had his friend Bina do some light research. If he was going to give up his career and freedom for the chance to stop the rise of Famine, better to know he was marrying the real heir-apparent. Unfortunately, despite Bina's experience skimming USELESS files—she'd been one of their techs—her queries had sent up a red flag about Ginny. When the four horsewomen rose, it was rumored they'd be more powerful than the gods. And the gods didn't want anyone edging in on their rapidly diminished power.

Which put Ginny in their crosshairs. There she—and he—would remain unless he could prove she wasn't a threat. Or nullify her menace. He shoved a hand back through his hair, then worked to smooth it out again.

Last night, Ginny Lack had seemed anything but dangerous. Other than to his resolve.

She'd been charming. Sweet. He'd picked her up and carried her across the gravel in a calculated move, but somehow, she'd curled against him and slid beneath his skin. So much for objectivity. He hadn't wanted to put her down, had taken his time letting her slide down his body. A smarmy move probably, but he hadn't been able to resist.

His father walked in, despite the closed door.

James drew in a frustrated breath at both the uncooperative tie and the invasion of privacy. Then again, his father had never had much respect for privacy, so why start now?

"Now don't you go and try any funny business and bollocks this wedding up for us." William pushed James's hands aside and went to work on the tie. He yanked it tight and leaned in close. "This is our ticket up, son. This marriage will keep our family floating pretty. Help turn the eye of some of the others who want to cause trouble for us." Dad had married Mom for her money in an arranged Famine marriage, common among the upper-class clans, though most of that wealth was long since gone.

James clenched his hands momentarily and resisted the urge to shake off dear old dad. No sense tipping his hand just now, and making it clear he wasn't exactly as reformed as he'd let them believe. He was and always would proudly be the family black sheep. The son with the least Famine ability and every need to prove he was nothing like Dad.

Dad would go to spare if he had an inkling of James's plan. "How strange that some people think debts should be repaid," he couldn't resist saying, voice dripping with sarcasm.

Dad swung him around and wagged a meaty finger in James's face. "You think that smart tongue will get you anywhere? What would you have, hmm? Your mother in the poorhouse?"

James readjusted the tie after Dad's fussing.

"Mother has no need to worry," he said mildly. He'd made sure of it. Three years ago he'd combined his certificate in Food Science and modest Famine ability to create a food bar no one could resist, and that could feed a family of four for a week. He'd made a mint when he'd sold the recipe to competitors who sold their version to NASA. The profits allowed him to give his bars away and reinvest the rest of the money back into his team's charity work. He'd concealed his success under the pseudonym James Short and set up a tidy nest egg for Mom.

"What're you going on about?" Dad demanded.

Dad and his older brothers would give anything to

get their greedy paws on that money. They'd skin James alive for going against the Famine tradition, which they thought meant using their abilities to hurt others and advance themselves. Like James, they could read a person's wants and desires. They could also read the patterns in crops and land, and used their abilities to exploit others. A taste of suffering would do them good. They were living proof of the corruption that ran rampant through the Famine bloodlines.

Of course, couldn't say any of that, either.

"Nothing, Dad," he said.

Dad might call the wedding off if he thought James would try to stop his bride from bringing about the suffering of others. Being back in the family fold was harder than it looked.

James set his hands on his father's shoulders and looked the older man in the eyes, trying not to notice how they shared the same shade of blue. Though Dad's were bloodshot from too much of the welcoming single malt the Lack's had left in the guesthouse and a fondness for liquid meals. The fact that Dad was mostly sober this late in the morning was something of an accomplishment.

"I know what's at stake here."

His life, Ginny's…maybe the whole damned world.

Dad grunted but took a step back and smoothed a hand through his thinning hair. "If only one of your older brothers had been single, this would have been easier."

James set his teeth at the thought of one of his older brothers pawing Ginny. Funny how quickly she'd become Ginny in his mind. How a part of him kept wanting to tack on "my" to her name.

The door to the room opened, and his baby brother, Charlie, strode in. He was handsome, blonde, and arrogant as hell in his usual dapper attire. His dove-gray morning tux to complement James's charcoal one. While Charlie wasn't yet as irredeemable as the others—

something that irritated Dad to no end—he'd never had much respect for doors or privacy, either.

"Oh, come on. You're not already starting a fight today, are you?" Charlie clanked the bottle of Glenfiddich onto the dresser, sloshed three fingers of it into three snifters, and offered one to James.

"It's eight in the morning." James waved off the snifter and inspected his baby brother. Accessorizing with sunglasses probably to hide bloodshot eyes and a bad hangover. Maybe if he could convince Charlie to stay here, far away from the rest of the family and their corruption, there'd be some chance for him. He'd broached the idea last night. Charlie had been noncommittal.

"It's your wedding day. Calls for a celebration." Charlie tossed back the snifter he'd offered to James, then another on the dresser. Dad grabbed the third and tossed it back.

"Maybe you should marry her, Charles," Dad suggested.

"Me?" Charlie snorted. "Not likely. I've never known a woman I wanted in my bed longer than a week, let alone forever. She's your problem, James."

James teeth clenched. Just marry her, as though Ginny was a thing, not a living, breathing, beautiful creature with skin like silk and breasts—

Desire sent blood southward. Better not to think about those right now.

He bit back the caustic remark. How could he berate Charlie for doing the same thing he had done just last night? Maybe he was as bad as the rest of his family. Up until the moment she'd introduced herself, he'd thought of his fiancée as little more than a means to an end. A spoiled Famine princess he was marrying for the sole purpose of defeating her.

Then he'd met her, and her introduction was like

opening Schrödinger's box expecting to find a cat, alive or dead, and instead finding a cute purple bunny. Who might be hiding claws. And the ability, if not the intention, to end the world with her fellow horsewomen of the apocalypse.

In that moment, holding her soft warmth in his arms, plans A through F flew out the window. G and H had died swift deaths when she'd sweetly confessed her desire to catch sight of him and know him better before the marriage.

She was so damned unguarded.

Vulnerable to him, and his plan to take advantage of her. Perhaps the apple didn't fall far from the tree. But he still had to ensure she never fully gained her abilities, no matter what it took. To bring down her friends, too, if necessary. Because power corrupted, and absolute power corrupted absolutely, to quote that old nugget.

The plan had seemed plausible...thousands of miles away in South Saharan Africa, plotting it with his best mate, Bina. And after three-too-many bottles of potent Akpeteshie from Ghana.

The same plan seemed impossible when he'd looked down into Ginny's wide eyes, those lips ripe and kissable. Waiting for him.

James grabbed the refilled snifter from Charlie's hand and tossed it back. He still needed to stop her, but he'd try again to lift the near death-sentence USELESS would have him deliver. Their involvement was his fault anyway. No matter her future, Ginny deserved better. Anyone deserved better. He considered calling his friends, too, to put together plan double-D if necessary. What was the sense involving more people in this mess?

"I have to make a phone call."

"You better not be thinking of running," Dad threatened.

Too late for that. "I said I'll do it, and I will. Go find

your seats."

ॐ

Ginny tried to smooth down her fiery hair, but it was no use. It didn't want to sit all neat and tidy in the chignon like in the picture. It wanted to puff up and look slightly crazy. Its usual thing. She also had an almost overwhelming urge to toss her breakfast, but that was to be expected considering the situation. T-minus-five minutes until she was supposed to walk down the aisle and become Mrs. Super-hot-James-she-didn't-know Derth.

Last time, she'd married a man she'd thought she'd loved…and she'd wanted to puke then, too. What if these were her instincts, warning her this James wasn't so different than Jimmy had been? She shuddered. *Frosting*, surely things couldn't turn out that badly twice.

How was she supposed to broach the whole "want to help me gain ultimate power and take out some bad guys" topic without sounding crazy? Because he was Famine clan, there was a chance he'd react as horrifically to one of her biggest secrets as badly or worse than her parents or her friends would if they found out. It probably wouldn't even matter that her secret sin could eventually lead to financial solvency. For once.

She was a Famine descendant who loved cooking and baking.

"Hello, I'm Ginny, and I love to cook," she whispered beneath her breath, like someone at an AA meeting. Though Mom and Dad would probably prefer she take up alcoholism.

A knock sounded on the bedroom door, and Ginny jumped. Even if it was knock four hundred and seven this morning.

"Genevieve, dear, can I be of any help?" Mom again.

The guilt twisted in the pit of Ginny's stomach. She glanced at her reflection and smoothed down the simple skirt of the dress she'd purchased online. She'd opted to wear it instead of the frilly cupcake-wrapper thing Mom had purchased. Cupcake wrappers were wonderful things. For cupcakes, not people.

"No, I'm fine. Thank you."

"But the guests—"

"I'll be out soon. Promise."

There was a pause. "If you've changed your mind…"

"I haven't. Please, Mom. I'm sure there's something else more important you could be doing."

Another pause, then Mom's footsteps retreated.

Ginny's shoulders slumped, and she tried pressing down her hair again. Still no luck. The hair and makeup lady had contained it as well as it would ever be contained.

"You did the right thing, love," Roger said from the desk. *"Now, lean over, pull the bodice down, and wiggle. Just a bit. Your tits aren't sitting quite right."*

Ginny did as the grasshopper suggested, which said something about her life. She was now taking fashion advice from an insect. Okay, not an ordinary insect, technically her horse, but how would taking fashion advice from an apocalyptic horse be better? She'd taken advice on the dress and the rest of her husband-wooing new wardrobe from her dead twin brother, so maybe a grasshopper was an improvement.

"Excellent." Roger crawled back and forth along the top of her dresser mirror, considering her. *"Tip the tiara slightly to the right. Yes, just like that. Well, luv, I think you're ready."*

"To puke? Definitely."

"Don't you dare. I don't think I'd survive another round of explaining to you how to fix your lipstick after that woman did such a shoddy job."

A chill traipsed down her spine, and her dead twin brother materialized next to her, his reflection wavering in the mirror. He was tall and red-haired like her, the same green eyes. But he was slim and muscular where she was not. There was a pale translucency to his form, like an echo of the man he would have been. If he hadn't died from a birth defect a few hours after they'd been born. Though that hadn't stopped him from somehow growing up at her side. A near constant companion.

A constant reminder she'd lived, leaving her in his debt to live her life for both of them.

"You look lovely, sister. You will make the groom we selected melt in your hands. Remember: you need to remain in control. This is not a romance. He is a business partner. A way for us to achieve our glorious potential."

"Whoa, now. What does he mean the groom 'we' selected? Is that the royal 'we'? Who is this dead guy anyway?" Roger said, giving Thomas a withering glower, his skinny little green arms crossed. *"Well, luv?"*

Ginny sighed, pitching her voice softly so Mom didn't overhear her talking to herself the morning of her wedding. "Thomas is my brother. We—Thomas and I—went through all the prospective groom dossiers together. To select the groom most suited to our needs." It was Thomas who'd pushed James Derth's profile to the top. Who'd said the work he'd achieved in famine-struck countries, ostensibly combatting famine with his close-knit team of friends and engineers, was obviously a cover for actually causing the damage in those same countries.

"Was it his genius idea not to look at the name and photo, too?" Roger said, sourness tingeing his words and warm spicy flavor.

"That was Ginny's preference, though I looked for her. To be sure his appearance would meet with approval," Thomas said smoothly. He smiled at her in the mirror. *"Mr. James Derth will do nicely. The fact he's not hideous should work in his favor, I think. If you can keep your heart unattached. We don't want a repeat of what*

happened with Jimmy."

Ginny's stomach clenched, memories and images of the worst days with her first husband flickering through her mind. She shook her head, a shudder rippling through her. If not for Thomas, she might not have survived. She certainly wouldn't have had the strength to consider a second marriage. Thomas had always been her strength, her reminder to try harder, to do better. To prove that somehow fate had been right in letting her live rather than him.

Unfortunately, so far, it was always Thomas who knew better than she. Thomas who seemed to prove in everything he did that he would have been more effectual, more loved, more worthy of having been the surviving Lack child.

"If this is your so-called horse, why is it green and not black?" Thomas asked, looking over Roger with disdain. *"The Famine horse is black."*

Roger looked himself over. Pointed a skinny limb at the black spots peppering his back. *"Green is a respectable color. And I have black spots. See?"* he said, pointing at black spots so miniscule Ginny could barely see them.

"Hmm," Thomas said, flicking his gaze away from Roger dismissively. *"Perhaps it's defective. It might turn into something more impressive—and black—as we come into our abilities. James will help us to do that."* His smile broadened, and he caressed her hair. *"Now, shall I walk you down the aisle?"*

"No!" Ginny cried, causing Thomas's eyebrows to rise, and Roger to straighten at attention. "I need chocolate," she muttered, rubbing her forehead. She blew out a breath, and faced both her brother and Roger in the mirror. "Look, I just…what if some of the guests can see you? How am I supposed to explain my dead twin walking me down the aisle without upsetting Mom? A-

31

and what about James?" She gestured toward Roger. "Somehow I already have to explain my pet grasshopper to him."

"You're still afraid of your friend Nia, the Death girl, finding out about me," Thomas said slowly.

"She might not understand that you're not just any ghost. And what about the League? What if they're there and they somehow try to hurt you?"

"Dear Ginny, you don't need to worry about either your friend hurting me, or the League. Once we have our abilities, we needn't worry about anything." He gave her shoulder a squeeze. *"Very well. I'll just watch. From a distance. Be sure you're not late to our wedding."* Thomas faded from sight, the temperature in the room climbing a few degrees at his departure.

Roger hopped down from the top of the mirror onto the dresser top. *"About time he's gone. Now, time to get you married. Pick me up, and I'll ride behind the tiara while we marry Mr. Shagtastic. You—we—can do this. You have a kickass, remarkably clever horse at your side, and I'm chock full of advice."*

"A bit too much advice maybe?" Ginny obligingly picked him up, the tickle of his tiny feet getting less disturbing all the time. Mostly. Grasshoppers still had to be the on the top ten of gross insects

"Deprive you of my titillating conversation? Never. Come now. Shoulders back, tits out. Time to go get you hitched!" Roger pulled on just enough strands of hair to cause a sting.

Roger was supposed to be confirmation that she really was coming into her Famine ability. A horse equal to their ability and suitable to the locale. She'd gotten a talking, gutter-minded grasshopper. Of course.

James Derth might have inspired some lustful imaginings over what might have happened last night if he had kissed her. But she was still entering this marriage with far too many secrets. "This is insane. I don't think I can do this."

"You're talking to a grasshopper about to be stuck in Canada in the middle of winter. And seriously? I've seen your wardrobe. If you want to talk about bad choices, you're way past that point. The new wardrobe, new husband, all of it's a good change for you. You need a good shag, sweet pea. For both our sakes. I've been afraid sometimes that you've become so uptight, you've thought of squashing me."

Too many times to count. Sounded like he could read her thoughts. Plus, he was a large bug, which would mean a lot of bug guts. Being a supernatural pseudo-apocalyptic-horse, he also wouldn't stay dead, so the effort would be wasted. Besides that he'd never let her hear the end of it.

"The sex will be good."

Yes, it probably would be, judging by the heated looks James had given her when she'd been in his arms, the way he might have noticed that tank was too small and thin, and it'd been pretty nippy outside. Then there'd been the heat that singed through her at even an innocent touch. She might combust if he touched her more. Although she would die happy…

She gave her head a shake. "This isn't a one-night stand. It's a marriage."

"Pfft. Who says it'll be that long before the world ends?"

"What do I know about seducing anyone? Maybe if I seduce him with food first. You know what they say about the way to a man's heart."

"There are other parts of his anatomy that take a quicker route." More hair pulling. *"Let's go. Time to get wedded and bedded."*

She really needed a different pet.

But, maybe this *was* her chance to find the ally she

craved. Maybe she could learn about her abilities and potential with him. Maybe he could help her finally defeat that horrible pattern where just when things started to go well, everything went down in flames.

Maybe James could become so much more than just an ally. With him at her side, she wouldn't have to look like a failure in front of her friends, but would only have to reveal her abilities once she'd figured it all out. Then she could help them save the world and prove she really was one of them. She was enough. She *was* the twin who should have lived.

She'd never know if she chickened out now.

Deep breath, and she headed for the door.

CHAPTER 4

This was not how James had pictured his wedding. Not that he'd given it a whole lot of thought before this morning. But there was no backing out now. USELESS refused to back down. He still had only ten days to decide his wife's fate, and it was because of him that she was in danger in the first place. What a cock up.

James blew out a shaky breath and stood alone in front of a crowd of strangers, about to pledge his life to a woman he'd vowed to defeat. A woman with the ability to starve the world.

Yet last night he'd dreamed of her. The feel of her curves against his body. How she might have tasted if he'd dare try.

He took slow breaths and focused on outwardly remaining calm, something he'd perfected years ago courtesy of his brothers and the fools at school. He could go through with this. For the villages and families in Sudan who might be spared another devastating year like 2011. For the children he'd met and watched grow in

Ethiopia. For his team, a group of five paranormals like himself who didn't fit in with their families or people, and who had instead dedicated their lives to trying to help others. Who'd become a family. They worked outside the official aid groups, went into areas deemed too dangerous by the others, and stopped supernatural causes of suffering when they found them. Other times, they acted more like traditional aid groups, building wells and schools. He and his team had fought famine and starvation so long and so hard, but all their efforts were like spitting at a forest fire.

All he had to do was stop one woman. Then everyone else would be saved.

Charlie was supposed to be his best man, but being Charlie, he lounged on one of the white folding chairs, sunglasses partially disguising his closed eyes. But the open mouth and loud snoring belayed any hope of consciousness. James winced. Here his parents were worried James would drop a clanger.

Mother sat primly beside Charlie in a swirly-looking hat and dove-gray dress, the perfect scion of respectability. Father glared at James, wrinkling his suit with his crossed arms, and daring his second youngest to bollocks this up for the family, too.

His three older brothers hadn't bothered coming. A cause for celebration. Gods forbid the family pretend they tolerated each other.

The rest of the guests filling the folding white seats must been the collective townspeople, because every one of over five hundred seats other than the front row was full. At least it looked like at least five hundred seats. It was challenging to focus on counting seats when the people sitting in them were more than distracting. Some had horns, a few sets of wings, skin of every hue imaginable. It had been a long time since he'd visited one of the sanctuaries for those with magical ability, and the paranormal bloodlines on display were even more obvious than he recalled.

He pulled at his collar and glanced toward the driveway and the rental cars. After thirty years of making mistakes, this one made the rest look easy. This was like Luke Skywalker taking on the whole Empire alone. Without R2D2. Or Yoda.

Geez, what he wouldn't give for a smart-talking robot sidekick about now. Or any sidekick.

But he hadn't told his team his intentions, aside from Bina, and he'd sworn her to secrecy. So far as they knew, he just had business here in Canada. He certainly hadn't told them about the wedding. They'd have tried to stop him. Most of his team were tougher than he was. Paranormal aid workers with experience manipulating Normals and paranormals alike, they were engineers and former soldiers. They'd never have believed he was ruthless enough for this mission.

The double French doors at the back of the house opened. Ginny's mother scurried out, her navy-blue suit pretty even as her heels stuck into the lawn and slowed her progress up to the front row.

Next came Ginny's dad. Brief scuffle near the door with him gesturing inside the doorway, pointing at the crowd. Finally, he threw his hands up and followed his wife, who'd just reached the front row and taken her seat.

James sucked in a deep breath.

A curvy vision in a simple white sheath dress and mostly obscured by the veil appeared in the doorway.

And didn't move.

One minute.

Three minutes. Possibly three years.

The back of his neck heated and he pulled at his collar again.

Nope. She wasn't budging.

The guests started to murmur.

Her parents poked at each other and argued in not-that-hushed-tones near the front about whether they should go get her, or if they did, who had to do it. There may have been a quick session of rock-paper-scissors.

With a final scowl at her husband, Ginny's mother jumped up from her seat.

Before she could run down the aisle, three figures broke away from the back of the guests.

One was tall, with a long dark braid, and dressed like she was probably part of some conservative religious group. Who liked floral tablecloths.

The next was blonde, model-hot with gentle curves in all the right places, wearing a pale green cocktail dress and hooker heels. Power emanated from her in the way she walked and held herself. In the way the crowd leaned away from her.

The last was tiny in comparison, so much so at first it looked like some kid. This one wore what looked like a black ill-fitting tuxedo, equally sharp black hair hanging around her face.

Then it hit him who they were. His skin tingled and his muscles tightened. As they gathered around his bride and held out their hands, she finally took the last few steps toward them.

Together, they were the four. The four bloody horsewomen of the apocalypse.

The women he'd come here to stop.

CHAPTER 5

"Breathe, luv, breathe," Roger said from atop Ginny's head, and she struggled to follow his directions. *"Everything's hunky dory. There will be no chundering on your dress. You've a little case of the collywobbles."*

Collywobbles? No. This was full-blown panic. Random thoughts floated off the crowd in a way she'd never experienced. They were wondering if there'd be any food at a Famine wedding. They also probably wondered how bad things would get, considering some of them had almost died when Piper rose and spread massive disease. Random flavors and tastes comingled on her tongue, increasing the nausea.

Worst of all, visions of her first wedding at that crappy chain hotel were making black creep in at the edges of her vision and her breath thick in her lungs. She could almost feel the itch of that cheap sundress, the nicest thing she'd owned at the time, and only Piper there to see her off. Mom and Dad had refused to come, instead choosing to draw up papers so Jimmy couldn't steal their money. Anna wouldn't leave Beckwell, and Nia, well, no one really knew where she'd been. But that day, sure Ginny had felt sick, but she'd gone through with it because she'd been convinced she loved him. That love would make it all okay.

She'd met this groom for the first time last night. There was no love. So what was going to make it all okay? Her plan to gain Famine powers? That might fail. Or the League might take over. Or this James might be as awful as Jimmy. Or, or...

Ginny drew in a shuddering breath and took a hesitant step out onto the patio as her three best friends walked toward her. All of them here this time. At the perfect wedding Mom had planned down to the color of the confetti.

The pain in her chest eased somewhat. Because she couldn't possibly choose one friend over another, she'd opted for neither a maid of honor nor bridesmaids. It had seemed like a good idea until about five minutes ago. When she'd been faced with walking down the aisle alone.

Here they all were anyway. For her.

The other three women destined to become the horsewomen of the apocalypse, ascending from their respective clans. Totally badass. Her friends. They would make everything okay. It was already better knowing they were here this time.

Frosting, if puking wasn't bad enough, now she wanted to cry, and her mascara would drip all over, and she'd look like a raccoon.

"Oh no you don't," Roger said from behind her tiara, where he'd taken up permanent residence and ran through a litany of fashion commentary on every outfit he could see to distract her. Unfortunately, he seemed to have very good eyesight.

And good taste. He whistled at Piper Bane, now the

embodiment of Pestilence, who came decked out like a super model.

She strutted ahead of the others, first to Ginny's side as she'd been last time, when she'd been the only one. Her heels somehow never got stuck in either the gravel or the cracks between the patio sections.

"Oh, sweetie. You look so beautiful!" she said, wrapping her arms around Ginny. That much perfection was just unnatural, the kind you'd have to hate if she hadn't been Ginny's best friend.

The soft herbal taste of lemon balm blossomed on Ginny's tongue at Piper's touch before the other woman stepped back.

"You look scared," Anna Fray, War clan, said, though her words were slightly softened by her protective tone. The only one with worse taste in clothes than Ginny's mom, Anna didn't give a fruitcake about fashion. Anna was like a big overprotective sister to all of them, especially Ginny…and she'd never understand that Ginny wanted her abilities. Anna held out her hands, and Ginny hesitated only a second before taking them. The sweet, heady taste of anise burst over Ginny's tongue at Anna's touch.

Along with a heavy dose of guilt. When they'd asked, Ginny had told the others she didn't have any Famine-abilities yet. Because telling her friends she could taste them was beyond creepy. The other three should have been immune to her abilities, but she could taste them all the same. What if they were frightened of her?

She dreaded what would happen when they found out Ginny wanted her abilities, wanted to become Famine with all the power that entailed. Anna had allowed them practice using their ability only with the intent to understand and suppress it because of how much she hated her own War-clan abilities.

Wasn't it possible they could use their powers for

good? Being stronger could make it easier to defeat their enemies.

"And easier for us to finally assume the position we deserve," Thomas whispered, his chill chasing up and down her neck, but mildly because he hadn't materialized.

Thank goodness, because last came Nia Amort, Death clan, dressed in what looked like a second-hand cheap black tux, over a black T-shirt. For Nia, it meant she'd gone all out. "All right. What's it going to be? I've got the car gassed up, and I figure we could make it halfway to Vancouver before we have to fill up. The alternative is we walk you down that aisle and make you Mrs. Blond-Brit-Hottie. Your choice."

Too bad they didn't feel the same way about her acquiring her powers. "Aww, that's so sweet." She waved her hands rapidly under her eyes. "I'm so glad you're all here." They'd all come this time. All three of them.

"There's nowhere I'd rather be," Piper said, squeezing Ginny's elbow. She looked Ginny up and down approvingly. "That dress…doesn't look like your Mom's typical taste."

Ginny flushed. "I chose it, actually." Well, mostly. Thomas had helped. All part of their plan to woo James to their side. Before they'd discovered the unfortunate hotness aspect.

"He is kinda cute, if you're into the blond, hot kind of thing," Nia said, likewise offering a hug, the taste now cool, sharp spearmint. "We have your back. Who needs groomsmen? You have us. Whatever you need—a push down the aisle, or swords to ward off the wedding guests while you run—we're here for you."

"Uh, you didn't bring swords, did you?" Ginny said, peeking uneasily around Nia's back.

"Meh," Nia shrugged. "Just saying."

Anna took Ginny's hands again, back to the anise taste. "You're sure about this? Absolutely positive? This one, at least, is nothing like the first. That I can assure you."

"You can assure me…" Ginny's eyes narrowed. "You went into research mode."

Anna shrugged, her gaze going down, and color blossoming on her cheekbones.

Ginny flung herself at the other woman. "Thank you for caring about me enough to do that. We…we have to talk. Later. I have a horse now. His name is Roger. He's a grasshopper." Her voice dropped to a whisper. "I should have fought to have three bridesmaids. And you should have been my maid of honor. You grew up in this house. You've always protected me. There's no one who deserves that honor more." And the truth. *Chocolate cupcakes*, she had to tell Anna the truth some time. Soon. Maybe it wouldn't be the stuff of nightmares she'd dreaded. A Famine cooking. It wasn't like she was a serial killer or something.

After a second, Anna squeezed back, her voice raspy. "I… Thank you." She pulled back and took a deep breath, her smile crooked and eyes shiny with moisture. Finally, she shook her head and settled her shoulders back. "Piper made me wear makeup, so don't you make me cry, either. So, down the aisle or down the highway?"

Ginny looked over Anna's shoulder, over the length of patio and lawn separating the wedding guests from the house. Then finally down the aisle to the man standing there, waiting for her, his sandy blond hair James Bond perfect, hot and steaming like Saskatoon pie fresh from the oven. There was no doubt in her mind that if she asked the girls to help her run, they'd be her getaway ride.

But…what if she didn't?

Her first marriage had almost broken her. She'd thought she'd loved the guy. She'd been so convinced that love would save her, that she'd gone against Mom and Dad's wishes. Against Anna's advice.

This time she was marrying the man everyone seemed to approve of. She wasn't stupid enough to fall in love so easily again. She'd keep her heart in lockdown. This time, she'd get what she really wanted, not what she thought everyone wanted for her. She'd gain her Famine abilities, and ascend as a true horsewoman, fulfilling the potential she and Thomas had been born for. Then she'd use those abilities to help her friends stop the League of Assholes and really be a help, not just a wannabe when all the rest of them had typical horsewomen abilities.

James could help her with that. Even if he was regrettably hot. He was Famine clan. He should be immune to her abilities, if she ever developed anything dangerous. Surely she could control herself around all that hotness.

"But why would you? Shag him. He'll be on your side then," Roger suggested.

"Or maybe I could start with cupcakes?" she communicated back.

Even way down the aisle, James shifted nervously. He didn't ogle Piper like most men did. Like her first husband Jimmy had, mere moments before they were married. James stared right at Ginny.

Only at her.

He was too far away to see his eyes, but she could feel his gaze on her. Her breathing slowed. Panic wafted away.

A strange calm settled over her, unlike anything she'd felt in her life. She stared down the aisle at James. Last night there'd certainly been chemistry between them. That was a good start to her plan to woo him to her side. As a bonus, he'd tasted of dark chocolate and coconut, possibly her favorite flavor profile.

"First cupcakes...then shagging," she communicated.

Roger whooped, even as Ginny started down the

aisle. Toward James. Toward her future, and the end of mistakes. "Come on, ladies," she said, and her friends ran to catch up with her. "I'm getting married today."

🕉

The four bloody horsewomen of the apocalypse were headed straight for him. James forced himself to stay rooted to the spot. His mouth dried, and all he could hear was the clatter of plastic wedding bells in the trees and the rustle of autumn leaves falling. Ginny's friends couldn't read minds, could they? Surely they didn't know about his plan, or about USELESS.

Bollocks, but the entire thing seemed ludicrous now, negotiating with USELESS. Marrying the Famine heiress. Coming here to investigate whether she was worthy of the gods' misgivings and should have her abilities extracted. Or if she really was the sweet woman she'd appeared last night. Bina's contacts and intel had bought him some time, but that would run out in nine days.

Her friends were unlikely to see him as the good guy in this matter. Frankly, with USELESS taking an interest in Ginny, they'd likely go after her friends soon, too. The gods weren't fond of any of the horsemen clans. Or anyone with the potential for real power.

The enormous audience clambered to their feet— someone knocking over a chair with their wings and starting a brief kerfuffle. Some of their desires and fears filtered over him. Most of them just wanted to be safe. Brilliant. So did he. Didn't seem likely to happen now.

The sun was hot on his shoulders. But not nearly as heated as the intensity on the faces of the four horsewomen, each studying him like he was an especially intriguing insect caught in their web. Even though they were clanswomen, he could still pick up small hints of their desires and needs, though he couldn't sort them easily. Redemption. A happy ending with her twins. Escape, freedom some darkness he couldn't quite make out. Finally, a strong desire to protect their own.

After the three of them came his bride, and he tried to clear their thoughts from his head. Her face was covered with a sheer veil that wafted lightly in the breeze and hid her face, but there was determination in her step as she made it to the end of the aisle and kept steaming onward. Those curves made his hands itch to touch them, but touching was against the rules. Stop Famine, stay objective. That was it.

James's palms dampened. Maybe his team was right. Maybe he wasn't ruthless enough, wasn't enough like his brothers and Dad.

She'd almost reached him. While the veil obscured her face, it sure did nothing to hide the look in the other threes' eyes. Three identical glares that said if he hurt their friend, he'd wish his great-grandfather had never been born. Three identical glares that said the end wouldn't come quick.

James swallowed. He didn't feel very bloody ruthless about now. But he'd have to be, have to channel the same blood that made the rest of his family as cruel as they were so he could figure out how to stop this woman. To protect his own life, but also prevent all those needless deaths and strife that were biproducts of famine. Stopping her would prevent starvation on levels his food bars could never hope to combat, suffering that no matter how fast and how hard his team worked they could never completely halt.

Ginny came to a stop at his side her face just visible beneath the haze of the veil. A warm smile curved her luscious berry-tinted lips. She was sweet softness and light. Almost as though to counter the thunder and fury of the other three.

The three other women each took a turn giving her a hug, starting with the blonde. After they finished their hugs, they stood to Ginny's right and each singed him with another glare.

The hair rose on the back of his neck. Nope, not glares. Something that seemed infinitely worse. Like hexes and curses. He tugged at his shirtsleeve.

He and Ginny turned to face the clergyman. Bollocks, it could have been a clown with blue hair, and James wouldn't have known the difference. Anything to turn away from those glares that still drilled into him.

He repeated the words, his voice wooden while Ginny's tone rang softly and clearly.

Last night, she'd promised she wanted to make this marriage real, while he had every intention of using her emotions, her very kindness, against her if it meant stopping her.

He glanced briefly at the sky, clear and blue, not a hint of the lightning that should have struck him down for using this woman.

Stop Famine, save the world. Seemed easy enough. Unless USELESS got him first. Or Ginny and the four horsewomen devoured him faster than any drought destroyed a crop.

What a cock up. He had to channel Yoda. There was no trying here. He had to do this.

CHAPTER 6

"I now pronounce you husband and wife. You may kiss your bride," the officiate said, and it was like Ginny woke from a fog.

She turned to James and blinked. At her husband. Glanced down at her finger, where he'd slid a simple gold band. *Holy spumoni.* They were married.

"Well, then," she breathed.

He offered a small smile, but a shadow lurked in his blue gaze. He stepped closer and glided the back of his hand against her jaw, the touch setting off flutters deep in her core.

"May I kiss you, Ginny Derth?"

She nodded, the movement jerky, because she'd forgotten how to breathe and it was hard to speak and move smoothly when you had no air in your lungs.

His lips twitched toward what looked like a genuine smile before he leaned closer and brushed his mouth against hers. Once. Twice.

Her breath shuddered out, and she breathed in James.

The chocolate-coconut essence of him, the taste of rich alcohol on his lips.

His lips settled on hers more firmly, moved against hers. She settled her hands on his firm chest, gripped the lapels of his evening jacket and tasted him. Felt the thrill of him, the danger and temptation of him, the promise of all they could have. The earth shuddered beneath their feet. If she could lose herself to this just a little longer, maybe she could believe, maybe she could trust...

He pulled back. Straightened. His retreat was more than just physical as he settled a hand at her waist and that faux smile back on his lips to turn them toward their audience.

As though the kiss had meant nothing to him. As though it, like the smile, was all part of a script she hadn't read.

Anna's gaze narrowed, enough of a warning for Ginny to paste on her own ready smile. The one everyone expected. The one that was supposed to be there. Her friends had given her a chance to run, and she hadn't wanted to take it.

"Stick to the plan. Every sacrifice will be worth it when we ascend," Thomas whispered from her side. *"Now enjoy our wedding."*

A frisson of ice slid through her veins. Of course, it was better if the kiss meant nothing. No falling in love this time.

The crowd clapped wildly, cheered, horns and wings quivering, a tail here and there. Their flavors were again almost overwhelming, the touch of their thoughts forming a general question: "What's next from the Lack girl?"

Lack girl. As though she were still a child. Still her parents' responsibility.

James led her down the aisle amid the congratulations. Next were the photos, which didn't require much attention. Mom posed and pushed everyone around as if they were garden statuary to be positioned as she liked.

An uneasy chorus circled through Ginny's head. *Was this a mistake? Is he really the partner I need?*

Thomas and Jimmy had convinced her with the first wedding that the flowers, the dress, none of the details mattered: they were in love, and that was all that mattered. Of course, it turned out Jimmy had been more interested in Mom and Dad's money that a future with Ginny.

So this time, all the details were perfect. She didn't love the groom. This time it was her who planned to use him for her goals. Did that make her as bad as Jimmy? *Cupcakes*, she couldn't possibly control all these variables. This might have been the kind of wedding she'd enacted with her dolls, but Barbie at least loved Ken. She hadn't married Ken just for the Barbie Palace and unimaginable power. At least, pretty sure that hadn't been the case.

"You look like you're a million miles away," James whispered as they headed to the cake table, her arm on his, his breath whispering against her ear and sending shockwaves through her nervous system.

His touch was like electric sparks dancing over her skin, sending heat straight to her core. She glanced up at him, then just as quickly away. *Frosting.* Maybe it would be easier to talk to him if he wasn't so blasted yummy.

He gave some excuse to Mom and the rest of the wedding party and tugged her aside, a tree offering some illusion of privacy. Then, his touch unspeakably gentle, once more touched her chin and raised her gaze to meet his. "What's wrong?"

"What's—" She frowned and shook her head, glancing quickly over her shoulder, though none of the guests seem to have noticed. They were too busy enjoying the plentiful champagne that had been dragged out, and decimating the two dessert tables. The brunch was long gone. They were insatiable.

James, on the other hand seemed to see no problem with their marriage. Certainly he had to have motives for marrying her, too. Was this Ken marrying her for the sake of the Barbie…er, Famine empire? *Chocolate chip cookie*, now even her metaphors were confused. But from where she stood, it looked a whole lot like she'd just married a stranger in what was quite possibly the most colossal mistake of her life since Jimmy. That included the whole Goth phase when she was sixteen.

"I'm fine," she said, the fake smile brittle as she settled it back on her lips. Another glance up found James studying her with unnerving intensity. His face seemed free of the happy mask he'd worn all morning. She leaned closer. "It's just… Are you fine with all of this?" She waved her hand to encompass the elaborate event that was all of Mom's dreams come true. "With us?" she swished a hand between the two of them.

He caught her hand in his, intertwined their fingers, and leaned closer, his voice a deep rumble that rolled through her causing all kinds of fluttering quakes of heat. "This might not be the norm, but it can be a start for us."

She dared to meet his blue gaze directly. "A start for us, or a start for a grand union of the Famine clan?"

He started to open his mouth.

"There you two are!" Mom's grip was firm as they landed on Ginny's shoulders and steered her toward the cake table, the only one with any food left on it. "Time to cut the cake. Before someone eats it first."

"Mom, can it wait?"

"No. It certainly cannot. I need to get packing. Do you know what your father said? He's finally agreed to that vacation we've been talking about. We're leaving tomorrow. Isn't that wonderful?"

Ginny flinched. The vacation her parents hadn't taken before because they had to stick around to take care

51

of her. But she didn't break her gaze from James.

He frowned, and firmed his lips to a thin line. Leaving her question unanswered.

ॐ

An hour later, Ginny swirled the champagne in her glass and sighed as she wandered away from the festivities and anyone else who dared try and congratulate her. Their thoughts and flavors were too distracting, so much harder to ignore than they'd ever been before. Besides, there seemed little need to celebrate. She'd just married a gorgeous Brit based on four print pages that read more like a resume than a bio.

"Cheer up, luv," Roger said, still perched on her head. *"It was a good resume, wasn't it? And I thought you wanted your abilities? They do come with an added perk: Moi."*

Yes, that's what she'd thought, too. But now… What if she'd married for the wrong reasons?

"So you don't love him. You could come to. Or enjoy some brilliant shagging, gain your powers, and leave him in the dust when the apocalypse party gets swinging," Roger said.

Most of the guests were washing down their horribly dry cake with champagne and starting to dance sloppily, even though the music and dancing portion of the event wasn't scheduled to begin for another few minutes yet. Wings bumped into wings, tails protruded from fancy cocktail dresses, but at least they were having fun. Even a local blogger and a newspaper circulated in the paranormal community had come out.

"I don't want to end the world. I don't want to love him. That's what will get me hurt." Especially when James found out, as everyone else seemed to, that she just wasn't in the same league. She was in some sub-basement league, with folding chairs, a dimly lit room, and other people too ashamed to even look at each other.

She rubbed the back of her neck and glanced over to where James and his brother—the cute baby-faced one she'd feared was James last night—were surrounded by a group of women all asking inane questions and for typically British phrases as they'd done since the moment the cake-cutting was over. It'd been almost a pleasure to be squeezed out of that crowd.

James met her gaze over the heads of his admirers, his gaze serious though inscrutable. Purple streamers fluttered in the rising breeze above him, the paper bells knocking together soundlessly.

She raised her half-empty champagne flute to him along with a pseudo-smile for the benefit of anyone who might be watching.

"You'll have to do more than just woo him. A man like that needs seduction. Then he'll be easy enough to lead. He can help you learn to use our abilities," Thomas said. *"This is what we wanted. It's what we always wanted."*

"How am I supposed to seduce him?" she replied in her head. Then glanced at her champagne, let her shoulders slump, and flagged down the nearest waiter. She handed him the half-full flute. Getting drunk was unlikely to make the day better.

"You've been married before. We've purchased the right wardrobe. Surely you can figure it out. I'm just trying to look out for you, little sister," Thomas's tone softened. *"Seduce him and focus on our abilities. On getting stronger."*

"Will that make all of this better? By the way, if anything ever does happen between James and I, neither you nor Roger are going to be anywhere nearby, is that clear?" Ginny murmured. It's not like anyone was close enough to hear her.

"Of course not," Thomas said, as though affronted.

"Oh. Well, whatever you want, luv," Roger said. He

sounded disappointed.

Ginny ignored both of them, and looked for her friends in the crowd.

Nia and Anna both lurked somewhere near the otherwise empty patio in deep conversation, which was convenient since the guests liked to keep an equally wide berth around both the Death and War clanswomen. The sound of Anna's voice could incite brawls, like it nearly had at the decorating party last week. Probably the other part of the reason Anna was only speaking to Nia and not any of the other guests.

Ginny's gaze searched out and found Piper, the beautiful blonde's soft smile full of love as she swayed gently in the arms of her brand-new fiancé, Doctor Daniel Quilan. There wasn't even any music.

Ginny sighed and had to look away.

They'd always been the perfect couple, even in the ten years they'd been apart before the Fates and her wedding invitation had brought them back together. What did it feel like knowing the person you were with really was the one? That, finally, you'd gotten it right?

"I could do without power. All I really wanted was that." She nodded to Piper and Daniel. That had been the potential bonus of choosing a husband based on his written profile alone: maybe she'd stand a better chance of finding someone compatible. More than a friend. A soul mate.

Thomas stepped in front of her and sniffed. *"Love won't last. True power, now that will last. A lifetime and beyond. Possibly even make us immortal."*

"Us? Has Mr. Chilly conveniently forgotten he's dead?" Roger scoffed.

Cherry cheesecake. Immortal? That kind of thing probably sounded good for the first hundred years…before everyone you loved got old and died. She chaffed her arms with a frown.

Maybe that was why it appealed to Thomas. Who'd never really had a chance to live.

"I have a surprise for you," Thomas said. *"Proof of our ascension, our coming power."* This with a sour-tasting sneer at Roger.

Then Thomas held out a ghostly translucent hand. Standing in his palm was a ghostly translucent grasshopper identical to Roger in size. This black grasshopper swept her a courtly bow.

"Our true horse," Thomas said.

"Greetings, mistress," the ghostly grasshopper said, his voice regal in her head. *"I am Barnabas. I hope I may render service."*

Roger forgot how to talk.

Ginny forgot how to breathe.

Thomas had a horse. Just like hers. Except elegant and helpful and… Better than hers. Like the true Famine horse, Thomas's grasshopper was completely Famine black.

Did that mean Thomas had been the true Famine all along?

Maybe he should have been the twin who lived.

"Oy! I'm helpful. Would you really prefer that…that…Mr. Perfect-Antennae? I was just about to suggest how you gather up Mr. Yummypants and find yourselves some privacy. To seduce him…and stuff," Roger said, though there was an edge of insecurity in his voice.

Thomas opened his mouth to speak, but then looked up with a start, and vanished with Barnabas.

"Oh, bollocks…" Roger's voice trailed off. He audibly gulped inside her head.

She stopped and pivoted, turning slowly to find the source of Roger's disquiet. Her gaze fell on Anna at the porch. She froze when Anna stiffened to her full height despite Nia's frantic actions to try and distract the War clanswoman.

Cupcake, cinnamon rolls, and sherbet! Don't get mad, Anna. Please, please, please. Ginny couldn't look away. Fortunately for the world, Anna was fairly good at holding her tongue if not her temper. Most of the time.

Anna's hands tightened to fists, and color crept up her face. Finding out exactly how much violence the War horsewoman could incite if she was angry was not something a wise person wondered about. Her gaze tracked something, or on the optimistic side, maybe someone, across the yard.

Right toward Ginny.

Frosting.

"Maybe we should run," Roger said.

Ginny stared steadfastly at Anna. She didn't want to look at the scary someone headed for her. From Roger's reaction, it wasn't James. Unless the town had invited some other scary demigods to visit, it could only be one person. Or being.

"You should have run when you had the chance," Roger squeaked.

There was also only one person Anna reacted that strangely and strongly to.

Loki.

"Genevieve Lack, pardon me, it's Derth now, isn't it? May I be among the first to offer you my sincere congratulations," said the sexy baritone that must have been capable of making women ovulate since the beginning of time. It rolled over her like chocolate ganache, a faint hint of something else in it. The sharp sweet spark of Pop Rocks crackled on her tongue.

It wasn't a choice. Ginny had to look up. And up a little bit more. Past a whole lot of masculine muscles and hotness barely made decent by his deep green shirt. Finally, her gaze reached a square jaw and bronzed skin that probably made a girl pregnant just for staring too long. All of that was before she even met those gray-blue quicksilver eyes.

Holy cupcake. Yep, Loki.

Ginny's knees turned soft as buttercream frosting. Loki caught her hand just before she went down.

"Sweetheart, I'm going to need you to breathe. Please," Loki said. No, begged. He shot a quick look toward the porch where Anna had been. Back to Ginny. "You did invite me, did you not?"

"I invited Lou, my old friend and the town bartender. Not you." Lou was Loki's alter ego. Maybe that made this man Lou-ki. He'd pretended to be Lou for years; a lie Piper's fiancé Daniel had recently uncovered and hadn't been able to forgive. Lou-ki was also the one person who knew at least one of Ginny's secrets.

"But it's me. It always has been."

Her eyes narrowed on him. Was that why he'd invited her into his kitchens? He'd given her cooking lessons and she'd discovered an incredible ability to create food no one could resist. Not only the town founder, his recent actions had set a plot into motion that had accentuated the magic lineage in every Beckwell citizen, hence the rise of visible horns, tails and the like— and may also have been the reason Ginny and the girls had become destined to rise as the four. With Loki, there was undoubtedly a game afoot. And a catch.

"You have some gall showing your face around here." This a growl from Daniel, Piper's new fiancé, coming up fast from the left. He'd gone from cute and handsome to horned, bronze, and demonic, courtesy of his Fomorian heritage. He looked ready to kill.

There were murmurs from the rest of the wedding guests, all eagerly watching to see what would happen next. Mom stood, hands clasped in front of her, the look on her face equal parts horrified at what might happen, and delighted Lou-ki had deigned to attend their event.

Anna's low growl came from the direction of the porch, but was getting a lot closer.

"Oh, crap," Loki whispered under his breath.

Then those remarkable gray-blue eyes—wait, the color swirled and changed—then he looked at her, and she kind of forgot everyone else again.

"I just…this has all gone tits up, hasn't it?" A rueful sparkle in his eyes. "Congrats, Genevieve. May this union bring you all that you deserve. May your abilities bring you all that you desire. And may you always place your trust wisely. I'll be watching."

He snapped her upright. A different set of masculine arms—James from the taste of chocolate and coconut on her tongue—encircled her waist.

Daniel and Piper stormed across the lawn toward them.

Anna was faster. Her fist connected with Loki's jaw with a crunch. "How dare you ruin her wedding?"

James's hands tightened on her arms.

There were shouts and fury erupting near the cake table.

Frosting. Anna's abilities. Exactly how bad was this going to turn out?

Horror blanked Anna's face.

Loki straightened.

More shouts.

He grabbed Anna's hands.

A charge of electricity sparked. The air stilled. Utter silence descended. Energy crackled between the demigod and Anna. Loki grit his teeth a moment as a shudder overtook him.

The sky darkened momentarily as a shadow blocked the sun. Anna stood frozen in shock, for once wordless and open-mouthed. Staring up at Loki.

Loki straightened, and the world seemed to right itself with him. The fighting and shouts had stopped. Only the usual joyful wedding-type noises as the guests mingled, seemingly unaware of Loki's presence.

He held Anna's hands a fraction of a minute longer than necessary. Until her expression cooled and hardened like burnt caramel. She yanked her hands away from his. He opened his mouth, then grimaced and smoothed a hand through his hair.

A glance back toward Daniel and Piper, who seemed locked in slow motion as they made their way toward Loki.

"My apologies," he said, ducking his head quickly toward both James and Ginny. Then he vanished.

Anna glared at the spot where he'd stood a moment or two longer, as though he stood there still. "The gall of that monster. To start a plague with his League of Assholes and then dare to show up at your wedding?" She grumbled to herself before she spun on her heel and marched back toward the confines of the porch.

Daniel and Piper made it to the group, Daniel's jaw tight, his skin tinted metallic bronze. "Damn. He's more slippery than a greased frog."

"How many frogs have you greased?" Piper teased and smoothed a comforting hand down Daniel's not unimpressive biceps, and the bronze color slowly receded along with his horns until he was once more handsome Doctor Daniel Quilan.

Ginny finally remembered how to breathe. Her body and every female instinct in it took note of the band of muscle still around her waist. The hard masculine body behind her that made her shiver with heat deep down inside.

James turned her slowly until she faced him, and he gently tucked a curl behind her ear. "Are you okay?"

She nodded. Even though she was feeling breathless all over again. This time she didn't mind so much.

"Care to explain?" he asked, his voice just as sexy as

Loki's. He wasn't a demigod, but there was something to be said for that sexy British accent, the deep rumble of his voice that she felt all the way to her toes. And the way he hadn't taken his hands off her waist yet, his fingers like hot brands she felt all the way through her gown.

It must have been his touch that melted her brain to wanting goo. And his nearness. And his scent. And his taste. In any case, she started babbling before she did something dumb, like ask him to kiss her again.

"Oh, well, that's Loki. He and a group of baddies are trying to end of the world, and they'd like us—the girls and I—to help."

"You're supposed to ease him into it, sugar. Not toss him upside down in a barrel of shit," Roger snarked.

Well, *cupcake*. For once, Roger was right.

Ginny forced a smile, and pointed. "Oh, look. Isn't it time for the first dance?"

Nia linked arms with Ginny. "Nu-uh. We need to have a little meeting first, just us girls. Dancing can wait."

CHAPTER 7

Dancing, and it seemed, her groom, were both on hold. Nia dragged Ginny over to the side yard where Anna was waiting, just out of view from most of the guests. James had looked like he wanted to follow, and it was clear from the look on his face he had a lot more questions. But not quite enough to overcome a healthy wariness of Anna and Nia.

The last she'd seen of him was waiting near the patio, his hoard of female followers and his brother finding and swallowing him in their midst again. His gaze had still been on her, not any of the other women.

Then when Lou-ki had arrived, James had somehow made it to her side and been there to catch her in his arms. Dare she dream he might even have been there to rescue her? Funny thing, but unlike her friends, she wasn't convinced Loki intended them harm. After all, if he wanted them dead, he was Lou-ki. They'd just be dead. Instead, he found ways to help them gain their powers.

"I can't believe Loki had the gall to show up. After

what he and the League of Extraordinary Assholes tried to pull at the bachelorette party yesterday." Anna fumed, though with much less violence-inducing power than usual. Like some of the steam had been let out.

Nor had Lou-ki caused any trouble. Anna had almost caused that. But mentioning that was unlikely to defuse Anna's temper.

"All I can say, Anna, is it's damned lucky Daniel didn't get there first." Piper shuddered. "He's still pissed Loki lied to him—to all of us—about being plain old Lou. Did you see the horns?"

Why would he expect that anyone in this town is normal? No one else does. Ginny bit her tongue.

"Speak up, then," Roger said inside her head, reading her thoughts without permission.

"No need to rock the cake bowl."

Roger snorted derisively.

"They're saying pockets of disease have broken out in several major cities around the world," Piper said quietly, staring down at her shoes. "We might have stopped the League for now, but they still took my disease and have managed to spread it somehow."

"There's something nasty going around the Senior Center," Anna confirmed, lips tight. "Maybe it's like Loki said: what happens in Beckwell, doesn't stay in Beckwell. We're a mirror state for the rest of the world. We might have broken the magical object that was holding us all prisoners, but there's still something else causing the mirror effect. I have several theories, but I haven't been able to locate any of the objects yet. Now that the barrier is completely down, it's possible the object isn't even in Beckwell any longer."

Gulp. Before the League had destroyed it, there'd been a magical barrier surrounding Beckwell that kept Normals out, and the paranormals who made their homes there safe from scrutiny. But it was long gone. So…if she lost control of her abilities, there was the possibility of hurting other people. Ginny gripped her forearm.

"Yeah, about that. We're attracting tourists. Actual tourists," Nia said. "Did you see that old couple who pulled up at the gas station this morning? I swear they must have swallowed a lot of bugs, the way they were standing around with their mouths hanging open. Next it will be the conspiracy nuts. Then the internet journalists. Beckwell is going to get famous fast, for all the wrong reasons. It won't be a sanctuary much longer."

Piper snorted. "Things weren't any better when everyone was trapped in here while we gained our powers. Most people won't believe what they're seeing is real anyway. People with horns don't exist according to Normals."

The arrival of outsiders would explain all the extra flavors and thoughts. Maybe Normals exuded them more than people with paranormal blood did.

"You know, you could actually be saying some of this aloud," Roger suggested.

"They've got this handled. It always sounds stupid when I say it out loud."

"How is that grasshopper I gave you, Gin?" Piper said.

"Um, annoying?" Ginny said.

Piper smiled, like she understood, when there was no way she could. There was no comparison between Queenie, Piper's horse, and Roger. Queenie was dignified and suited her name. Like Thomas's horse, Barnabas, suited his. Roger… well, he probably suited his name, too.

Roger sniffed. *"I was just fine until you met that imposter. Barn-ass."*

"Well, as long as you keep us updated on the progress of your abilities," Nia said. "'Cause you wouldn't keep secrets like that from us, would you?" There was an odd edge to Nia's words, the kind that suggested she knew or had guessed at some of Ginny's secrets.

Which one?

Safer not to answer. Anna hadn't seemed to notice. Yet. Ginny offered a confused smile.

Ginny cleared her throat. "Look, I don't mean to be a bother, but the dance is supposed to be starting soon—"

"Oh, Gin, of course. Go!" Anna said.

Piper said something the same.

Nia made similar sounds, but when Ginny smiled and started off toward James and his entourage, Nia grabbed onto Ginny's arm with the tenacity of dried batter in the mixing bowl.

"I'll just make sure she doesn't get lost," Nia called back to the others.

"Nia, what's going on?" Ginny asked, as Nia led her in a wide loop away from James, toward the other side of the house instead.

Once they had a bit of privacy, Nia turned and confronted her. "Why haven't you ever told me you're being haunted? I mean, hello, Death? I can help."

Ginny stiffened and tugged at her arm. *Oh, cupcake.* Thomas was strictly her business. Keeping him that way was why she'd never invited Nia over to the house as often as she had Piper. And why she'd always insisted Thomas hide himself from Nia, as she had today. Thomas might think Nia was harmless, but Nia had always had different relationship with ghosts, probably because of her natural affinity with them. This conversation was only proving all of Ginny's fears about telling Nia the truth. Nia had always kind of been a bit scary. Maybe it was a Death clan sort of thing. Although quite possible it was just a Nia thing.

"It's not like that." Ginny glanced back toward the cake table. James was headed their way.

Nia released Ginny's arm, and stepped back. "Not

like— Oh. I see. I'm good enough for other people's ghosts, but not your own?"

"That's not what I mean."

James had picked up speed, an intent look on his face.

"Then what, Ginny? Because this spirit? He's bad news. He needs to pass over. Do you know what kinds of trouble a spirit attaching to you for long can cause?"

"Maybe other spirits, but not Thomas." He'd only lived a few hours after their birth, and his ghost had grown up beside her. She'd been the one to survive. But he'd also been her only childhood companion until she started school and Anna moved to town. She'd lived, and for so long, Thomas had been her everything: best friend, brother, confident. She owed him something for that.

Her Famine abilities might have been what killed him. Which seemed doubly unfair since it was Thomas who'd always seemed to "get" their abilities better. Look at the difference between Roger and Barnabas.

"I'm doing the best that I can," Roger said tightly. *"In case you don't know, it's not like I received training before showing up here as an insect."*

Nia raised a brow.

Ginny gulped, but tried to cross her arms over her chest and look tough. Nia couldn't possibly understand how different Thomas was. Why it was Ginny's job to protect him, and give him as much of a life as he could have. She had to protect him…even from a friend.

Nia broke the stare first.

"Sure. Whatever." Nia glanced up at James, who was almost on them, and pitched her voice lower. "Look, you change your mind—which you should—you let me know. I hope to hell it's soon. Before you gain any serious power for that ghost to feed off. Or the League finds out about him and sees the exact vulnerability they've probably been looking for." She mock saluted James as he came to their side. "She's all yours. But just remember: I'm not known as Death for nothing."

∞

James didn't have time to say anything in response before the scary little horsewoman strutted off—and honestly, what was he supposed to say? Death had just threatened his life. That was probably the kind of warning to take seriously.

Although recently, in the whole scope of things, probably not that unexpected. He'd been in town for less than two days, he was marrying the woman poised to become the incarnation of Famine, Loki had just crashed his wedding, and when he stopped Ginny from gaining her powers, he'd undoubtedly piss off War, Pestilence, *and* Death.

That was, if he figured out a way to convince her not to rise, or to let the USELESS agents drain her of her abilities. Never mind the other scenario if he didn't, and the agents hunted he and Ginny down. Then it would be a race to see if the horsewomen or the USELESS agents got him first.

He might as well have been Han Solo facing off against the Hutts: totally buggered.

Maybe he should have invited his mates here for backup. But that would have been a Dad move: unfathomably selfish.

"Are you all right?" Ginny's touch jerked him back to the moment.

He looked down to find his lovely bride staring up at him with impossibly huge, luminous green eyes. The worst part was she seemed genuinely sweet.

He was not feeling even remotely ruthless. Nor objective. Not good.

"Isn't that my line?" He took her hand and tucked it under his arm. The action drew her against him, enveloped him in her sweet scent, and wow did she smell scrummy. Like cake and chocolate, like the most mouth-watering dessert he just hadn't sampled yet.

Down, boy. And which you can't sample. At least…not a real taste if you want to remain objective. If you want to succeed.

"I haven't been the best groom today, have I?" he said, surprising both of them with the truth.

Ginny's mom's voice boomed over the speakers, announcing the first dance. A spotlight found them, hiding in the shadows near the house.

Everyone turned to stare, all five hundred pairs of eyes on them. Piercing. Expectant.

Ginny clenched his arm, frozen.

He covered her fingers with his, and squeezed gently. "Shall we, or shall I make up some reason we can't dance? I might have a gammy knee from an old rugby injury I could invent." He smiled down at her.

"I'd…I'd like to dance. With you. I'm just not very good at it."

"I'm mostly rubbish," he lied. Mother's dance lessons in childhood had made certain of that. Mostly, he hated the idea of them dancing while everyone else watched. It had never made a difference before, at any one of those charity balls where he'd danced and charmed the donations out of the guests, everyone watching. But with Ginny, he wanted to get to know her better. In private. "I'd like to dance with you, too."

The smile she gave back to him was luminescent. It drew him closer, toward the center of a flame. His breath caught. That had never worked out well for moths in the end, and it wouldn't work out well for him, either.

"Then let's dance," she said.

He didn't say anything else. If he did, it would probably be something stupid like how she could be his Leia to his Han, or how he'd be thrilled to be her He-man to her She-ra. Instead, he led his bride out to the dance

67

floor and took her in his arms.

She fit there like she'd been made for him. The perfect height, which made it easy to maintain proper form. There was a soft curve at her waist to rest his hand, and her long fingers closed with his. The music began, and it wouldn't have mattered what the hell it was, because the first dance he had with his bride was going to be a waltz.

The music was some country-western tune he'd never heard before, but with Ginny in his arms, he didn't even notice everyone watching. Well, mostly not. The stunning woman moved gracefully in his arms, following his lead, her hand on his shoulder, and that was all that mattered.

They danced alone and silent for the first bit of the song before, thankfully, everyone else joined in and they were less conspicuous.

"You're a liar," Ginny whispered.

He almost stumbled, but quickly repaired the misstep. "I'm sorry?" How had she found out so quickly?

"You're an excellent dancer. You almost make me look good." Another gorgeous smile. She was so damned intoxicating.

His insides twisted. If only that were the only thing he'd had to lie about. He could fall for her all too easily if he wasn't careful.

"It's definitely the other way 'round," he said. "Have I told you how beautiful you look today?"

A flush crept up her cheekbones, and she glanced away. "Mom picked out a different dress for me. I probably should have worn that one. It made me look smaller."

"I like this one." Not that he'd ever thought a lot about dresses before. But the gown was simple yet elegant, pretty and a touch sweet with the relatively high neckline that just hinted at collarbones but curved over her generous breasts. Stretches of flawless ivory skin. Long, muscular legs to wrap around his waist. His grip tightened, and his wits scattered.

The silence grew and hovered like a thick fog between them, the kind of thing you'd expect after, oh, two perfect strangers agreed to an arranged marriage in the modern era.

The music for the first dance ended, and a new song began, something a bit faster, but still with a tempo that was waltzable. If you pretended. So, James kept dancing. And she didn't try to pull away, so perhaps she hadn't noticed...or perhaps she didn't want their dance to end, either.

"So, um, the house Mom and Dad bought us is nice. It's cute. There's a little garden. And the bedroom is pretty, with this big bed..." Ginny's words petered off in direct proportion to the darkening flush on her face. "I mean, I wasn't sure if you knew about the house. Maybe you've seen it?" She wouldn't meet his eyes now.

Was it because of her enthusiasm...or because she'd started talking about the bed? He skipped a step, and had to adjust quickly to catch up. There was an intriguing and unexpected concept.

Did his bride want to sleep with him? Tonight?

ജ

Well, *frosting*. Now her shiny new, mostly-a-stranger husband knew she wanted to sleep with him. Ginny's face burned. Roger's chuckle from inside her handbag was not helpful.

She swayed in James's arms and tried to think of something clever to say. She was supposed to woo him, not suggest they jump in the sack. They barely knew each other. But that hadn't stopped other people before throughout history. Did it have to stop them?

Okay, so none of this was leading to any remotely clever thought on how to save the conversation. The new song was winding down, and now neither she nor James had said anything for long, stretching minutes.

Boy, did he smell good. His own spicy, unique scent, probably sandalwood or cedar, along with something wholesome and warm, like the kind of baking perfection just before you pulled it out of the oven. He was also the best dancer she'd ever been with. There was something very sexy about a man who was good at dancing. The powerful yet graceful way he could move his body, lead her over the dance floor. Thoughts flooded through her of all the other ways he'd probably be able to use his body.

Nope, that wasn't helping her think of anything useful to say.

James cleared his throat. He opened his mouth, frowned, then faked a smile before he closed his lips again. A small sexy dimple peeked at her from his right cheek.

"We can leave to drive over to the house whenever we want. We don't... I don't expect... I have no expectations about tonight," she lied. Expectations, no. Hopes, dreams, wild, irresponsible visions of his sexy back and all that naked bronzed flesh? Yeah, there were lots of those. "The house has two bedrooms. Two beds."

So much for something clever. Or seductive. Gah!

When was the last time she'd seduced a man? Especially a man of this calibre? Basically, never.

"We have plenty of time to get to know each other," he said, more smoothly than she'd managed. He drew her closer to him, so her skirt twined with his legs as they moved across the dance floor Mom had rented. A few other couples danced with them, but already the crowd had begun to thin.

The only one that mattered was him. The way she fit so well in his arms. Jimmy hadn't been as tall, and as soon as he'd stopped playing football, he'd lost most of his muscle bulk relatively quickly. Along with any hint of patience.

James wasn't bodybuilder big, but there was definite tone and definition beneath that tux. Plus, he had maybe four inches on her, which was rare in a world that seemed mostly made up of short men. If that wasn't enough to make him dreamy, he held her in his arms as though she could have been petite. Even when he'd carried her yesterday. The meeting of feminine and masculine was heady stuff.

Hmm. Maybe he was a gym rat. Into healthy eating and dieting. A body like that probably didn't get a lot of baking and yummy treats. Nope. That just created a body like, well, hers.

She traced the hard outline of his jaw with her gaze, studied the golden-brown length of his lashes that should have been pretty but weren't.

"Why did you marry me?" popped out of her mouth.

She'd meant to ask something innocuous, like "do you like to read?" Or "tell me about yourself." *Oops*.

His gaze collided with hers. A hint of panic rushed through his eyes before he quickly glanced away, and a hint of burned chocolate grazed her tongue. The taste of a partial lie. The bigger the lie, the bigger the bad taste always was. It all happened in less than a second, but long enough to make Ginny's shoulders tense.

"I wanted to finally do something to make my family proud, to mend some of the tears we have in our relationship. I also wanted to do something important for the Famine clan." More burned chocolate. "Why did you marry me?"

"I wanted to make my family proud, too. But if I really am going to become the embodiment of Famine, I need a partner who knows about our history and can help me." She paused a moment before she added the last. "I wanted a partner I could trust."

The look he gave her was inscrutable, and they

finished their dance in silence before James said something about having to see his family off and strode away. Nothing like making him look even guiltier.

Ginny watched him retreat through the late afternoon sun, her palms damp.

In her case, at least her response was true. He was lying when he said he wanted to make his family proud or do anything for the Famine clan. The question was: How big were his lies?

Lou-ki's warning to be careful who she trusted floated back through her mind.

Did that include her new husband?

CHAPTER 8

The darkness turned his new wife's skin to gray porcelain, spirals of hair caressing her neck as Ginny peered out into the dark woods marching along either side of the narrow roadway. James tightened his fingers on the wheel and tried to focus on driving—on the wrong side of the road no less—but his gaze kept drifting back to her. Thank the gods they seemed to be the only ones out on this lonely stretch of road.

She worried that luscious lower lip of hers, a frown flickering over her face every so often, though she'd said hardly a word since they'd left the wedding reception. Bollocks, but not being able to read Ginny left him playing blind.

Something had happened during their dance, when she'd asked why he'd married her. She'd stiffened in his arms at his answer, iridescent light flashing in her green eyes. If his abilities allowed him to read the desires of others, maybe her abilities told her he was circling but avoiding the truth.

Question was: How much of that truth did she know?

Perhaps she was naturally nervous because this was their wedding night and they were still virtually strangers.

Or perhaps her thoughts took a much darker path.

James tried to focus on the twin ribbons of light unfurling from the car onto the dark curving roadway as they headed toward the cottage her parents had purchased for them. He'd made a quick trip there yesterday evening, just to take a look at what was supposed to be his new home. At least for the time being.

He slowed the car as they came to the little post with balloons fluttering in the breeze, marking the drive to the cottage. The signal ticked loudly in the car before they bumped off the highway onto the grassy drive.

Blast, but all this uncertainty had his neck tight and his stomach in knots. "So, the wedding was nice." Bollocks, why had he said something so inane?

Only years of negotiations with war lords, demigods, and big-headed local supernaturals let James keep his expression detached, his actions smooth as he went through the motions of pulling the car up next to the tiny white cottage.

Ginny chuckled, the sound deep and throaty, far too sexy. "The part where the guests devoured all the food like locusts, or Lou-ki showing up and Anna almost causing a riot?"

"I meant you, mostly." Bollocks. Now he sounded like a green lad with his first crush.

"I…oh. Thank you," she whispered.

He couldn't look at her. Couldn't see those beautiful eyes widen, the way the moonlight caressed her skin, hinted at mouth-watering curves beneath the vintage-style navy-blue cocktail dress she'd surprised him with just before they'd departed beneath a hail of paper confetti. She looked like a pinup girl, and all he wanted to do was unpin her hair and see it around her shoulders. Preferably without the dress.

He cleared his throat, cut the engine, and climbed out of the car. He came around and held open the door for her before she headed for the porch and he strode to the boot and retrieved their overnight bags. The rest of their things were supposed to have been delivered.

He met Ginny on the stoop, where she fumbled with the key in the uneven glare of the porchlight.

He couldn't read her, but he'd read other women. Ginny exhibited all the signs of a woman who wanted him. It was in the way she touched him, the stolen heated looks, the tremble in her fingertips.

Easy enough to recognize, especially when he felt the same.

She'd basically said she wanted a partner to lead the Famine portion of the apocalypse. But that depended on how she defined partner. That could mean a lover. Or a business associate. Outright seducing her might be too smarmy. But if she wanted to be seduced? She might trust him more if they were intimate. Perhaps she'd forget any hint of whatever she'd read off of him when they were dancing.

It was somehow natural to reach around and cup her hand in his, her softness sheltered against his chest. Her soft curls tickled his chin, and gods help him, she smelled like fresh baked strawberry shortcake with clotted cream, his favorite dessert. Cool cream sliding and melting over ripe lusciousness. His breath grew rough.

Together, they guided the key into the lock, and turned. He paused there, his hand and body still wrapped around her. Her eyes glittered up at him in the darkness, but he couldn't make out the expression. "May I? It *is* tradition."

"What is?" she asked, breathless.

"Carrying you over the threshold," he said, his voice husky at the thought of touching her again, at the thought that this was his bride. And what else was tradition on the wedding night.

"Oh. Yes. If you like," she said, voice small.

He scooped her into his arms for the second time in as many nights, the soft scent of her crushed against him, all those curves pressed against his chest. Her hands went to his shoulders, and his hand accidentally found the edge of a lace stocking and what felt like a garter strap. His tongue thickened, and it was difficult to remember to breathe, since he was too busy thinking about what she'd look like with just the stockings and garter straps. Nothing else.

Other parts of his anatomy were very intrigued, too.

Stay in control. Your lives depend on it. Your dick does not get a say in the matter, he tried to tell himself as they stepped through the doorway.

Strong disagreement from other parts of his anatomy.

They stepped inside, a few lights on inside lending the small cottage a soft glow.

The light enabled him to see Ginny's expression clearly, the soft flush of color tinting her cheekbones, the dilation of her sage eyes, the tip of her tongue as it traced her lush, damp lips.

It was far too tempting to kick the door shut and head straight for the bedroom. But that might scare the hell out of Ginny. Instead, he slowly lowered her to her feet.

She held onto his shoulders and slid down his body. She boldly met his gaze the entire time as they slid against each other, inch by tortuous, exquisite inch, until her feet finally touched the floor. She couldn't have missed evidence of how much he'd enjoyed the process. Her hands still rested lightly on his shoulders. "I think that's a highly underrated tradition," she said, her voice like mellow scotch.

There was a good reason tonight was supposed to end by tossing the bride on the bed and enjoying the rest of the night. His body was so tight and hard, and he kept picturing her red curls trailing over ivory skin, down over those glorious breasts. And of course, that bloody garter belt.

The cottage trembled and shuddered, the floor jumping beneath them.

Ginny flushed and jumped back. The ground stilled. She looked up at him. "I… Are you okay?"

"It was just a little tremor. I'm certain we're fine." Although…were earthquakes normal in this area of the world? They did seem to be occurring with some regularity, and he was fairly certain he hadn't imagined this one.

She flushed, ducked her head, and spun away, heading down the warm glow of the hallway toward the source of the light, presumably the living room. He hadn't memorized the layout yesterday…and he was too mesmerized by the sway of her hips, unable to do anything but follow.

Ginny trailed her hand slowly against the wall, drawing his attention to their progress through the cottage and not just the sway of her perfect ass.

The cottage was cozy. There was the door they'd entered through, a miniscule closet on one side, a bathroom on the other, then two bedroom doors faced each other. Next came the cut-out for the kitchen. Ginny paused there, glancing inside, turning to give him a come-hither look before she continued.

He quickened his pace to intercept, but she slipped into the room on the end, the generous living room with basics for furniture—a small dining table, sofa, two arm chairs, a modern flat-screen on the wall, and a lamp. Somehow, she'd managed to put the table between them. The table held a basket covered in a plaid dish towel, and a bottle of single malt with a bow.

None of which satisfied the craving he'd developed.

The one which the hint of those garter straps had further whetted.

The kiss during the ceremony was supposed to be sweet, charm her, her family, and her scary friends. But she'd tasted sweet and forbidden, like luxurious and exotic fruit he could never get enough of. He'd caught her gasp in his mouth, and gods help him, even with all those people watching, he'd been sorely tempted to deepen the kiss, to seduce his bride right there with first his mouth, then his hands.

Probably not the wisest course of action, all things considered.

They were alone now. Actually, it seemed like a really good idea to seduce his bride. Then he'd know if she really was as sweet as she appeared, and building intimacy would begin trust, so he might be able to convince her to promise no harm or give up her famine abilities.

He came around the side of the table.

She thrust a basket between them. "Hungry?"

He stared directly at her, let his gaze drift down the modest inviting top of the dress that left just the tiniest hint of delicious, creamy décolletage, before he met her gaze again. "Famished."

Her lips parted, then color flushed over her face again, and she looked away. "I, um, oh look! There are some muffins in here. Do you like muffins? What kind?"

Well, bollocks. She'd seemed eager too, but now seemed much keener on…muffins. He rocked back on his heels. "I'm not keen on muffins, actually." So how should he play this, then?

Ginny's smile wavered. "Oh. Of course you're not," she said, and her gaze fell.

She seemed to take her muffins very seriously. "But then, I haven't tried these ones," he said, holding out his hand.

She peeked up at him from beneath her lashes. "What type?"

"Surprise me." She'd already done a fair bit of that since the beginning.

She looked inside, then after a moment, reached into the basket and pulled out a golden-brown muffin. It had a spicy scent that curled around his senses, something like pumpkin pie and a reprieve from the chill of autumn beside a roaring fire.

Her gaze held his as he took a bite. Then blinked at the explosion of flavor inside his mouth, the tart burst of cranberry, the warmth of the spices. There was also a creaminess just on the edge of sweet, and a curious hint of something else, just at the edge of his senses that made him take another bite. This time there was the crunch of nuts, the tang and sharpness of an autumn breeze, the crackle of leaves beneath his feet. He had to take another bite. Then another. Trying to understand the flavor, to encompass it.

Suddenly…he was holding the empty wrapper. His eyes went to the basket before he could help himself. He gave his head a shake, frowned, then looked up at Ginny. He knew when he'd tasted that flavor, the indescribable spicy-sweetness. It was the taste of her lips when he'd kissed her, the forbidden hint of wildness he'd tasted on her.

His voice was husky again. "Well. That was unexpected." As had been everything about her. How could the muffins have tasted of her?

She stared at him, her lips slightly parted, her gaze wide. "Were they?" Her breath shuddered out, the action drawing his eyes back to the rapid rise and fall of her chest. "Is that…a bad thing?"

"No." But it could be dangerous. He must have imagined the taste, put them and the heat of the evening together somehow. So much for objectivity. That had gone up in smoke the second he'd lifted her into his arms.

She still clutched the basket like a shield.

He took a step back. "Ginny," he said, his voice sandpaper. "Nothing is going to happen tonight that you don't want to happen. We can wait. As long as you want, as long as you need, whatever speed you need."

She nodded. Then nodded again. "I, uh, I think I need that. To take it slow. Thank you." She edged around the other side of the table, emerging again out at the entrance to the hall. "I'll take the bedroom to the right. You can take the master; it's to the left." She backed down the hall as she spoke, in full retreat, while he followed more slowly, unthreateningly. "I'm, um, really tired. You must be, too. I'll see you tomorrow. Good night." She backed into the room on the left, and shut the door.

He stood outside the door and dropped his head. On the other side, he could hear Ginny's heavy, shuddering exhale before she walked farther into the room.

James blew out a breath and shoved his hand back through his hair, then circled back to the living room. He contemplated the single malt and the basket of muffins. Brilliant. He now had nine days to figure out how to not get killed by USELESS, and to somehow deliver them the results they wanted. He'd completely cocked up tonight's efforts. He considered the muffins again. Project one tomorrow: Uncover just what his new wife's abilities were. And be careful not to run afoul of any of them. He couldn't let her out of his sight.

CHAPTER 9

Ginny was up, dressed for escape, and bleary-eyed by seven a.m. after not getting a wink of sleep. Sadly, not for the right reasons. *Cupcakes.* A certain magical grasshopper with a fondness for show tunes had begun his serenade at the early edges of dawn. She'd thrown several pillows at him, but the little bugger moved fast. She glared out the window at the fluttering gold leaves that hemmed her and the cottage in. She had to get out of here. Figure out her next move. How to make James her partner and gain her abilities. And gain control over them.

"I thought you'd appreciate my choice. 'Touch-a, Touch-a, Touch-a, Touch me' is a classic. And would have worked better to have gotten you a good shag last night," Roger said, and began humming the tune again.

Ginny growled and finished off the braid to contain her unruly curls. *"Don't you break into that chorus,"* she said, cutting Roger off before he bellowed through her head again, high, squeaky, and with a British accent. *"And yeah, okay, things didn't go so well last night."*

In other words, she'd completely backed out of her seduction plan when it became obvious James was so much better at it than her and out of her league, probably as interested in her as he was in muffins…and the part where she was pretty sure she'd caused a small earthquake. The ability to manipulate the earth was one of the Famine abilities. Who else would have caused it? She grabbed her phone and did a quick search, but there'd been no serious earthquakes reported anywhere in the world. Her shoulders sagged in relief.

Roger broke into Carole King. *"I feel the earth move—"*

Ginny scooped up the grasshopper and dangled him over a glass of water. *"No more show tunes before nine. Got it?"* Then she put the huge green bug back on the white dresser. *"And I'm serious. What if this little earthquake was a bigger earthquake somewhere else? Remember what the girls said? Everything that happens in Beckwell is still reflected out into the rest of the world."*

She'd thought a couple of times at the wedding she'd felt the earth move, but it had seemed more like a metaphorical thing. Not a literal the-earth-is-trembling thing. It seemed to be triggered by her feelings for her husband.

"That would be lust, luv. A strong desire for a good ol' round of rumpy pumpy," Roger said, seemingly unperturbed by her threat.

Yes, which had been one of the reasons she'd stayed in her bed, not sleeping, instead of going across the hall and knocking on James's door. To do much more interesting things than not sleep. *Frosting*, last night when he'd scooped her into his arms, she'd wondered if maybe they would just continue the trek straight into the bedroom. She could have shown him some of the sexy lingerie that went with the rest of her new clothes.

But she still didn't know what he wanted from the

marriage.

"You could try talking to him. Or wild monkey sex. Yes, that's my vote," Roger said.

"How is that going to tell me what he wants?" Although, about the same as trying to get him to tell her the truth about his motives. She'd been honest about hers…mostly. If you excluded the Thomas part. And the cooking part. And maybe the just wanting a partner, not really a husband part.

Ugh. What she needed to do was bake. It was the only thing that always cleared her head.

Of course, first problem was that she didn't have a car, and there were no ingredients in the house. James had driven last night, and while Mom might have left a fruit basket, she'd never leave raw ingredients for cooking in the house. She'd had the kitchen removed in their house. Because Famines didn't cook.

Problem two was that no one knew she baked—and after James's reaction to her muffins last night, she wasn't sure she should tell him. She licked her lips. It'd never seemed all that sexy, watching someone eat…but the way James savored her food? The raw aggressive need he'd demonstrated…yeah, that had been sexy. She could go to the Senior Center, where she rented the secondary kitchen. If James was awake, maybe he'd drive her there.

Roger started humming another show tune.

She turned and glared at him, pitching her voice low enough hopefully James couldn't hear her from across the hall. If he was even awake. Maybe better she just borrowed the car keys.

"Tonight, you're sleeping outside."

"Lack of monkey sex makes you grouchy," Roger said.

"No, early morning show tunes make me grouchy," she lied, her voice soft. That description: Monkey sex. What did that entail, exactly? The monkey part was either dirty…or fun. Sex with Jimmy had never been especially fun. She grimaced, memories of heaving and groaning on top of her, while she'd wondered: is this it? It'd been mostly…exhausting.

"Oh, but Mr. Sexypants would make it a good kind of exhausting. My poor, sheltered Ginny. What am I going to do about you? I came into existence three days ago, and even I know what monkey sex is. And that I want to have some." The grasshopper hopped over until it settled on the window ledge beside her. *"It's decided. Let's go into the city. Find a strip club. Loosen you up, murder some of that naivety."*

"I'm not going into either the city or a strip club with you." She grabbed the light jacket she'd worn last night off the bed and threw it on over the pale gray, pink-flowered dress that cinched at the waist and flared to a full swing skirt. One advantage to the new wardrobe—she felt different in them. Not like she was trying to fit into the perfect daughter's wardrobe but more like…her. She tossed her purse over her shoulder. "Besides, the goal of your existence isn't supposed to be to live in the gutter. You're supposed to be my horse. Help me fulfill my destiny…or something."

"You mean you'd prefer a horse like Barn-ass? I'm trying to help you, puss." The sour tang of hurt flared on her tongue and in his voice. Surely he didn't worry about Barnabas the same way she worried about Thomas, did she? That the wrong duo were gaining the power?

She softened her tone. "I know. It's just—"

"The strip club would be more fun."

Aaand…she was done for this morning. She rolled her eyes before closing the door, hopefully trapping the grasshopper.

She turned and collided with a wall of damp, warm, muscular male flesh. Naked, bronzed flesh. Only a yellow towel slung low around James's hips, barely riding his hipbones. And the bulge beneath the towel.

She stumbled a step back and her gaze went on a quick journey southward. *Hot cinnamon rolls…*and *dumplings*. Her breath whooshed out, and the words monkey sex circled through her head in neon colors.

Nope. Definitely hadn't imagined those muscles beneath the tux.

Ginny forced her gaze upward. Back over that rippling flesh. Six pack? Oh yeah. Definitely a cupcake no-fly zone. Her mouth was damp and she licked her lips by the time she made it back to his face, the quirked brow beneath hair that was spiked and dark with water.

"Good morning, love," he said.

The sound rumbled through her. Warmed and coiled into aching pools of want deep inside her.

Oh, frosting. If only there'd been wild monkey-sex.

"Told you," said Roger from the other side of the door.

Great. Now she was staring. Probably drooling. Still staring. Oh, yum. So. Much. Man.

"Morning," she managed to squeak out, her thighs, knees, and other parts turned to quivering pools of desire. The ground might have been shaking. Or maybe just her knees.

He crossed his arms, making his pecs do a sexy jumpy thing.

Ginny's lady parts replied with a similar bump and groove.

"I didn't wake you, did I? I like to get an early start on the day," he said. At least, probably. Words were hard to focus on right now when there were all those muscles and naked flesh…and naked James.

"Oh. Um. Me, too." *Don't stare, don't stare*. Roger's show tune antics might have woken her earlier than usual, but getting up early had always been her thing. Unlike everyone else she knew. Mornings had always been hers.

Sacred alone time.

His gaze skimmed over her, potent as a touch. "I like the dress." He pointed at her purse. "Were you headed out?"

A nod. *Don't stare at his chest. For frosting's sake, don't drool, either.*

"Brilliant. Give me a second to get dressed and I'll give you a lift. I wanted to get a better look at the town today, see where my brother ended up." He smiled, the sole dimple peeking at her and making her insides do a flip. He took a step closer, their bodies almost pressed against each other.

Heat seared through her like the flare of burning sugar. Her pulse thundered. She'd probably stopped breathing. Who needed air?

Oh, *frosted cupcake*. He was going to kiss her. *Yes. No. Yes!*

Another dimple sighting.

Then evidence of just how narrow the hall was as he slid past her. He smelled of soap, that spiciness, and ohmigod, warm, melted dark chocolate that had her puddled, confused, and wanting.

He had to turn sideways to get those shoulders past her. Bringing them face-to-face, practically lip-to-lip. She clenched the handle of her purse so she didn't reach out and grab something that didn't belong to her.

It probably only took half a second for him to pass her, but it might have been centuries. Almost like he'd paused in front of her. Waited for her to reach out and grab him. Maybe grab his shoulders, jump up, and wrap her legs around his waist so they could stumble back into his room and fall onto the bed together. To enjoy a very satisfying bout of monkey sex.

A perfect opportunity to be bold, like Thomas suggested. To seduce James and make him her ally.

Except…could she become the kind of woman who

could do that? More than in her dreams at any rate.

Fantasies firmly entrenched only in her dreams, she could only watch as James gave her one last heated glance and stepped into his room. Alone.

Ginny remembered she needed to breathe again, and gasped in air. *Holy gingersnaps*. Physically, she couldn't jump that high anyway to grind herself against him. She'd be more likely to knock him over, smash his head against the wall, and give him a concussion rather than a sexy romp.

She glanced down the hall, toward the rear door. Toward escape. Her hands tightened on her purse handle. How wrong would it be to borrow slash steal the car and abandon her new husband the morning after their wedding?

"It's amazing how quiet it is out here," James called, his voice carrying through the not-quite-closed bedroom door.

Ginny jumped, guilt shooting through her.

Now evidently, they were talking through the door while he dressed. *Isn't that one of those stages of intimacy things we're not ready for yet?* Either that, or he'd guessed her plan of running out on him, and thought conversation would keep her still.

Sigh. *Doughnut holes* on him for using her good manners against her. "Um, yeah. I guess so." A thought occurred to her that might buy her some time. "Don't you have to take your family to the airport?"

"No. They left last night," he said, as though it didn't matter at all.

Hmm. At least part of his lie was that he'd married her to please his family.

"So what sights does Beckwell offer that you'd recommend?" he continued.

A soft plop of what was probably the towel to the floor had Ginny swallowing hard. And unable to keep her gaze from the gap between the door and the frame. The brief glimpse of a long body passing by the door. Had that been one toned and bronzed butt-cheek? Not too much hair anywhere. The sound of a zipper came next—probably his suitcase—then one foot coming down. Then the next. Guess he wasn't going commando.

Why was that suddenly a bit of a disappointment?

"Ginny? You there?"

"Oh. Umhmm. Yes." *Totally peeping on you like some shameless hussy.* Not that she could drag her gaze away. He'd been saying something about what to see. "There's the school, I suppose. And the library—my friend Anna works there. I heard someone has opened an antique shop in their house, but I'm not sure where." No use pretending she was used to this.

A gentle thunk of clothes hitting the bed, then another brief glimpse as he walked over to the bed. Dark blue boxer-briefs gripped muscular thighs. Poor butt cheeks hidden from sight and unable to be worshipped. A belt buckle clanged lightly, more movement, then a zipper.

"Beckwell is unlike any of the other paranormal sanctuaries I've visited. I've been in rural areas before, but rural Africa is rather different than rural Canada I suppose," he said with a soft chuckle.

"You lived in Africa? Yet you'd still want to live here?"

The door opened, and her eyes zipped up to his. Oh, *frosting.* Her guilt was probably written all over her face.

Oh wow. He hadn't put on his shirt yet.

"For a few years, yes. I was with Engineers without Borders. A Canadian invention, actually. I've enjoyed life in the smaller villages, which is why I thought Beckwell would suit me. Have you ever been?" He pulled a dark blue polo over his head. For a few seconds, Ginny was mesmerized by the play and pull of muscles in his chest and abs as he worked the shirt over his shoulders and pulled it down.

She blinked and shook her head a moment, bringing his face into focus. Because it was rude to stare at people's bodies. Their glorious, bronzed, muscular bodies. You were supposed to look them in the eye. "Have I been an engineer?"

As the dimple peeked and a slow smile spread over his face, heat spread over hers. "I meant, have you ever been to Africa?"

Great. It wasn't even eight in the morning and she'd already made an idiot of herself.

"Um, no."

"There wasn't any food, so I thought we could catch a bite together later. Is that all right?" Again, he didn't really wait for an answer—though after her last reply, it was probably just as well. Instead, he pulled on a wool sports coat, and they both slipped on their shoes at the door before he held it open for her.

There went that flutter in her belly again. *Frosting!*

Outside, the lawn sparkled with a light early morning frost that likewise coated the windshield of the dark blue compact sedan parked out front. In the stilted conversation as they'd left the wedding last night, James had told her how he'd bought it online, something about fuel efficiency, still more she couldn't really remember.

He unlocked the car door and held it open for her. The action unreasonably made her skin tight and hot. First he had to be too good looking, and now he was a gentleman too? Sigh.

He started the car and reversed down the short driveway away from the perky little white and red house that seemed almost sad to see them go. Finally, he turned around and pulled onto the narrow two-lane highway that would take them into town. "So where have you been? Europe? Asia?"

Ginny struggled not to squirm, instead rearranging her purse on her lap. "No."

"South America? Australia?"

"Actually...I've never left North America."

"I see."

She deflated like a leaking balloon, and started speaking quickly, as though somehow she could still save this. "I mean, I planned lots of trips, but they all got cancelled for one reason or another. Then I traveled quite a bit in the US for the first company I worked for...before they went bankrupt. Then I had my own business, a restaurant supply chain. That didn't work out too well, either." Wow. How impressive she must sound. She pasted on a bright smile. "So, you like to travel?"

"I do, yes." A very long, awkward pause that took them most of the way into town and to the four-way stop, dead center of downtown Beckwell. Downtown Beckwell comprising the corner store and bar, school, emergency center, and library, each of them occupying a respective corner of the intersection. "You didn't tell me where you were headed."

"You didn't ask."

"I'm sorry, I didn't—

"I'm sorry. I didn't mean that to come out so harsh. I just—" She pointed, straight ahead. "The Senior Center. Just to the right of that log building, that's the library. The Center is the big white one on the other side."

Another pregnant pause while James stopped and waited studiously at the four-way, despite being the only one around for miles. It was lovely to find someone else who followed the rules like that, not just when other people were looking.

With her directions, he pulled into the nearly empty parking lot—only a few cars and trucks from the overnight staff available, since most of the residents didn't have cars of their own.

"Would you want to travel?" James asked, putting the car into park.

Instantly an island paradise popped to mind. James in a pair of swim trunks and nothing else. Her in... Well, a mumu maybe. Just the sun, the sand, and the two of them together. Her throat thickened making it difficult to reply. "I'd like to." Oh *cupcake*. What if he hadn't meant with her? "I mean, someday. When I've saved enough." *Frosting. Just get out of the car.* She fumbled for her belt.

He shut the car off. Then reached for his own belt.

Ginny froze. Was this just about being a gentleman and opening her car door again? He didn't have to shut the car off to do that.

Oh, *frosting*. It looked like he thought he was coming in with *her*.

"I'm working!"

He paused, his thumb on the belt release. "I'm sorry?"

"I mean, not working exactly, kind of volunteering? Yes, I volunteer here. I'm sorry. I wasn't thinking. I should have explained before. You know what, why don't you go across the street to the bar and have something to eat there? We can catch up later."

He straightened in his seat. "You haven't eaten either."

"I, er, I'm fine. I'll have one of those food bar things. You know, the meal substitutes."

He cocked a brow. "I've heard of them."

She unbuckled, popped open the door, and scrambled out, leaning back in to see him. "I'm really sorry. I just... Um, health code rules and security checks and stuff, you know?"

"Uh huh." He wasn't buying it.

"You know what? I'll call you when I'm done. It'll only be an hour. Or two?"

He leaned across the seat and reached for her hand.

She froze.

There was a peek of dimple. "Then shouldn't I give you my number?"

"Oh. Yeah. Of course." Oh, *cupcake*. She didn't even know her husband's cell number. She jammed her hand into her purse, fumbled around until she found it, swiped to open it. Then promptly dropped it back onto the passenger seat.

James picked it up. "May I?" At her nod, he punched in his number quickly, then held it out to her.

Their fingers brushed and energy crackled between them. Sparks and lightning in the veins, the flavor of caramelized sugar suddenly so real, she could taste it dissolving on her tongue. All of it not just metaphor, but real. Hopefully the sparks hadn't killed her phone.

He'd paused a second, like maybe he'd sensed the sparks, too.

If he hadn't, she probably better stop in and make an appointment with Daniel, Piper's fiancé and the local doctor. Because that kind of sensory overload couldn't be good for her brain. Especially if she was making it up.

"Well…if you're sure," he said, his brow lowered.

Crumpets. She needed to tell him her secret, about the baking and cooking. How else would he be able to help her learn to use the rest of her abilities? Especially the more common Famine ones. Yet, she'd been keeping it secret for so long. And after his reaction to the muffins last night, and the disastrous seduction failure…she needed some time to herself. To regroup. Replot.

She straightened, and waggled her phone. "I'll call." Then she turned, and raced into the Senior Center before she let the guilt from abandoning her day-old husband change her mind. *Cupcakes*, she needed a mixing bowl.

CHAPTER 10

James sat in the car outside the Senior Center a few moments after Ginny disappeared inside. He tapped his fingers on the steering wheel. So much for keeping his new wife in his sights, and for his plan to charm her today. She seemed determined to run from him, which seemed especially unfair that she'd dressed in that sexy frock. It was like he'd become as mutton-handed as his brothers when it came to women. What was she hiding from him?

He undid his belt and climbed out of the car. The Senior Center in front of him appeared to be a modern facility with generous windows and a large layout. He could wait inside for her. Though she'd made it clear she didn't want him in there. If he put her off, so much for building that trust. Blast. He'd just have to bide his time and go find her when she was willing.

He turned and strode the other direction, across the graveled car park, then cut diagonally across the tarmac and deserted four-way stop to the only other building with an open sign—the wee grocers. The building next to it looked like a bar, but judging from the plywood boarding up the front, it wasn't open.

The bell tinkled above the door, and a tall, slim redhead with glasses waved from the till where she perched on a tall stool, though she didn't look up from her book. Despite the store's small size, it was unusually well-stocked. Everything from a modest supply of alcohol, a small bakery section, fresh produce, and pantry items. He poured himself some hot water from the convenience section, adding a tea bag, and reached for an apple.

"You know, many people believe the apple was the fruit Eve ate that got she and Adam kicked out of the Garden of Eden. It was also an apple that the evil queen gives to Snow White to poison her," a man's deep voice said from behind him.

The hair on the back of James's neck tickled, and he froze. His senses reached out first, finding only a desire to protect, lightning-fast images of Ginny and her friends, and flames. A lot of flames. The punch of raw power there was like a physical blow, and he tensed to hide his reaction. On several missions, he and his team had encountered lesser deities causing trouble for the local population. He'd gotten used to how they felt.

But he'd never encountered one this strong before. This was definitely no "lesser deity." He withdrew his hand from the apples and slowly turned.

A large plaid-clad man, the overhead lights catching on his bald pate, smiled. Although there was something not entirely friendly in his unusual gray-blue gaze, that couldn't seem to settle on just one color. "Mornin'."

"And to you," James replied, still cautious. "You don't like apples?"

The man reached past James, grabbed one, and contemplated it. A perfectly round, smooth, gleaming example. "Oh, I like them well-enough. It's just...sometimes it's so hard to know what you're going to get under all that pretty exterior until you bite in. The darned thing can be rotten to the core, and you can't even tell." His gaze flicked up to James. "Know what I mean?"

They weren't talking about apples. Perhaps the god knew about James's family, the corruption that ran deep through their bloodlines that James had spent so long fighting. He swallowed, and pulled on all his experience of negotiating with gods who'd wanted to intimidate him and caused suffering for the humans living in range. From what he knew of Beckwell, the only real god in the area was Loki, who was a known trickster and shapeshifter. Who'd seemed very interested in Ginny yesterday at the wedding.

"I do. One never can trust appearances," James replied.

Loki's smile, as it was almost certainly him, broadened. Then he raised the apple again. "This apple is also kind of like this town. Not the most exciting on first glance, but with a little effort, it can turn into something truly spectacular. Just as the people who live here can. Mr. Derth, we're a welcoming bunch here in Beckwell for the most part. But we also protect our own, and I have a particular fondness for Genevieve Lack and her friends. I wouldn't take it well if, say, someone came here bringing a threat to any of them."

Bollocks. Either the god suggested James was a threat, or he'd somehow uncovered the threat from USELESS. And their arrival in nine days if James couldn't figure out how to convince them otherwise. Wonderful. It looked like he got to add someone else to the list of people out to end him if he turned Ginny over or she got hurt. "Ginny is special. I don't want any harm to come to her. Nor to her friends."

"Then we have an understanding." The god offered a small, tight smile that didn't reach his eyes. He took a few steps away, then turned and tossed the apple toward

James.

James caught it in one hand.

"The apple and tea are on me. Now, I suggest you go find your wife across in the Senior Center. She'll be down the hall from the medical clinic, the purple door with a green triangle, third from the right. There isn't a lot of time, and you two are going to need to come to an understanding a bit quickly, I'm afraid. After that, you might want to ask your wife about the bachelorette party. It was…quite the smash." Loki inclined his head slightly, then turned and strode toward the door. The bell tinkled as he departed.

James took an uneasy breath.

"He's good for it. You'd better get a move on, Mr. Derth," the girl at the counter called, drawing his gaze. She removed her glasses, straightening on her stool. "After what happened at the bachelorette, people are getting antsy. Some are perfectly ready to take on the gods and end this world, but others are just scared for their families. Ginny's a sweet girl, but some might blame her if things go badly."

He grabbed his tea and lifted it and the apple as he strode toward the door. "Thanks for the warning." Sod it. Ginny might not want him over at the Senior Center, but looked like they needed to have a good long chat.

Frosted sugar cookies, but she'd needed this! Ginny sighed in satisfaction, humming to herself, and drove her spoon into the batter, churning and combining the wet ingredients with the dry, letting the scents and feel of the kitchen well around her. The secondary industrial kitchen in the Beckwell Senior Center was her special haven, and a steal for what she paid. Although the two ovens were aging, the sterile, cheap white cupboards and countertop weren't exactly pretty, and the walls were a dingy pink. The income from her muffins had paid for her new wardrobe, and in a few months she could probably afford a car. The rental of the kitchens was a steal, but the ingredients weren't.

Still, it was worth any cost for this freedom.

She bit her lip, closed her eyes, and let her ability flow through her.

Some people meditated. Some people did drugs. She baked.

Heat spread from the center of Ginny's belly out to each fingertip, each toe. It climbed up her neck and warmed her skin, soaked through every strand of hair. The dull murmur of voices pulsed through her, louder today than they had been. Different tastes, some sweet, some sour, everything in between, danced over her tongue. The hypersensitivity was almost painful, but *holy cupcake*, it was exhilarating, too. A lightning storm inside her skin.

She sucked in an unsteady breath and let the energy travel down her fingertips, down the wooden spoon handle, and into the batter. It eased the dull headache she had from wondering when and how much she'd have to tell her friends. What in *honey cakes* she was supposed to do about James. When she baked, the tastes and textures carried her away. Into a place where there was no time, there were no friends to please, no family to disappoint, no husbands to avoid.

It was the one time and place she knew who she was, and that she was enough.

She slid the last tray of muffins into the oven and the ability whirling through her that surged when she cooked slowly slid out of her, leaving an ache where it had been. Cooking anything brought out the ability, but baking was a particularly sweet indulgence. Though if she didn't want her secrets spilled like a dropped bag of flour, one she had to be careful not to indulge in too often.

She headed to the sink and started washing up, hands deep in sudsy water.

Just the memory of what had happened when Anna had caught her cooking in the back of Lou-ki's place when she was seventeen churned her stomach. He'd been the one to supply all her family's meals, and out of curiosity, she'd started picking them up. She'd been fascinated, watching the way the big man worked the grill, diced the ingredients. That had led to him teaching her a few things, until before she knew it, she was sneaking over to the bar during spares between classes and cooking specials everyone in town came out for. No one ever knew who the mystery cook was, thanks to Thomas helping keep watch, and despite Lou-ki's suggestion she tell them. He'd even suggested she apply to culinary school.

That all ended the day Thomas didn't tell her Anna was looking for her, and Anna had caught Ginny, apron on, hands deep in raw chicken. The disgust on her face... It was like she'd caught Ginny having sex with Lou-ki, not just cooking. The way she'd hustled Ginny out of there. *Lou can do his own damned cooking, or find another cook,* she'd said. *You won't be going back there. It's...it's anti-Famine. It's not safe. Can you imagine what your parents would say?*

Ginny shuddered. Yeah, she could imagine. Mom's reaction would probably be something like the time Ginny had, at six, accidentally let Thomas's name slip. Mom had paled, gripped Ginny's arm, and shaken her until she repeated it, then sent Ginny to her room for the day. Mom couldn't ground her anymore, but cooking would be a sin akin to murder. Just further proof the wrong twin had lived and that Ginny wasn't the Famine she was supposed to be.

Further good reason she hadn't told any of her friends or family that she was back to cooking again, like she'd taken up drugs again. Her best-selling muffins and cupcakes were sold through the Senior Center and everyone seemed to assume they were baked by someone on staff in the kitchens, not Ginny. Would James possibly understand any better?

She stacked the trays to dry, and wiped her hands on the towel before going to the oven and opening the door to check on her babies. Almost done.

"Helll-lllloo? Earth to Ginny?"

The oven door slammed shut as she let go and spun.

Roger perched on the kitchen island in all his bright green ugly glory.

"How did you get in here?" And out of the closed bedroom where she'd trapped him.

"Magic, duh." He stood on his rear legs and crossed green little stick arms. All he needed was a top hat and a cane and she'd name him Jiminy. *"How do you get off ditching me without even a word as to where you're going? And I'm a grasshopper, not a cricket."*

She shook her head and turned back to the oven, making sure she'd set the timer. Her back and feet ached a little, and—she glanced at the clock on the oven. *Maraschino cherries!* It was almost nine. James would be expecting her call. She was supposed to have a plan with how to deal with him. Maybe she could stuff him full of muffins until he submitted to her plans.

"What about a little slap and tickle instead?" Roger suggested.

"Roger, I'm busy."

She headed to check on the first six trays worth of muffins on the cooling racks. Good. They were cool enough to touch, so they'd be ready for the morning tea rush in the cafeteria. She wasn't making enough money with her baking to live on yet, but she didn't have the shame of having to rely on Mom and Dad like a kid who needed an allowance. Unlike Jimmy and everyone else who envied their money, she'd always wanted to make her own, prove she could. Even though most of the time she'd barely scraped by, and Jimmy had taken the little she had in the divorce. She didn't want to have to rely on James for the money either. Yet another way they wouldn't be on equal footing.

"Can I have one?"

"No." She grabbed the baskets out of the cupboard and lined them with fresh napkins. Her hands shook as she gently piled the cooled and fragrant muffins into the baskets. She would have to tell James about this secret, though, if she wanted him to help her learn to access more of her abilities. Especially the more typical Famine ones. Next, she set the timer on her phone to go off one minute before the timer on the oven. She unlocked the heavy industrial door. She really needed to get a door stop to hold it open, but the fact that she could rent the kitchens whenever she wanted made them practically perfect anyway. She could open the door with her butt.

Finally, six baskets stacked in her hands and along her arms, there was no choice but to face the bug. "Are you coming or going?"

"Can I ride on your head?"

"No."

"Pocket?"

"Ugh. Fine. Just...don't let anyone see you. Insects and health codes don't mix." Outside, footsteps shuffled toward the cafeteria, and the hard of hearing yelled disjointed sentences at each other. If she didn't hurry, she'd miss the crowd. And all those sales.

"You have hang-ups. Have I mentioned that? Now could we go to the strip club?"

"No, I don't." *Liar.* "And absolutely not." She helped the insect into the pocket of her apron before she re-gathered her baskets. "Coming through!" she shouted, so hopefully she didn't collide with any seniors. Then she backed out the door.

She had to step quickly to avoid the back-swish of the steel door knocking any of the precious muffins to the ground, and the move was almost graceful until she turned.

And almost collided with James. For the second time that morning. She froze. *Sugar cookies*.

He caught the door before it walloped her, his arm brushing her hair, his body leaned over hers. That rush of salted dark chocolate and coconut rushed over her again, along with a flood of want hotter than her ability had been. "Hello, love," he said, that delicious accent rolling over her.

"Hi," she squeaked, and glanced at the muffins. Would he believe these weren't hers?

"Why not tell him the truth?" Roger suggested.

"Can I lend assistance?" James asked.

Since it was unlikely he'd agree to turn around and pretend he hadn't seen anything, might as well make the most of it. Besides, the longer she delayed, maybe she could come up with some reason why she, the Famine heir who was supposed to destroy all food and basically starve people, was carrying fresh-baked muffins. The same kind as she'd arranged to have waiting in the house for the wedding night. "Uh, okay." Wow. Her sparkling wit kept getting better.

He took a few of the baskets, and she pointed toward the staff entrance to the cafeteria on the other side of the hall, just a little way down. She glanced over her shoulder at James, then knocked on the door.

Barely a breath later, Megan, a petite blonde with a cute pixie cut and a chef's uniform opened the door.

"Thank God!" She leaned against the door to hold it open, taking two of Ginny's baskets and waving her into the larger industrial kitchen. "I thought for a minute I'd have a riot on my hands."

Please don't ask, please don't ask! Ginny silently begged James. She and James followed Megan inside. Ginny showed James where to set the baskets on the gleaming steel prep table. This kitchen was drool-worthy, equipped with every modern appliance, four ovens, and a bustling staff preparing meals for the seniors. Because the secondary kitchen had been intended for catering purposes but then never used until Ginny, it had never received the same spiffy upgrades.

Of course, with James there, she couldn't ogle the appliances as much as she normally did. He followed her lead, setting his baskets down, while Megan disappeared up front to the service counter.

"A riot?" James asked, simultaneously proving either he wasn't telepathic…or he just wasn't susceptible to her telepathy.

"She's joking," Ginny tried desperately.

Megan snorted as she came back around the corner, and dug inside a nearby cupboard. "The hell I am. The line started even earlier today. And not just the residents. Word is out. People come in from all over town if they know it's Muffin Day. As soon as you came in today, I let them know."

Oh, *snickerdoodle*. The day kept getting better. Nothing subtle about having a day with capitalized words to expose her secret.

"Quick, snog him! Maybe it'll distract him," Roger suggested from her pocket.

"Brilliant," James said, with a direct look that suggested kissing him would probably not be enough to distract him from this latest revelation. "Did you supply the basket left at our house last night by any chance?"

Megan turned with a grin. "Of course. Ginny insisted." The situation got even better as she pressed six red and pink wrinkled polymer bills into Ginny's hand, the face of Prime Minister Mackenzie King staring up at her, judging her. Six Canadian fifty-dollar bills.

Ginny glanced down at the cash just long enough for her eyes to widen before frantically trying to throw it back at Megan. "This is too much. We agreed on a dollar apiece."

Megan raised her hands and backed away. "That isn't enough. Sweetie, I'm feeling guilty about ripping you off as it is, but I don't have more cash on hand. Maybe we could work out a new deal for you using the other kitchen and you could come in more often and make even more. You really should consider setting up shop. When even the hunger strike set can't resist these, you know you've got a winner."

Yes, setting up shop would be a dream come true. Except for the nightmarish aspect where everyone would know her secret and that she was the one baking.

"Surely not everyone loves them," James asked, far too curious. Of course he would be.

"We should get out of your way." Ginny grabbed his arm and tugged.

He might as well have been made of stone. An especially dense and heavy variety, as he didn't budge and instead stood, waiting for Megan's reply.

"Not a soul can resist these." Megan laughed. "Me included. If I'm not careful, she'll shut me down. It's all anyone wants. Maybe you'd agree to come work for me, Ginny. I swear I need lessons from you."

Yep, not getting better. Especially with the heavy look James pinned her with.

Megan didn't seem to notice. "Okay, I better run, guys. There's still a few more I take it?"

"Yes, four batches in the ovens right now. I'll bring them over as soon as they're ready." Megan might not know just how wrong it was for a daughter of Famine to be a baking whiz.

But guessing from the look in James's eyes, he did. He wrapped his arm firmly around her waist, and guided her out of the kitchens after a polite wave at Megan.

"Let's chat," he said, iron in his voice.

MUST LOVE FAMINE

Hot fudge sundae. This couldn't be good.

CHAPTER 11

James pulled Ginny back through the hall, through the thinning crowd of pensioners, and across the other kitchen. It was the only purple door with a green triangle, just as Loki had said. Bollocks, he was acting like a brainless ape, like one of his brothers, but she'd completely blindsided him. What kind of game was she playing here? Pretending to cook and, what? Polluting and spoiling the food maybe, possibly making the old and weak sick. Famine was a corrupting factor. Was this proof of that corruption? His stomach clenched, and adrenalin raced through his body. He needed an explanation. Now.

He released her as soon as they made it into the kitchen, and she regarded him warily while he paced back and forth on the opposite side of the counter, his thoughts racing. It could mean she wasn't as dangerous as he'd feared…or much more dangerous than he'd feared. Maybe it was best he turn her over to USELESS. He grimaced, the thought making him nauseous.

She sighed, and he stole a glance at her as she bent

over and checked on her baking. The skirt of her dress hugged her bottom and revealed toned, creamy legs. She looked shagtastic. Not that there'd been much doubt after feeling it in his palms that first night when he'd caught her, then again last night when he'd carried her over the threshold.

He gave his head a shake and rubbed a hand down his face. Not that it mattered a whit. Nor should it have mattered that the entire kitchen smelled heavenly. Cranberries and some kind of spice. His mouth watered.

He may or may not have had a hard time taking his eyes off her ass. Again.

She turned and wrapped her arms around herself, but glanced at him only sparingly, instead staring at either the scuffed floor or her red Mary Janes. "So. Are you going to tell my parents?"

"Tell your…?" He'd lost track of reality somewhere along the line. He put his hands on his hips, scrubbed his hair again. "What game are you playing here? You could hurt those pensioners by spoiling the food."

Her mouth opened, then she snapped it shut. "I…you think I'm *spoiling* the muffins?"

Well, he had up until two seconds ago. "Then what are you doing with them?"

Color climbed her pale cheeks, and her gaze skittered away. "I…" She took a breath, and met his eyes. "I bake them. And you didn't seem to mind last night. Those were my muffins at the house."

He let out a bark of laughter at the joke. But she wasn't joining him. His skin began to tingle. "*You* bake them? Are you actually a Famine heir?"

She put her hands on her hips. "I'm sorry. Did you just accuse my family and I of lying about our heritage?"

"No! Well, maybe. Are you?"

"Yes, I'm Famine clan. Much good that it's ever done me," she grumbled.

106

This was getting them nowhere. He stepped forward and braced both hands on the counter top across from her, then waited until she met his gaze. "Sod it. I'm a Famine heir, and you're *the* Famine heir, but you're telling me you can cook? And no one can resist your food?"

She leaned over and braced her elbows on the table, and balanced her chin in her hand.

He tried really hard not to notice the way it allowed him a very tempting glimpse down the front of her dress.

"For the record, I'm not telling you any of that...not that it makes much difference at this point. But yes, I can cook. And bake. And do all kinds of wonderful things with food that have nothing to do with making it green and fuzzy."

Still not exactly clear what that meant...or could mean. She was the Famine heir. They destroyed food and sustenance. Starved people. According to family lore, it was their raison d'être.

Maybe if he went at the topic sideways. Loki's suggestion bubbled up to him again, even as James's stomach growled at the smell of the muffins. One would think he'd never eaten the way his mouth watered for the things.

"What happened at your bachelorette party?"

She straightened and blinked. "The bachelorette party?"

"Yes. The one where, from what little I know, your friend ascended to become the personification of Pestilence. Perhaps it rings a bell?" he drawled, a brow rising.

She crossed her arms over her chest again, pushing up the bounty of her...muffins. Bloody hell, she seemed unaware of how appealing she was in that dress, how it hugged her figure to perfection.

"Someone's been whispering secrets to you, have they? Fine. Yes, Piper gained her abilities. She's risen to be the first of the four. She may have unintentionally unleashed a plague. The whispers about our rising started late last year among the seers, and I'm up next. It's because of those rumors that your family agreed to the match in the first place, isn't it?"

"That's direct."

"It's faster that way. The timer is going to go off soon, and I don't want my muffins to burn because we're fighting."

"Is that what this is? A lover's quarrel?"

The air thickened around them. Along with other parts of his anatomy. Ginny's eyes rounded, while he wondered if she was still wearing the garter strap.

She swallowed, and frowned at him, her irritation forced. "I'm not sure this is a fight, but I suppose we have to clear the air." She glanced back at the oven. "Three minutes. Why did you marry me?"

He opened his mouth, but she stopped him with a raised hand.

"Please, no nonsense of pleasing your family. You hardly said two words to them all of yesterday, and you didn't even want to say goodbye even though your parents flew out last night."

She was a hell of a lot more observant than he'd given her credit for. Mistake number...bollocks, at this point it was probably mistake two million and three or so.

"Do you have any proof or reason to believe you're rising next?" If she was willing to be so open, all the better to find out what he could.

She hesitated, then reached into her pocket. Then plonked the biggest, ugliest grasshopper he'd ever seen down on the counter between them.

A squidgy feeling made the apple and tea less comfortable in his stomach. In the places he'd worked, he'd seen some ugly insects, even a literal plague of locusts. But then the bright green insect in front of him stood up on hind legs and seemed to cross its enormous front legs and twitch its antennae at him. As though waiting for a response.

"You've taken up bug collecting? And carrying them around?" he asked, lacking the courage to take his eyes off the thing.

Ginny snorted. "Hardly. This is…" She gestured toward the bug, then shrugged and crossed her arms again. "He's my horse."

Hmm. Maybe it wasn't just him feeling like he'd lost the plot today. Ginny hadn't been stealing the pensioners' meds, had she? "The grasshopper…is a horse?"

"His name is Roger. He's more metaphorical than actually…horse-like." She shifted, as though perhaps even she realized how ridiculous her story was. "My friend has a book about all this stuff. You know—the horsemen, the legends, whatever she's been able to track down. And it says the horses will arrive in a clan-related form appropriate to the horseman's—me, in this case— level of ability. The fact that Roger's an insect should tell you something."

That book sounded like something he'd very much like to see in person. Though for now, James dared to lean closer and study the insect. Grasshopper, like the crop eating locusts, perhaps, who caused famine. The bug seemed to study James back with unnervingly human-like intensity. "Will he stay an insect?"

Ginny leaned down, and their gazes met over the grasshopper named Roger. "Probably not. Piper had a toad to start, but it grew as her abilities did. Next into a skunk, then a truck." She bit her lip a second and took a little breath, as though preparing herself for the next words. "Did you marry me just because of my ability? To try and find some way to steal them, or use me?"

Bloody hell, but she was direct. Dangerously so. She'd been able to tell the last time he'd lied. So how could he answer and not get himself in trouble?

"I don't want to steal your abilities," he hedged. True enough. He didn't want to steal them. USELESS wanted to, or rather, to render her harmless.

But, wait. Maybe after all this, he could convince her to see reason. Maybe they were on the same side after all. Maybe he could convince her to give up her abilities to USELESS, or vow an oath of non-harm. "Do you want to use your abilities to hurt anyone?"

"Why would I—" The buzzer on the oven cut off Ginny's words, and she blinked, then turned back around and busied herself with oven mitts and pulling out steaming trays of those muffins, almost as delectable as the woman herself. She put all but one on wire racks, then reached up for a plate in one of the cupboards, and brought one of the treats back to the counter, splitting it open with her fingers.

She hissed and dropped it back onto the plate, cradling her injured digits.

He acted before he thought, and reached for her hand. Tugged her closer, even across the counter. And brought her fingers to his mouth.

They were both half leaning across the counter, a giant grasshopper and a steaming muffin between them. Her fingertips tasted like sugar, cinnamon, with just the slightest hint of something tart, possibly the cranberries. He'd been wrong last night. The muffin last night was a pale comparison in flavor to her. He suckled gently.

Her eyes widened, her lips parted.

Heat and lust shot through him with an intensity he'd never felt before, like he'd been struck by lightning. It'd never felt this good. He was aching and hard. He licked again at her fingertip, pulling her ever closer.

He leaned his free hand on the counter and felt the tickle of antennae against his wrist. A glance down showed the grasshopper...caressing him.

This kiss, letting desire distract him, was utterly mad. He'd finally been getting answers from Ginny, the answers he'd come half a world to find out, and maybe find an ally instead of an enemy, and he was willing to throw it all away because he was feeling randy?

He took her fingers from his mouth. "Ginny, I'm—"

She lunged the short distance across the countertop and pressed her lips to his, swallowing his words.

After a moment of acute shock, and the discovery his bride was a bit inexperienced in the kissing department— what the hell had been wrong with her first husband?—he twitched his hand away from the smarmy bug, and instead wrapped his hands around Ginny to pull her closer. And then deepened the kiss, tasted her.

He'd been mistaken about the taste on her fingertips being from her baking. It was her. She really tasted of sugar and spice…and something not quite as nice, but tart and challenging. Wild. Irresistible. It spurred on the wanting, the lust.

He angled her lips for better access and continued to explore while little mewls of pleasure vibrated up her throat. The blasted countertop was suddenly too big a barricade between them. Somehow it was natural to pull back only long enough to hop the counter, slide over onto the other side, and pull Ginny's softness against him. Those breasts, those brilliant breasts. He might take up writing odes as he slid his hand up the soft cotton of her dress and tested the weight of those precious orbs.

Maybe not odes. That sounded a tad cheesy. Though true.

She pulled back for a moment, and they both panted for breath. "I'm sorry. I…I know we said we'd take it slow."

"Bollocks slow," he said, and stole her lips again. He tugged her more firmly against the ridge of his erection, her softness perfectly cuddling him, her skirts leaving little barrier. Was there a lock on this kitchen door?

The door swung open. "We ran out! Are those muffins re— Oh! I, um, sorry. I'm sorry," the chef from the main kitchen said, her face bright pink. She stumbled back into the wall rather than the door, since she was trying to shield her eyes.

"*Cupcakes*," Ginny muttered and pulled away, the mood cooling faster than the muffin on the counter. It still steamed. "Megan. Wait. I'm sorry." Now it was Ginny's face that was hot. "I know this is completely unprofessional. And in your kitchen…"

"Oh. No. You're newlyweds. He's hot. I, um, I… Can I look now?" The petite blonde faltered.

James cleared his throat, and swiftly put the counter to good use to hide what his trousers could not. "Quite all right. You're here for your muffins? Ginny just pulled them from the oven a moment ago. None of this is her fault. I…"

Ginny stared at him, her face bright pink, her gaze faltering, making it clearer than words that she'd likely never been caught making out before. Why the hell not? Her first husband must have been a complete wanker. Another surge of lust, accompanied by thoughts of what he could teach her and what fun they could have with some ingredients from her kitchen. Whipped cream and cherries to start.

He should feel bad that she was embarrassed, but he'd happily repeat the kiss. Then again, there was growing evidence he was a complete prat.

"It was completely my fault," he said.

Ginny's gaze flashed up to meet his, and it didn't matter that there was someone else in the room.

"Not that I can be honest and say I regret it," he said, his voice raspy. "Because given half a chance, I'm likely to repeat my actions." Only this time, he'd lock the door first.

A small, hopeful smile blossomed on Ginny's face, and it felt like he'd hung the moon.

"O-kay. So, I'll just gather up my muffins and leave you two alone, shall I?" Megan said, gathering muffins in the empty baskets she carried at incredible speed. She never looked up. "Or know what? Why not go back to your place? These seniors will probably be listening at the door." The blonde promptly escaped as quickly as she'd collected her edibles.

Leaving he and Ginny once more alone. The spicy, delectable steam of the muffins swirled around them. The heat zipped through their bodies. Last night, he'd wondered if seducing her would be too smarmy. But today? It was clear her first husband had been a sad arse. She deserved all the pleasure he could give her. If she really was a Famine capable of cooking, maybe she wasn't dangerous at all. Maybe this was the evidence he needed to convince USELESS to leave her be.

He just needed to be sure. "Ginny, about the baking…" He said, his voice thick with lust. He'd much rather have asked her where the nearest bed was rather than if she planned to end the world.

Ginny reached for the lone remaining muffin, the one on the plate beside—yep, the grasshopper was still there, too.

Still, even the bug couldn't completely dampen the desire surging through James as Ginny picked a small piece of muffin off between her fingers, and held it up toward his lips. "Want to try my muffin?"

Now was it just him, or did that sound like a whole lot more than an offer to sample her baking? Gods help him if it was just wishful thinking.

James took the bite of muffin, no more able to refuse than Darth Vadar had been able to resist the dark side. His lips brushed Ginny's fingers, and color deepened on her pale face. His bride and her…muffins were too much of a temptation. He might have made more of it if not for the heavenly fusion of flavor, spice and sweetness, just the perfect touch of tartness that exploded on his tongue. He groaned.

The taste of these would drive him barmy. The muffin tasted only half as good as his Ginny herself. He opened his lips to speak. "I have to ask you some questions."

"Want more?" Ginny said, and without waiting for an answer, stuffed another piece of moist, warm muffin between his lips.

It was delicious, but he had to have answers first. It could mean they weren't in danger. "Ginny, please—"

She tried to stuff another piece of muffin into his mouth. Instead, he caught her wrist and drew her closer. Then his gaze locked with hers, brought her fingers to his mouth and licked off the icing. Her gasp was shaky. He turned her hand slowly and licked off the icing sugar from the underside of her wrist, her pulse pounding beneath his tongue. Ginny made a small whimpering sound, and the taste of her consumed him, made him hunger with an intensity he'd never encountered before. He struggled to remember what he'd been trying to ask her, but what was the use? She could bake. This was no dangerous Famine heir.

He would report his findings to USELESS…in a few hours or so. After he'd satisfied his craving.

"I-I don't suppose you'd like a tour of the town," she said.

He shook his head slowly, pressing a kiss to the underside of her wrist.

She shuddered, and her eyes fell closed. She opened them with effort, took a deep breath, and faced him head on. "Then what about a tour of the bedroom instead?"

James smiled.

CHAPTER 12

Her plan to seduce James lasted almost until they pulled into the yard of their cheery little white house with the cherry-red trim and Thomas materialized in the backseat. His chill on her neck cooled her ardor.

"What are you doing, little sister? Don't make the same mistake you did before. We need this man, and any seduction is only for the purposes of aligning him to our goals," Thomas whispered.

"Are you sure of his motives? Are you sure you can trust him?" Barnabas, the other grasshopper, suggested.

"Oy. Corpse-face and Barn-ass. This is my show, not yours. This lady needs a good shagging," Roger piped up. He then began to sing "Sexual Healing." Very. Loudly.

Cupcake, but between Roger's singing and all these voices in her head, she was getting a serious headache. No, fine, she hadn't gotten a straight answer from James about why he'd married her. So maybe she needed to do that first. Without seducing him. Or maybe before.

Ginny jumped out of the car first with her purse and

the basket of muffins she'd brought home. She'd unlocked the front door and stepped inside before James had even gotten out of the car. It gave her a second to take a deep breath in the front hall of the little house.

"Okay, everyone, out of my head," she communicated. *"Just…I can handle this. But not with all of you giving me a headache."*

"As you wish," Barnabas said, and he and Thomas retreated, taking the chill of their presence with them.

"Are you sure you don't need any pointers?" Roger asked.

"I'm sure."

"But I'm supposed to guide you, help you. What if I—"

"Roger, make yourself scarce. Now." She hung her purse—with Roger in it—on one of the hooks by the door, and toed off her shoes. Roger could rescue himself later.

Heavy footsteps sounded on the stoop outside, and James came in behind her. "Ginny?"

She hurried into the kitchen. Answers first.

Then tour of the bedroom.

"Just putting the muffins in the kitchen," she lied, and ducked into the tiny kitchen. Despite her distraction, the room pulled at her attention. She had a kitchen addiction. Her brow furrowed.

She'd thought the Senior Center kitchen was looking its age. She set the muffins on the counter, then opened and closed some of the yellowing, once-white cupboards. A few of the cupboard doors were loose. She rubbed the stickiness between her fingers. They could also use a scrubbing. And something in them. Every cupboard had been bare. The stove was stained and not even large enough for a standard cookie sheet. The small window above the shallow, single sink had a yellowed lace curtain, and there wasn't even dish soap. She bent over to check one of the lower cupboards.

"I must say, I appreciate the view. However, is there a particular reason you're inspecting our kitchen in such detail right now?" James said.

She popped upright, her face heating, and just barely missed smashing her head into the countertop. *Cupcakes*. She was supposed to be getting answers, not planning a reno. She spun around to face James. "It has good bones. But the cupboards are literally bare. And...I got distracted."

He'd removed his shoes, too, and set the car keys on the countertop. Then he leisurely unbuttoned his wool sports coat as he advanced toward her. "We can buy food later. I thought...we were talking about a tour," he said, his voice husky and deep, that accent rolling over her again and sending heat soaring through her all over again. This close, his spicy scent and the deep chocolate taste of him rolled over her.

She bit back a moan. She had to focus. "You asked if I want to hurt anyone. I don't. What about you? Why did you marry me really?"

He froze in the middle of the kitchen. "I'm glad to hear it." Then began to advance again. "Perhaps we could continue where we left off? There's no one to interrupt us this time."

A shiver went through her at the low timbre of his voice, and his appreciative gaze skimmed over her. "You're avoiding the question," she said, inserting an edge to her voice, and waiting until his gaze met hers.

"I don't want to hurt you," he said, and there was no hint in his flavor to suggest he was lying.

Okay, that part was good. She hesitated a moment, then nodded, shifting her stance against the opposite countertop. Her plate of muffins was behind her and slowly filled the room with their delicious fragrance. "What *do* you want?"

There was the barest instant of hesitation, the tiniest

tang of guilt in his flavor. Before he straightened and slowly began to close the distance between them, his voice husky. "I thought I'd made that very clear back at the pensioner facility." He stopped only when they were almost toe-to-toe, Ginny trapped between him and the counter, though he didn't touch her in any way. Yet.

Her eyes widened, and her lips parted. "I, um, that wasn't—"

He caught her lips in his. *Donut holes.* He'd interrupted her again, and he was trying to distract her. Oh, he tasted good. Her hands came up to his chest, and she clutched handfuls of his polo, the muscle tensing beneath the cloth and her fingers. She opened for him, to let him taste and conquer her. Because she was doing some conquering of her own.

She brought one hand to the back of his neck, so she could better angle her lips against his. Her other hand crept lower, explored the hard expanse of his chest.

James distracted her from that purpose, too, when his fingers found her breast. He teased her a moment, letting his thumb brush once, twice over her nipple, flicking it as it hardened to a firm peak.

She made a soft mewling sound in her throat, and he rewarded her by taking her breast firmly in his hand, massaging it, squeezing, finding the size and weight. She was left grasping handfuls of his shirt, the sensations rushing over her too much to think of any other plan.

He angled his mouth, deepened the kiss, and pressed his hips into hers. She leaned into him, her softness cushioning the hard ridge of his arousal and dragging another groan from his throat. Then his hands found her ass, and he lifted her against the counter and pushed up her dress. He pressed himself against her in just the right place. She gasped and saw stars. And this was with clothes *on*. She tangled her fingers in the hair at his nape, pulling him closer and rubbing herself against his shaft with a breathy moan. Tension coiled and built inside of her, hotter and hotter.

James groaned against her.

Her fingers slid into the gaps between the buttons on his shirt, rubbing against bare flesh, finding the hard disks of his nipples. Her other hand she slid downward and grabbed his butt cheek. His fingers found the zipper on the back of her dress and edged it downward. Cool air caressed her flesh and the lacy edges of her bra, before James loosened it, and then, *frosting* yes, cupped her bare breast. His fingers were warm and rough against her, tearing another moan from her throat when he pulled gently on the nipple. He moved to give the other breast the same loving attention, and ducked his head to take her nipple into his mouth. Liquid heat and fireworks went off throughout her body.

She cried out, holding him against her chest. This was taking too long. He wasn't close enough. Her free hand searched for the catch on his trousers. His fingers slid over her mound, the dampness of her panties, and her head fell back.

Someone tapped on the window.

One tap. Two. Then someone rapping hard enough to rattle the glass.

"James, there's no time for that now. The others are coming!"

Hot fudge sundae!

CHAPTER 13

"Bloody hell." James swore and turned to block Ginny from the kitchen window and view of his friend, Bina. What was she doing here? She was supposed to be safe in sodding South Africa.

Ginny shrieked, tried to cover herself and twist. She lost her balance and fell off the kitchen countertop with another shriek.

He caught her by the shoulders and set her on her feet. Then, just as quickly, he pulled her bra down, refastened it, and pulled up her dress, doing the zip. His heart pounded, his knob still ached with want. But if one of his team members was here, where were the others? Over the years they'd become closer than family, and they usually traveled together. Especially when it was to protect one of the other members. He intentionally hadn't called them in because he could handle this. If what Ginny had told him back at the Senior Center was true, and she could cook, maybe she wasn't Famine at all.

There was more tapping on the window. "James, you

need to—"

"Bina, sod off for half a minute. I'll meet you by the front door." His hands shook, and he tried to smooth them down Ginny's bare arms. His brain was not working at top speed—other than thinking of ways he'd much rather continue to seduce his wife. "Ginny, love, it's all right."

Her face was bright red, her arms wrapped around herself, and she wouldn't look him in the eye. "All right? Someone was spying on us through the window. And you *know* them?"

James gently lifted her chin until their gazes met. "It's my mate. Today is my fault. Both times. I'm sure all any of them are thinking is that we're very happily newlywed." He tried to smile, hoping for a smile.

She dropped her gaze again to study the kitchen floor.

Banging came from the down the hall on the front door. "James, open the damned door. We don't have much time!"

He wanted to growl. Instead, he lifted Ginny's hand, and pressed a kiss to her fingers. "To be continued. Until then…I'm afraid I have to see to this." She wouldn't look at him before he stalked down the hall, flipped the lock, and ripped the door open.

Bina rushed inside, shivering and jumping up and down wearing her red superhero jumper, zipper up to her chin, and bright blue yoga pants. Her short dark hair stuck out from her head in pigtails, her glasses steamy and accentuating her large, dark eyes.

His ability told him just how desperate she was to keep him safe. Bloody hell, talk about a way to make him feel guiltier. And was confirmation of why she should have stayed in Africa. She'd been his friend for the longest of any of the team members, the little sister he'd never had, and she was equally protective of him. But she was much handier behind a computer keyboard than in a potentially dangerous real-life situation, where she was more likely to forget face-to-face interactions weren't the same thing as online ones.

"This is red-alert territory," she said, closing the door on a shiver. "I'm sorry I interrupted you guys, but seriously." Her dark eyes met his. "The others found out."

His pulse jumped into his throat. "What do you mean found out? How much?" The answer would define just how deep the river of shit was.

"Everything!" Bina chaffed her arms. "I'm sorry. I swear, I didn't want to tell them. But there was all this chatter online, and then I found out you went ahead and married the woman? James, what were you thinking?"

"Never mind that." He'd explain how different Ginny was than he'd expected later. Right now, he needed to know how much time they had, because they were at least chest deep in shit. "Where are the others? What's the red alert?"

"You have maybe ten minutes. I jumped in a cab ahead of all of them—do you have any idea how expensive it was to take a cab all the way out here to the sticks? I think Maddox stole a bus. Not sure about the others. I had to tell them, I swear. Maddox, you know how he is. He went all smoke and sparks when he heard. The others think you can't handle this." Bina cringed. "James, they think the best solution is if they kill her first. Then USELESS won't take you, too."

"What's useless? Who thinks they should kill who, exactly?" Ginny's voice was soft. And directly behind him.

Well, fuck a duck.

❧

Ginny's brain had misfired somewhere around the "kill her first" part of the sentence, but it felt as though her entire being depended on the answer to that question. She squeezed her hands into fists, the jangle of James's car keys smothered in her palm, the sharp edges digging into her skin. She needed to understand this situation and just what she'd gotten herself into this time.

James turned to face her slowly, and raised his hands like people do when they're afraid they're probably going to get hit with something. Or deserve to be. "Ginny, I can explain."

"Do it fast. Start with the killing part," she said. Because it sounded like his friends wanted to kill her.

"Questions later. Run now," Roger said, pulling hard on her hair from where he perched on her shoulder.

The stranger who'd spied on them through the window stepped around James, a waif-like creature in a red superhero zippered hoodie and blue cropped pants. She barely reached James's chest and looked like she needed a cheeseburger, stat. Her arms were the size of Ginny's wrist, but she did have enormous brown eyes behind her glasses that some people might have considered rather pretty. There was also her luxurious butterscotch pudding skin.

A sharp spike of jealousy followed by a cold douse of hurt shot through Ginny. *Snickerdoodle*, maybe she was James's "type."

The tiny stranger stuck her hand out, and when their fingers touched, Ginny's mouth filled with the welcoming and surprising taste of creamy vanilla chai. "Hi. I'm Bina. You're a lot prettier in person. You really should have sent a proper profile photo. I hope you won't take it personally that our friends want to kill you. But it's you or James."

Ginny's mouth fell open. Maybe she'd fallen off the counter and had a concussion. Because what the *frosting*?

James grimaced. "Bina…misunderstood. Ginny, I—"

"The hell I did," the tiny woman piped up, rounding on James. "After those rumors cropped up about her rising, we agreed you'd find a way to stop Famine. Not marry her. I brokered the deal only because I didn't think you'd be stupid enough to let yourself get killed."

"I never said kill. Ever," James said, his gaze only on Ginny. He stepped toward her. "I can explain."

She backed away, her insides flipping. *Sugar cookies*, she knew that look. Oh, why did he have to have *that* look? He was going to "explain." Or rather, feed her more lies. It was the same look Jimmy always had when he'd explained why he'd missed another dinner, stayed late at work again…or smelled of some other woman's perfume.

"I never wanted to hurt you, Ginny. I swear it." James was holding out his hands to her again, palms up, as though she'd forgive him. "I thought maybe we could work out a deal. I could help you learn how to control your abilities, so you don't cause any harm. I never wanted to turn you over to USELESS. Not after I'd met you."

"What's useless? And does he think you're a muppet? Time to leave, luv," Roger communicated.

He might not have wanted to hurt her, but just who was he going to turn her over to? Maybe he meant he'd intended to turn her over, but then he'd met her, and what? Decided he could control her instead? The keys bit into her palm as she squeezed. Control her like Jimmy had. Jimmy wanted Mom and Dad's money. James only wanted her Famine abilities. Her insides ached. She'd planned to stay objective, to keep her heart safe to avoid exactly that kind of hurt.

James continued, inching toward her. "Now that I've gotten to know you—"

"Gotten to know me? Hardly." They'd just gotten married yesterday. She'd been so stupid to think she could seduce him, that she might have found a partner. He hadn't even waited more than a day to turn on her. She jerked away, and slid against the wall toward the door.

She groped for her purse. "I'm not staying here. I won't listen to more of your lies."

"Or for his friends to show up. Go. Now!" Roger said.

Ginny turned and raced down the hallway.

James swore. "Ginny, wait!"

She ran with a speed she hadn't known she possessed, though the usual grace as she stumbled. Stupid panic tears burned her eyes, blurred her vision. But she still smashed through the back door faster than James did, and took some pleasure in throwing it back at him. It gave her the few extra seconds to dive for the car, rip the door open and jump in, jamming in the keys and roaring the engine.

James stood on the front porch of the little white cottage, a stiff figure as she threw the car into reverse, hit the gas and spun backward before throwing it into drive and tearing down the driveway and onto the highway. In the rearview mirror, he still stood stock still, hands at his sides and watching. He made no attempt to come after her. Her ribs constricted, and she couldn't draw in a full breath. At least she didn't have to try and get away from him, see what else he was capable of. *Frosting*, why did it have to hurt that she mattered so little to him?

CHAPTER 14

Ginny rammed her foot on the gas harder, the little sedan racing down the highway. She didn't know where she was going, other than away from James and the house. She could go find Anna and the girls. But they hadn't been keen on the marriage in the first place. They could be full of "told you so's." The gold hue of the trees was a blur on both sides, part from speed, and part from the moisture that burned her eyes.

What had happened to keeping her distance from James? She was supposed to be the one in charge this time. She was supposed to keep her heart out of it. She wasn't supposed to be in this position, where her insides ached because she'd been dumb enough to let a sliver of hope into her heart that the attraction they shared could grow into something more. Instead, it looked like she'd found another liar, who'd leave her broken and alone like Jimmy had. She blinked rapidly, but that only seemed to make it worse. She could barely see the school on the rise ahead.

"Ginny, you can slow down now," Roger said from her shoulder, where he clung for dear life.

A chill slid down her neck, and goosebumps rose on her arms. Thomas materialized in the passenger seat, almost as solid-looking as her, every dark auburn hair in place, his eyes a clear green. It wasn't often that he appeared in full form. He had his own grasshopper, Barnabas, on his shoulder.

"Darling, Ginny. We knew his motives weren't pure. But you were doing excellent on the seduction front. I'm very impressed. Soon he'll be putty in our hands," Thomas said, his voice a whisper in her head. *"He said he wouldn't kill you. Remember, we need him. For training. To become stronger."*

Ginny cringed and wished she could melt into the seat. "You were…watching?" Just how many witnesses had there been to what had happened? And oh, *meringue*, a lot had happened. Everywhere James touched her turned to liquid heat, and she turned into a woman gone mad for sex.

Ugh! Flavors of all kinds, from fish soup to chocolate chips all rose into her mouth at the same time, along with a dull but steady drone of muttering voices. She'd lived in the city before, but the inundation of other people's thoughts and tastes had never been like this before. A pounding ache started behind her eyes, and she blinked to focus on the road through her tears, the voices, the tastes, and the three males in the car with her. She eased off the gas just a tiny bit. All those extra voices and crud in her head probably counted as distracted driving.

"What has happened does not mean one must abandon all hope. It is but a setback," Barnabas the grasshopper said, wise and monk-like. Just like you'd expect a venerable apocalypse horse to talk.

"Oy! Dead guys, shove off!" Roger shouted, a vibration that tasted sour on her tongue emanating from

him toward Thomas. *"What about what Ginny wants, huh? Stop pimping your sister. I mean, thou dost not, er, pimp."*

Thomas huffed. *"Barnabas and I will be back when you've calmed down."* He and the other grasshopper vanished.

"Don't worry. I was the only one there when things got interesting, and I only watched the really good parts. I kept them away, just as promised," Roger supplied, patting her shoulder. *"If you want venerable, I can do that. I am your real horse. Even if I don't talk all snooty."*

"Oh, I have no doubt you're my horse. What other kind would I deserve?" she told the bug, and wiped at her eyes. The voices were like someone playing their music too loud next door. A dull but impossible-to-ignore rumble.

Thomas had a smart horse, well, still a grasshopper, but Barnabas seemed more…official. Wise. The kind of horse a genuine rising horseman should have. Ginny's shoulders sank. Everyone seemed to think she shouldn't have her abilities. Was that what James had been getting at when he'd said they'd work out a deal? Her plan to get him on her side had been flawed from the start, especially when she'd met him and he was so obviously out of her league. She didn't even understand who it was he planned to turn her over to—

"Brake!" Roger squealed.

"Frosting!" Ginny screamed at the same time she spotted the obstruction ahead. She slammed her foot on the brake. The car fishtailed for a moment, the tires screaming, her knuckles white against the steering wheel.

She stopped before she hit either the large city bus parked diagonally in the four-way stop, the little old woman…or the large man prostrate on the asphalt at the end of her glowing leash.

She didn't recognize the large, dark-skinned man,

but since the barrier had come down and made it easier for both Normals—non-magical people—and others from near and far to visit Beckwell, there were a lot more strangers.

Mostly it looked like someone else was having a cruddy day. Although the skinny little old woman, her hair completely white and put up in pigtails, was definitely not the man's wife, so at least this didn't look like another of those new-marriages-gone-bad like her own.

The voices hadn't gone away, and from the little old woman she picked up the equivalent of a delighted, erotic giggle. Just pain and humiliation from the man.

Cupcake. Ginny bit her lip. The bus blocked the entire intersection. She could probably drive around it if she cut through the parking lot that served Lou-ki's bar, the gas station, and minimart. But there were no other cars in sight.

No one else to help the poor guy on the leash.

She shut off the car and climbed out. No matter who they were, it was wrong to leave anyone at the mercy of a Beckwell senior citizen.

"Fear not the old people," Roger piped up, in a forced tone. *"Even if we were running for our lives and you were about to kill us both."*

"I'm not suicidal."

Roger snorted. *"Your driving technique says otherwise."*

She closed the car door and started toward the little old woman and her prisoner. Uh oh. She was close enough now to tell who it was. When Ginny had started working in the Senior Center, she'd been warned about a few of the residents. This resident had required at least five separate and carefully worded cautions. The most repeated being to never accept food from her—it was probably enchanted. Oh, and never go to one of her parties. She made the free-love hippies look repressed.

Probably part of why this particular resident was not free to wander around unsupervised. Not that many of the Beckwell Senior Center residents should have been wandering around unsupervised. Most were powerful, curmudgeonly, and prone to believing everyone under the age of seventy should probably be taught a lesson.

Ginny blew out a breath but approached with caution. Around here, people looked out for one another, which meant she could do no less. Even if she was muffin-less, and therefore had nothing available to bribe the old woman.

"Good morning, Sister Marguerite," she called, lifting her hand in a small wave and trying to smile through her fear. In those warnings, hadn't there been something about fireballs too when it came to Sister Marguerite? The first two points had been so distracting, she'd forgotten the others.

The wren-like woman blinked through thick lenses. "You're that Lack girl, one of the four. What do you want?"

The man down on his knees was bigger than he'd looked from far away, even down on his knees, and he groaned. "This fiend is a nun?"

She pulled harder on the leash, and the big man groaned again. "Who are you calling a fiend?"

Ginny sighed. "Wrong kind of sister. She's a disciple of Eros," she explained to the man, then turned her attention to the woman. "You know you're not supposed to kidnap any more men, Sister Marguerite."

The tiny woman pulled on the large man, who was forced to crawl behind her on the asphalt toward the Senior Center. "You have your new husband, this one's mine. I caught him, and you can't have him."

"I belong to no one, woman," the big guy growled. The action only got him dragged a few more feet toward the Senior Center.

"Didn't you hear? There's an apocalypse coming, boy. Time to cash in your chips, tally up that bucket list. Me? I'm finally having me an orgy!" She whooped with delight, her wrinkled face wreathed in smiles.

Well, *cupcakes*. The man did look like decent orgy material, all muscles, smooth skin, and that pretty face. How was Ginny supposed to convince her otherwise?

"Convince her of what? Let's see if we can get an invite!" Roger added his own whoop.

A touch on her elbow made Ginny jump, even as the taste of Pop Rocks exploded on her tongue. She narrowed her eyes on the large, plaid clad man who stood beside her. "Where did you come from? I see you put on your Lou face today, huh? Or do you prefer Loki? I think I'll just go with Lou-ki to cover my bases."

The stormy blue eyes had been the same no matter which role he played, and now, if anything, a shadow of hurt darkened the blue. "You may know one of my secrets, dear Ginny, but it doesn't change who I have always been. I saw the trouble and came out of the bar to see if I could help." He nodded toward the imprisoned large man, who was trying to argue with Sister Marguerite. That technique was getting him dragged back to the Senior Center. "What about I give you a hand with this, hmm? I'll deal with Marguerite and the bus, you feed the guy. That leash will have sapped his strength."

He didn't wait for an answer, like the fact that she didn't have time for feeding strangers, but the idea of cooking through the latest debacle was appealing—not the problem where little old women were kidnapping strangers, but the part where her own husband evidently was in on some plot to stop or kill her.

She glanced toward the bar. It was still boarded up with plywood after the whole bachelorette party debacle. But the door had been rehung and the open sign glowed in the only remaining window.

Lou-ki strode confidently toward the intersection, casting a quick look at the bus. A grin flitted over his lips, before he focused on the tableau. "Margie, my sweet, you know you're just too much woman for a simple creature such as this." He inserted himself between the man and the old woman.

The imprisoned man growled something, and Lou-ki whacked the guy absently in the back of the head, still giving all his attention to the old woman.

Sister Marguerite patted her hair back, smiled up at Lou-ki, and batted her cloudy blue eyes. "But not too much for you?"

The demigod touched the glowing leash, and the bright orange faded to gray. Marguerite barely seemed to notice, too rapt on her newest prey. The leash snapped, and Lou-ki waved a free hand indicating Ginny come to help, while he put his arms around the frail old woman's shoulders and led her back toward the Senior Center. "Oh, too much for any one man, I think. Though I have heard Albert is quite the catch."

"I was planning the most wonderful orgy. There was going to be Jell-O shots," Ginny heard the old woman say as Lou-ki led her away. She shut out the rest. There were some things you just couldn't unhear.

The big guy was still down on his knees, fighting weakly against the leash. Ginny helped untangle it from around his large shoulders, barely contained by the tight black T-shirt, and from around his camo-clad legs. She coiled up the leash, now seemingly as inert as electrical cord, while the man struggled to stand. He fell back onto his knees.

She knelt and helped him to his feet. He leaned heavily on her and they limped their way toward Lou's Place, otherwise known as the town watering hole. Good thing she was built for this kind of thing, or the guy would have squashed her. As it was, her knees still ached. And the touch of her hand against his filled her mouth with his flavor—Tabasco with a hint of ghost pepper. Good in a chili, maybe, but not her thing.

Although Beckwell was developing a crazy-high population of hot men. This guy included.

She'd even married one of them.

"This is…shameful," he said, as they painfully made their way up the stairs. His complexion was too dark to be certain, but she had a feeling there might have been a hint of color on those high cheekbones.

"It's just Beckwell. Sorry about that. You really need to be extra careful around the seniors."

He grunted, and she tried not to roll her eyes. Well, at least James wasn't a grunter. Seriously, were men incapable of speech?

That whole quagmire of thought made her scowl as she pushed open the temporary door held up by plywood blocking the hole in the front wall of the bar when Piper's horse—in the form of a large truck—had driven through said wall. To run over Lou-ki, as a matter of fact. Funny. He hadn't looked worse for the wear at the wedding yesterday, or this morning.

Then again, it would probably take more than a horse of the apocalypse disguised as a Porta Potty truck to take down a demigod.

After getting the big guy seated on one of the stools at the bar, Ginny stepped behind it. "You just sit there and catch your breath, okay? I'm going to cook up something for you, high protein, some extra iron. That should help."

She didn't wait for another grunt but instead strode behind the bar, through the swinging doors, and back to the kitchens, the feeling familiar though it'd been years since she'd last been back here. She tied on the white apron hanging near the sink and scrubbed up before she assessed the fridge and supplies.

Not much had changed since Lou-ki had invited her back here as a teenager and introduced her to her gift for cuisine. She fell back into the familiar patterns with ease, a tiny curl of some extra energy and her ability spiraling through her. But here, at least, she belonged. Here she knew what she was doing.

Even grilling the steak while mixing up a quick batch of biscuits was calming.

James had said he didn't want to hurt her, and no, he hadn't been lying. Maybe this was just clearing the air for them, finding out his intentions. At least she didn't have to keep wondering what he was lying about.

She needed to talk this through with the one person other than Thomas who could make her feel safe: Anna.

Just so long as she didn't have to tell Anna about the cooking and baking quite yet.

Less than fifteen minutes later, she piled the plate high with the steak—something told her this guy was a "I like my steak mooing" kind of man—along with potato, some grilled spinach and veggies from the stock she'd found in the pantry, and a steaming biscuit. The rest she covered and put aside for Lou like she'd always done. *Donut holes*. Lou-ki. Lou didn't exist.

Unless...maybe Loki wasn't lying, either. Maybe he was the same man, just a different aspect she hadn't known about.

Ugh. She must have been stupid, to even think of trusting *Loki*.

"Why would he lie? Easier to flatten you like a bug if he wanted to," Roger said.

She picked up the plate, cutlery, and a napkin and carried it out toward the stranger, opening the swinging door with her butt, and expertly moving aside before it swished into her. The big guy's dark eyes zeroed in on the plate and his nostrils flared. He dug in before she had a chance to come back with a glass of water for him. He made groaning and appreciative sounds, his eyes occasionally closed in rhapsody, the merest hint of a smile on his lips with each bite.

She smiled and went back to tidy the kitchen quickly before coming back to find him finishing off the last of his plate, eating the last few bites.

"This food. It is fit for the gods," he said, his unusual gold eyes meeting hers. He took another bite, shook his head. "No, it is too good for them."

She chuckled. "Feeling better, then?"

He nodded, finishing off the steak. "Greatly restored, yes. Thanks to your feast." He cleared his throat. "I offer thanks for your assistance with the dangerous old woman. I owe you a debt."

She leaned back against the edge of the opposite bar, in front of the shelves of liquor. "It's no big deal."

He crossed his utensils carefully on his plate and shook his head slowly. "No, milady. It is indeed a big deal. It is a matter of honor that I repay my debt to you."

What was he, an escapee from a Renaissance fair? "We don't even know each other. Although I am curious why you've come to Beckwell."

Although, wait a minute…hadn't the woman at the house said James's friends were coming? They'd be strangers in town.

Ginny straightened, a tingle of apprehension on the back of her neck. She smoothed down her flowered skirt with damp hands. Wow, was this sounding dangerously familiar. She was already getting a bad feeling about whom he might be.

James she might be able to trust. In time. But his friends? Especially that Maddox fellow?

He pushed his plate away. "I had to…borrow the bus in my haste to reach a good friend who has made a grievous error. I have come to save him. But once I have done that, I will repay my debt to you. However you see

135

fit."

Yep, not looking good.

She glanced at her wrist, pretending to glance at the time. Remembered she wasn't wearing a watch. "You know what? Why don't we table that for now. I was on my way to meet a friend of my own." She edged out from behind the bar, and closer to the door.

"We should be running, shouldn't we?" Roger said.

"Of course." The big man stood, towering over her, and bowed low in front of her. "Then 'til we meet again. I am in your debt. My name is Maddox. Maddox Drake."

"Of course it is," Ginny said faintly, her smile gone faint. *"Yeah, now we run."*

CHAPTER 15

After a sneaky trying-not-to-look-sneaky escape from the bar, Ginny didn't bother with the car. She made the short dash on foot across the four-way to the welcoming front porch of the log-cabin-style library. It was Sunday, but Anna spent most of her free time at the library. Ginny banged on the front door.

"Anna, open up!" More banging, and a quick glance behind her, but no sign that the Tabasco-flavored Maddox had followed her.

Okay, fine. Maddox wasn't a completely unheard of name. Another Maddox *might* have come to Beckwell and gotten captured by Sister Marguerite. That Maddox might be completely unrelated to the one who James's friend said wanted to kill Ginny. Which, on the whole, seemed rather unfair—she'd never even met him.

"We're getting that a lot lately, luv." Roger said from where he'd snuggled down into her hair. *"You're about to inherit powers that will make the gods shiver in their boots. Probably should get used to it."*

"I am not getting used to people wanting to kill me." Nor to the steady thrum of voices still in her head, and the confusing mix of flavors on her tongue, the effect of which made her nauseous and her head ache.

She raised her hand to bang again when the door cracked open, and Anna peeked out, her long braid of dark hair loose and frizzy, her bedhead broadcasting that she'd slept in the library. Anna blinked, stepped back, and opened the door for Ginny. "Gin, you okay?"

Ginny hurried inside and locked the door, peeking through the blind, just to make sure the big guy hadn't changed his mind about following her. "No. James hates Famine. And his friends are here to kill me. And something about something useless that also wants to kill me. We kissed, which was wonderful, only not, because what kind of man has friends who want to kill his new wife? Unless the sort of make out session was a distraction, if I've married a psycho. Oh, and I don't think Lou-ki is as bad as you all do, because he just helped me. Although, he didn't mention that the guy I was cooking for was also the one who probably wants to kill me the most. Though, come to think of it, that is kind of suspicious. I mean, Lou is Loki, and Loki can read minds and stuff. I think? Anyway, did he actually put me in danger?"

She struggled to catch her breath, inhaling the taste of the library: Anna's dark roast coffee, old books, a hint of mildew, and a strange spiciness that always sparked on her tongue the moment she stepped over the threshold.

Anna pulled out one of the chairs at the massive scarred conference table near the front of the library, and gently pushed Ginny down into it. "Take a breath. Sit. We'll figure this out."

Ginny sat for almost half a second before she hopped up to peek out the window again. Nope, no sign of the big guy yet. Or Lou-ki. Or the bus. Where had the bus come from? "Did you see a bus drive off? Like a big city one."

"No, but I've been deep into research," Anna said from near the rear of the library with the coffee maker.

The library wasn't huge, maybe half the size of a gymnasium, and although Anna had conceded to allow a half-dozen computer stations along with the requisite DVDs and CDs, about a third of the space was dedicated to what they all referred to as "Beckwell weirdness." It was filled with overstuffed shelves that groaned with the weight of scrolls and ancient looking leather tomes, only the circulation desk standing between it and everyone else. Well, and the War clanswoman.

For as long as Ginny had known Anna, since just before kindergarten, Anna had hunted down bullies, protected her horsewomen sisters, and fought fiercely for the underdog, no matter who that put her in conflict with. Probably why no one on the town council, not even Lou-ki, had the guts to ask Anna to change how she ran her library. Or to remind her that it was supposed to be a public library, not "Anna's" library.

Anna caught Ginny's elbow and again guided her back to the table, this time pressing a green mug of steaming coffee into her hands.

"I heard a lot of questions and not many answers. Slow down, and just tell me what happened. Did James hurt you?" There was a hint of darkness in her tone and a sharpness to Anna's anise taste.

"No. He wouldn't…" Ginny broke off. Did she really know that? "One of his friends arrived at a rather…unfortunate time."

One of Anna's dark brown brows quirked upward.

Ginny flushed, and stared into her coffee. "She warned us his other friends were coming. That one of them, a Maddox, was going to kill me."

"Did James seem surprised by this?"

Ginny turned her mug round and round. He'd

139

seemed plenty surprised, judging from the swears and sharp tone. Yet he'd also still taken the time to make sure she was decent first. "I think so."

"How *many friends* are we talking about?"

"Well, I met two."

"Are they armed?"

Ginny stared at her friend, her response a squeak. "Armed? As in, with weapons?"

"No, with breadsticks. Of course with weapons," Roger piped up. *"Did you see the muscles on the big guy? His hands were weapons."*

Anna leaned close, pushing Ginny's mug aside so she could take both of Ginny's cold hands in hers. "I need to know what we're up against. I hoped James would prove to be an ally, but I won't let him or anyone else hurt you. Now, do you remember if you saw any weapons? What are James's abilities? Are there any other details you can tell me? Anything else I should know?"

Like about Ginny's secret abilities? Like her unbelievable culinary skills, even though she'd promised Anna years ago she'd stop cooking?

"James said he'd never wanted to hurt me. But I ran anyway, and I don't know what abilities he has. Then there was a bus in the middle of the four-way, and this huge man, Maddox, had been taken prisoner by Sister Marguerite. Lou-ki and I helped him and then, I, um, came here."

Anna stared patiently at her for a few moments longer, as if she knew Ginny wasn't telling her everything. Then she squeezed Ginny's fingers and nodded. "All right. Let's start with that." She headed off to the circulation desk and rooted around a bit. She finally emerged with both her giant brown Four Horsemen scrapbook with all its bulging pages. Nia and the others liked to call it the Bigass Book of Scary. She also held a manila file. She hesitated a moment, then slid the file toward Ginny.

"I know I said I wouldn't…but I couldn't let you, the closest thing I have to a sister, marry a stranger without knowing more about him. So, I…researched him a little," Anna confessed, avoiding Ginny's gaze. She opened the cover of the Bigass Book of Scary and hefted through tabbed sections until she reached a particular bookmark.

"Research" in Anna's vocabulary probably meant she'd dug deeper than the CIA.

She didn't even know Ginny and Thomas had selected James specifically to be their ally. One more secret. Ginny frowned a moment, stared down at the manila file for only a second longer, then opened it.

James's piercing blue gaze stared out at her from a slightly grainy photo. Ginny's breath caught. "You knew what he looked like." Then again, with Anna's methods, she'd probably known his underwear size and whether he preferred boxers or briefs.

"That's not all I knew," Anna confirmed quietly. "Do you want to read it, or should I give you the short version?"

Ginny paged through the file, her eyes darting over the words. Some she'd known before, like that he was fourth child of five boys. Others were a surprise, like the bouts of illness when he'd been young that had often confined James to bed, private tutors, then Eton College when he was in his early teens, then onto Oxford University. Doctorate in Agricultural Engineering, Biological Engineering, a certificate in Food Science, graduate studies in hydrology. Various detailed reports about clashes with his family, especially his father and older brothers. Then some details about the team he worked with in famine-struck areas. Combating famine, finding ways to save people. Not causing it. Why had she been so foolish to think he'd help her gain her abilities?

There was a black and white copy of a photo showing

six people. She recognized only three of them. The tiny woman who'd interrupted them today crouched in the right. Behind her was Maddox, glaring at the camera. There were two other men, both good-looking, and a woman who looked like she'd walked off a fashion runway somewhere. James stood in the center of them all, that intense gaze of his staring straight at the camera.

She closed the file without reading everything and massaged her forehead, the headache behind her eyes growing. "You knew he worked to combat famine," Ginny said, her words barely more than a whisper. Oh, *lemon bars*, what had she done? James wasn't the ally she'd been looking for, but a dangerous enemy. He wanted her to suppress her abilities even more than the girls did.

"Precisely," Anna said, and leaned closer again. "Are you sure there's nothing else you should tell me?"

Gulp.

"Come on, luv. Get on with it," Roger said.

He was right. She took a deep breath, set down her coffee. But couldn't bring herself to meet Anna's eyes. "I...haven't been completely honest when it comes to my abilities. Because they're not really Famine-like at all. I, um..."

"You've been cooking again," Anna said quietly.

Ginny's gaze flashed up. "You *knew*?"

Anna raised an eyebrow, her tone dry. "You had noticed the library isn't very far from the Senior Center, right? And that everyone in town is talking about your muffins?"

"Oh." The word stole Ginny's breath, and her shoulders sagged. "You're really disappointed, I imagine." Although it was also a huge weight gone knowing Anna knew the truth.

"Why would I be disappointed?" Anna asked, as though she didn't remember that scene at Lou's Place years ago, and calling Ginny's abilities "anti-Famine."

Ginny straightened. Wait a minute. Now that meant her friends could help her gain her abilities. She didn't need James. "So maybe we could work together on understanding my abilities?"

Anna gave Ginny a long-pained look. "I thought we had been."

It was too hard to hold her gaze.

The War clanswoman cleared her throat. "I'd hoped if we didn't use our abilities we wouldn't have to rise as the four and become the target of the danger that will entail. Seeing as that doesn't seem to have mattered, at least you're still safe. I resumed my research of companion abilities after what happened at the bachelor party." She flipped through the Bigass Book of Scary some more. She looked up at Ginny through her lashes. "It was after that first time I found you the kitchens that I came across the idea. Companion abilities are the equal yet opposed abilities to typical horseman abilities. Like the graces balance the seven deadly sins. In your case, it seems you're more proficient at creating than destroying."

"Companion abilities? You mean, like I can destroy food and create it?"

Anna ran her finger down a page, then looked up, her eyes bright. "No. More that you don't seem to have the typical Famine abilities at all. Don't you see, Ginny? If you rise, you won't be Famine. You'll be, I don't know, Abundance?"

Anna's words were like a whollop to the chest, and it took a couple of breaths before Ginny could speak. "Then I won't be one of the horsemen. I won't be one of you at all," she whispered. That's why Thomas's grasshopper Barnabas was more official. Thomas really was the one who should have been Famine.

Thomas *was* the one who should have lived.

Anna was on a roll, and so excited she didn't even

seem to notice Ginny's heartbreak. Of course, for Anna, nothing would be better than the news that she'd never gain her full abilities. "I wasn't certain at first, and I'd hoped James would be the perfect partner for you, another measure to keep you safe, keep you from rising. Although maybe you don't have any typical Famine abilities at all, if we're lucky. It's like Daniel and Piper—a doctor paired with Pestilence? Now we've found you someone who can help control and dissipate *your* abilities. He's studied famine, knows it inside and out and how to stop it. He's fought it all his life. He's perfect for you. All you need to do is tell him you have no intention of using your abilities, that you're on the same side. This is how we defeat the League. This is how we prevent the apocalypse and prevent the rise of the four. This is how you get your happily ever after."

"You've really thought this through," Ginny said weakly. Her stomach ached like she'd swallowed acid. It seemed like Anna thought Ginny should sit happily on the sidelines and watch her friends become powerful and stop the League. She'd never wanted to start an apocalypse or starve people, but she'd always thought she was one of them. That her abilities would help them and everyone else to see that when she helped stop the bad guys. If she wasn't one of the four, who and what was she?

She scooted to the front of her seat and leaned forward. "Um, do you think maybe we should get a second opinion? Or, hey, maybe all of us should get together and really dig into who the League of Extraordinary Assholes might be. We could figure out how to stop them, how to find the rest of the objects they're using to reflect what happens in Beckwell out into the broader world."

Anna waved the suggestions off. "Oh, we're on it, don't worry. Piper is helping Daniel at the Senior Center where there've been the largest number of illnesses relating to her disease, though thankfully everyone has recovered so far. Nia is…well, I'm not certain what Nia is up to, besides talking to dead people, but she's still using her network to find the rest of the Fates on the League so we can stop them. The League doesn't know that you don't have typical Famine ability, so they may still target you. The best thing you can do is go home and clarify all this for James, get him up to speed. Who knows? Maybe his friends could even prove helpful."

Now that they know I'm basically useless. Unless the war party needs snacks. "What about practicing our abilities? Learning to use them so we can defeat the League?"

"Why don't you just tell her what you want?" Roger said.

"I'm trying," Ginny communicated back.

"Ah, here we are," Anna said, running her finger down the open page of the Bigass Book of Scary. "'Famine, the third horse'—well, not this time, hmm?"

Yep. Because Ginny was such a failure at being one of the horsewomen, she couldn't even get the order right.

Anna continued without noticing. "'The black horse, carries a pair of balances or weighing scales either said to measure out food during famine, or possibly dispense justice. Unleashes aggravated distress and mourning, a hunger that cannot be quenched. Earth element, telepathic, affinity with plague insects and animals.'" The War horsewoman looked up. "I wonder how your companion abilities will manifest. I'd suggest James, with his studies in agricultural engineering and hydrology, may be tapping into some of his earth element abilities. He seems to have found ways to use his Famine abilities for good. Have you tried to communicate with him telepathically?"

"I, um, no?" So far, she had none of the described abilities.

"Except for telepathy and an affinity for beautiful creatures like moi," Roger said.

"Yes, but I think Anna's right. I'm better at making food than destroying it. I can make plants grow instead of killing them. I'm like...anti-Famine." But wait. When James was at the house, he had said something about helping train her so she couldn't hurt anyone. And she didn't want to hurt anyone, but maybe he still could help her gain Famine abilities. Like maybe they'd been suppressed. She could make it clear to he and his friends that she wanted to help her friends, protect her town, and in no way hurt anyone. Surely then they wouldn't want to hurt her.

"Don't forget me, your valiant steed. You must be Famine. We can figure this out. Perhaps you're doing something wrong?" Roger said.

That much was obvious.

"Ginny?" Anna touched Ginny's wrist.

Ginny jumped and blinked. "Sorry!" *Cupcakes*, but the whole having more than one conversation at a time was confusing.

James was still the answer. Now he knew about her cooking, and she knew why he'd married her. Now they really could be partners. No more half-baked plans to seduce him into helping her. No more getting too close to him and possibly getting hurt. He'd be like her personal trainer. Her Famine trainer. He'd said he didn't want to see her hurt, so he could help protect her from his friends and whatever useless-whatevers were after her, too.

"Umm, are you sure about this? Help you lose your knickers? I'm certain he'd be into that. Help with the rise of the four? Not sure he'll be into that, luv." Roger said.

Ginny ignored him and stood.

Anna blinked up at her. "Where were you? Did you hear what I said?"

"Sure. Yes. I mean, you know what? I think you're

right. I should get home. Talk to James about all of this."
She stood, and headed for the door.

"Well, of course. That's a good idea. I just, you'd
mentioned Loki…"

"Yes, he was at the bar. Helped me with Maddox.
Well, if that was helping. Thank you, Anna. Nice talk."

She unlocked the door and stepped outside.

Directly into the arms of her new husband.

CHAPTER 16

James's arms closed around Ginny, the feel of her against his chest somehow right. Like she belonged there. For a moment, she looked up at him, her hands on his shoulders, and he wondered if he might get away with a kiss.

"We have to stop running into each other this way," he murmured, not that he minded. Anything to get her back in his arms again, which was moronic, but was the truth nonetheless. He felt like a prat after the disaster back at the house, and had spent the last two hours searching for his lovely bride. On foot, seeing as she'd taken his car. There were advantages to a town this small.

She pushed out of his arms and closed the library door behind her. She rubbed bare arms and the autumn breeze sent golden leaves dancing across the library porch, the light pale as day turned to evening. "I guess I'd better start looking both ways before running through doors."

He slipped off his sports jacket and draped it over her shoulders, pulling it closed around the front. It was purely coincidental that his fingers brushed against the soft exposed skin of her collarbone.

She sucked in a sharp breath.

Remember where you are, you fool. Out front of the library, run by the War horsewoman. And as much as he'd rather take Ginny home and make love to her all afternoon, he couldn't. Bollocks, if what Bina said about the salt-damaged fields she'd passed on her way into town were any indication, Ginny was lying to him and she'd been manifesting more than just the ability to bake heavenly muffins. When the hell she'd had time to do that he couldn't say. But he needed to keep a closer eye on her. He needed to get her to come with him. So he could keep her safe…and keep the rest of the world safe from her.

There was also the strange headache he'd had after Ginny had left. Practically like a hangover. Had she done something to him?

Never mind Maddox and the others coming to interfere. Although maybe it was just as well they were coming. Because he lacked all objectivity when it came to his new wife.

He took a step back from Ginny and jammed his hands in his pockets as he stepped down from the library porch. Away from temptation. "I apologize again for Bina…and probably for the others before you meet them." He held out a hand, indicating she precede him down the sidewalk.

She gave him a long look but stepped off the library porch to stand beside him. She didn't take a farther step down the narrow concrete path. "So, you married me to stop the rise of Famine. Because you thought I was dangerous."

He sidestepped the question. "I've experienced the worst that famine can dole out on a nation, on a people. I've seen starving children and parents who must decide who eats and who doesn't. In my family, I've also seen the cruelty that can be inflicted using inherited ability. When I saw an opportunity to stop at least some of that suffering, I had to take it."

"What about your friends? The ones who want to kill me?"

He chose his words with great care, like Kirk negotiating with Klingons. "They're a bit…overprotective. I didn't invite them in here, but they were concerned."

"Because I'm dangerous."

He reached out a hand and slid it slowly down her upper arm. "No. When they meet you, I know they'll see things differently. As I do."

She shivered at his touch, but didn't move away.

She was caving. Good. He stepped closer, and cradled her jaw in his hand, her soft curls brushing his knuckles.

"Love, I'm so sorry I wasn't honest with you from the beginning. Please believe me. I want to keep you safe. And I will. From my friends…and USELESS."

It hadn't felt right, using her as he had from the beginning. This would be better. They could work together to make sure she didn't develop dangerous abilities. He'd find a way to convince USELESS to either take those abilities or that she was harmless. He wouldn't let them harm her.

"Is Useless a person? A thing? I don't understand why you keep talking about them."

He stroked his fingers over her cheek and took a moment to appreciate the softness of her skin. He tried to decide how much to tell her. She already didn't trust him. If she knew the truth, that it was his fault USELESS was after her in the first place, she wouldn't come with him. With the damage to the fields, there was the alarming possibility she knew more than she let on and she was trying to use him.

But he had to at the very least warn her of the threat USELESS posed.

"USELESS is the legal enforcement agency of the gods. The United Supernatural Exalted Law Enforcement Secret Service."

"That's a dumb name and doesn't sound all that scary." Ginny quirked an eyebrow.

"USED, basically the UN of the gods, took almost fifty years to agree on a name in the first place. They didn't think anyone could possibly mistake the term with their acronym. Their name aside, they are dangerous. It means the tribunal of the gods has heard about you and your friends. And they'll be coming after you. All four of you."

Ginny gulped. "You mean…like angels?"

Obviously, her parents had told her some of the scary stories about angels, but not enough about the gods. "No, not nearly as bad. Whereas angels believe they're on a divine quest for destiny, most of the agents aren't bad people. So long as your case doesn't get in front of the tribunal of the gods, there's a chance for survival."

"If it does go before the tribunal?" she whispered, the breeze catching at her bright hair and sending it dancing.

"They've never found anyone innocent before," he said quietly, clinging to the words of the deal he'd been promised. He couldn't possibly turn her over now. He wanted to trust her. He'd find a way to save her. "But you won't ever see the tribunal. Because we have eight days left to train you before agents arrive and convince them you're not a threat."

"Eight days? What do you mean 'before agents arrive'? What about my friends? Are they in danger?" She practically shrieked, pushing his hand down.

He kept his hands on her forearms so she couldn't run. "Bina used to work for them, and she still has inside contacts, so she monitors them for us. They're concerned about Pestilence, but now that she's risen, there's little they can do to stop her, especially with the Fomorian clans backing her. It's not certain yet that this Death or War will rise, at least, not immediately. It's your rising that's imminent and that has them worried." He shoved the lump of cold guilt further down in his belly that they might not be arriving at all if not for him. And that he withheld pieces of the truth. "Listen, this is why my teams' arrival could make all the difference. They trained me to survive and thrive out on our missions in the most dangerous and inhospitable environments. Teaching you about your abilities and how to use them can't be that different."

He slid his hand down to her hands, and caressed her fingers with his. "We don't have much time. We need to start training immediately." He dropped her one hand, and tugged her gently toward the sidewalk. "We should go. Please."

Her wide green eyes searched his gaze for a moment, then she slowly followed him. Leaves crunched beneath their footsteps as they crossed the tarmac and the four-way stop to where the car stood. They'd reached his car, but she made no move to reach the passenger door or get in. Instead, they stood near the front hood, her arms still wrapped around herself, the cold wind chilling him through the thin cotton of his shirt.

"You've known the agents were coming for a while. Haven't you?" she said bluntly.

He winced. "Since before the wedding."

"I told you I don't want to hurt anyone, and I, at least, wasn't lying. What if you're wrong about me? What if you're wrong about what the rise of Famine could mean entirely?"

"Come again?"

She took a small step closer, bit her lip a second, then looked him dead in the eyes. "What if my Famine abilities aren't dangerous? What if by ascending, I could actually help the world?"

"Help? How?"

"Well, for starters—"

"James Derth, is that really you? What are the chances?" The bubbly female voice cut off Ginny, and she frowned, snapping her mouth shut.

They both turned to watch the petite, perky brunette cross the road toward them from the school.

Well, bloody hell.

೮౩

Ginny turned to glare at the intruder. Could she not just have a conversation or make out with her husband without interruptions?

The woman had perfect curls bouncing on her shoulders that couldn't have been natural—or shouldn't have been. The same went for her boobs. Little Miss Perky indeed.

"You look at other women's tits? Since when? Why was I not involved?" Roger cried.

Of all the horses she could have gotten, why did hers have to be a porn fanatic? *"I meant, she looks fake."*

Miss Perky's gaze was locked on James like he was the biggest, ripest strawberry in the field.

He took a small step toward Ginny. "Can I add another advance apology to my tally?" he said quietly.

Ginny didn't have time to reply before Miss Perky was on them like meringue on lemon curd. Despite the chill, she wore only a thin T-shirt—probably the better to show off her assets. She flung open her arms to wrap them around James.

James caught her forearms firmly in his, holding her off, and offered a tight smile. "Daphne. How unexpected." He pushed her away gently, and took up position next to Ginny, wrapping his arm lightly around her waist. "Have you met my wife?"

Roger pulled on Ginny's hair as he leaned over her

forehead, evidently for a better look. *"Hubby is not happy to see her, is he?"*

Ginny pretended to brush back hair from her forehead, pushing Roger farther back into her curls. James stood stiff, his one hand fisted at his side, a tick starting in his jaw. Hmm…just how daring was she, and how willing to do whatever it took for some private time with James? Although when she was around James, she felt daring enough to do anything.

"Whatever you're planning, luv, it sounds fun. Can I play, too?"

She finally had a way for the little green bugger to prove himself useful in a way that didn't involve riding in her hair or giving her bad advice. *"Yes, please."*

Roger cackled in her head.

Miss Perky, aka Daphne, looked ready to lunge at James again, but turned a sparkling smile on Ginny.

Ginny was waiting with a dazzling smile of her own. "Daphne?" She cast a quick glance back at James, who looked momentarily alarmed before his expression cleared. "This is *the* Daphne?" She improvised, her words suggesting she and James had thoroughly discussed the woman when in fact, she'd never seen or heard of her before today. She grasped Daphne's hand in her own before the other woman had finished widening her eyes. Then Ginny had to hold on tight to her smile and composure as the taste of rotting tomato and mold filled her mouth.

She dropped the other woman's hand as fast as possible, turning and wrapping her hand around James's muscular bicep. "Darling, you didn't tell me she lived here," she said to James.

"I just recently arrived. Perhaps that was why I didn't receive an invite to the wedding," the other woman snarked.

Ginny kept her smile fixed, and focused on James's

heavenly taste of dark chocolate and coconut. It still wasn't enough to completely get rid of the taste of rot.

Whatever kind of being Daphne was under those perky boobs and perfect hair, it was nasty.

"I didn't know myself," he said, his expression somewhat bemused.

Daphne's gaze, meanwhile, had narrowed, even while the smile stayed plastered on her face. "You've talked about me, James?"

"Talked about you? Of course not," Ginny said. *Blech, blech, blech.* She needed some water. Or mouthwash. "You know James—far too much of a gentleman for that. We've just shared *all* our secrets. And regrets." She squeezed James's arm and looked up at him. *Chocolate chip cookies*, but he was gorgeous.

"Every one," he murmured, staring down at her. He brought his arm around her.

She shivered and couldn't seem to help herself from pressing closer against him, the way he'd touched her in the kitchen, the taste of him practically overwhelming. She could lose herself in those blue eyes of his, the feel of him beneath her fingertips.

Too bad they hadn't really told each other all their secrets. Because she'd tasted deception during his explanation of USELESS. She also hadn't exactly told him about Thomas and her precise plans, either.

"We were just going, weren't we? Somewhere private." Her voice had gone breathy with anticipation that was one hundred percent genuine.

His arm tightened around her, and his gaze riveted on her lips. "Definitely." He spoke to Daphne, but his raspy words were focused completely on Ginny. "It's still our honeymoon."

Daphne cleared her throat, loudly. "You couldn't make time for—eeee!" She tried to grab her back, twisting and jumping around like she was having a bizarre kind of seizure. "What is that? Oh no, it's on me. It's gone down my shirt!" She shrieked. She jumped and twisted, tearing at her T-shirt.

"Off you go, luv. I've got this," Roger said with a cackle.

"Get it off me. Get it off!" Daphne now danced around in the gravel trying to pull off her shirt.

"Yep, these are fake. You called it."

"That's our cue," Ginny whispered to James.

He cocked a brow. "Should we help her?"

"It's just my grasshopper, Roger. She'll be fine. Unless…you want to stick around?"

"Gods, no. It's not a problem leaving the, er, insect here?" He strode around the car and opened the door for her, his eyes a deeper stormy blue-gray color as he watched her fold her legs into the car.

"I left him in the bedroom this morning, and he still managed to end up at the Senior Center. He'll be fine."

James closed the door behind her, climbed in, and they drove off and escaped before Daphne had fully pulled off her T-shirt.

She glared at them both as they drove away, and her thoughts telegraphed themselves to Ginny's mind with unnerving accuracy. *"You will regret this. Your time is coming, bitch."*

Ginny's breath caught. Now that seemed like a lot more than just someone who was a tad competitive.

They already knew that one of the League members was an aging soccer-mom type with terminal cancer named Louise Dole. And Piper's fiancé had told Piper he was a suspicious of a new woman in town who'd as much as threatened him. Could that be Daphne? Could she be part of the League of Assholes?

James's dark chocolate flavor and the secluded privacy of the car distracted Ginny from any serious thoughts. Other than what they could do with all that privacy on a little back road.

Strudel. This man made her forget every moral she thought she'd possessed. Along with every lick of sense. She was supposed to be questioning him, straightening things out between them. The plan to seduce him was out. It'd probably never been a very good plan in the first place. She knew next to nothing about seduction.

She definitely wasn't thinking about licking. Or tasting. Or how easy it would be to reach over, slide her hand up his pant leg, and cup his—

"Thank you for that back there," he said, his voice stiff. "I'm sorry. For that." He paused, a frown flickering over his face, though he stared out the windshield. "And for earlier. With Bina."

Do not reach over and fondle anything. Big girl panties, Gin...sexy panties for when I know it's safe. "It's...fine." But they'd just stood together, like a real couple, and it felt very empowering. Very sexy. "I have to say, I'm a little surprised you didn't want to rescue her. Daphne, I mean. She's an ex?"

He snorted, cast a glance at Ginny, then back to the road. "Surely your grasshopper can't cause any real damage. I'm starting to see his usefulness, by the way, other than a charming fashion accessory. Daphne likely would have invented some catastrophe. And ex would imply we had a real relationship. We didn't. But Daphne thought we did." They passed onto a quieter section of road, and unexpectedly, James pulled them off onto a quiet little laneway.

Her pulse revved. Huh. Had he telepathically read her mind about looking for a little privacy and time together?

Instead, he turned to her, his hands loosely lying overtop of the steering wheel. "She and I were never together. In any way, despite what she might insinuate."

Cinnamon roll, but he'd just gone and made himself

even sexier. "Oh. I mean, that's good to know. Of course, we both have histories…" She shut her mouth before she said anything stupider.

"Like your first husband."

She groaned. "He was my high school sweetheart, a Beckwell local, and a mistake. A terrible one. I'm pretty sure he had leprechaun ancestry, because all he cared about was my parents' money."

"You'll pardon my presumption, but from why I can tell, he definitely didn't treat you as you deserve. He was a fool for valuing money over the treasure he'd married instead."

She turned to just stare at him, her throat thick. "I…wow."

"I know how a woman like you should be treated." His gaze was on her lips again. Then burned a path down toward her chest.

It was really tempting to push back her jacket and bare more skin for him.

He blinked and closed his eyes with a low growl that she'd swear had a hint of Scot in it. He turned back toward the steering wheel. "You were saying how you're ascending, how if you became Famine, you could help."

Was she? 'Cause pretty sure she'd been thinking about how the gearshift wasn't that bulky, and she could totally crawl over that thing and into James's lap.

Oh, *cupcake*. Roger wasn't here, and those dirty thoughts were completely and entirely her own.

She tried to think of Anna. Of how scary it'd been at the bachelorette party when the League had tried to take over Piper's abilities, and Daniel had almost died, and everyone else had gotten sick, and there was puke and…

Okay, lust gone.

She opened her eyes. Saw James.

Okay, mostly gone.

She raised her chin. "I don't believe I have typical

Famine abilities. I've told you before, I don't want to hurt anyone. What if I rise…and I help stop the spread of famine? With your help."

He leaned back. "I'm listening."

She blew out a breath. "All we—I mean my friends and I—know about our abilities is what we've learned from old texts and legend. But when my friend rose as Pestilence, many of the abilities weren't exactly as described. For me, they're almost nothing like described. I don't even know for sure what abilities I should have, but I don't think anyone was expecting I'd be better at creating food than destroying it."

"Is that your only ability?"

Strudel, but this was harder than she'd thought it would be. She'd never told anyone who wasn't dead or a grasshopper the truth. "I can hear Roger's thoughts. A-and sometimes, if I'm really upset, I've heard other people's thoughts, too," she said, thinking of the whisper of thought she'd gotten from Daniel after Piper had been kidnapped. The fear of the guests at the bachelorette party when they'd become ill.

"Is that all?"

She dropped her gaze to her lap, and fiddled with a fingernail. "I can taste people," she whispered.

"You can *what*?" His voice turned to gravel, and he was staring at her mouth.

She struggled to clear her throat. "I mean, I don't go around licking people." Yep. Not better. Oh, *buttercream frosting*. She was thinking of licking James.

He made a strangled sound and clenched the wheel.

She had to look away, her face on fire. She'd just run from him earlier because she was afraid of falling for him, because their attraction was messing with her head. Plus, his friends and USELESS still wanted to kill her. She wrung her hands in her lap.

"I mean, I taste people. When I meet them, I get a

distinct association of a flavor. How the taste changes also tells me if they're lying or not."

James's touch was gentle as he touched her jaw, slowly raised her chin until her gaze met his. Found the kindness in those stormy blue eyes. He brushed his thumb over her lips, the pad rough against her sensitive flesh. "I've always been able to tell what a person wants and needs when I meet them. For everyone but you. What do you want, Ginny?"

"You," she said softly, the word slipping out before she could stop herself.

His gaze darkened, and his grip tightened very slightly on her chin. He leaned closer, his voice rough. "This could get very complicated."

"Isn't it already?"

His lips almost tipped into a smile, and he stroked his fingers over her jaw, as though memorizing the shape. Again, he brushed her lips with the roughness of his thumbpad. "I would like nothing better than to take you home to bed. To taste you. To teach you about pleasure. However, seeing as our home is currently overrun with my team who wrong-headedly want to attack you, I fear we'll have to deal with that problem first, don't you agree?"

She whole-heartedly did not. Maybe her plan to make them partners and keep things professional could expand a bit. Because while her plan to seduce him had been half-baked, she was more than halfway seduced by him. Maybe she could still find a way to use that to her advantage. And pleasure.

CHAPTER 17

Ginny was still trying to figure out how to convince James not to involve his friends when they rolled up to their cheerful little cottage. She wanted James. The way he set her body on fire, the way he made her feel somehow important. She wanted him in bed, in the car, in the kitchen, with green eggs and ham if necessary, whatever.

She did not want his friends. What if they took one look at her and knew she wasn't good enough for James?

A large gray and yellow tent was set up just to the left of the house. Much worse were the five people who stepped out from it, blocking the entry.

Well, *chocolate cupcakes with cherries on top.* They looked even scarier than they had in the photo. There was huge, dark Maddox next to tiny Bina, who was like a tiny Halle Berry. Next to them was a gorgeous model wearing camo—a scary Zoe Saldana. Two other heartthrobs, one as dark as the other was light, looked like they'd stepped off the shoot of some Hollywood war movie...and forgotten to leave their prop army gear and weapons behind. One wore some kind of gun across his chest, while the other was into knives.

"Um…guess you haven't explained to your friends yet how they're supposed to help me, not kill me." She locked her car door. It might not stop them, but at least it'd slow them down.

"No, I didn't have a chance," James said, his voice low, his gaze likewise on the waiting group. "They're…a bit intimidating, I admit. But that's only until you get to know them. We're all close. For some of us, our friendship is the closest thing to real family we have. It means they're protective. They'll see reason…eventually. None of us are fans of USELESS."

A good-looking blond man stepped out of the house, turned to the five scary people, seemed to exchanged words with them, then threw his hands in the air and jogged toward the car. When he was close enough, Ginny recognized him as James's brother.

"What the hell, Charlie," James muttered, before he popped his door.

James's brother braced his hand on the top of the car and leaned inside. He had the same sandy blond hair and masculine features as James, but there was a spoiled softness to the younger brother, like everything had always come easy to him, which James had either grown out of, or never had to begin with. Still, there was kindness to his smile, and he gave Ginny a roguish wink.

"Hi, luv. Sorry, didn't introduce myself yesterday. I'm Chas, James's brother. The only good-looking one of the lot. Don't you just look scrumptious today. Sure you married the right Derth?"

"You're family now. This is Charlie," James said, shifting so his shoulders blocked her view of his brother. He pulled the keys from the ignition, then turned to his brother. "You were supposed to be on a plane yesterday. Not enough for excitement around here for you, wasn't that how you put it?"

"Wouldn't you know it, I ran into a bunch of your friends at the airport. Now, I wouldn't have known they were your friends and all, seeing as you've never bothered to introduce me, but judging from their surliness and the amount of dust coating their clothes, I figured they matched you. Then that little cutie, Bina, isn't it? I overheard her looking for a cab to this place and how she might be able to slow the others down. I thought, what are the chances anyone else would want to come here? She left, I introduced myself, and here we all are."

He leaned around and gave Ginny another charming smile. "I could take this lovely lady somewhere safe for a while and entertain her, if you like."

James opened the door, forcing his brother to jump back. "That's all right, thanks." He leaned back in to speak to Ginny. "Give me a moment, and I'll straighten everything out." He tried to give her a smile, but it was so tight, there wasn't even a hint of dimple.

Frosting, the scary group was closing in.

They didn't broadcast their thoughts or flavors like Normals, suggesting all of them probably had some level of paranormal ability, though they were not pleased with James. They gathered around him, hands on weapons or on their hips. The huge dark man in the middle, Maddox, was even a head taller than James now that he was standing instead of imprisoned and on his knees.

Probably should have let Sister Marguerite have him. Saved herself some trouble. Though, in good conscience, could she have left anyone to Sister Marguerite?

James spoke to them, his brother Charlie at his side. From the way he speared his hand through his hair and glanced in her direction, things weren't going well. He rubbed the back of his neck, then turned back to the intruders.

If today had proved nothing else, it was that rising

was not going to be as easy as she'd thought. All these people trying to kill her was ample proof of that.

Goosebumps rose on her neck, and the temperature inside the car dropped several degrees, broadcasting Thomas's arrival.

"There will be no threat we can't conquer once we rise, and we need James to do that," he said from the backseat.

"This must be very overwhelming, Genevieve. Remember, great reward does not arrive without great effort and challenge. We will be nearby to assist whenever you require," Barnabas the Wise Grasshopper added from Thomas's shoulder.

James knocked on her window.

Reluctantly, she unlocked the door.

Another tight smile from him. "Look, I will work this out. I promise. It just might take a bit longer than I thought. Why don't you go inside? It's brass monkeys out here."

Guess that meant cold. She did still have his coat. She nodded, missing Roger's smartass remarks about now to lighten the mood. Her fingers shook as she freed her belt, and it was difficult not to break into a run as seven pairs of eyes from James and his team all watched her progress into the house. Yet, he'd still be out here for who knew how long. She slipped off his coat, and handed it to him, before she dashed toward the front stoop.

She slammed the door behind her and leaned against it, letting her breath sag out. Were her abilities worth this? *Cupcakes*, she'd so much rather be baking muffins.

☞

James pulled on his coat, still warm from Ginny's body, and waited for her to close the cottage door before he rounded on his team.

"What the hell do you mean you won't help me train her? I told you. She's not dangerous. She wants to cooperate. She doesn't want to hurt anyone."

He'd expected a bit of resistance, but not outright rebellion. They didn't have time to waste with in-fighting. Ginny had to start her training ASAP. Surely, they had to see what she was really like. She'd stopped to give him back his coat when she certainly had needed to.

"Not dangerous? My friend, perhaps you've been too distracted by your new wife's assets to see the truth, but the signs of famine are all around us. Fields are white with salt starting near the edge of town. Crops are failing, and we passed herds of starvation-thin cattle," Asher said, an edge to his usual smooth tone, though his pretty-boy blond looks were as usual, flawless. He was their PR guy, since he could charm the panties off the Queen. Just your garden-variety siren.

Probably better he didn't have too much time alone with Ginny. James tried to ignore the sliver of jealousy that made him want to keep his wife and friend separate.

He could feel his mates' fierce desire to protect him, and how antsy they were to be here, but surely Ginny couldn't be guilty. "When did you have time to do all that investigating?"

"You weren't exactly quick in coming back after finding the woman," Nahla said, her arms crossed over her chest, lips set in a firm line. Like the rest of her nymph line, she was both beautiful and deadly, with a deep connection to the earth. She might have come wrapped in a super-model exterior, but there was no doubt Nahla was one of their fiercest warriors, capable of taking on even Maddox if pushed. Her bad side was never a comfortable place to be, and he'd definitely landed there today. Her rich, caramel voice almost made her angry words sound less insulting. "Did you stop for a quick slap and tickle? Honestly, James. I thought you were smarter than to allow yourself to be led by your dick."

"James? Stop and do something not in his ten-year

plan? Perish the thought," Charlie piped up.

"Sod off, Charlie," James said, though there was no heat behind his words. If he got Nahla to see reason, he might be able to convince the rest of the team too. "I gave her my word that we'd help train her to use her abilities so I can prove to USELESS she's no threat."

"Train her to use her abilities? What's to stop her from using them against you and to start her own apocalypse after that?" Nahla said. She shook her head angrily, her dark braid shaking. "In all our journeys, all our negotiations, we've encountered no greater threat. There's a reason she and her compatriots make the gods nervous. They're dangerous. We should stop them while they're still human and weak enough that we can."

James shoved a hand through his hair again, which at this point probably stood on end. "Will any of you help with her training? Because I refuse to turn her over to the gods. Ginny isn't what I, what any of you, expect. She's kind and sweet. She wants to start her own cupcake and muffin business, for Pete's sake."

"She actually did seem very nice," Bina offered, trying to help.

Asher snorted. "I'm certain she'll be very nice about taking over the world and starving children, too. How many times have you said that the horsemen clans aren't to be trusted? Your clan in particular."

James swore below his breath. "Sod it. I guess you can all go home then. Find a new mission."

"Oh, don't get so pissy," Nahla said. "We said we wouldn't help train her. We didn't say we wouldn't help. You're going to need intel when the USELESS agents arrive in a week, then someone to run interference. Bina says there was some kerfuffle with someone else starting trouble in the town? The League of something?"

Blast. He had been too distracted by Ginny and the desire coursing through him to get more information on the League. "The League of Arseholes, I believe she and her friends call them." Although, if his team investigated them, at least if Ginny did tell him anything about them, he could confirm whether she was telling the truth or not. "They want to use Ginny and her friends to start the apocalypse from what I can tell."

"Gee, and you mean they didn't marry her first, before they found out her intentions?" Nahla said dryly.

"It seemed like the best way to get close to her at the time," he said. Marrying Ginny was one regret he didn't have. True, things weren't precisely ideal, but if she'd been looking for a Famine partner to help her achieve her goals, far better it had turned out to be him than one of those other dodgy wankers in the family tree.

Nahla sighed. "Now it's me being pissy. Look, just watch yourself, will you? I can't believe she's as nice as you seem to think. They never are. I don't want to see you go down for it. We'll look into what else is going on in town and report back. We'll also need to monitor and analyze the damage caused by your wife, and how far it's spread. At least we're close by for backup when you come to your senses."

James shook his head. "None of you will help me set up a Famine boot camp for her?"

Bina's hand shot into the air. She looked around, saw that no one else was similarly inclined. "Geez. This is like civil war, but I'm definitely on team Cap." She shifted closer to James. "That's you, by the way. Do you suppose your wife will mind if I experiment on her a little? Just a few electrodes to measure her ability and record her aura's activity."

"No experimenting. But thank you." He squeezed Bina's shoulder briefly. They'd met shortly after he graduated Oxford and joined Engineers without Borders. He'd been a completely green and naïve fool who was lucky to have survived that first year working in India before he'd met Bina. She'd introduced him to her friends, who, with the addition of Maddox, had become his team. Outcasts and rebels against their respective families and species, they'd formed a tight bond on the oftentimes dangerous missions they'd worked together, handling sometimes natural and more often supernatural destruction that caused harm to surrounding communities. Until today, they'd always found a way to work together toward the same goals.

He hadn't given returning to Africa and their work much thought beyond stopping Famine. Then he'd met Ginny, and it was becoming clear he wouldn't be leaving anytime soon. He'd left England to give back and escape his family, while somehow making up for the harm his family caused. He and the team moved around so often, they'd become his home. For the first time in a long time, he was exactly where he wanted to be, not just where he had to be.

Just so long as he found a way to explain to Ginny his part in USELESS's interest in her. A way that didn't paint him as the villain that had painted a target on her back, however inadvertently.

"Tahiti is overrated at this time of year. I'll stick around just to make sure you don't cock this up," Charlie volunteered, knocking James on the back. Maybe James wasn't the only Derth black sheep who could find a way to use his abilities that didn't hurt people. There was hope for little brother yet.

The same kind of knowledge he needed to ensure Ginny had, especially when she'd soon be inheriting all the Famine clan's abilities.

James stuck his hand out and shook his brother's hand. "Cheers, mate."

"You are certain this beautiful goddess you've brought back is the Famine bitch we've come here to kill?" Maddox said, his massive arms crossed over his chest. The good sign was he wasn't smoking, and no sparks came from either his mouth or his ears. The hazards of working with dragons. That, and a distinct disdain for modern language and society. The only thing Maddox seemed to like about the modern world was ketchup. He still preferred his broadsword over modern weapons, though as the team's "muscle," he grudgingly made some concessions.

"I'd ask you to watch your language when it comes to my wife," James said, trying to keep his tone mild.

"As I am in her debt, I cannot in good conscience kill her until it is repaid. I will remain to assist with training and watch for my opportunity," Maddox said solemnly.

Just what had Ginny done to save Maddox and get him in her debt? James shook his head. Whatever the case, at least it meant he didn't have to protect Ginny from Maddox for a little while.

"I'm going to say this for the last time: no one is killing anyone. Especially not my wife," James said tightly, meeting the eyes of every member of his team. He didn't need to have to protect Ginny from them, this supposed League, *and* the USELESS agents.

He turned last to Caspian, the most easygoing of the bunch, and Nahla's older brother.

The ultra-rare variety of nymph, a male, Caspian was the team strategist as he rarely let emotion dictate his actions and could think both quickly and broadly. His expression was unreadable behind silver aviators that concealed his distinctly inhuman eyes.

"Caspian, come on, mate. Help me out. Surely you don't want to kill an innocent woman," James said.

Nahla snorted at the innocent remark.

Her brother was slower to reply, smoothing his chin thoughtfully for a moment. "You know my feelings on violence. We have seen too often the heavy cost famine brings to the most vulnerable. That said, we cannot ignore the threat posed by USELESS. Maddox is correct: if we kill her or turn her over to the agency, the less chance they will come for you. Our work is valuable. Together, between ground force missions and innovation like your food bar, we can save thousands of lives. You've told us yourself the legends of the horsemen clans, how they eagerly anticipate the apocalypse and the destruction it will bring. As it is, I too am surprised at your impetuousness. The gods and their ilk are known to renege on their contracts. At this point, I'm not certain whether we can save you or your wife."

This was not a promising start to Ginny's training.

CHAPTER 18

Ginny stood in the center of her tiny kitchen, all the cupboard doors open, and frowned down at the red Fiestaware mixing bowl in her hand. One of the first bowls she'd used when Lou-ki first invited her back into his kitchens and she learned to cook. What was next? Flying monkeys coming after her? The League of Assholes was after her. Plus, agents from the gods. Plus, James's friends. She'd never in a million years imagined rising to become Famine would be so...dangerous.

And now her kitchen had been stocked by the mischievous demigod, Lou-ki, who could be one more new problem. She might have wanted to run when confronted with James's team, but she needed his help too much for that. She needed a partner other than just a smut-talking grasshopper if she had any hope of rising as Famine...and staying alive.

The front door opened, and there was the sound of shoes being kicked off, a jacket shucked, and then the smooth, heavy footstep she recognized as James. Her heartbeat kicked up a beat, and she turned and put the bowl back in the cupboard with the others. She'd closed most of the cupboard doors by the time James cleared his throat. Of course, when she was bent over closing one of the lower cabinets.

She turned, and caught his heavy-lidded gaze on her butt. A pleasurable little purr rippled through her. Which was dumb. Partners, remember? Without benefits would be the more sensible, though much less fun, way to go. *Frosting*, he made that blue button-down look so darned sexy, the way it flexed over his chest.

She blinked and forced herself to meet his eyes, to focus on more important matters at hand. "So, do your friends still want to kill me? Lou-ki seems to have stocked our kitchen, and I can't quite decide why. He's either being helpful, so we don't starve…or he wants me to start an apocalypse."

James let his gaze slowly rove over her until he met her gaze, his eyes dark. Then he rocked back on his heels, as though he'd just processed her words. "I'm sorry…Lou-ki?"

"The name I've decided on for Loki. Because he used to disguise himself as the friendly neighborhood bartender, Lou, when he was actually Loki all the time. Hence, Lou-ki. I don't really think he stocked the kitchen in a 'women belong in the kitchen' way, but more a 'the four women of the apocalypse could end the world' kind of way. The food is probably fine. Whatever his goal, I doubt he wants to kill us. Your friends?"

James frowned. "They won't be a problem. They'll investigate this group you told me wants to start trouble in town, and I can put them on Loki if you like. Bina, Charlie, Maddox, and I will see to your training." He stepped forward, holding out his closed hand, palm up. "I have a surprise for you."

Her chest tightened at his approach, and her breath

came faster. She stared at his fingers, and thought of the last time they'd been in this kitchen. How those fingers had felt on her breasts. "A-a surprise?"

He stepped close enough she could catch his masculine scent, the dark chocolate taste of him on her tongue. It was heaven, blotting out the mess of others she kept picking up. Just his presence seemed like a distraction from the cacophony of other thoughts too.

"A peace offering," he said, his voice raspy. "To start our new partnership."

Now she wanted him to be holding a condom in his hand. Maybe a flavored one. "Really?"

He opened his fingers. "Look who I found outside."

A large green grasshopper sat there. *"He does taste dreamy. I've been licking him since he picked me up, and he doesn't seem to have noticed,"* Roger said.

"Stop licking my husband." If she couldn't, neither could Roger. *Frosting.* She had been hoping for a condom. She brought her hand close to James, and their fingers brushed. Sparks of heat and electricity shot through her, sending little quakes up her arm and straight to her core. The hair rose on her arms and nape, her skin hypersensitive. And waiting.

He was close enough she could see the little silver flecks in his eyes, and smell the hint of some expensive, yet subtle aftershave he'd used. His gaze darkened and dropped to her lips.

Roger started singing "Let's Get it On." Really. Loudly.

The back door opened and closed, and there were more voices. Two men, and Bina's higher voice, two of them arguing.

James broke their shared gaze. He transferred Roger to her hand and backed away. "Well. Glad we've found him then. Let's get started with training."

A day and a half into training, and James was getting antsy. Ginny wasn't progressing as quickly as he'd hoped, and sleeping across the hall from her but not being able to touch her only aggravated his sour mood. He'd had an email from his accountant, and there were discrepancies in his books. As though someone might have been skimming some of the money that should have been going to the charity. He pulled his wool coat around him against the wintry chill in the air and watched as Ginny knelt on the snow-dusted ground a few feet away and tried to unsuccessfully kill the plant she'd grown. For the seventh time that day.

Its leaves were looking lusher and greener all the time.

This was what he had to focus on—finding a way to protect Ginny. Not the damned money or catching a thief.

She held out her hands, as though that might help, and bit her already torn lip. "Come on, you stupid plant. Die."

Bina's fingers tapped away at her keyboard, as she typed up her observations of Ginny's aura and the rise of her ability. "Does cursing at the plant help?" she asked.

Ginny shot Bina a withering glare, dark circles underlining her eyes. The glare had as much effect on Bina as it'd had on the plant.

Maddox, Bina, and Charlie had all tried in their own way to help Ginny access her abilities. Bina observed and questioned. Maddox taunted. And Charlie flirted. Explaining why Charlie was inside, doing research under James's orders. Other than when Ginny entered her kitchen, she seemed incapable of accessing her abilities.

Or unwilling, Nahla claimed.

Bina pushed her glasses up her nose, sniffed, then continued to tap away on the keyboard. "When you enter the kitchen with the intent to cook, you call upon your ability almost instantly. Open a cupboard? Your aura lights up like a Christmas tree. You need to tap into that same energy without the kitchen as a prop. To access true Famine ability rather than the inverse you use for cooking."

Ginny rubbed the back of her neck. "I know that. I've been trying. It's not working."

Maddox shifted against the wall of the house. "The USELESS agents arrive in seven days, and with this pitiful show of ability, they'll kill you quickly and deprive me of my chance to repay my debt to you first. I had hoped to be able to kill you myself."

The ground may have trembled, just slightly. Ginny picked up the plant and hurled it at Maddox.

He caught the pot and inspected the plant closely. He raised a dark eyebrow, and glanced at James. "You and your brother considered all possible Famine abilities. Have you considered if she is simply the wrong woman?" He turned to Ginny. "Or, that she is lying and concealing her true abilities."

A low growl rose from Ginny's throat. She stood, stalked over, and jerked the plant out of Maddox's grip. "Why would I do that? I don't want to die because of you or the agents, or whoever decides to add me to their hit list next." She plunked the pot back down on the brown grass, sat down on the snow-dusted grass, and hunched over the plant, glaring at it. The leaves quivered, but it might have been the wind.

"Does—" Bina began.

Ginny turned on her with a glower.

James blew out a breath and shoved a hand through his hair. His ability told him Bina, and even Maddox, wanted to help Ginny. Even if so far, their methods left something to be desired.

"Why don't you and Maddox go inside," he said to Bina, giving Maddox a pointed look that said this wasn't a request. "Ginny baked apple cinnamon muffins this

175

morning."

That news had both of his mates rushing inside.

He turned back to Ginny. "I saw the fields my friends told me about yesterday. They have the unmistakable white sediment that marks salt poisoning, every trace of plant life gray and powdery. The damage spreads out in a circumference from Beckwell." He paused a moment. She deserved to know the truth. Along with the truth about what they all suspected. "Specifically, it spreads out from the cottage as the point of origin." USELESS would see the damage as proof of Ginny's threat. Yet Ginny was with him, or at least, she hadn't left the house. Nahla had suggested he seduce her, so she was in his bed and he could be certain of her location 24/7, but treating her so callously was a dick Dad-type move.

"You think I somehow salted the fields with my power? When I can't even kill this plant?" Ginny's shoulders slumped, her back to him. She picked it up, and turned it toward him. "This is the healthiest freaking marigold I've ever seen." As if to prove the point, a bud formed and then unfurled, revealing a frilly orange flower. "I can make it grow from a seed. I can read Bina's stray thoughts. But I can't make the earth shake on purpose. I can't kill the stupid marigold. Well, other than with neglect. I don't think that's the superpower either of us is hoping for."

He was almost certain she had made the earth tremble a few times they'd touched, possibly a moment ago in her anger at Maddox. But experimenting with any increased intimacy wasn't a good idea. For either of them. It just made him remember the taste of her and crave more. The taste of her muffins was nothing in comparison.

He cleared his throat. "My team found the League you told us about. It's a group of three women, a group of Fates. Daphne Spinner is one of them. The oldest is the school principal, Deirdre Boniface. The last, a middle aged woman named Louise Dole. You were right. They are monitoring your progress, and they're also aware USELESS is involved, and concerned the agents could take you out of their reach. I wanted you to know: we're on them now. They won't be a threat for long." His stomach twisted at the part he held back. The fact that they were using someone close to her to manipulate her. But he and his team didn't yet know if it was her parents, or possibly even one or more of the other horsewomen. Or if Ginny colluded on the whole bloody thing.

She snorted. "We should have suspected mean old Mrs. Boniface. We knew about Louise Dole. And Daphne Spinner? Figures. I mean, at least we know where all that crazy is pointed." She frowned. "Unfortunately, at us." She shook her head, and focused on the plant. "Whatever. If I figure all this out, it won't matter. I'll be able to help stop them. They won't be able to hurt me or my friends." She glowered at the marigold. Her hand trembled. Her shoulders shook.

The marigold didn't appear to give a damn.

Hell. He didn't think she was an actress. Worse, he hated seeing her practically in tears, still trying to do as they'd asked.

"Enough. Let's take a break," he said, pushing away from the wall and approaching Ginny.

She shook her head, and knelt on the ground in the light snow. She tucked back unruly red curls with trembling fingers and concentrated on the plant.

"No. I haven't learned anything yet. And I need to know how to use my abilities when the agents come, right? So I can protect myself. And my friends."

He was about to tell her there was no sense working herself until she was ill, she started focusing again. Her hands started to tremble. Sweat broke out on her face.

Black crept around the edge of one of the marigold's leaves.

Ginny grimaced, and her hand shook now. A tiny trickle of blood started from one nostril.

A single leaf curled and turned black.

He held his breath.

Two more bright green leaves suddenly burst from the plant, followed by a bud that formed and popped open in orange glory.

Ginny dropped her hand and rocked back on her heels. "*Frosting!*" She wiped away the tiny trickle of blood.

He strode to her side and held out a hand to her. Damn the plan to train her hard. It wouldn't help any of them if he broke her. Besides, he didn't think she was lying.

She looked up at him, and something inside him cracked to see moisture gathering in her beautiful eyes.

Her fingers closed in his, sending a streak of lust straight to his cock as he pulled her upward.

She grabbed the plant off the ground, and tumbled against his chest as she reached her feet. Her hand pressed against his chest. Her breath caught. Their legs were separated by a hair's width.

His gaze went straight to her lips. The gap at the top of her jacket allowed him a look at the sweetheart neckline of another dress that did everything for her breasts and legs, and nothing good for his brain. He inhaled a lungful of her sweet spicy scent, hungrier for her than he could remember ever having hungered for anything before.

Ginny cleared her throat, stepped back and broke contact between them. She massaged her forehead. "I'm still not able to manifest actual Famine ability. I won't be able to protect anyone when the agents get here."

Then I'll protect you, he wanted to say. But did he have the right to? It was his fault she was in danger in the first place. Because he'd started looking into Ginny, had raised her name out of mere rumor that the gods ignored into something more that USELESS felt worthy of investigation. If he hadn't interfered, Ginny might have been safe to rise before the gods found out about her.

He clenched his hands against the temptation to grab her and kiss the daylights out of her. It was like she hadn't a clue how bloody sexy she was. Most people would have asked for a break, but not Ginny. She tried everything he, Maddox, Bina, or Charlie suggested. Kept trying, despite the dark circles beneath her eyes that suggested she wasn't sleeping. And her lack of success.

He cupped the side of her jaw. "This is progress. You did make the leaf blacken."

She snorted, and held out the plant. "For a moment before it all grew back." She sighed. "What if I don't have real Famine ability? What if I just have...something else?"

"I know I have Famine abilities, but I was still able to help develop a food bar to combat hunger. You have a choice in how you use your abilities, I'm sure of it. We'll figure it out," he said, his throat thick. He saw a hell of a lot of grit and strength beneath Ginny's sweetness. What he didn't see was the inherent Famine corruption he looked for, had expected to see some sign of by now. Unlike his family and any other Famine he'd met at family reunions, Ginny seemed completely unable to cause harm without causing pain to herself. Look at what had happened when she had blackened the plant? Perhaps the corruption was family specific, confined to the Derths.

Worse, despite his best intentions, he was falling for her. Not only had he not found a way to tell her the truth about why USELESS was after her, he didn't deserve her. Deep down, he was probably as corrupt as Dad.

"Come on, let's go inside," he said roughly, not trusting himself to touch her. He wanted too badly to drag her into his arms. He might hunger for her, but he didn't deserve that satiation.

ഒ

Ginny stared after James for a minute, willing him to turn around and walk back to her. To look at her like he had a couple of seconds ago, to pull her into his arms, kiss the living daylights out of her.

Instead, he strode briskly for the front door, up the front stoop, and disappeared inside.

She hugged the marigold's pot, and her shoulders slumped. Maybe she was the only one who seemed to feel that pull toward him, like no matter how much she ate, what she did, there was still a part of her missing that needed James. Plus, his touch offered some relief from all the voices and random flavors in her head. When she touched James, it was only his taste that flooded her mouth, only his thoughts she wished she heard.

"Well, I think you did jolly good. Aside from the part where you couldn't do most of the things they wanted you to," Roger said from where he'd curled up in his warm little nest inside the pocket of her heavy wool coat.

"Thanks, Roger. But if I want to be able to protect myself and my friends, I need to be able to do more than wilt a solitary leaf." She kicked at the snow on the ground, speaking aloud since at least alone outside, no one was around to hear her and question her sanity. She was doing enough of that these days as it was. How did she think she could maintain objectivity around James or ever learn to use actual Famine abilities in under a week when she'd never been able to before? Even knowing who the League members were didn't help if she was too weak to face them.

Her entire body ached with exhaustion. More and more now, stranger's thoughts and flavors filtered into her mind, as welcome as ants at a picnic. They disturbed her sleep, woke her up nauseous after all those comingling flavors, like she'd attended an all-night smorgasbord.

According to James's friend Bina, Beckwell was trending on the internet, with a rash of photos everyone so far, thankfully, believed were Photoshopped. Instead, they were just pictures of tourists snapping shots of the beleaguered locals, especially the ones who couldn't blend in as she and her friends could. With the protective barrier gone around Beckwell, what was once a paranormal sanctuary was quickly becoming an internet sensation.

It became more important all the time that she figure out how to protect herself, her town, and her friends. She wouldn't do it if she gave up.

She marched back over to where she'd been working, set the plant on the ground, and glowered at it. She rubbed her chilled hands together and focused on the lush green leaves. When she'd made it wither, it had felt different. Painful. She closed her eyes and tried to focus on that pain, envisioned the plant blackening. It was like she reached for air rather than the deep rise of her ability when she cooked.

"You need to rest," Roger said. *"Have you considered shagging your husband? It's quite common in marriages. I believe a very clever grasshopper suggested it very early on."*

Straining to reach that other ability drove spikes driving into her skull and pressed a heavy weight on her lungs. If she could just reach a little further, hold on a little longer… There was the earth in the pot, the roots of the plant spreading like a tangled web. The nutrients and even microbes feeding the plant. Tears pressed past her closed eyelids. The pain increased until she gasped and opened her eyes. The plant was still green. Her shoulders slumped. "It's not that easy, Roger."

A shiver traveled along the back of her neck, and Thomas's cold fingers massaged her skin, sending prickles of ice through her.

She'd wondered when he and Barnabas would show up. They monitored every practice session she had. In fact, Thomas was around more now than he'd ever been her entire life.

Thomas clucked his tongue sympathetically. *"Poor Ginny. Trying so hard. You're wise to keep the relationship with James platonic. It makes you partners without the complications sex could create. Here. Let me help."* He took her hand, his icy fingers barely more substantial that her frosted breath, and together they held their hands over the marigold.

A sharp spike of pain drove through Ginny; ice followed immediately by searing heat.

The hapless marigold's leaves curled and blackened as it dissolved into itself. Black, then gray, then white. The very soil and the microbes seemed to cry out as they too blackened and shriveled. The soil paled in color. White gathered around the edges as it cracked and compressed.

The pot shattered. Ginny sagged onto her knees, grasping her pounding head. Her vision was blurry and her stomach did somersaults. She couldn't seem to catch her breath. Couldn't stop the tears that rolled down her face. She wiped away the blood that dribbled from her nose to her chin. There was nothing left of the marigold but dust, carried away in the wind.

Thomas barely touched her, and with his help, she'd accessed true Famine abilities.

Oh, *frosting*. Who was she kidding? She hadn't accessed those abilities. He had. If that wasn't further proof that he should have lived, that he should have been Famine, she didn't know what was.

"Ginny? Luv? You're hurting yourself. Stop. This isn't right," Roger insisted.

"You are making progress," Thomas's grasshopper, Barnabas said, as if she didn't have enough voices in her

head. *"With our help, you will achieve your potential."*

"Oy! Dead guys! Shove off. You're hurting her," Roger shouted at Thomas and Barnabas, crawling out of her jacket pocket to face them.

Thomas seemed to completely ignore him. He knelt in front of Ginny and smoothed back her hair. *"The pain is necessary. We're getting stronger. I can feel it. But you do need rest."* He touched his finger to her face and came back with her blood on his fingertip. He considered it a moment, then looked up at her, his green eyes brighter.

Ginny shivered.

"Perhaps the false horse is correct. You should get to bed earlier tonight. Rest." Thomas's lips curled up. *"There is much to be done. Together, we will be unstoppable."*

Roger flapped his front legs at Barnabas and Thomas. *"Back. Off,"* he snarled.

This time, they seemed to acknowledge him. The air fluttered, and Thomas and Barnabas vanished from sight, their accompanying chill replaced only by a wintry cold wind that suggested more cold was in the forecast.

"Come on, luv. Let's get you inside. I'm freezing my arse off. And you need to rest," Roger said gently.

She nodded and forced her gaze away from the remains of the marigold. It was an unsteady climb to her feet, and she swayed a moment before she made her way to the front door of the little house, the front stoop as difficult to ascend as Everest. She stepped inside and pulled off her coat and boots, every muscle burning.

"Luv, what happens to ol' Barn-ass and Toad-face when we rise, exactly?" Roger said, hopping down from the coatrack where he'd waited while she hung her coat, and onto her shoulder. *"What do they have to gain out of this?"*

"Thomas is my brother. Please don't call him names. I know he can come off a bit heavy-handed, but he's been

there for me when no one else was." The whole Thomas topic hadn't been something she'd been ready to discuss with James. Or anyone. Especially after Nia's strange reaction at the wedding.

Before Anna had come to live with them, Thomas had been her only friend. The only true friend, at any rate. The only one she knew wasn't over because of her parents' money, or their influence in town. The only one who could always find her and keep her company, all day, all night. The only one who believed someday they'd be something important.

"Uh-huh. You sure about that? Because I'm not sure he's as good of a friend as you think. I don't trust him, and I don't think you should, either," Roger said, hopping off her shoulder when they walked past the kitchen, probably to help himself to the muffin he'd started eating this morning that they left in the corner of the counter for him.

Ginny paused just outside the living room door, her back to the wall, just out of sight of the sofa and chairs, but able to see James. He was in the midst of discussing something serious with Bina and Maddox, and Charlie, as usual, was giving him a hard time.

She didn't even listen to the words. There were enough voices in her head clamoring for attention and giving her a constant headache. Instead, she leaned back against the wall and took the opportunity to study James, from the dark gray T-shirt he wore that accentuated every muscle, and the designer jeans that just showed his thighs were every bit as muscular as the rest of him.

This was what she'd said she wanted from her marriage—a partnership, no emotions involved. All of that so she could get her abilities.

Although, right now, staring at James, all she could think of was that kiss they'd shared in the Senior Center kitchen. The scent of fresh muffins surrounding them, the heat of the kitchen, James's appreciation for the taste of her food.

Followed by his appreciation for the taste of her. The way he'd suckled her finger and tasted her lips, his body moving expertly against hers.

All the other Famine powers seemed to involve destruction and literally left a terrible taste in her mouth. Right that instant, she'd have given all of them up to be back in that kitchen with James. Maybe teaching him how to bake.

Oh, *frosting*. She curled her arms around her, but it didn't stop the slow spread of cold through her insides, nor the pinch of moisture at her eyes.

She'd started out determined to keep her heart locked up, but she'd started to fall for James anyway. Question was, would he break her heart as badly as Jimmy had?

CHAPTER 19

Two more days had passed in intensive Famine boot camp, and Ginny was still bombing every class without Thomas's help, no matter how hard she tried. Although truthfully, the only class she'd really like to work on was Husband Seduction 101. She rubbed her forehead with the back of her hand and whisked the eggs for yet another batch of muffins, her tiny kitchen cleaner thanks to Maddox, who'd gotten bored waiting for her to endanger her life and started scrubbing. James continued to frustratingly keep his distance, and she was starting to think Roger was right—she and James needed to shag.

She'd started to fantasize about accidentally shrinking all his clothes in the dryer so he had to walk around naked. Admittedly, that could be a bit awkward with Bina, Charlie, and Maddox around. Perhaps she'd bake a huge batch of muffins for the Senior Center so they'd all have to take them. Leaving she and James alone. She'd lock the door and have her wicked way with James. The plan for which she had come up with in enough detail, she could make up cue cards.

She put the extra eggs back in the fridge and let the batter rest.

Too bad she couldn't tell the girls about James and everything that was going on, even if they would tease her. She'd been so busy with training she hadn't seen Anna in four days and hadn't seen Piper and Nia since the wedding. It felt like forever. Maybe Anna missed her, too, because she'd started sending hourly text messages. Even though all of them only said she'd found something interesting in her research.

She paused to rub her forehead again, though it did nothing to dispel the tension building there from all those voices who kept getting louder. Which sucked, since it was almost dinner, and she finally had some time to herself. When even Bina let up on the observation and went instead to watch paranormal activity and movement on the internet, or what Bina called "reading the data stream." It meant she wasn't observing and asking questions that would make a psychologist squirm, so it was fab.

It was also the time when James, Maddox, and Charlie met with James's team to have their conversation, reporting on Ginny's progress with her abilities. Or lack thereof, according to Roger. They tracked every movement of the League, aka Mrs. Boniface, Louise Dole, and Daphne Spinner, and were making plans to stop them. One less enemy would be nice.

She pulled out the muffin sheets from a lower cabinet and greased each compartment.

Today, even Roger had made himself scarce. They'd had another argument about Thomas. Roger wanted to ask Nia to exorcise Thomas. He said he wasn't sleeping well and blamed Thomas and Barnabas for it. Roger seemed to believe he disappeared whenever he went to sleep, and he was certain Thomas was behind it. The entire idea was ridiculous, surely.

Ginny leaned down to check on the roast. It was almost dinner, her favorite time of the day. The only time in her life she'd ever actively been *encouraged* to cook, and everyone raved over her food. Bina and James would bicker over sci-fi or superheroes. Then Bina would tell them about other unusual happenings in paranormal sanctuaries around the world. James and Maddox sometimes shared stories about the missions he and his team ran, about building wells and schools mostly, with the occasional negotiating with troublesome local gods.

But sometimes, if she were lucky, she'd turn and catch James's deep blue gaze on her, heavy lidded and hungry in a way that had nothing to do with food. His lips were completely kissable, so good-looking it hurt, and perfectly at home in their little living room. Like he belonged there. Like he belonged to her. With that thought, she'd add another step to her having her wicked way plan.

Then he'd turn away and change the subject, and she'd wonder if she'd imagined it all.

She rubbed her forehead again with a small moan. Stupid voices. Why couldn't people keep their thoughts to themselves?

"You are too unguarded. Too psychically open," Maddox said from the kitchen doorway.

Ginny jumped, knocking her bowl of batter, and narrowly catching it. She scowled at him. "What are you doing here anyway? Shouldn't you be at the team meeting?"

She began scooping out her batter. The roast in the oven was almost done, so she'd be able to get the muffins in soon. Her ability whirred through her in a way it never did when she was supposed to be training.

"Someone needs to keep an eye on you. My people are similarly psychically gifted. You must better arm yourself. I have not been blind to the sacrifices you have made, the effort you have exerted. I have no desire to kill you, but I owe James my life many times over. My loyalty is to him. If he doesn't turn you over to the puppets of the gods, they will take his life as well. I won't allow that to happen."

She turned and stared. "You mean…if James doesn't turn me over, they'll kill him?"

Maddox nodded. "Either before or after they do the same to you, yes. James is an honorable man and feels duty-bound to protect you. He's also, I imagine, become quite attached to you."

"Gee, poor guy," she said dryly. Though inside, something fluttered to life. Even James's friends thought he might have become "quite attached." It probably wasn't on the same level to what she felt—stupidly and completely head over heels in love. Most people weren't as foolish as her.

"I have taught him a method to teach you to protect yourself psychically. You needn't suffer pain due to open telepathic pathways."

Muffin pans all filled—she only had three, and they weren't big—she turned to face the big guy. "Sorry, what?"

Maddox was gone, and James stood in his place, quietly watching her.

She swallowed, every step of her plan to have her way with him flooding through her head. She tried not to stare at the way his charcoal sweater hugged his shoulders, or that the collar of the shirt he wore underneath was unbuttoned just enough to see his Adam's apple. *Chocolate cream pie*, she definitely wasn't loving the way he leaned casually against the archway wall, one hand tucked inside his pocket, his ankles crossed.

Nor the dark intensity of his gaze. The way he took in her navy-blue dress and lingered at the way it crisscrossed over her breasts, giving her just the tiniest bit of cleavage. His gaze wandered back up to her face, and no, she hadn't imagined all that heat.

"Maddox told me you're in pain because of the telepathic input you're receiving. He also said I could help. I wish you'd told me sooner," James said, his voice raspy.

She nodded. "I, uh, didn't think you could."

He pushed away from the wall and sauntered toward her, muscle rippling beneath his sweater. He stopped less than a step from her, and reached out a hand to touch her jaw. "He said it's better when I touch you. That I shield you."

Headache gone, lust firmly in place. She nodded, because words were well beyond her. It was possible she wouldn't have noticed the other voices and tastes. Because James filled all her senses with dark chocolate and man and sex, and all the hot fantasies that left her aching. She lifted a hand to her lip. Oh good. No drool.

"I want you close your eyes and feel what it's like when I touch you. What that touch feels like. Memorize it."

Her eyes drifted shut. Oh, but she had memorized it. The way it was like tiny flames licking her skin where he touched, the gentle caress of his fingers against her cheek, down over her lip. She was drenched in dark chocolate, want, and James.

"Have you memorized it?" he said, his voice rough.

Another nod. *Cupcakes*. She'd look like a bobble head soon. She cleared her throat. "Yes."

"Keep picturing it, feeling it. My touch. The way it makes you feel. The way it blocks out all the others." He traced the outline of her lips, and her knees trembled.

Frosting, she wanted to lick him. To taste his fingers, his lips, kiss a path down his body and take him into her mouth.

"Do you still feel it?" he said.

Another nod. His fingers were on her lips, caressed her face, slid down her arms. So close, and he could take her breasts into his hand. Unzip her dress and—

"Open your eyes."

She opened her eyes. Then blinked.

James stood back near the entrance of the kitchen, his hands clenched at his sides, his breathing rough. "You still felt me. Even when I wasn't touching you anymore."

"Yes." How much had she imagined? Surely she hadn't merely fantasized about the way he'd touched her lips.

No, his gaze still traced up and down her body in a way that said he wanted to touch her, that he wanted to press her back against the counters, lift her up, and bury himself inside her.

She'd vote for that.

He rubbed a hand over his face and cleared his throat, staring at a point somewhere just left of her shoulder.

"Good," he said, his voice stiff. "I hoped it would help you sleep. It doesn't look like you've been getting enough. Maybe I've been pushing too hard. I'm sorry on both counts."

Well, *shortbread*. Looked like no sex on the counter after all. "Oh, no. It isn't your fault." Okay, the part where sometimes she tossed and turned because she was fantasizing about him, that was kind of his fault. She flushed. "I mean, we both know why I need to train hard. Before USELESS arrives. Even though I think they'll see ample evidence that I'm hardly a threat." Surely he wasn't completely unaffected. She leaned back against the sink, tossed her hair back, and pushed out her chest. "I appreciate all the help you've been."

James's gaze darkened, and he gripped the archway wall. "Ginny," he growled warningly, though didn't follow through on exactly what he meant.

Her knees wobbled at his dark gaze. Oh, *hot fudge sundae*, preserve her from sexy husbands with intense, brooding, sensual gazes. "Yes, James?"

He closed his eyes and squeezed his lips together for a moment before he spoke. "The weather is forecast to be worse tonight. The team's tent might collapse in the snow and wind. I thought perhaps the rest of the team could stay here for the night. If that's all right with you."

She tried not to let her disappointment show in her face, struggling to keep it as blank as she could. A chill rushed through her.

Because she'd tasted the bitterness of a lie in James's words.

"Of course. No problem," she lied back. Why would he lie to her when he knew she could tell? Then again, Jimmy never had figured that out, either.

He opened his eyes, and studied the counter next to him. "I thought Caspian and Asher could have the living room. If Bina and Nahla can have your room. Which leaves you with me."

She blinked a few times, wondering if she'd heard correctly. "I'm sorry…what?"

This time he met her gaze directly, and it stole her breath. "You and I will share a room. If that's okay with you."

What was she going to say? No?

ॐ

James stood, arms crossed, and glared as he watched his team officially take over his house from just outside his bedroom door. Not only were they taking over, but they'd shortened dinner, too, his favorite time of the day, when he could listen to the glorious sound of Ginny's laugh as Charlie told ridiculous stories, or he and Bina bickered about nothing.

Sometimes, if he was lucky, she'd pause, her chin on her hand, this little half smile just touching her lips, as if just waiting to blossom across her face. He could stare at her unabashed and wish she could really be his. That he was just a man in love with his wife, and tomorrow he'd help her run her muffin business, and the world was brilliance and light.

He cleared his throat and shifted, trying to shake off his own thoughts, earning a glare from Nahla as she passed with her kit.

Ginny should have refused to let his team invade, and then he'd have had a viable reason why this couldn't happen. Why they couldn't force Ginny into his bedroom. Right where he would breathe in her scent all night long. And not be able to touch her all night through.

But his team was reporting increased incidents of damage throughout and around Beckwell. Entire swathes of forest, eradicated. Herds of cattle were losing weight drastically, looking more like mooing skeletons than what had been a few days ago healthy, thriving animals. Worse, that same damage was popping up in pockets all over the world, according to Bina's intel.

He'd told his team he'd been with Ginny every day, and she hadn't caused any harm. Furthermore, he didn't believe she could, nor would, cause any harm.

It was Asher this time who'd asked if he'd been with her all the time, even at night.

James rolled his shoulders, and continued to glare at his friends. So tonight, Ginny would move into his bedroom, and he was supposed to ignore the ever-present desire between them, the way that no matter how hard he looked, Ginny wasn't tainted by the corruption of Famine.

Yet his suspicion of his own bloodlines and his research into her had led to her being added to USELESS's watch list. The truth of which he still hadn't had the balls to tell her about. Could she ever forgive the fact that she and her friends were in more danger because of him?

"Well, let's all turn in," Nahla said, faking a large yawn, and giving him a meaningful look. It was probably supposed to mean keep his dick in his trousers.

He looked away from her and found Ginny headed down the hallway from the kitchen, where she'd been directing Charlie and Asher in tidying up the kitchen. She hesitated in her step, and her face flushed.

He stepped back to allow her to pass, but the part of him that was a right bastard, and quite possibly masochistic, stayed in her way enough that she had to edge past him. Her skirts against his legs, her hair tickling his chin, her breasts just brushing his chest. He grit his teeth as fire roared through him.

Every member of his team chose that instant to shut their respective doors and flick off the lights, like a well-rehearsed movement. He growled beneath his breath and stepped back into the room, closing the door behind him.

Ginny stood near the bed, her hands clasped nervously. She looked between the bed, to him.

Bollocks. He had to make it clear nothing was going to happen tonight. He took a step toward her. No, wait. Bad idea. If he was close to her, he'd want to kiss her. He'd want to more than kiss her. Hell, he already wanted to do that. The trouble was that there was nothing to stop him from carrying through. If he was close enough to touch her, he would.

"I'll just take the floor, shall I?" he said, and edged around the room in the most ridiculous move known to man.

"Oh. I mean, there's plenty of room in the bed—"

"No! I mean…" He scrubbed a hand over his face. "Ginny, if I come over to that bed, I'm going to want to kiss you. If I kiss you, I'm probably going to make love to you."

She made a strangled little squeak, and when he peeked over his hand, her eyes had widened.

"Which would be a problem," he confirmed. For both their sakes.

She cocked her head. "Would it?"

Holy hell. His dick hardened. "Yes. A serious problem. We need to focus all our attention on preparing you for USELESS and making a concerted plan to keep you safe."

"All of our attention?" she said, sounding disappointed.

He wanted to smash his head into something hard. "Definitely."

"Oh, I see." She sighed. "Well, if you're sure. I suppose we should just try to get some sleep then." She turned her back to him, pulling all those red curls forward, and looking at him over her shoulder. "I don't suppose you could unzip my dress, could you?"

Bloody hell. His mind filled with images of unzipping that navy-blue dress, kissing his way down the creamy flesh exposed to his gaze, and then peeling her out of those clothes and making her moan through all of it.

He clenched the doorknob. "Ginny, if you knew half how much I wanted you, I'm not sure you'd be comfortable with me in this room right now," he said, voice gravely. "Tonight, I'm not turning you down because I want to, but because I am determined to keep you safe, and this is how I prove to everyone that you're innocent. If we share the room tonight, I have proof you haven't been out at night spreading famine. Proof my team needs. With that proof they'll finally help me develop the plan to keep you safe. Because I will be damned before I'll let anyone that isn't me get their hands on you. Do you understand?"

She blinked and nodded. "I...yes," she said, breathless.

He nodded and turned away, hands clenched at his side. "Good. Then please sleep in your dress. Or maybe a really ugly robe if you have one. Because I'm trying hard to be a good man tonight, but I'm not sure how much of that there is left right now."

"Okay." Bed covers rustled.

Probably best if he slept in his clothes, too. The more layers between them the better. He stalked stiffly over to the chair, where he'd piled a spare pillow and some blankets. He spread them out on the old shag carpet, and sure enough, laying there, staring at the ceiling, was just as uncomfortable as he'd hoped, his shaft aching.

"Shall I shut off the light?" Ginny called from the bed. His bed. All alone. And quite possibly waiting for him.

"Please," he said, his voice strangled.

The light flicked off, leaving them both in darkness.

Her voice floated out toward him, a disembodied quality to it. "James, when this is all over, I just want you to know that I really would like us to be man and wife. For real. In every way."

His throat and other anatomy thickened painfully so he couldn't reply.

"James? You are a good man. The best I've ever known." The sheets rustled again, and the mattress creaked as Ginny made herself comfortable.

It wasn't as easy for James, as he lay staring up into the darkness. If he'd never had delusions of herodom, never looked into her name and sent up red flags for USELESS, Ginny might not be in danger now. Would she still believe he was a good man when she found out the truth?

CHAPTER 20

It was still pitch black in the room when James jerked awake. For a couple of disorienting moments, he tried to remember where he was and what had woken him.

The bedroom door creaked open quietly.

He sat up, taking care not to make a sound, and narrowed his eyes on the widening space the open door left, the slightly grayer dimness of the hallway outside creating a fuzzy silhouette. A curvy silhouette. Ginny.

He climbed to his feet and followed her out of the room, then down the hall.

She didn't pause at the front door to grab a jacket or shoes, simply opened the door and walked out, quietly closing the door behind her. He grabbed his coat and tossed it on, shoving his feet into shoes as he followed her outside.

Fresh snow blanketed everything in thick fluffiness even as the wet flakes tickled the back of his neck where they feathered down from the dark sky. The surrounding trees cast tall black shadows.

Yes, it was Ginny ahead of him. She padded through the snow, her thick curls colorless in the pale light, her footsteps seeped in shadow. Bollocks. She wore only her navy-blue dress he'd asked her to sleep in, but the chill of the night air seeped through his trousers and under his skin.

She continued onward, out among the towering trees that made up their back garden, winding through them. A slightly off-tune hum, something broken and disjointed just beneath her breath, carried through the air to James.

It wasn't snow that tickled the hair on the back of his neck this time, but awareness of something "other" in the atmosphere. It was something he'd never quite been able to define as triggered by a particular set of stimuli, but the like of which he'd experienced before, when supernatural forces were at work against the natural order.

That sense of other, and that he needed to know what she was up to, stopped him from calling out or catching up to her to wrap her coat around her. Canadians might claim a near immunity to cold weather, but this was ridiculous.

The pungent aroma of mildew and fungus thickened his throat. James stumbled. Bloody hell. The trees around Ginny. They were blackening, sap bleeding from their cracking bark. He jumped aside to avoid being crushed. The thirty-foot-high monster tree compressed in on itself, breaking into smaller pieces as it tumbled to the forest floor.

Three more trees in Ginny's path followed the first. James dove left to avoid being flattened by one of the timbers. They fell, disintegrating into further rot that turned not into something to feed the ecosystem, but rotten ash that melted into a dark muck. A putrid odor bubbled up from it, singing the insides of James nostrils. He covered his nose and mouth with the back of his sleeves to keep from gaging. It spread like oil over the ground, swallowing everything in its path that withered and sank into the goop, more inexorable than lava.

Whatever she was doing, he couldn't let her continue. He picked up his pace, ducking and dodging the falling trees and closing the distance between them.

Her off-tune hum increased in volume, the rumble of Ginny's voice peculiarly deep. She emerged from the edge of the trees into a gently rolling field brightened by moonlight over the fresh snow.

He was almost close enough to reach out and grab her.

She raised her arms in the air, hands at shoulder height, the movement jerky, marionette-like. The snow melted away off the field, steam rising off the field. The stubble from the harvest poked through the snow around her pale toes. Bare feet, out in the snow. The earth rumbled beneath their feet. She opened her mouth in a wide "O."

James grabbed her, swung her around to face him, and placed his hand over her mouth. Nope, nothing noxious was coming out on his watch.

"Ginny, what are you doing? What happened to causing no harm?" His voice shook but remained pitched low.

Her head lolled to the left, and her lips curved into a smile beneath his palm while the skin crinkled around her eyes. Eyes whose gaze was flat, a strange green glitter to her eyes that held no warmth, no emotion.

No Ginny.

He wrapped her coat around her and gave her a gentle shake. "Ginny. Answer me."

Her eyes shut, and a breath sighed out of her. She sagged in his arms.

His heart stuttered, and he scooped her up against his chest. "Ginny?"

A loud "oink, oink, reeee!" burst out from behind

him along with small racing feet, and a medium-sized pig banged into his leg. It snuffled up at Ginny with a short whine, and its snout touched her dangling fingers.

Her eyes flickered open and it was Ginny who stared out at him again. Who looked around her in some bemusement, down at the pig, then at him again, full-out bafflement filling her expression. She opened her mouth to ask a question but began to shiver so violently, her teeth chattered. Then her eyes rolled back in her head, and she went limp. Again.

"Bloody hell." He scooped her into his arms and marched back toward the cottage, cuddling her against his chilled chest, but at least he had a shirt whereas she only wore the petal-soft dress that slid against her skin, against his skin. It must have done nothing to keep her warm.

The pig continued to snuffle and whine, trotting after him.

"What the hell happened?" Charlie said, stumbling through the snow toward him.

If only he knew for sure. All he did know was that she'd had no problem destroying things tonight, proving how much of a Famine heir she truly was. Coincidentally providing all the evidence USELESS would need to drain her of her abilities…or worse.

He'd always expected the corruption of her Famine blood would show itself at some point. He hadn't expected to be so damned disappointed when it did.

☙

Ginny woke up the next morning, the sun shining in between the master bedroom curtains. She licked her lips. There was an awful taste in her mouth. At first it had seemed kind of like morning-breath-from-hell, but it was worse than that. Acrid and sour, dry and smoky like she'd licked a log from the campfire. Yuck. It was getting worse.

She lifted the blanket, and found she still wore her

navy-blue dress from last night. Along with her parka. Every muscle ached like she'd run a marathon.

And there was a pink pig with black spots on the end of the bed.

She scrambled up near the headboard, away from the pig. *Crepe Suzette*, what was going on?

"Good, you're finally awake. How are you feeling?" James said.

The pig at the end of the bed made a snuffling sound, woke up, and jumped off the bed.

She twisted to find James in a kitchen chair on the other side of the bed, his arms crossed over his broad chest, sexy as ever in another dark blue button-down, sleeves rolled up to his elbows. Not a friendly dimple in sight.

"I, uh, did you sleep in that chair?"

He shook his head. "Do you remember what happened last night?"

"Roger, what's going on?" she communicated to the insect in panicked thought.

A slightly wet nose reached up over the edge of the bed and nudged her hand, and the dark brown eyes of the pig looked up at her. *"I will get back to you about that just as soon as I know, luv,"* the pig said. In Roger's voice. It turned in circles. *"Look. Black spots. You can see them this time, right? Black spots for Famine. We're getting stronger."*

She jerked her hand away. *Coconut cream pie*. Ginny breathed out. Her grasshopper seemed to have turned into a pig. That should only have happened if her abilities had somehow grown.

It was hard to swallow.

The chair creaked as James stood. "Get changed, wash up. I'll meet you in the kitchen and we can talk." He padded out of the room, his gray pants lovingly cupping that gorgeous ass, proving she could lust after her husband even as the world fell apart.

She threw back the blankets, grabbed the first outfit her fingers closed on inside her suitcase, and dove into the ensuite bathroom to get dressed, brush her teeth, and splash cold water on her face. It didn't help. As she emerged into the bedroom, dressed in black stretch slacks that hugged her hips, a red and white striped shirt with sweetheart neckline, and a mint sweater, she might have looked cute, but the world had turned topsy-turvy. A pig still sat square in the middle of the bedroom floor waiting for her. And James was waiting for her in the kitchen.

The pig snuffled up to her, those big brown eyes ringed with long, pale lashes. *"Don't you recognize me, luv? It's still me. This means we're gaining our abilities. This is what you wanted."*

She edged around the animal. *"Just...give me a bit to get used to the idea."* She'd wanted to rise as Famine, to prove she was one of the horsewomen like her friends. She hadn't expected it to mean people were hunting her down. Or for her husband to look at her with such suspicion. Or to wake up in strange clothes with strange animals on her bed.

Ginny emerged from the bedroom, peeking around the corner out into the hall to look for the others. No sign of anyone else, the bedroom across from hers empty, beds made, not a sound from the living room and kitchen, either. Her stomach growled, and she crept toward the kitchen.

She'd just poked her head into the fridge when James spoke.

"Feel better?"

Ginny jumped and spun, clutching the fridge door.

James leaned in the entryway to the kitchen, legs crossed at the ankles, and sipped a steaming cup of coffee. He nodded toward the counter. "There's porridge on the cooker, still warm. Coffee, too, if you want some."

He didn't sound especially happy...but he didn't look pissed. How could he look so good after a night like last night? The fabric of his dark blue shirt accentuated every muscle that flexed with as he brought the mug to his lips, his gray slacks fit to perfection, and gray socks shouldn't have been sexy but somehow were.

"Are you going to tell me what happened last night?" she asked.

"Eat first. Then I'll show you." He took another sip of coffee, his deep blue gaze steady on her.

She licked dry lips, her insides quivery. Was that a "we can wait for me to show you because it's not all that bad?" or "you'd better eat first, because you're never going to want to eat again after I show you" kind of deal?

"Okay." She pulled a bowl out of the cupboard and dished herself up some hot porridge but skipped the coffee. Like she needed anything else to make her hands shake.

He padded out of the kitchen to the dining table in the living room, and she followed. Although following him seemed oddly risky, like this was all waaaayyy too easy a wake up after the mystery of the parka and Roger turning into a pig. And the interrogation that was likely to come. Mom and Jimmy had always done that—play nice just to lull her into a sense of false security before they snapped the trap and reamed her out.

Still, she followed him into the living room. He pulled a chair out for her before sitting next to her.

She perched on the edge of the chair next to him, their knees brushing. She took nervous bites of her porridge, waiting for the inevitable attack.

The bowl of porridge was nearly finished, and James still said nothing. She glanced up to see him leaning back in the chair, arms crossed over that broad chest, his gaze half-hooded and focused on her.

She almost choked and spewed porridge back into

her bowl. Her face burned as she reached for a napkin and dabbed at her face. The porridge particulates that had escaped onto the table. *Cupcake*, couldn't she do anything right?

"W-where are the others?" She'd better prepare herself if they were going to jump out any minute. Because she'd rather not be eating and choke if they were.

"Reconnoitering. Procuring vehicles if possible, and provisions. They'll need something better than the tent with this weather."

The pig settled down at her feet under the table, its head on her foot.

James leaned his forearms on the table and closed some of the distance between them. "Are you ready to tell me what happened last night?"

Gulp. The spoon chattered against the bowl in her fingers. She dropped it, and clasped her hands in her lap instead, her gaze flitting away from James, then back. "I-I have no idea. You said you were going to tell me." She tried to piece together what little she remembered about last night. "I had a strange dream. Something about being outside. And you."

"That's all?"

She nodded, a sick twisting inside her stomach that made the porridge uneasy.

"Hmm," he said. Then reached for her bowl. "Let's go outside then, shall we?"

He rinsed out her bowl in the sink while she went past him toward the back door, slipping her feet into her shoes and pulling on her jacket. Only his shoes and hers waited at the door. He came up behind her to pull on his own jacket, a dark brown leather jacket worn to buttery soft perfection.

She groped for the door and burst outside into the crisp, dripping morning before she was tempted to see just how soft the coat was. Or got lost in James's eyes again.

Thomas's chill crept across her neck. *"Now is not the time for stupid, little sister. Watch yourself."*

The beginnings of a headache slid through her, then just as quickly it and Thomas's chill vanished.

James came through the door and bumped against, catching her elbow to steady her and prevent her fall from the little porch. She looked up and fell into those beautiful eyes again. Eyes that matched the cool blue sky above today. His brow quirked up.

"Let's take a walk."

She hugged her coat around her and nodded, stumbling down the steps. James quickly took the lead, and she followed him. Still, glancing around, while there were footprints in the snow, no sign of his team or brother anywhere. *Frosting*, this was giving her a bad feeling.

James stopped, turning to look back at her. "Coming?"

She nodded, and hurried after him, though for once, she wanted to keep her distance.

They stepped only a short distance into the woods when the blackened puddles and gaps between the standing trees drew her eyes. Ginny gasped, turning to look all around her. The puddles were almost like elongated remains of fire, where the trees had stood...and melted.

There was a pattern to the destruction. A path. A set of footprints traipsed through the center of all that destruction. Footprints that had burned away the snow and any hint of green or healthy soil color. The soil beneath the footprints was bleached and beige, barren of life.

Her gaze followed the footsteps back to her own feet. Where she stood in one of the footprints. She lifted her foot. A perfect fit. Her stomach lurched.

James walked back to her. "This is what happened last night. This is the mark of Famine." There was a hard edge to his voice, but pain in his eyes. "This is what you did."

"No, but—" She broke off, bit her lip, and forced herself to meet James's eyes squarely. "I swear to you, if I did this, I don't know how. I don't remember any of it."

He stepped closer to her, until he was close enough to touch. "What do you remember specifically?"

"I remember us, going to bed." Her face heated further as she recalled the part where she'd tried to seduce him, and he'd turned her down. She dropped her gaze, frowning. "I had that strange dream, of you and I outside in the snow. I remember hearing your voice, but then nothing else until this morning."

"I followed you out here last night and watched you cause this damage. You gained consciousness only for a moment or two but then fell into a deep sleep and didn't wake until this morning." His lips pressed together, he considered her, his brow lowered, as though trying to work out the truth. "I want to believe you. You promised me you didn't want to hurt anyone."

She smoothed her hand up and down the rough fabric of her coat. "But?"

He stepped closer still, his fingers gentle beneath her jaw as he lifted her chin to face him. They lingered there, sliding against her skin as he tucked an errant curl behind her ear. "But, this is Famine. I recognize its work. This is the destruction I came to stop."

"The kind of destruction I don't want to cause, I swear."

"You say that, but how can I believe you? You don't even remember causing this, but I was there, Ginny. I saw *you* do it."

Her eyes burned and blurred. Good. She didn't want to see the disappointment in his eyes. She'd tried so hard to focus on her abilities during Famine boot camp, and hadn't been able to kill a marigold, but somehow, she'd been able to reduce a section of forest to melted goop. How could she have done it without even remembering it?

"M-maybe I didn't do it. Maybe the abilities are getting too powerful for me." Maybe everyone was right. She was never supposed to rise as Famine. Thomas should have lived. Thomas and Barnabas should have had all this power. "Maybe it was an accident. I told you I needed a partner. Maybe you can help me prevent this from happening again."

"How? We've worked on trying to teach you to control your abilities with little result, and this?" He gestured toward the destruction, the acrid taste of smoke and devastation burning her tongue. "I can't control your abilities for you. I don't even fully know what they are. If this was an accident, the result of a few short moments, what if it happens again? It could be so much worse. This is the evidence USELESS will be looking for. Evidence of your power."

Yeah, like the power to accidentally start the apocalypse.

Moisture pooled in her eyes, and she wiped it away before it could escape. "I know. I'm sorry." Her voice shrank into a quiver, and she squeezed her arms tightly around herself. She waited for the rest of the tirade.

Instead, James sighed and gently pulled her into his arms.

She froze there a moment, before letting herself lean into his warmth, his steadiness. She released a shaky breath.

"Then I guess we're in this together," he said. "The team is gathering supplies to clean this up. We won't give USELESS the ammunition they want. We'll continue to work on your skills. Get control of your abilities."

She squeezed her eyes shut, and just inhaled his scent, the feel of his hard chest against her, under her fingertips. Memorizing it. Because she didn't deserve to hold onto him.

"As you say, I haven't learned how to control them. I…I think I've made a terrible mistake. I don't think I'm supposed to be Famine. I can't control this. I'm not…enough."

James pulled back, stroking a finger along her jaw and lifting her chin to look her in the eyes. He took a deep breath, then met her gaze steadily. "I have grown up seeing only the terrible things famine can do. When I was a lad, desperate for my older brothers' approval, I even played lookout while they spoiled all the food in a local man's stall. I watched my father grow rich on the suffering of our tenants, whose crops and herds he'd never let make it to market successfully. I was certain there was nothing redeemable about famine, and it had to be stopped. That everyone with our family's blood was tainted." He tucked her hair behind her ears, his touch sending tingles through her, his words even more so. "Then I met you. And all the things I thought I knew? They went up in smoke. You are nothing like I expected. In all the most wonderful ways."

Her throat thickened, and her fingers closed around handfuls of his jacket. She didn't know what to say in response without blurting out her feelings.

He blew out an unsteady breath, and gripped her face gently so her gaze met his. "I promise you, that I will do everything in my power and then some to make sure USELESS doesn't get near you. I will keep you safe. Even if that's from your own abilities."

She stared up in his beautiful blue-gray eyes, and her heart swelled at his promise, the sincerity of his words that seemed to enrich the taste of him. He'd worked so hard to help her, no matter how often she'd failed. Now, when the abilities seemed to control her instead of the other way around, he still vowed to find a way to help her.

She couldn't disappoint him now. Even if in the end, as she eventually disappointed everyone, she would disappoint him.

She leaned up, and pressed her lips to his. The dark chocolate taste of him, the heat of his mouth, it flooded her senses. He wrapped his arms around her, and pulled her against his hard length. There was a desperation in their kiss on both sides. Something that seemed to know they were running out of time. Yet something green and fresh, too.

It whirled and spiraled through her, tugging at her ability, it sang through her blood, down through her legs, and out into the ground beneath her feet. Into the destruction that sapped the life from the soil, and instead let new life blossom and flow. New saplings emerged and sprang from the earth where the others had fallen. New leaves sprang from the buds. The salt and destruction were swallowed by the soil and absorbed.

There, standing in his arms, for that precious moment, she was exactly where she needed to be, exactly who she wanted to be.

Should have known it couldn't last.

"Oh, gracious. What happened? I, uh…" Someone cleared her throat loudly.

Ginny sighed. That sounded like Anna. But she wasn't done enjoying the last few moments of the kiss with James.

"Maybe we should just go," Piper said.

Someone else let out a very long, low whistle. "Ginny. I am very glad you and your husband are getting to know each other. But we have a problem. And its name is Thomas."

CHAPTER 21

Ginny pulled back from James and took in three things. First, her friends all stood staring at she and James. Well actually, at the blackened husks of trees and the ruin of forest on one side…and the vibrantly green new growth forest and shrubs on the other side, green peeking out from beneath where she'd stood. Holy *hotcakes*, that was…new. And, ugh. Green leaves in autumn? Especially next to all that black mess? She'd wanted to make things better, but this had every sign of having only made it worse. More evidence for USELESS to find.

Her shoulders slumped, and she took in the third problem.

Roger, rubbing himself from head down to his curly little tail all along James's leg, and making a low nasal *arf, arf, arf* noise that was distinctly sexual in feel. Ew.

James looked up at her. "Uh, Ginny…"

"Roger. Back off," she said aloud, then communicated telepathically, *"If anyone gets to rub themselves all over my husband, it's me. Got it?"*

The spotted pig gave James one more loving oink, a wink, and then sashayed off with what could only be described as a chuckle. *"Then get to it, luv. About time, isn't it?"*

"Um, wasn't your horse a grasshopper?" Piper said, she and everyone else watching the spotted pig dance around in the snow.

Ginny sighed. "He was."

"Now we get a pork chop with attitude," James murmured.

"It must mean you're channeling your abilities," Piper said, rushing through the snow to give Ginny a quick squeeze. "Go you!"

Anna frowned, her enormous coat something between a mossy blanket and a worn-out bearskin. She could barely cross her arms to look stern, it was so massive. "Is that what's happening here?"

"Yeah...I vote we talk about Thomas. Now," Nia said, easily crossing her arms in her black puffer jacket. She gestured toward the house, and they all moved toward the front door.

Ginny's chest tightened, and she glanced at each of her friends, her gaze finally resting on James. All this time she'd thought having Famine abilities would make her feel more powerful, more like she was enough. Instead, she felt more overwhelmed, and frankly, sick to her stomach. The second she stepped away from James, the thoughts and tastes filtering toward her were enough to almost knock her off her feet. She grabbed for James hand. Yes, fine, she could imagine he was there and try the trick he'd showed her last night, but right now, she wanted to hold his hand.

James squeezed her hand.

"We agreed you'd behave," Anna said quietly to Nia.

"No, you agreed to that. I didn't. But we all agreed we were worried about Ginny. So here we are, Gin. Tell us what's with the dead trees and what you need," Nia said.

"I...don't remember doing it," she confessed.

Anna and Nia exchanged a dark look, and goosebumps rose on the back of Ginny's neck.

She felt downright nauseous when Nia stepped forward and linked arms with hers, tugging her toward the house.

"Let's go inside. Because I think you're going to need to sit down when we tell you what we found."

❧

James followed the four horsewomen of the apocalypse into the house cautiously. The pig kept him company, following more slowly. And giving him long, flirtatious looks.

James paused just outside the front door and pitched his voice low. Best no one else saw him talking to a pig.

"Listen, Pork Chop, I need to find a way to protect Ginny, which means I don't need any distractions." He indicated the forest behind them, the worst of the damage and new growth almost invisible from the front stoop. "That back there? It will be all the evidence USELESS agents will need to forcibly remove Ginny's abilities...or worse. I don't want anything happening to her. Do you?"

The pig shook its head.

"Then we're in agreement—we find a way to keep Ginny safe. From any and all threats. That means I need your help to convince her to choose the right path. Even if that means not using her abilities at all." His voice dropped. "We both know she's special."

The pig definitely smiled, then nodded again.

James scrubbed a hand through his hair and headed into the house after the girls. He might have been certifiably insane, but it felt like he'd just formed a bond with the pig. Frankly, he could use all the help he could get. It'd been a tough sell last night, convincing his team

Ginny wasn't dangerous and that she hadn't intentionally caused the harm outside.

Especially when he wasn't certain himself. What he wouldn't give for Ginny's ability to sense the truth about now. No, he'd never seen her melt trees. But there had been the incinerated marigold he'd found beside the house. If she hadn't destroyed it, who had?

On top of that, Bina had shot him a text this morning that his accountants were frantically trying to get ahold of him. Because of the time zone differences, they'd only been able to leave a message. There was definitely a problem with his books, and a substantial portion of money that should have gone to his charities had somehow vanished. Worse, the information had already been leaked and was bound to attract unwanted media attention. Evidently the reclusive philanthropist James Short had become something of a media sensation. Frankly, he didn't give two figs about the money, but it rankled if he'd been as negligent as Dad when it came to his finances. He didn't need a scandal now.

He hadn't told Ginny about that part of his life yet. Damn, but they needed to have a good long chat.

He and the pig stepped inside the house. He slipped off his shoes, while the little porker was polite enough to wipe its trotters. Then both of them followed the sound of voices down the long, narrow hallway to the living room, where Ginny and her friends were gathered around the dining room table. Only the tea candle Bina had brought out last night for dinner remained on the table.

Ginny held out a hand to him as he came in, and he pulled up a chair next to hers, their fingers intertwined.

She wouldn't quite meet his eyes when she spoke. "I…I've told the girls what your team says. About the spreading Famine destruction." She grimaced and sent darting glances back toward her friends. "About the cooking, and the lessons you've tried to give me. And our plan. To figure out a way to control my abilities before the USELESS agents arrive."

Anna came in from the kitchen, much smaller without her massive coat. She carried a teapot and five teacups. "Thank you, Ginny. For finally trusting us with the truth."

Ginny nodded miserably, picking at a scratch in the table. "I'm sorry. I just...all of you seemed to know exactly what you were doing all the time. How your abilities worked. What would happen when you gained them." She gestured at Anna. "You don't even want your abilities, but you're more powerful than I am. I..." Her shoulders slumped. "I still seem to have anti-Famine abilities. Like I'm not even one of you."

The petite, dark-haired Nia leaned over and squeezed Ginny's hand. "Ginny, you could have no abilities at all, or be turned into some kind of goddess, and we'd love you and know you were one of us. Got it? Now, let's talk about your ghost."

He blinked at Ginny. "Ghost?"

She avoided his eyes, and picked at her cuticle. "There's nothing to talk about, Nia. I told you."

"Wait a minute, people can be haunted? I thought it was just houses, places, that kind of thing," Piper said. Least scary of the four, she reminded him a bit of Mom. "Anna, please don't tell me to read a book. I'm the personification of Pestilence, not ghosts, so give me a break."

"There's a dead person attached to Ginny, a dangerous one—that's how they haunt you, Piper." Nia glanced at Anna, as though for backup. "I saw him the first time at the wedding. She basically told me to mind my own business."

"Yes, because he's no big deal," Ginny said. She glared at Nia. "This is why I didn't want you to find out about him." She turned to each of her friends. "His name is Thomas. He's not bad news. He's my brother. My twin brother." She turned to him, her words soft. "Thomas only lived a few hours after birth." Her voice faltered and she couldn't hold his gaze. "He…he started out developing fine, like me. But something happened and development didn't progress normally. I've wondered if he died because of me. Like a hopeful crop that failed, because he gestated next to Famine."

Ginny swallowed. "He's grown up beside me." She first met his gaze, then that of her friends. "He might be a ghost, but he's also my big brother. And my friend. It's my job to take care of him, too." Finally, she faced Nia.

Nia's brown gaze held some sympathy, but her lips were also compressed in an immoveable thin line. "Yeah, sure," she said, unconvinced. "You've hidden Casper from me because he's such a nice ghost? Nice ghosts don't suck your energy—which could be very bad when you gain your full abilities, by the way. And they also don't possess people, like I'm pretty sure he did last night."

Ginny was already shaking her head. "No. You're crazy."

Nia flinched at the last word, and an odd, shimmering charcoal mask, part gossamer shadow, hung around the petite woman's eyes. Only making her glare more off-putting. "Yeah, I might be. But not about this." She swung her gaze toward him.

James forced himself to stay still. Because this was definitely Death staring at him.

"What was she like last night, when she was melting trees? Describe her." Nia demanded.

"You don't have to do anything, James," Ginny said, her eyes sparking with green iridescence.

"I'd like to hear it, too, James," Anna said.

He swung his gaze between the women, dampness gathering at the back of his neck, his toes nervously tapping. Well, bugger. He hadn't figured on getting caught between all of them. He didn't want to destroy the fragile trust he and Ginny had just found. But there had been something off about her last night. His family had never associated with the other horsemen clans…and now he had a fair idea why.

He shifted, and glanced at Ginny, bright color burning on her cheekbones.

Ginny pulled her hand out of his, leaving his fingers cold.

Damn it. If Ginny was in danger, her friends couldn't help if they didn't have the information. He cleared his throat. "Her expression was almost blank, a bit mad if I'm honest. She walked out into the snow in bare feet and no jacket. She…didn't seem like herself."

"Just what I thought." Nia turned on Ginny now. "You said yourself you don't remember anything, right, Gin?"

Damn. If Ginny was haunted and her brother had possessed her, how dangerous was he? Because it was sounding like he was the real threat.

"No. You're wrong." Ginny glared down at the table.

The pig got up and snuffled at her feet.

"Ginny, I wouldn't have believed it myself," Anna said gently. "But when Nia came to me with her concerns about this spirit, I put it all together. It makes sense that somehow, your abilities were split. Perhaps in the womb. You don't have Famine abilities. He does."

Ginny flinched. "No. That can't be true," she said, her voice a whisper. She shook her head again. "No. It's not true. Look at what happened outside. A ghost couldn't rise as Famine. We weren't even supposed to rise until now, because of the League." She shoved her chair back with a loud squeak, and pointed at the pig at her feet. "And there's Roger. He's proof I'm becoming Famine. You said it yourself Anna. That's why you found him, right

Piper? M-maybe what happened last night, maybe I went into some kind of trance or something using my abilities. Thomas had nothing to do with it."

"Um, I've never gone into a trance with my abilities," Piper said quietly, earning a hot glare from Ginny. "I'm sorry, Gin, but I haven't. Look, maybe this not having abilities isn't a bad thing."

"Precisely," Anna said. "It means you're safe."

"Except from this spirit," Nia insisted. "I don't know how he has your abilities. If he's a spirit, he can't use most of them without physical form, which is why he possesses you. When he's strong enough, he won't need a body. He won't need you. Because he'll have absorbed your life force and your abilities. Look at Piper. She needed both parts of her abilities to rise. We should get rid of him now. Before he possesses you again."

"We're just trying to help you. Because the stronger you get, the stronger he gets," Anna said, reaching for Ginny's hands.

Ginny pulled out of reach. "Find a different theory. This one stinks."

The Death horsewoman growled and squeezed her hands into fists, slowly letting them out and meeting Ginny's gaze. "I understand he's your brother, and I'm sorry for your loss. I can't even imagine what that must have been like for your parents." She pulled her hood back up over her hair, shadowing her face, and pushed back the chair before standing behind it, her hands gripping the chair back, her gaze dark. "But we need to do something about him. He's tied to you, so I doubt I could exorcise him without your consent and possibly help. I wish you'd listen to me now, rather than wait and find out yourself. Because brother or not, he is dangerous."

"Please, Ginny. Our abilities are linked to our life force. I know. I've felt it," Piper added, standing likewise, her expression pleading as she clenched the chair back.

"Anna and Nia know what they're talking about. If he's willing to cause this kind of destruction, he's probably willing to cause an apocalypse. Which means he'll need your abilities, too. And if he takes your abilities, he takes your life. You're my best friend. I don't want anything to happen to you."

Cold hit James's core and his skin tingled. The abilities and their life force were linked. That meant USELESS couldn't drain or take away Ginny's abilities. Not without killing her. Convincing them she was harmless had always been a long shot, especially with what had happened last night.

Which meant USELESS would come. And they'd want to kill her. Because of him.

She might not even have Famine abilities. If this Thomas existed, then by teaching Ginny to use her abilities, he'd inadvertently made Thomas stronger.

He'd made Famine stronger.

His head spun.

Ginny slowly climbed to her feet. She gripped the table, and faced her friends. "I think you should leave," she said, a small tremble in her voice.

"No. We need to find a way to exorcise this bastard before he gets really dangerous," Nia argued, taking a step toward Ginny.

"We're your friends. Your sisters," Piper said, the last to stand.

"I meant all of you. It's time for you to get out of my house. Now," Ginny said, louder this time, her knuckles white where she pressed her fingers down into the table.

Anna stood, a small frown on her face. "We're trying to help you, Ginny. If you don't inherit your abilities, you'll be free," she said, as though baffled by Ginny's response. "USELESS and the gods won't be after you. The League won't be after you."

Ginny blinked, and a tear slid down her face. The

house began to tremble. Glass rattled in the windows, pots and pans rattled in the kitchen cabinets. "Yes, well, I'm sure that seems wonderful when you've experienced your powers and have grown up never doubting your inheritance and ability. But for the rest of us, maybe we'd like proof we're not just pretenders. Maybe not all of us are like you, Anna." The shaking increased. Something clattered to the floor in the kitchen.

The War horsewoman stiffened, and squeezed her hands into fists. Her voice was sub-arctic. "That's what you think? That I'm *lucky* to have my abilities?" The candle flared to life on the table, the flame almost four inches high.

The house shook harder. The chairs tipped over, the table danced. James fought to keep upright.

Bloody hell.

"You all need to go. Now," James said, wrapping his arm around Ginny. Despite his better judgment, despite every plan to stay objective, Ginny had come to mean a lot to him. It seemed impossible to both protect her *and* stop Famine.

The Pork Chop squealed and started shoving at the girls. Piper grabbed Anna and dragged her toward the door. Fire flared in the kitchen, hopefully from the range cooker.

"Anna, cool it!" Piper said, dragging her friend outside, through the shaking house.

"Please, Ginny, let me help you stop him," Nia begged again, holding onto the shaking table.

"Go!" James shouted.

The other three horsewomen ran for the door.

James did the only thing he knew to distract his wife. He kissed her.

CHAPTER 22

The world stilled and settled into a place of warmth and desire as James's lips moved over hers. Ginny curled against his hard chest, wrapped her arms around his neck, and pulled closer to him. Heat flared and spread through her, and she was more than eager to lose herself completely in her husband.

"Woohoo!" Roger cheered from somewhere under the table.

Unfortunately, James pulled back, stroking a hand down her cheek. "Better?"

"It was when you were still kissing me," she said, all the things the girls had said, what they thought about Thomas flooding through her. She tried to blink them away. This morning it had finally seemed like she was becoming Famine... Even if she didn't remember using her abilities. It was what she'd thought she'd wanted for so long. But now her friends thought it was Thomas somehow using those abilities. Thomas who was causing harm. And that she needed to get rid of him.

They couldn't possibly understand what he was to her. He was the only one who'd always been there.

A chill rose on her neck, and she felt Thomas's presence near her, though he didn't materialize.

"Of course, they can't understand. Only one of them bothered to attend your first wedding, when you were so sure you'd find your happy ending. None of them were there when Jimmy turned so cruel, when he humiliated you."

The shiver that went through Ginny had little to do with Thomas, and more to do with the memory of that day. Her twenty-first birthday, almost a year since they'd been married. And what Jimmy had done to her.

"I was there for you, wasn't I?" Thomas said. *"I was there when you had to wear those awful yellow and green athletic shorts home. I was there when you called Dad to pick you up. I've always been there. I've protected you, and you protect me. You help get us the life we deserve."*

Ah, yes. "Their" life. The one she had to live for the both of them. The birthday they had to share, where Mom and Dad faked their cheer, and Mom spent most of the night with a bottle of wine and Thomas's photo album, a tiny album filled with the photos, fingerprints, and the tiny lock of hair the hospital had helped make in the short hours he'd lived. Mom had obsessed over that tiny album a lot more than twenty-eight years of photos of Ginny.

"He's dead. It's your life, luv. Back off, dead boy," Roger said, with a rough coughing noise.

"Ginny, what's going on?" James asked, clearly taking note of Roger's behavior, the little pig stiff with fury, and facing a seemingly empty corner of the room.

"You need to tell the Death girl I'm none of her business. And you need to keep your distance from this man. You know better than to let yourself get hurt again. He'll hurt you just like Jimmy did. We're close. We can become Famine," Thomas said.

"Or he can," Roger said. *"Ask him what he remembers last night. What did he do to us?"*

The rough pads of James's fingertips against her skin, tracing her jawline pulled her back to him, back to their living room. Where the chairs lay, tipped and tossed on their sides on the floor, and the tiny tea light had burnt itself out on the tabletop.

"You're miles away right now. Is there anything I can do?"

His touch made her breath quicken, and a pleasurable shiver coursed through her. His eyes were like stormy waters. She didn't know how to convince the girls they were wrong about Thomas. *Cherry cheesecake*, she wasn't even certain she wanted to the powers of Famine anymore. The stronger she got certainly hadn't equated to feeling more confident in her abilities, and it seemed to just add more levels of danger to her life that she could do without.

"Ginny, he's—" Thomas began.

"No, Thomas. Tonight, I get to live my life." She reached a hand up and cupped James's jaw, then stroked the pad of her thumb over his cheek. She let his scent, the dark chocolate taste of him, the strength of him fill her, to force out all the other voices, the tastes.

Even Thomas.

Her brother's chill disappeared.

"Roger, make yourself scarce," she told the pig.

"About damned time," Roger said, pride in his voice as he trotted off.

James was nothing like Jimmy. With him, she was always enough. Even now, when her insides were all torn up because of the fight with the girls and she didn't know what she wanted, or what end was up. The prickle of James's stubble tickled her fingers. The way his eyes darkened sent a thrill through her, the headiness of the power she had when she touched him. Now that was a power worth having.

"Do you still think you just need to focus on keeping

me safe?" she said, her voice rougher than she'd expected, thick with all the ways she imagined touching her husband, the many ways she'd discover his taste.

He cleared his throat and caught her hand. "I said I wanted you, but that I didn't think it was wise if we were intimate."

She stepped up closer, her toes touching his, her chest against the soft fabric of his dark blue button-down. She splayed her hand over the silky fabric, feeling the thud of his heart beneath her palm, the tension in his muscles. "What about now? Is this too intimate for you? You already know what I'm capable of, maybe more than I am."

"Ginny..." he said, a combination of roughness and warning in his tone.

She leaned closer, brought her hands against his chest, and slid them slowly up the soft fabric of his shirt. Over his ribs, hard pecs, up onto his shoulders. Her hands followed the lines of his body, and she bent down and traced a line of kisses down his flat, hard belly.

He hissed out a breath, and gripped her shoulders.

She changed direction, and kissed her way upward until she cupped his face in her hands, massaged that firm jaw with her fingers. "What about this? Is this too intimate for you?"

He caught her hands in his. "I said it wouldn't be wise," he rasped.

"Oh...well then. Gods forbid," she whispered. A moment before she pulled him close and pressed her lips against his. She caught his breath in her mouth as she slipped her tongue between his lips, and tested his limits of intimate.

She continued to test him, taste him, pressing herself against his chest only a few moments past "What have I done now?" to enter her mind before his hands slid down her arms, over her back, and cupped her butt, pulling her up against him.

Against a— *Cupcake*! Very hard, clear evidence of the effects of her test. He deepened the kiss and she arched against him, all the better to feel him. All those delicious muscles and hardness against her. All hers.

The sound of the lock flipping closed was faint. Then he turned and pressed her against the wall, his hardness fitting between her legs, every inch finding answering softness. Bright lights sparked behind her eyes, and she gripped his shoulders, sliding herself against him in a long slide.

James groaned and squeezed handfuls of her ass. Then he slid his hands up beneath her mint-green sweater, pushing it down her shoulders. His fingers were gentle but rough against her soft skin as he found bottom of her shirt and then found the lines of her bra, the thin lace hardly a barricade at all to his questing fingertips. *Frosting*, but he knew what he was doing as he found her nipple and turned it to a hard, aching nub. She writhed against him again, and he thrust gently against her, hitting just the right mark. More sparks and heat pooled in her core.

He pulled back to stare down at her, his hands still working at the edges of her bra, pinching her nipples gently.

"We really shouldn't do this," he rasped.

"Uh-huh." Her eyes half-closed, she ached with need as she slid a hand down and boldly cupped him, rubbed up and down his length before giving him a gentle squeeze. "You're not going to stop, are you?"

He pressed into her hand with another rough groan. "Not unless you want me to."

She found the pull for his zipper. "Thank gods."

Everything had been going great…until James put his hand on hers, stopping her from unzipping his fly. And he. Stopped. Ginny stared at him for a second. For *frosting*—

He took her hand in his, and walked backward toward the bedroom, a small smile playing over his lips and in his eyes. "You deserve so much better than for me to take you the first time out in the hall," he said, voice still rough.

How sweet. Even if she was perfectly fine with out in the hall, on the table, against the wall. Just so long as they finally touched.

But she left her fingers in his and let him lead her toward the bedroom. The problem, of course, was that the brief pause let those doubts creep back in. The ones that asked what she was thinking, that said of course this was probably a dumb idea to top all remarkably stupid ideas. Why not just let the heat of the moment remove responsibility and rational thought? Pretty sure that was the definition of passion.

Of course, as he closed the bedroom door and faced her, the confidence and to-hell-with-it attitude she'd felt out in the hall that had her rubbing herself against her husband had pretty much evaporated.

Rushing also meant she didn't need to keep seeing how sweet he was. She was already falling for him. She didn't need any help.

She bit her lip and wondered what she was supposed to do next. *Sweet potato pie*, how moronic. She'd been married. She'd had sex. In the past tense. It had just been, well, a while.

James stepped up to her and slid his hands up and down her arms. "You still sure about this?"

She nodded stupidly, since words were impossible. At least, any words that would have been useful at the time. She wanted this. She wanted him. Of that she had no doubt.

He cupped her jaw gently, his thumb stroking her skin. "You're my wife. There is plenty of time for us to shag out in the hall, on the table, wherever else you want, love. But not this first time."

That all had kind of a long-term sound to it, didn't it? It sent a trill of pleasure sailing through her. And freed her words and reheated her desire. "I just want you. I'm not too picky."

"Oh, Ginny, but you deserve to be. You deserve to be worshiped, love." Seemingly taking utmost care, his lips found hers again in a soft, chocolate-melting kiss that left her gasping for more.

He stopped again, his gaze direct as he reached for the buttons on his shirt and slowly undid them, one at a time, revealing inch by inch of tantalizing flesh.

Oh, gods above. Clearly, not only did he never imbibe in sweets and work out constantly, he must do it naked, outside in the sun, because every inch he revealed was hard and toned beneath bronzed skin. Hope he used sunscreen, which was a bizarre thought, but she did not want anything bad happening to this man.

Muscle rippled as he pushed the shirt back off his shoulders and let it drop onto the floor. There was only a light dusting of blond hair, but so. Many. Muscles.

Then he reached for his fly.

Her breath caught.

Flicked the button free. Then the zipper.

She struggled to swallow.

His smile was slow and teasing. But then he left it there, his fly undone but pants still on, just a hint of blue underwear beneath.

Cupcake.

He chuckled, and stepped forward to reach her again. "We've all the time in the world. Where's the rush?"

Uh, what about the fact where she might change her mind first? Or he might. Or his friends might come home. Or one of them might realize this was foolish and they should have just rushed through it because the foreplay was usually the most fun anyway.

Or at least, it had been.

"Can I help you with that?" he said, nodding at her striped shirt.

Gulp. She nodded.

His eyes darkened, and he slowly lifted the hem, his knuckles brushing her bare skin. Her breath came faster as he lifted higher, his gaze locked with hers. His knuckles brushed the underside of her breast, and she gasped. Then again. Nope, that hadn't been an accident.

"Oh, *banana cream pie*," she said, grabbed her shirt, and ripped it off over her head.

The heat of his mouth closed over her breast. He tightened and twisted the shirt, trapping her arms behind her as she gasped, thrusting her breasts out more.

"Now this was a view worth waiting for," he said, his eyes dark and heavy lidded.

He walked them back to the bed, his gaze hot as it moved over her chest.

Was she ever glad she'd picked the pretty lace bra this morning instead of just one of the boring everyday ones.

He gently pushed her back onto the bed, following her down between her legs. "Purple and black lace. Lovely," he rasped, running his lips over her nipple that was peaked and waiting for him. Then he sucked her nipple into his mouth.

She arched up against him with a breathless moan. His tongue was like combined heaven against her as he suckled her. Then he moved onto the other breast, squeezing and massaging the neglected one with his fingers.

Everything he did was wonderful, but she wanted to touch him, too. She tugged at her hands and pulled them free of the shirt. Then she could feel those smooth, hard shoulders beneath her fingertips, his skin hot. Hold him against her as his fingers found the clasp on her bra and tossed it away, his mouth now raw against her bared flesh.

She moaned and arched up against him until she found his hardness and could rub herself against him.

It was his turn to groan.

Her fingers found the waistband of his pants, then the elastic of his shorts, and she slid her hands beneath, cupping his ass and pulling him and his erection toward her.

He groaned again, cold air circling her wet nipple as he pulled back and met her gaze. "You're not making worship easy," he rasped.

She pushed at his pants. "I'm all for worship. So long as it's a fast service."

He chuckled. "I suppose we do have time. For repeat performances."

Wait, what? Her eyes widened before his lips found hers. Then it was all about the kiss. Oh, *frosting!* Was there anything better than a man who knew how to use his tongue, his hands, and tasted like chocolate? If there was, she'd never heard of it.

She slid her hand up and down his shaft until he unzipped her jeans and slid a hand and some very nimble fingers down her pants, inside her panties, and along her seam. This while he lavished more loving attention on her breasts, weighing them, seeming to memorize and adore every detail about them.

"You are so damned gorgeous," James said before stealing her breath again. First with the kiss. Then with one long finger as he slid inside her.

Sensation took over as they fought to get rid of their pants and underwear, and still he continued to tease her, to urge her closer and closer to the edge. He quickened his pace, helping her find nirvana not only with those fingers, but his mouth on her breasts, tasting and caressing every inch of flesh.

His fingers shifted inside her, color flashed behind

her eyes, she might even have died a second, the pleasure was so great, and she tightened her legs around his thighs. Waves of pleasure cycled over and through her. Still he pushed her onward, still he kissed and teased her. A second wave rose and made her tighter, hotter, riding higher, higher.

He traded his hand for his erection and thrust inside her, sending her over the edge and spiraling into heaven. They stole each other's breath, her thighs wrapped around his waist as he pressed into her. Again, and again. Deeper and deeper. Tension again grew and twined inside her, and this time when she flew. James, with a deep guttural groan, came with her.

Eventually, her thoughts settled like floating petals on the water. *Chocolate cupcakes*, but she'd been missing this all her life. Sex before had always been "good enough." But now she was spoiled. That would never be enough again. She had seriously underestimated the need for more worship in her life.

CHAPTER 23

Sun burned in around the edges of the blackout curtains, just enough light to find the beautiful redhead curled against him. The light turned the edges of her hair gold and fiery.

James's lips turned up. The unbelievably sexy, full-of-surprises redhead. Last night had been…cosmic? What was better than incredible, better than any night of sex he'd ever experienced or dreamed of? He'd never felt chemistry like with Ginny. She was rapidly becoming so much more than just a mission. They may have gotten into this marriage on false pretenses, there was the tree-melting episode, and the fact that she was set to become one of the most powerful creatures in the human realm. He was supposed to be here to stop her.

She was also the woman with the soft, sweet smile who he'd caught spying on him with a stepladder. Or trying to. A woman who claimed to want ultimate power but knuckled under with her friends and appeared more determined to defend her dead twin than her own tender feelings. A woman who had curves in all the right places, but who clearly hadn't seen the benefit and power of all those curves.

There went that internal warning alarm clanging away in his head, the same one that had gone off before he even knew who she was. The one that said this woman could be dangerous to him in so many ways. Hell, he'd already fallen for her. Her Famine heritage was no more her fault than his was. But he still had to find a way to protect her. From USELESS, after her because of his own arrogance, to think he could single-handedly stop a horseman. From his alter ego James Short, which could draw even further attention to Ginny and her friends. From his own team, who still believed she was dangerous.

He smoothed his hand down her arm and she curled against him more closely. The urge to protect her was darned near irresistible.

She was so much stronger than she knew, both in her abilities and the rest of her life. But if the way she'd interacted with her friends was any indication, she seemed far too used to letting other people tell her what to do.

His brow lowered.

He was doing the same, telling her what she should or shouldn't do. Hiding the truth about exactly why USELESS was after her. Weighing every action with how he might use it to convince her to see his side.

Manipulating her like Dad and his brothers manipulated others for their gain. His throat thickened and his skin chilled.

Granted, his original intention had been to stop her because he'd believed she was dangerous. But during the tree-melting incident and all the time they'd trained together, he'd seen for himself that destruction wasn't in Ginny's heart. He couldn't believe she wanted to hurt anyone. He'd deepened the danger she and her friends were in, and he was running out of time to find a way to protect her. Now he knew USELESS had lied to him. There was no alternate means to save her. He turned her over, and they killed her.

Or he found a way to save her.

Now there was this mysterious ghostly brother, who was definitely trouble. The stronger Ginny and her abilities became, the stronger the brother would become. Whether Ginny wanted to believe it or not.

It almost seemed like Ginny needed protection from her own good heart. His lips thinned. Maybe that was something he could do. If she'd allow him.

He couldn't stop himself from stroking his hand through those silky, riotous curls and down her back. What a fool he'd been to think last night he'd been in control, when his beautiful wife had completely overwhelmed him. She had no idea how incredible she was.

She stretched, froze a moment—perhaps her moment of figuring out where she was and what had happened last night—before she propped herself up on one arm and peeked up at him from beneath her hair.

"Good morning," he said.

He gently reached forward and smoothed her hair back from her face, tucking it behind her ears. Bloody hell, even her ears were sexy. Then there was the way her curls curved against her pale skin, and down over her breasts. Those coral nipples peeking out at him.

After last night's performances, he should not have been getting hard. It should have been physiologically impossible.

His body proved otherwise. It was like he just couldn't get enough of her. He slid his hand down her soft shoulder, then up, letting his fingertips trail over her breasts.

"Good morning," she said, ending on a soft gasp as his fingers found her nipple.

"Any regrets?" he rasped, kissing a trail down the side of her neck.

"That we waited this long?" she breathed.

He laughed quietly. "I hope I've made up for it." He turned his attention to the second perfect breast.

She grasped his shoulder with one hand, while the other slid down his body, over his abs and wrapped around his length. She squeezed, and a soft groan broke through his lips.

He was more than just interested. Especially when she curled her thigh over his. He found her ass and pulled her closer.

Things were just getting interesting when an annoying buzzing sound started. Insistent and repetitive from out in the hall. He tried to ignore it, and thank gods, it finally stopped.

Until the dingle of a cheery pop song chimed, repeating the same chorus. Again. And again.

Ginny pulled back, her brows rising. "I think that's my cell."

He groaned, and flopped back onto the bed. "Mine's on vibrate." That had probably been the first insistent buzzing.

"It's odd that anyone would call me this early," she said, pushing her hair back and sitting up.

The chiming stopped. To be replaced a moment later with a loud telephone ring.

He pushed himself upright and turned to her. "We have a telephone?"

Ginny got up, tugging the loose blanket around her like a toga and padding toward the door. "I think Mom said something about having one installed."

He pulled on a pair of trousers, grabbed his cell, and followed her out into the hall and down toward the kitchen. Sure enough, a small white wall telephone hung just inside the kitchen, ringing. It paused. Then started ringing again. Along with her cell down the hall. The hair rose on the back of his neck.

Not touching her, he wasn't as hungry for her.

Much more sated. What if part of his attraction to her the same kind of reaction people had to her food. That inability to feel satiation. He should have been immune to her.

Unless…she really was gaining her abilities. And therefore, absorbing his.

He touched the screen of his cell, and swiped it open. His eyes scanned the text back from his solicitor. <Charity and accounts manager siphoning off funds. Millions lost. Building case. Story leaked to media. PR nightmare. Go into damage control mode.>

Fuck.

The chances of the media finding him here should have been small. But so were the chances the story had been leaked this quickly to them in the first place.

He still hadn't told Ginny about the food bar and his charitable, much wealthier alter ego.

Or about the much worse secret. His part in bringing USELESS here.

That inherent corruption was the trouble with Famine. Something he'd never been able to outrun. Something perhaps Ginny wouldn't be able to outrun, either.

The shrillness of the telephone seemed to double. Ginny tossed her hair. "This is ridiculous. It's just a phone." She grabbed the receiver off the wall and held it to her ear. "Hello?"

Dumb or not, an uneasy feeling still gripped him.

It didn't get better as Ginny's face paled, and the receiver trembled in her hand. "Can you tell me anything more?" She swallowed. "I see," she whispered. "W-we'll be right there." She reached to hang up, fumbling the receiver and almost dropping it. Her gaze still downcast, she slipped past him headed for the bedroom. "We need to get dressed and leave. Something's happened at the bar."

❧

A chill shivered through Ginny from the inside out, leaving her fingers shaking. Of course she wanted to know what was going on…but that desire was having a serious smackdown with her terror of knowing. Maybe this was the League, enacting some new scary plan in town. Had she told the girls who the League members were? Maybe she should have told his team to arrest the Fates or something.

Or maybe something happened to one of her friends, and their abilities had gone haywire. *Frosting*, Anna might have accidentally caused another brawl. Or Piper another mini-plague.

Or worse, maybe it wasn't any of them at all. Maybe she'd somehow done something without knowing again, like the tree melting. She didn't remember that and it had still happened.

Roger leaned forward from the backseat, and rested his head against her arm. *"I remember last night and the porno I watched, so I don't think it was you. At least…not directly. We'll figure this out, luv. Together."*

James frowned out over the steering wheel, and his grip tightened.

She and James had hardly said another word to each other as they'd gotten dressed, then headed out. His knuckles were white against the steering wheel, a small tick starting in his jaw. He hadn't asked any further questions but had seemed in just as much hurry to get out of the house and see for himself what had happened.

It'd been Anna on the phone who'd just said they needed to get downtown, ASAP. Something had happened at the bar. The last time "something had happened at the bar" Piper had gained her abilities, then diseased and almost killed about a third of the town.

"I think…maybe you should try not to use your abilities," James said, his voice low.

"Not use them? But…we've been practicing so I could learn to control them."

"That hasn't gone especially well, has it?"

She flinched at his words, and wrapped her arms around herself. "I guess not," she said, her voice small.

He glanced her way, then back out the windshield. "I didn't mean… Bollocks." He hit his hands on the steering wheel. "Look, what if your friends are only partially right? Maybe your brother is trying to steal your abilities. You do have some Famine abilities of your own. Like the way no one can get enough of your food…and the way I can't seem to get enough of you. You make me insatiable."

She stole another glance at him, the hard line of his jaw. He didn't seem especially happy about it if that was the case. *Donut holes.* Last night had seemed so promising. At least the part where she tried to ignore Thomas and the threat he possibly posed, and the fight with the girls, and the fact that maybe after all this, she didn't really want the powers of Famine anyway.

She twisted her hands together in the lap of her eggplant colored skirt. It wouldn't really hurt for her not to use her abilities. It's not like she'd perfected them. And she hated the way it felt like she'd somehow disappointed James.

"Who bloody well cares?" Roger snapped, with a raucous snort.

"Just until we figure out what's happening." She paused, feeling guilty even for saying it. *"And until we know for sure what's going on with Thomas."*

"I…I'll try not to use them." Maybe it was for the best. Especially if Thomas really had been somehow using them. But it was still so hard to believe he'd ever hurt her.

James blew out a breath, and glanced down at the pig, who now glared at him with fiery intensity. "Does Pork Chop…talk by any chance?"

She blinked. "To me he does."

James shook his head, and squeezed the wheel again, his knuckles white. "I think…I can hear him."

"You can hear Roger?" Oh, *hot fudge sundae*. Well, never underestimate the magical powers of sex. This sounded like the kind of thing the girls—especially Anna—would not be pleased about. Something she needed to discuss with them.

The pig cocked its head.

James winced and gave the pig a light shove into the backseat, evidently responding to a private conversation with Roger. "I didn't need to know any details of what he was up to last night."

"It's as if you two had a sexy baby, and it was me! He really can hear me," Roger crowed. He popped his head up between the two seats again with an excited squeal. *"Oh, this is all kinds of fun."* The pig batted his eyelashes at James.

Her husband massaged an eyebrow, then glanced at her and squeezed her knee. "After we untangle this latest debacle, we need to sit down and have a long chat. There are…things I need to tell you."

"Well, don't everyone go and cheer at once. A little appreciation sure is rare as rocking horse shit," Roger grumbled.

Her pulse skipped, and she opened her mouth to ask what James wanted to talk about. But a wall of tastes and thoughts hit her like a physical blow. She wheezed and grabbed for his arm to try and block it out, her eyes watering. *Frosting*, so many flavors. All those thoughts.

Confused and disoriented, they caused the same feelings in her.

She looked up, blinking back tears as they rounded the last bend in the road. Ahead was a visible road jam of vehicles in and around the four-way stop. It was a pretty good guess where trouble was centered.

Because all the people who milled around were partially to completely nude.

"Is. That. An. Orgy?" Roger gasped.

Whatever it was, there were an awful lot of people wandering around. Many more than she recognized, and was that a newsman and camera crew?

A very strong urge to run for the nearest kitchen and cook until all this craziness passed grew inside and she squeezed her toes up in her shoes.

James pulled over to the side of the road, the car parked on a slant. He frowned, but his gaze was distracted. "I'll come around and help you out," he said, but he was looking toward the four-way and the small clutch of businesses, including the gas station, the mini-mart, and Lou-ki's pub.

She opened the door, and then promptly almost rolled out. "No, I'm fine," she lied, grabbing for the door and trying not to roll down into the ditch at the side. Although…there was something to be said for breaking her leg as a convincing reason why she couldn't get involved in whatever was going on. She struggled to focus on bringing back the memory of James to block out all the extra thoughts and tastes, enough that she could climb to her feet.

She hadn't even been here. Surely, she couldn't have caused this.

James came around and, with the apparent agility of a mountain goat, seemed to have no problem at all keeping his balance and offering her a hand. She closed the door of the car, and she and James made their way to the level roadway. Then, either because of his distraction or because he knew she needed the help to block out all the flavors and thoughts, he still held her hand in his, and together they walked toward the four-way.

The gravel parking lot near the bar was standing room only, between the handful of cars and all the people spilled out of Lou-ki's place. People who, despite the crisp late-autumn temperatures, seemed to have all misplaced most of their clothes. There was a lot of bare skin. A lot of bare, wrinkly skin.

Ginny raised her eyes higher than the parking lot—and all the things she didn't want to see and have nightmares about later—and found Lou-ki himself, wearing his Lou face. He stood, arms crossed over his broad, plaid-covered chest on the front porch of the bar. The newly repaired door—hadn't they just fixed that yesterday? Was propped up against the wall.

Lou-ki's glare landed on her. "Genevieve Lack, do you have an explanation for this?" he called. "Because all the food in my kitchens is spoiled."

"I have no idea what's going on," she said. People seemed to be drifting aimlessly, confused. The sick whirling feeling in her stomach grew.

Next door, the door to the mini-mart burst open, and five people tumbled out, behind them one of the cashiers, a pretty red-head with a pixie cut. She shooed more half-naked people out of the store. "I told you, there's no more junk food. You're all causing a mess, so we're closed until further notice."

The redhead looked up and spotted Ginny. Her lips tightened, and she sent Ginny a black glare before turning and slamming the glass door shut on a tinkle. A few seconds later she shoved out more half-naked confused people. Then slammed the door again. This time she blocked it from inside with what looked like a large sheet of plywood.

Oh, *cupcake*.

Ginny spotted Anna's tall, slim form on the other side of the road, arms crossed...glaring back across the road at Lou-ki, it looked like. Though with Anna, it could be a general crowd glare. The tiny dark figure near her could only be Nia. Oh, and there, striding through the crowd, nearly a head taller than most of them, looked like Daniel rather than his twin brother. Especially judging from the smaller blonde, Piper, at his heels.

A small distance away, standing all alone and evidently invisible to everyone else, stood Thomas and his pig, Barnabas. Watching.

He'd never appeared anywhere so public before. He looked so...solid.

She shivered and looked away. Things had gone badly yesterday with the girls, but Nia had said yesterday that no matter if Ginny had abilities or not, that they'd always be her friends. Frankly, with the strangeness of this morning, she needed to talk to them. It shouldn't have been possible that James could hear Roger. Or that she'd somehow influenced him with her ability.

Coldness filled her stomach. Surely that wasn't the only reason he'd wanted her last night.

"There are the girls," she said, tugging on James's arm.

"There's my team," he said at almost the same moment, pulling her in the opposite direction.

Anna flagged her over. Daniel, Piper, and Nia all stood at her side now, along with Piper's horse, a small skunk.

"I have to go find my friends," Ginny said, turning to James.

His lips narrowed to a thin line.

Who the heck were all these people?

The crush of mostly naked people had closed the gap she and James had used to come into their midst. The ones in the parking lot she recognized as largely locals. A large number had escaped from the Senior Center. Many more were looking very Beckwellian, with the requisite paranormal oddities that had become more prevalent since Piper had gained her abilities. That is, extra wings, horns, tails. Very nonhuman additions.

Uh-oh. That was a news crew, the cameraman now up on top of the news van. Judging from the bright light on the camera, they were filming. If this footage got out, it could be a disaster if Normals who saw it believed what they saw.

The crowd was either growing, moving, or both. Thomas had vanished, or at least she couldn't see him anymore. She could barely see the girls over all the people surrounding them, the movement of the crowd starting to make it disorienting which direction she was even pointed. She and James were suddenly amid people who seemed to wander, their expressions dazed. Still not enough clothes among them, and they seemed curiously unaware of the cold.

"I've got to get to the girls," Ginny had to practically shout, dropping James's hand and stepping away.

The shifting crowd seemed to almost immediately fill in the space between them, and she had to stand on tiptoe to see James above the other heads.

"I'll gather my team and come to meet you," James shouted back, and headed in the opposite direction.

The crowd squeezed around her, and she slid and excused her way through them, trying not to flinch every time she brushed bare flesh. Nearly naked stranger flesh. Ugh, and they all had strange flavors. Pumpkin spice here, boiled eggs there, all with a hint of charcoal. Ew on all fronts.

A group of cowboys stepped between her and the girls. Well, maybe strippers dressed as cowboys. All they wore were low-slung denim, holsters, and cowboy hats, nothing else. Though from the looks of those six-packs, the no-shirts thing was a norm for them. Okay, sure, Beckwell didn't boast that many strippers—or any, so far as she knew—but from the strong bacon, cheeseburger, and greasy-spoon pan steak taste of the three of them that was nearly enough to make her gag, the three of them were Normals.

Which made them relatively unthreatening. Until their gazes latched onto her. And they moved determinedly closer.

Oh, *cupcake*. The squidgy feeling in her belly returned.

"Well, hello, darling," one of them drawled.

Her skin prickled, the bitter taste of burned toast and oranges bursting on her tongue, her distraction making her lose the shield of James's flavor.

"Sorry, not interested." She gave him and each of his friends a dark glare and lifted on tiptoe to spot Anna again. Waved frantically. *"Roger, we've got a problem here."*

"On it," Roger said. Then a moment later. *"Ow. Okay, less on it. Your friends are grumpy."*

She didn't have time to analyze what that meant. Or say anything back, since her tongue was stuck in the back of her throat. The burning taste grew worse.

The four cowboys seemed to be drawing attention. More people drew closer. They seemed to have too many nearly naked friends, and all of them seemed interested in her suddenly.

Yeah, okay, it could have been flattering…if it wasn't so creepy.

"You smell so good," a woman moaned. She reached out and slid her hand down Ginny's arm. She tasted of peach-apple cobbler coupled with that burning flavor.

Ginny jerked away. "I've got to—no! Please, stop. No touching."

"I saw her first," someone else said. Cheerios and bananas combined with that burning.

More hands, reaching for her. Eggs. Turkey. Creamed corn. Toothpaste. The taste of burning made her gag, all the different flavors even worse. A wall of bodies surrounded her. Their desires. Their Want, their Need for an unnamed something, flooded through her like physical blows that knocked the wind from her lungs. *Black forest cake*, this was bad. Especially since it all seemed to be focused on her.

"Let me through!" Forget being nice. She pushed and shoved at them, her movements more restricted the more of them there were, the closer they surrounded her.

"Help!" She screamed as hands and bodies cut off all movement. And then air.

CHAPTER 24

James had just reached his team when Ginny's scream cut through the din of the crowd. His adrenaline spiked and the hair lifted on the back of his neck. He had to get to her.

"It's Ginny," he said to them, then turned, and raced back into the throng. There was never any doubt that his team would back him up, no more than he'd never doubted it was Ginny who'd cried out. Which was completely illogical—definitely channeling Kirk lately more than Spock—yet he just...knew.

The half-naked people had clumped together, and from that glimpse of copper hair, he had a bad feeling about whom they'd gathered around. As a group, they seemed to all shuffle toward her, that glazed look in their eyes, unsteady movements making them disturbingly zombie-like despite the heat of their bodies and huffing breaths that clearly marked them among the living.

Bollocks. He shouldn't have left her there alone. Should have seen her to her friends.

"Step aside," he said brusquely, trying to politely shove a big man who was all sweaty flesh and hair aside. There was no moving the brute.

"Allow me," Maddox said with a growl. He took the lead and barreled a bruising path toward that flash of copper hair.

"Pork Chop? Pork Chop, do you hear me?" he tried to communicate to Ginny's pet or horse, or whatever it was supposed to be. Roger. Its name was Roger. *"Roger? Can you help her?"*

He followed close on Maddox's heels, Charlie, Caspian, Asher, and Nahla at his back.

Either he'd done something wrong with his first attempt at telepathy, or there was some other reason the pig didn't answer. Hopefully because he'd already reached Ginny's side.

"Do you see her?" he shouted at Maddox, the crowd pushing back, growing more aggressive now. He elbowed someone aside. The closer they should have gotten, the more the crowd would surge and the more people were between them.

"A sword would be helpful," Maddox said, shoving two large men aside at once.

"No sword. Something's wrong with these people."

Maddox grunted, and went back to clearing a path for their group.

"I. Said. Back. Off," a booming voice shouted from the other side of the crowd, the sound of the voice sending chills through the air and a strange unsettled feeling in his stomach.

He could just make out the tall brunette head of the War horsewoman, Anna, and the wide berth even the crazed crowd gave she and her friends. It wasn't her speaking, but the tiny Death horsewoman, Nia. The three women seemed to have cleared their own path, as the crowd edged away from them. Unfortunately, it hadn't freed Ginny, who seemed to be at the center of a thick clutch, carried along by the crowd.

"Do you see her?" he shouted to the three women.

Anna's head shot up. She pointed, indeed, to the thick throng.

The blonde Pestilence horsewoman lifted on her tiptoes. "Can you get to her? They're not even scared of Nia's Death voice."

That explained the unsettling feeling the voice had invoked. "Where's the pig?"

With each body Maddox and he moved aside, another seemed to shift into their way. He could just barely hear Ginny's muffled cries from inside.

"Get us the hell out of here!" Roger shouted in his head, loud enough James winced.

"Tell the sausage we are trying," Maddox said through gritted teeth, tossing aside what looked to be the same two people he'd removed only a minute ago. No time to ask now how Maddox heard Roger...or how long he'd been able to hear Roger.

"There are too many of them," Nahla said. "They're like water. We can't break through this way."

Desperation gripped him, tightened his muscles, made him push through strangers with more force, anything to reach Ginny. He'd promised to protect her. Yet his own arrogance and ignorance had put her in danger again. He couldn't do this alone. He'd need all the help he could get to keep Ginny safe.

"Can you do anything?" he shouted desperately to the horsewomen.

Pestilence's boyfriend had grown horns and changed color to a deep bronze—well, that was disturbing, though somehow not that surprising—and was tossing aside people as quickly as Maddox, with the same lack of result. The women pushed and shoved at the crowd, shouting at them too, but got no further, despite Death's scary voice.

"Ginny, I'm coming." Somehow.

ဆ

Ginny sucked in small quick breaths and struggled to stay conscious. Black spots gathered in her vision. Oh *frosting*, they'd smother her. She'd die, smothered because people finally wanted her. What stupid irony. Was that irony?

She heard James's voice, as though far away. The murmur of the voices, their thoughts about how much they wanted her, how good she tasted, and below that the whisper of their needs and wants soaking through her at every touch. Tears wet her face and she'd curled into the smallest ball she could, pressed into the ground and curled around Roger's warm little body. The pig had an essence of eau de barnyard.

"Hang in there, luv. They're trying," Roger said.

She was feeling floatier all the time, disconnected from herself and from all those hands on her, all those tastes.

Oh, wait, she could feel the others. James's friends maybe, Piper's Daniel was there, too. Their desires and needs, too. The frantic need to reach her. To understand what was happening. To control it, but losing each battle. The growing anger.

She was feeling more and more floaty. Hardly tasted the people anymore. The eau de barnyard grew faint. Her breathing came in slow puffs. Her heart stuttered. She wasn't enough for this. She'd failed.

"You do know this IS your doing, don't you?" Came a different voice in her head. A cultured masculine voice, tinted with the slightest accent she couldn't place, but that made her feel warm and melty.

It was starting to get crowded in there. Couldn't they leave her alone? The floatiness was kind of nice. Peaceful even.

"Genevieve Lack, are you really going to take the

easy way out?" the same cultured and annoyed male voice said in her head.

Huh. Only her mom called her Genevieve.

And sometimes...Loki. Or was that Lou-ki? Hehe. Lou-ki. Had she told the girls about that?

"Genevieve Lack. YOU started this. Now go on and DO something about it," Lou-ki snapped.

This time, along with the irritation, there was a push that forced a breath of air into her lungs and the peace of the floatiness away. All those flavors, those needs, and desires flooded over her again. Her heart raced. Too many hands. The sick feeling in her stomach. The ringing sound in her ears.

What did he mean she started it? She was pretty certain she hadn't. Which made it hard to figure out what she was supposed to do about it.

Below the ringing sound in her ears, a whirling, thickening feeling built and grew, soaking up through the earth into her body. It soaked through her as rapidly as she noticed it, almost as though it had been waiting permission. Warmth dimming all those whispers and murmurs, the tastes and the sounds. It was like when she started a batch of muffins, and yet so much more than that. The well of power deep and without end, as deep and steady as the earth. It quieted in her head and in her heart. She became that steadiness. Complete.

"Enough," she said. Whispered really, maybe she hadn't even said it aloud.

"Think it. Feel it. Will it," Roger said.

She closed her eyes, willing the emotion of enough through her. *Enough.* Enough of the hands reaching and touching her. Enough of the wanting and the raw need for something the people surrounding her couldn't even express. *Enough.* Their bellies were full, their bodies were sated, they were alive and at peace. *Enough.*

Hands fell away from her. The whispers of wants and

needs faded like they'd been brushed away by the wind. Fresh air rushed in and she opened her eyes to see the deep blue cloudless sky above.

"Enough," she said.

The last few stragglers surrounding her parted, blinked their eyes clear, and looked around in confusion. Some of them shivered in the cold, brought their hands up to cover themselves.

James's warm arms surrounded her. "Ginny, are you all right? What happened? How did you stop them?"

She would have answered, but bright lights were suddenly shone in her face. "What brings you to Canada, Mr. Short? Are you planning to set up operations here?"

"Mr. Short, could you answer a few questions about the accountancy discrepancies? Is it true you've been stealing money from your own charity?"

"What kind of—Maddox. A little help please," James said tightly, never looking away from her.

The bright lights and the people with their questions disappeared. Well, not like "poof," but they went away.

James didn't. He cradled her with utmost care in his arms and caressed her cheek with his fingers. They were moving. He was carrying her somewhere.

Frosting, but he had the most incredible eyes. There were little silver flecks in all that cool blue, and his lashes, though pale, were long and lush. A lot of women would have killed for lashes like that. Probably his bone structure and perfect ass, too. *Hotcakes*, they'd probably want him, too, if they saw him.

Oh, hey. The floatiness was back. James's lips moved—he had really nice lips. Not too thin, not too thick, just right. Like the perfect porridge and little bear and goldilocks. Sadly the ringing, whooshing sound in her ears swallowed his words. Her head felt like it was filled with helium and soaring fast.

"Well, *frosting*," she mumbled, and let the blackness

swallow her.

෨

The darkness lifted. Her eyelids were still heavy, stuck closed. But she wasn't relaxed and unaware. There was a weight on her, not a physical pressing of her body...but like a weight on her spirit. An awareness of that something else.

She wasn't alone.

It felt cramped, crushed in her head and in her body. Like she'd been squished down and compressed to make room.

"Shh...sleep," the voice said, but it was trying to be calm, when there was an edge of anxiety to it.

"Thomas? What's happening? Where are we?" At least, it sounded like Thomas, only his voice wasn't in her head, but echoed around her in the darkness, louder than her own.

"This will be easier if you sleep." Then aside, not to her. "Why is she aware, Barnabas?"

"It is puzzling," said her brother's horse. His voice wasn't just in her head, but echoed in the darkness around her.

Of course, if she was in her head, then their voices wouldn't sound like they were there. Would they?

Speaking of her head, it throbbed, and it felt like bruises up and down her arms, all over her. *Frosting*, she wanted to puke just thinking about what had happened, all those people touching her. Fortunately, her mind scuttled away from that back to this darkness, to trying to figure out what was happening.

"Thomas, where are you? Why can't I see you?"

"Why can't you just GO TO SLEEP!" he roared.

Ginny flinched and stumbled back. Wait. She looked down. She was standing, she had a body, and she stood in the darkness, the nothingness. But how was that even possible? What was Thomas doing?

"Well, that's hardly helpful," Barnabas said. A large black pig appeared beside her. Wearing spectacles.

Of course it was. This was some kind of weird dream, wasn't it? Maybe she'd hit her head.

"Yes, that's all it is," the spectacle-wearing pig said with Barnabas's soothing voice. "Lay down, dear heart. Yes, right there on the ground. You just have a sleep now. It will all be fine. Don't you worry about a thing. Thomas, don't you have something to say to your sister?"

Thomas appeared beside the large black horse. He was large and solid, his hair a darker auburn than hers, and he was almost as muscular as James. It could have been Thomas's head superimposed over James's body.

Her brother knelt at her side, and stroked her hair. "Hush now. You need to sleep, Ginny."

"I don't want to sleep. I want to see James." Her thoughts tumbled away. "I have...things to tell him."

"You can tell him later. It's my turn right now. I deserve a turn, don't I? After all I've done for you. All I've given up for you. It was because of you I didn't develop properly. Because of you that I've never felt the rush of air against my face, the touch of a lover. I deserve at least a few hours to feel what it's like to be alive. What you get to feel all the time."

Curled up on the ground, or where the ground would have been if there'd been anything but blackness, her mind wouldn't shut off. Because she hadn't hit her head. Even if she had, why would she dream of Thomas?

The memory of playing whispered through her mind. Playing tag with Thomas...only no matter how many times she caught him, she always had to be it. If she didn't he'd sulk all day and she'd be alone. It was always Thomas's choice of game. Thomas who got to choose what "they" wanted. All her life, playing his games, living for him.

She didn't climb to her feet, but was suddenly just

standing, as though the thought of action had created reality. Oh, her headache was getting worse. "Thomas, I don't like this."

"Ginny, come on, love. Open your eyes. Please, open your eyes," James said, as though very far away. Yet she could feel the echo of his fingers on her face, the warmth of his arms around her, taste his chocolate coconut essence on her tongue.

What in the *chocolate-covered cheesecake* was going on?

"If you'd just calm down..." the massive black pig with spectacles said.

"Knock her out or something," Thomas snapped.

"No," her voice firm.

She opened her eyes, and stared up at James. Her heart started racing all over again, and her head felt fuzzy. The weight was gone...but, dear gods, what had just happened?

CHAPTER 25

Ginny perched on the edge of the chair beside the scarred library conference table, the smell of old books and that spicy something extra curling around her. James had his coat and his arm around her, even though she still wore a coat of her own. She couldn't seem to shake the chill settled deep inside her that wouldn't go away, even though they'd escaped the crowd outside for the library some time ago. She didn't want to be warm. She didn't want any of this to have been real. Because of what that would mean.

Piper's fiancé, Doctor Daniel Quilan, finished staring into her eyes, making her follow a light while he moved it, checking for other injuries. He said something about shock but that she was recovering well. It didn't matter. The others listened for her. He left to see to other patients. More of the people who'd been outside, just as confused and frightened as she was maybe.

"Here, Ginny. Drink this," James said, gently pressing a mug of something warm into her hand.

She drank it, even if she couldn't have said whether it was tea or coffee. Her entire body ached with an exhaustion that went well beyond lack of sleep. Her soul was tired.

Her friends murmured around her, worried sounds.

"Do you think any of them hurt her out there?" Piper whispered.

"I think some of them were holding her down," Anna growled back.

"One of those bastards shoved her over," Nia said, a snarl in her voice. "I bet the League of Assholes was behind this."

"I'm not certain of that," Anna said. "James's team has been monitoring them. They appear to be composed of three Fates: Mrs. Boniface, Louise Dole, and Daphne Spinner. Orchestrating something like what happened outside seems well outside the abilities of the Fates. They influence larger scale events—like our rising. Not smaller things like a group of crazed nudes."

"Ginny is likely overcome by the stress of the event," James said, gently squeezing her shoulder.

"You think? Being randomly attacked by a crowd can't be good for anyone," Nia said.

"I'm quite aware of that, thank you," James snapped back.

James's team came and went, some of them outside. There was the Tabasco flavor of Maddox nearby, the chocolate chip cookies that meant Charlie.

Down near the end of the table, to accompany the clickity-click on the laptop keys, was Bina's vanilla chai flavor. "Beckwell is definitely trending. Along with James Short and the scandal. Videos are popping up with footage from the town here. Most comments about how fake it looks, thoughts on what movie it's a publicity stunt for. Oh, but here's a couple from USELESS associates. All this media coverage has definitely upped USELESS's interest in Beckwell. Yeah, they're not happy. And—"

"Bina, that's enough," James said, stroking his hand up and down Ginny's back beneath both her coats. The small tingles and reverberations that went through her were almost enough to melt some of the chill, but not quite. "Piper, do you think we should have the doctor assess Ginny again? Just to be sure?"

"I can call him back—" Piper started.

"No." Ginny shook her head. "I'm fine. Why don't you, um, discuss what happened out there." The doctor couldn't help her. Not with this problem.

"Luv, you're not fine. If you just told them—" Roger asked softly, snuffling next to her and laying his head on her feet.

"No! I mean, not yet." Not until she could figure it out herself. Not until it didn't hurt so much.

"We think it all started yesterday evening. Not long after we left your house," Anna was telling the others. "First there was the run on the cafeteria in the Senior Center, Lou's Place, the minimart. People carrying out bags of junk food, other strange things."

The suffocating feeling of being trapped shortened Ginny's breath. She dug her fingers into her arms and tried to slow the feeling. Tried to stem the flow of tears she couldn't seem to stop.

"That's when the other people started arriving. Townspeople, walking, driving, horseback riding," Nia continued, her voice soft, the weight of her gaze heavy though she cleared her throat and continued with the explanation. "Some of them were Beckwellians. Others were Normals. But as soon as they got here, they'd just stop and start taking off their clothes. Hardly aware of what they were doing."

Roger stood up with an aggrieved kind of grrr, grrr growl. *"You mean...there was an orgy, I was there...and I don't remember it?"*

Cravings. They'd all had cravings. They hadn't even understood what they'd wanted. What they'd needed to fill that hole inside. They'd been afraid their sanctuary wouldn't protect them anymore. That they'd be exposed. They'd felt this strange emptiness in their bellies they couldn't even explain. And they'd turned to her to fill it.

"Yeah, and that's when the snogging started," Charlie said. "The team and I showed up about then, just to see what the fuss was about. You couldn't stop any of them, though. Hell, we were lucky we didn't get caught up in it. We'd gone into the next town for supplies."

Their hands, all reaching out for her. Grabbing her. All that need. All those things they wanted but couldn't have. As though she could make them safe, as though she could fill in all that want. Ginny tried to smother a whimper with her hand, her lips wet with tears.

James found her hand and squeezed her fingers. "I'm here, love. We're all here."

She just shook her head, kept shaking it. It had started yesterday evening. When she'd seduced James. When she had caused all this suffering.

Maddox cleared his throat. "We tracked the so-called League most of yesterday. The unhealthy woman and the silver-haired woman with the face of the gorgon—"

Nia snorted. "That describes Mrs. Boniface perfectly."

"—and the younger one with brown curls and the stench of rot have not met, nor done anything suspicious in the past few days," Maddox continued, as though Nia hadn't interrupted. "They were not responsible for this…although perhaps we should have put an end to their machinations before they harmed Lady Famine."

"I suspected Daphne Spinner was a sociopath but doubted she was clever enough for machinations. I shouldn't have underestimated her," James agreed.

Their conversation floated around her, and even

though they were discussing the identity of the League, Ginny couldn't seem to focus, couldn't seem to participate. She closed her eyes to try and slow her breathing, to stop the rapid panting her pounding heart demanded. But that just put her back in the darkness. Trapped back in the suffocating darkness. She popped open her eyes, stared at the table. Spread out her fingers to prove that she could. She wasn't there. She was in the light. With her friends. With James. Not down in the dark. Barnabas the horse telling her to sleep.

She put her hands over her lips, but couldn't prevent the small whimper. Her stomach flipped and her throat was too tight for air.

Thomas had been there. Thomas telling her it was his turn. Telling Barnabas to just knock her out. Wondering why she was conscious.

Wondering why she'd fight back as he possessed her.

"We're going to figure this out, luv," Roger said, bumping her leg.

"You tried to tell me, didn't you? All those nights. 'I disappeared,' you said. I didn't listen. How long, Roger? How long has he been doing this?" She bit back a sob.

James held her tightly. "Just tell us what we can do for you. What you need," he said, an edge of desperation in his voice.

She ducked her head into his jacket to hide there right now. In his dark chocolate flavor. In his warmth and his strength. In her feelings for him. Beside her, she could feel her friends gather. Anna's anise, Nia's sharp spearmint, Piper's soft lemon balm.

She wanted to hide forever. But she couldn't. Because this was her fault. She had to stop it.

She had to stop Thomas.

She pulled back from James, swiped her eyes clear, then took a shaky breath. She faced her friends, catching each of their gazes and holding it for a moment. She faced

Nia last, hardly able to meet her friend's eyes.

"You were right," she said, her voice breaking.

Nia bit her lip to stop the tremble. "Ginny…"

Ginny shook her head. "No. I don't deserve your pity." She tried to smile, to show some of her gratitude, even if she'd been too foolish to listen. "You tried to warn me. I didn't listen." She blinked rapidly to clear the moisture, and blew out a slow breath. Then faced James. "Because I thought I wanted my abilities, because I thought somehow it would make me feel better about myself, more like the rest of you, Thomas is stronger. All I've been doing all this time is helping Thomas achieve his goals, and I've been too stupid to realize it. I—"

Coldness enveloped her, froze her limbs, sucked away her breath.

Thomas tsked. *"Now, Ginny. We don't want to go sharing family secrets, do we? I told you. It's my turn. Now be a good girl and give me a turn feeling alive."*

She clawed at her throat, her friends and James panicking around her. *"Why are you doing this, Thomas? What did I do wrong?"*

It was James's gaze she froze on. She stared at James even as Thomas froze her out of control of her own body, stole control over her own hands. *Frosting*, it was like she had to remember it was her hand touching James, her brain telling the rest of her body what to do.

She focused on his warmth, on the rumbling tone of James's voice. The roughness of the tips of his fingers against the top of her hand. The fine hairs on his knuckles. The gentleness she remembered when he'd touched her in bed. The taste of him, dark chocolate and coconut and sea salt.

James held her hand against his face. "Ginny, come on, love. Fight this. You're stronger than this. You're stronger than him."

She fought to choke out words, fighting the

blackness. There was only one being she thought might be able to help her. With her last awareness, she choked out his name.

"Loki."

CHAPTER 26

James clutched Ginny's hand and had never felt more powerless as her knees gave out and the panicked expression in her face grew. He carefully lowered her down to the library floor.

"Someone get Loki," he shouted at her friends.

Anna was already running out the library door. Asher and Caspian were looking in wondering what was happening.

"What do I do to make this better, Pork Chop?" he demanded of the pig, desperate for answers.

But the pig had vanished.

Ginny still stared up at him, the awareness in her eyes was fading. There was the flicker of something else in her expression. Some*one* else.

"Ginny, sweetheart, fight him."

Nia knelt at his side, pushed back her hood, and took Ginny's hand in hers. Her fingers looked small and dark next to Ginny's long pale fingers. Her eyes were shaded with a dark metallic mask that seemed part of her face, part shadow. Her voice held a dark, ancient quality that sent chills up and down his neck.

"Get the fuck out of my friend," Nia growled.

Ginny inhaled sharply and sat upright. She looked at him, but there was a fuzziness to her gaze. A look like she'd black out again.

Nia shoved up Ginny's long sleeves, and caught her with a pinch on the inside of her biceps.

"Ow!" Ginny yanked away.

Nia raised a slim dark brow. "Better?"

Ginny frowned. "Yes. Thank you."

He remembered how to breathe again, put an arm around her back, and helped her to her feet. She sank down into the nearest chair, and he pulled his closer until their knees bumped. This close, he could keep an eye on her, ensure she wasn't going to black out again.

Holding her, willing her to open her eyes, every bone in his body, every cell, knew that he didn't give a good goddamn whether she was Famine or not. It wasn't her ability that drew him to her, or made him want her more than he wanted air. It was the sweetness of her smile. The way she'd try again and again at whatever task was put in front of her, no matter how many times she failed. It was in the way she'd toss her glorious red mane and her gaze would light with fire, and he'd have gladly spent the rest of his life worshiping her with this body. It was the way she made him feel, the way she looked at him. Her look seemed to say she saw more than a former geek hiding from his family, but a man worthy of her attention, a man who could make the world better.

For her, he would. Starting with whatever was necessary to protect her. From the media. From his own idiotic mistakes. From USELESS. From whatever threats she faced.

But for now, all he could do, surrounded by her friends and his team, was hold her damn hand.

He didn't know how to protect her from this. The scandal surrounding his alter ego, philanthropist James Short complicated things further, attracting unwanted attention. Outside, he couldn't feel any of the thoughts or desires of the crowd, and still couldn't surrounded by his team and her friends. Which meant Famine was rising. And absorbing with it all the abilities of other members of the Famine clan.

Was it Ginny gaining those abilities, or Thomas? Thomas was unquestionably corrupt. If Ginny gained the abilities instead, would complete power still corrupt her? Hell, whatever the case, he needed to protect her. But he didn't know how to fight a ghost.

He tried to ignore the chest in his ache, and lowered his head until their eyes met. "Better?"

She nodded, massaging her forehead. "It feels like I was dumb enough to run a marathon. Twice," she said, her voice raspy. Then she stiffened. "Roger. Where's Roger?"

"Blimey, disappearing is enough to give a pig a damned bad case of the collywobbles," Roger replied. The pig wandered out from under the table and looked up at her with a soft grunt.

Both James and Ginny sighed in relief, their fingers entwined.

"See? Told you he'd like me," Roger said. *"Now...I'm taking a nap. Promise you'll wake me up for the next orgy."*

Ginny shuddered, and James pulled her closer. "Are you sure you're all right?"

"She's good. For now. But he'll probably try to attack again," Nia said, taking her seat across the table, frowning. Then she got up and wandered over to the library circulation desk. "I can't believe I've got to do this, but I think I need to look something up."

He turned to find Ginny frowning at her hands a

minute before she slowly raised her green gaze to his. "This is all our fault," she said softly. "No. It's my fault. Somehow, I have to put it right."

When Ginny had needed him the most, he hadn't been able to do a damned thing. He'd taught her to use her abilities, probably making Thomas stronger in the process, and then he'd told her not to use them. Possibly put her in more danger from that crowd outside. He'd dragged his brother and his team into this mess and put them all at risk. All because he'd been convinced he could somehow stop Famine and prove once and for all he was nothing like Dad and his brothers.

Only instead, he'd made her brother strong enough to try and possess her while she was conscious. Thomas might rise as Famine himself if he grew any stronger.

Yes, this needed to be put right. But hell if he knew how.

⁖

James frowned at her like she was speaking another language, his look intense, and he took a moment to find his coat and wrap it around her again before he spoke. "Caused what? How?"

Frosting, it didn't seem fair. That finally she'd had a taste of happiness with James…and that taste led to trouble for everyone else.

Or maybe it was fair. She'd spent so long wanting her abilities and believing Thomas wasn't dangerous. Now she knew she'd basically armed a paranormal nuke. If she didn't find a way to control her abilities and in turn her brother, Thomas would rise as Famine. Judging from the damage he'd already caused in the fields, the tree-melting incident, and the orgy outside, he'd be more than happy to watch the world burn.

"The orgy," Bina piped up, answering before Ginny could. "The sudden influx of out-of-towners. And the run on the grocers." His friend frowned at her laptop screen, her fingers flying over the keyboard almost too fast to watch. "Beckwell is currently trending number one. Hmm, that's even over the latest celebrity sex scandal. Though this latest news attachment to James has contributed to the popularity. Huh. I didn't think there was an airport in town, yet this travel agency is offering discount flights here... Ah, here's the article I was looking for. Yep, it's a good hotspot for sex—"

James stopped her with a hand on her shoulder. "Bina. Focus a minute."

The small woman flashed a look up at him and pushed her glasses up her nose, blinking away the peculiar glaze over her eyes until she frowned up at him.

Yeah, well, that's probably what came of reading all the news in a dazzling display of green letters and arcane symbols that had reeled past faster than Ginny could see more than a blurry green stripe.

The petite woman looked around at the others, who were all staring at her. She scowled, like what she saw was obvious. "They had sex. Famine plus Famine equals, well, an orgy apparently."

Ginny's face burned, even though she'd figured that out a little while ago.

As everyone else including James still looked confused, Bina sighed and tried again. "One of Famine's abilities is to create insatiable hunger, correct? Hunger can take many forms other than wanting food. Particularly if the personification of Famine happens to be hungry for sex with another Famine clansman. James and Ginny's lovemaking caused a ripple effect in town." She glanced at her screen. "As well as one in Barcelona, another in Montreal, oh, and Dunkirk, too. Huh. Who knew."

"Which is probably why Ginny was able to stop the chaos," Anna said slowly, catching on faster than most of the others. "Because of her companion abilities, she can create satiation."

Bina nodded in agreement.

"So only you get to plan orgies? That seems very unfair." Roger pouted, proving he hadn't actually gone to sleep.

James cleared his throat. "Ah. Well." He cleared his throat again, and sat down abruptly in the chair next to her.

Bina returned to her news feed of green streaming across her screen. "Oh, one in Milan, too. My, it was an interesting morning around the world."

Nia raised a hand. "So…just so we're clear here. Every time one of us finally gets to have sex, weirdness ensues? All the co-mingling of powers B.S." She shrugged at James. "You're probably lucky. Daniel Do-right changed colors."

James blinked at that.

"Bollocks," Charlie said. "My brother finally has sex, and now we're saying it really will end the world?"

Ginny cleared her throat. "I believe it wasn't specifically sexual in nature." Her face grew impossibly warmer. "But, our hunger for, um, each other, translated to sexual hunger for others." *Cupcake.* Probably meant no more sex with James. At least, not until they figured out how to control their influence on Thomas.

"Well then," James said, his gaze dark and intense as it met hers.

The door banged open. Anna, with Lou-ki at her heels, burst through the front door, and almost bowled Maddox down. Daniel and Piper were right behind them.

Lou-ki came to an abrupt stop.

Daniel veered to avoid the collision, and grabbed Piper to keep her clear.

Anna collided with Lou-ki's back with a soft "Oomph."

He twisted so fast, it was hard to see the movement and caught her in the arms. The movement so graceful yet incredibly gentle.

For a second, Anna stared up at him.

He stared back.

It probably would have been less weird if he wasn't wearing his Lou disguise and face, and appeared to be an overweight bald lumberjack at least twice Anna's age.

Then again, seeing as he was Loki, no telling just how many times Anna's age he was.

"Luv, being in your head is a strange and swirly place," Roger commented.

Lou-ki cleared his throat, his gaze locked on Anna.

Anna jumped out of his arms and spun away from him.

His gaze lingered a moment longer on the War horsewoman, before he turned to the rest of them, his expression hardening. "Okay, everyone. This party needs to move. Now." He nodded at James, his expression fierce. "We're about to have company. The unfriendly kind. Agents, media, you name it. Unless you fancy a trip to meet the gods, get moving. Out the back door."

Oh, *cupcake*. Would people please stop trying to attack and kill them for at least a couple of days? It didn't even seem worth the effort to ask right now who it was this time.

Daniel grabbed Lou-ki roughly by the shoulder, and pushed. "Why the hell should we listen—"

Lou-ki returned the move and shoved the other man back, with the ease of facing a child. "You can shout at me later, even take a swing if it helps. But right now, I'm trying to keep your wife, her friends, and your unborn children alive. Move. Now."

"Unborn children?" Ginny said, gaping at Piper.

James had already climbed to his feet, and tugged Ginny to hers. "I'm sure that can wait. We should go."

Maddox and Charlie were already headed for the door. "We'll hold them off."

"You'll *help* hold them off," Lou-ki corrected, sending the men a hard look. He tossed Anna a set of keys. "Take them to my place."

Wait…Anna knew where Loki lived? Wonder if she'd been there. The first of a lot more questions. Ginny massaged her aching forehead. Her knees were still shaky, and *frosting*, today was like someone had turned the bizarreness factor in Beckwell up to extra-high.

Lou-ki turned to her.

James's grip around her waist tightened.

Lou-ki didn't seem to notice, and his voice softened. "Your brother won't be able to hurt you in my home. You'll be safe there."

Ginny broke eye contact almost immediately, and shivered. She didn't want to think about Thomas right now. About all the implications of what he'd done. She'd lived her life for him for so long. Somehow she'd been foolish enough to think she could rise as Famine and he'd stand happily at her side. Maybe he *should* be the one to rise. He seemed to cause trouble like what happened outside and the destruction in the fields so effortlessly, whereas she had to concentrate just to make a marigold bloom.

Unless she was standing with James, and she could make half a forest spring back to life.

Chairs pushed back. Anna strode to the emergency exit at the back of the library, Bina following with her laptop under her arm, along with Daniel and Piper. James helped Ginny in that direction.

"Wait a minute," Nia said, making everyone turn. "You mean, we're going to trust this ass." She tossed a dismissive hand in Lou-ki's direction. "No questions asked? No promises made? What if this is all a trap by the League of Assholes?" Then her glare settled directly on Lou-ki. "Or at least, a trap by one particular asshole."

"You do have a way with words, Petunia. Have you

considered poetry?" Lou-ki said, quirking a brow. He looked like Lou, the oversized bartender with a deep-seated love for plaid shirts. But he sounded different, more cultured. The same almost-accented voice she'd heard in her head.

Nia sent him a searing glare. Probably first, for calling her on her nonsense which no one outside the girls was generally brave or stupid enough to do, and second for using her real name. She opened her mouth, likely with something biting to say.

"I-I think we can trust him," Ginny said.

Everyone turning to stare at her, the weight of those gazes heavy.

She forced herself to look at Lou-ki, that patient, familiar blue gaze…and yet unfamiliar, too. She took a breath. "He's stocked my kitchen. He helped me learn about my abilities before I knew I had any. He helped me. Outside." She took a deep breath. "We could use an ally like you."

The big man gave her a small bow. "You've always had one."

Nahla swung the library door in, scowled at all of them. "What are you still doing here? They're headed in this direction. Get out." She settled back her shoulders, and unzipped her jacket to show off her deep V-neck tank top. "I'll head them off." She slammed the door closed again.

"Start moving," Anna barked from near the rear door. "Daniel, I'm with you and Piper in your truck. We'll take lead. Ginny, you, James, Nia, and Bina follow. We'll make a wide circle to avoid detection, so keep up." She headed out the back door, followed by Piper, Daniel, and Bina.

Nia still glowered at Lou-ki.

Ginny pulled away from James enough to reach for Nia's shoulder.

The smaller woman flinched at the gentle touch and swung toward Ginny, her fists up.

Ginny held out her hand, forced a small smile and tried to ignore the exhaustion. *Chocolate chip cookies*, but she owed this woman so much.

"Please, Nia. We can trust him. Even if we can't? We're the four freakin' horsewomen of the apocalypse. You think we couldn't take him?"

It was enough to get the tiniest glimpse of a smile from the Death horsewoman. She snorted at Ginny's hand and swung a wiry arm around Ginny's waist. James, Roger, and the two women hurried toward the back door and out into the bright crispness of the late morning before they climbed into James's sedan. Ginny in the front seat, Nia and Bina in the back.

Bina put on her headphones, pulled open her laptop, and continued typing in her corner of the backseat almost as soon as they climbed in. James shoved the car into gear and they followed Daniel's battered old blue pickup truck ahead of them. They bounced onto a narrow dirt road, behind the library and community center, and then into the shuttered agricultural grounds, a back way out of the library parking lot.

Nia leaned forward from the backseat, pulling at her seatbelt, and squeezed Ginny's shoulder, the click of Bina's keys somewhat comforting.

"Do you really think we could take out Loki? We tried to run him over a little over a week ago, and it didn't stick. Whatever happens, I am sticking close to you. Because can we talk a moment about the fact that you were possessed—*twice*—today?"

All the strength drained out of Ginny like a falling cake. She dropped her gaze to her hands. "Do we have to?"

"Yeah. I think we should," Nia said, shooting a brief glare under her lashes toward James, and tugged on her hood a moment. "Which means I have good news, and I have bad news."

Ginny's stomach lurched, and it wasn't just the dip in the road that made the car bounce. She twisted to meet Nia's dark gaze. "Um, good news first?"

James flicked a quick glance in their direction, but his expression was serious, his jaw tight.

Nia's smile was dark. "The good news is that I was right about who's trying to steal your abilities and, it would seem, your body. Your brother."

"*That's* the good news?" Piper said.

Yeah...this didn't bode well for the bad news. Especially since they already knew that part.

Ginny couldn't break away from Nia's dark gaze.

"The bad news," the Death horsewoman said, "is that whatever he is, he's not a ghost."

CHAPTER 27

Ginny sucked in a shuddering breath and stared out the windshield of James's car a moment or two. The weight of the day settled heavy on her shoulders as she and her friends bounced through the field, running for their lives. All she'd wanted was to be useful, to be important. Oh, she was important now. Enough that the gods were paying attention. And her brother wanted to steal her life.

Daniel's pale, battered blue truck bounced along the dirt road ahead of them, the road cutting through the agricultural grounds. The soft clicking of Bina's keyboard was almost like the patter of rain.

James's expression was still hard, his fingers on the wheel white. He glared out the windshield ahead and kept close to the truck. They rumbled onto the asphalt of the secondary highway, then ducked down another road.

Frosting. She'd been such a fool. She'd believed all this time that she needed to gain her abilities, rise as Famine to make her life better. To feel equal to her friends. She glanced at James's sandy blond hair in the driver's seat. To deserve the life she wanted.

Yet all it had caused was trouble. Agents were after her for powers she didn't possess. She finally got to have sex with her husband and caused who knew what damage in town, to locals and Normals. She didn't want her abilities anymore. But now she had to learn to control them so she could stop Thomas. Thomas, who somehow, wasn't a ghost.

"How can he not be a ghost?" she said, half to Nia, half to herself.

Nia leaned forward from the backseat. "The worse news is that if he isn't a ghost, I can't control him. Nor can I get rid of him," she said quietly.

It was Thomas. He was her brother. He'd always been there for her. Right from the beginning, their literal conception.

"He was my only friend until I met all of you in kindergarten. He's always encouraged me, been there for me."

"Was he? I think the only one Thomas wants to help is himself," Roger said, sticking his head through the space between the seats.

The memory of the suffocating blackness returned. The way he'd tried to force her down into her own body, stolen control of it. So how could he have done what he did? Crawled inside of her, held her down in the suffocating blackness. He'd invaded her, made her body his. Nausea rolled through her.

She'd wondered what she'd done wrong to deserve it.

Just as she had when Jimmy attacked her.

It was Thomas who'd told her she didn't deserve it. Thomas who'd helped her out of that dark place of guilt and shame, to pack up some clothes in a knapsack and leave the house before Jimmy got home.

This morning she'd woken up, all warm and achy

after the incredible night with James. And now? It was like she needed to somehow be clean of what had happened before they could ever have a repeat. As though being possessed by Thomas would somehow taint what she and James had.

What did they have? A great night in bed, definitely. But he still wanted to end famine and her abilities. At least, he had this morning when he'd asked her not to use them. She wanted a partner, needed that from him. Maybe, like with Thomas, she was looking in the wrong place.

"Gin?" Nia squeezed her elbow, bringing Ginny back to the present.

James turned the car another corner down a gravel road.

"This isn't your fault either, luv," Roger said. He stuck his head between the seats from his place on the floor of the backseat. He nudged her arm with his snout.

Ginny blinked, pulled her coat more firmly around herself.

Nia continued to squeeze her shoulder. "I'll figure out what he is and how we get rid of him. And I'll teach you to fight him, okay? He won't ever do this to you again. Not on my watch."

Ginny shivered, then frowned, and twisted to see the Death horsewoman. "Has it happened to you? Have you been possessed?"

Her friend's smile was heartbreakingly fragile, her voice raspy. "Yes. The first time when I was six."

The first time? A cold lump settled in Ginny's stomach. *Frosting*, one and a half times had been awful. Although those were the times she remembered. All these years, and Nia had never said anything.

Nia cleared her throat and pasted on her usual cocky half-smile. Her mask. "I can kick any ghost or non-ghost asshole to the curb now, so it's all good." She leaned back against the seatback and crossed her arms. "Though whatever magic horse beans Loki's using to keep his house ghost-free, I'm totally making off with some, because I need some ghost-free space. Like the bathroom. You would not believe how awkward."

"Nia, I'm so sorry. I had no idea," Ginny said softly, as James turned them another corner. "If there's anything any of us can ever do—"

"You can end this conversation and not mention it again," Nia said tightly. Then, more jovially. "Think you could help me scope out Loki's digs for the magic horse beans, or whatever he's using to keep the ghosts away? Do you think Anna's been there before? Did you see the way he just tossed her his keys, like she was over there all the time. You don't think they have some kind of fucktationship, do you?"

That was that. Nia had shut down as she usually did when it came to talking about her past or the dark things in her life. Like her dad. Like all the reasons she'd turned to drugs, alcohol, and any other kind of escape she could find back in high school.

"Fucktationship. How do you get one of those? I want one," Roger said, nudging her arm again.

Both were also doing what they could to distract her from thoughts about what had happened.

"Anna? Definitely not." At least, probably not. Although from vague things Anna had sometimes said, it was clear she and Lou-ki had shared history. He was also the one who'd brought her to Beckwell after her parents died.

They turned down another corner, then another in quick succession. The road was rumbly and bumpy in a soft way, as though rarely used.

Roger let out a low whistle. *"Well, would you look at that. Why don't we have digs like that?"*

Ginny leaned over to look, and even the click of

Bina's laptop stopped. Her lips parted on a gasp. *Ladyfingers*. "Because we're not rich enough...and we're not demigods. Although I'm definitely seeing the benefits."

She craned her neck to see more of Lou-ki's home as he drove them up the driveway. It might have been the potential head trauma from too many attempted possessions and blackouts today, but the place had a positively magical look to it. The giant Gothic Revival was like a smaller, slightly less crazy version of the Winchester mansion she'd seen on TV.

This one had turrets and cupolas, too—that's what those little almost-tower things were, wasn't it? There were little windows at odd heights, and different parts of the building seemed to jut out here and there. It was almost as though someone had decided on all the rooms they wanted, then haphazardly stacked them to form a house and thrown on a whole bunch of windows and other decorative features to disguise the fact it was anything but a standard house.

Then again, of course it wasn't a standard house. This home belonged to Lou-ki.

Hopefully she hadn't just encouraged her friends and James into a trap.

಄

James gave the house a curious once-over, following the doctor and his old blue truck around the generous curved driveway, two graveled ruts that curved around to the front of the house. Daniel stopped the truck and shut off its lights, so James reluctantly did the same.

All the way there he'd paid half an ear to Ginny and Nia's conversation while following the lead vehicle and trying to ignore the tightness in his chest and the thrum in his ears. That look Loki had given him in the library said whoever the unwelcome guests were, they were James's fault.

Loki was right. It didn't matter how many times he'd tried to get USELESS to call off their investigation. It didn't matter that his alter ego of James Short was about philanthropy and keeping his money out of his family's greedy paws. He hadn't told Ginny the complete truth yet—about his other identity and worse, about the real reason USELESS was after her and his part in painting the target on her back. Now he was out of time, and she sure the hell didn't need the extra complication, what with her brother's attack.

He stole a glance at Ginny, her face still a pale shade between green and chalk. He'd never considered the threat of a non-ghost entity trying to attack her as one of the things he'd have to protect his new wife from. Most of the threats seemed to be protecting her from herself and everyone—including her—from her abilities. Had he really been so stupid not to have realized how complicated this could get?

If this wasn't proof why he didn't deserve her, he didn't know what was. He'd endangered her. He'd lied to her.

He was just as bad as Dad.

Now he had to rely on the others to protect her because they knew more about it all than he did. It was like letting R2D2 take the definitive shot on the Death Star. And he wasn't entirely certain they hadn't just made a deal with Darth Vader himself when they'd decided to trust Loki.

The large double doors at the front of the house opened, and a slim man with dark hair stepped out onto the veranda. The occupants in the front truck, led by dark-haired Anna, climbed out of their vehicle.

James pressed his lips together and leaned forward over the wheel. He'd feel better if his team had been with him. Hell, if he even knew whether they were safe or not. But they were taking care of his mess for now. The media and the agents.

The back door clicked open. Then the other back door.

"Well, are we just going to sit here, or are we going to check it out?" Nia climbed out of the car.

"I confess, I am curious," Bina said, doing the same. "I'm also hoping as a demigod Loki has better wifi than I've been able to get. The data stream is showing some unusual fluctuations, and I need to analyze more of it, and faster."

"What's the trouble?" The pig stuck its head between the seats again and looked from James to Ginny. *"Are you all mouth and no trousers? I want to see Loki's digs. And I have to wee."* Roger climbed out of the car and trotted after the others.

Ginny cracked open her door.

He stilled her with a hand on her arm.

She stared at his hand a moment, then slowly raised her eyes to his.

Gods, he could see the pain there. The indecision. From the sounds of what she'd said to her friend, what had happened had been much worse than he'd realized. And there wasn't a damn thing he knew about how to protect her from that threat. He opened his mouth to tell her he'd do whatever it took to help her through it, to tell her the truth about his secrets.

Instead, he said, "Are you sure about this? Sure we can trust Loki?"

She bit her lip. "No." She gestured toward the door and the others climbing the steps to the front porch. "But it's at least partially because of me that my friends are going in there. I have to go with them." She climbed out of the car.

He rushed around to meet her, putting his arm around her waist for support.

She flinched, almost banging into Daniel's truck

behind her.

He pulled back his hand and took a step back to give her space. "I'm sorry. Would you prefer I call one of your friends?"

She stopped, squeezed her hands into fists for a moment. "You heard what I said to Nia."

He caught her hand. "I heard some," he said softly. He'd heard enough to infer the kind of trauma the possession experience caused. He'd seen the same kind of shattered look on a friend's face, when they'd experienced some of the worst humanity had to offer.

She dropped her gaze. "You don't understand."

"I'm trying to."

"You're probably frustrated with me, like Nia was. For not telling you about Thomas earlier." She shook her head. "I never thought he'd hurt me."

He gently touched her chin, lifting it until she met his eyes. "I know it's complicated. That he's important to you."

She tugged at her coat, pulling it more tightly around her. "He's been there for me when no one else has." She took a deep breath. "My birthday has always been hard, especially for my parents, since it was also the day Thomas died. When I turned twenty-one, about a year into my marriage with Jimmy, I thought things would be different. Better." Her smile was sad. "Even if it had been clear early on the marriage was mistake, and his weight gain only made him more difficult since he blamed me for it. I don't know, maybe it was my fault. Anyway, I was hopeful that day. But when he missed dinner, Thomas encouraged me to go find him at work, in the Physical Education department at the university."

The way she seemed to shrink into herself made the back of James's throat ache with dread.

"We found him. Having sex with one of his students on his desk. The girl was embarrassed and ran. Jimmy was…angry. He, um…" Her voice faltered, but she forced herself to continue. "He threw me against the desk. Then he ripped off my pants…and my panties. He said the only reason he wouldn't rape me was because he preferred his dietician over me. Because I wasn't good enough for him. Even good enough to rape."

James balled his hands into fists as he pictured the scene, and he ached for what she'd gone through, wanted to pull her into his arms and comfort her. But he held back. She wasn't ready for that. She might not even want to be touched, after her bastard brother had basically made her go through something like that again when he'd forcibly possessed her.

Ginny cleared her throat. "He told me he wanted me out of the house, and took my clothes with him. I finally found a pair of gym shorts to wear home." She paused a moment, her gaze firmly on the snow-dusted ground. "Thomas was the only one there, and the one who helped me find the courage to leave that room. Then to go home, gather my things, and call my parents to pick me up."

She finally raised her gaze to his, and the strength in her gaze stole his breath.

"He's always been my brother. I thought we protected each other. Now I don't even know what he is. Thomas was the one who encouraged me to find Jimmy that night. I wonder now, how much of my life, and how many times Thomas has saved me because he put me in that position in the first place." She shook her head quickly, still avoiding his gaze, and started for the door. "We should go inside."

James reached out and gently caught her fingers, intertwining her fingers. He ached for her, wanted to punch something—preferably her brother or first husband.

"Ginny," he began.

She kept shaking her head. "I don't know what else

I can tell you," she said, her voice cracking. "I've messed this all up. Badly. Worse than I've ever messed up before. This is my fault."

"Ginny, love, look at me. Please."

Slowly, reluctantly, she raised eyes that shimmered with unshed tears to meet his gaze.

He didn't deserve her; he'd been the cause of more pain and danger, just like that bastard Jimmy. But he also loved her, and even if he didn't deserve her, he would move heaven, earth, and all realms in between to keep her safe. "You are the most incredible woman I have ever met. You're generous and kind to a fault, you have an uncanny ability to see the best in people, and a strength to carry on I can hardly fathom."

She rubbed her chin and glanced away. "James…"

"Listen. Please. I just…I want you to know that. Whatever happens after this, I want you to remember that. To know I believe in you."

She slowly turned to look up at him again, her lips tight, her eyes wide, and the desire to believe him so strong in her gaze. Then she turned away, gestured toward the house. "We should go. The others are probably wondering where we are." She let go of his hand, and walked quickly toward the house.

He had little choice but to follow her. Now she'd told him more of her secrets, and he still hadn't told her his. He'd been such a fool. Ginny wasn't corrupted by Famine, but her connection to it and her brother had certainly been harmful.

Just as her connection to another Famine—him— might prove just as damaging. He needed to make the time to tell her everything. To prepare her.

But for now, they both headed for the front door, and into Loki's lair.

This didn't seem promising.

CHAPTER 28

Ginny hurried up the front steps to the sweeping porch, the giant carved double doors flanked by two urns. She wanted to outrun James's words. He might have meant what he said, but maybe it was just a pep talk, a way to encourage her for the battle ahead. As much as she wanted to believe him, she was far from incredible. She didn't see the best in people. She was just usually too scared to say what she really thought. She blinked back moisture, her hand running along the smooth railing up the stairs. As for strength... *Frosting*, James had to be missing something. She wanted to give up and hide all the time, including now.

He was the one who was strong. He was the one who was incredible, sexy, kind, patient, and who could make a plan like stopping famine and carry through with it. Instead of her foolish plans. Or her naivety in trusting Thomas.

The massive carved front doors opened, standing behind it a skinny, attractive-ish man.

James caught up to her as she stepped over the threshold, his dark chocolate taste mingling with the taste of the house. That same hint of spiciness she got from the library, and something expensive, like fine, aged wine.

James tried to give her a significant look, but she turned away first. How was she supposed to answer him? Because she was terrified she'd accidentally blurt out how much she cared about him. That would be a mistake. She'd made too big of a mess of things. Before she could even think of a future with James, she needed to clean it up. Plus make sure she hadn't led her friends into a trap by daring to trust Lou-ki.

"Would you take a gander at these digs?" Roger said, trotting up beside her. *"It's like a bleedin' men's club. The expensive kind, not the strip-joint kind."*

"How do you even know what a men's club is? Or about any of the things you know? Yet you didn't know Thomas had the Famine abilities, while I had the companion ones. Why don't you know more about Famine abilities, and what I need to know to stop Thomas, or control my abilities, or anything remotely useful?" she snapped at the pig.

Roger scuttled back a few steps with a soft snuffling sound, his head and ears down. *"I...I don't know. I just know some things, and not others. I'm sorry. I want to help you. I'm doing the best I can. But I know it's not enough."*

Hot fudge sundae. She knelt to try to catch his gaze. "Roger, I'm sorry. I know you try. I just..."

"Would prefer a horse like Barnabas. Yeah, well, you'd probably be better off with that bloke. Possibly evil, but more powerful and all." He backed away from her touch. *"The others are waiting. We should go in,"* he said. His trotters slipped on the polished hardwood floor as he raced through the polished wood-paneled foyer toward the sound of her friends' voices in a nearby room.

Ginny rubbed her forehead, and her aching head. As Roger left, other voices and flavors assailed her. Pretty much what she deserved after taking out her frustration and fear on the poor pig.

"Shall we?" James said, gesturing toward the open door.

She just nodded, since she couldn't trust herself to speak and not say something stupid.

Instead, she and James walked together over wood floors polished to a satin shine, into the next room. Tasteful antiques were arranged around it, and a large window let in daylight through velvet drapes. The room was dominated by a large stone fireplace with carved figures on both side. Fire crackled inside, and it was flanked by a couple of club chairs and matching buttoned-leather loveseats in deep chestnut leather. Her friends stood around the chairs, though no one had taken a seat.

Unfortunately, the little verse "step into my parlor, said the spider to the fly" spiraled through her head.

Anna spotted her and immediately came to her side and led her to one of the loveseats. Her warm hands cupped Ginny's icy ones. "You must be exhausted after your ordeal. I'm sorry. Is there anything I can do?"

More tears stung Ginny's eyes. Her chest ached. She didn't deserve anyone's sympathy. She'd brought this on herself. "If I'd just believed you all before, told you about Thomas—"

Anna squeezed Ginny's hand to silence. "It's fine. I know better than anyone what it's like to make a mistake."

The loveseat dipped and James's warm flavor flowed over her, lending comfort and strength.

Enough that Ginny took a breath, and addressed Anna directly. "But what I said yesterday—"

"About you wanting your powers anyway?" Piper said, her hand in Daniel's as they came and took a seat on the opposite loveseat.

"Is anyone going to let me finish a sentence?" Ginny grumbled. Although it felt good to feel like she and Anna were okay again. Especially when it was one of the few things in the universe that was.

"You're right. I realize we haven't—*I* haven't listened to you properly," Anna said, looking down a moment, before she looked up again. "But that's going to change. Starting today." She glanced at the other women. "That goes for all of you. I know not all of you feel the same way about your abilities as I do. And…it appears increasingly useless to try to deny them."

"Gee, you think? I mean, I've only been saying that for, like, ever." Nia lounged in one of the club chairs, her short legs dangling over one of the arms. "Well, he might be an asshole, but Loki's an asshole with taste, isn't he?"

Bina plunked down in front of the fireplace cross-legged, tapping away on her laptop. "I've been monitoring the chatter online, and there's definitely word about your rising." She peeked up over the laptop screen and through the bottom of her glasses. "About all of you, actually. After that plague business—" she turned to Piper, "—the gods and other paranormals are worried this might be real. Worried they should probably stop you. Before you're too powerful."

Piper flushed. "But I didn't do that on purpose. Maybe I'm not supposed to ask, but who are you, and why are you monitoring us?"

The petite woman glanced around. "Oh, I'm Bina. James's friend. I've been monitoring chatter about all of you for much longer than just today, almost three years now. It's one of the reasons they tried to recruit me to the USELESS agency on a permanent basis. Consensus is for now, at least, you're all pretty human-y," Bina continued and started typing again. "But even immortals can be killed with the right weapon. And USELESS has a frightening selection of weapons. They're also really proficient at using them." She cringed at something she saw on her screen, then shook it off, and looked up at the others. "There's good news, though."

"You mean other than the fact that the douches after us are good at torture and killing us pretty much no matter what our state of mortality? Gee. Who'd a thunk," Nia said.

"Nia. Drink your coffee. You're friendlier with coffee," Anna said, then cleared her throat. "Ginny, I wanted to explain. About what I said yesterday. I know you want your abilities, even if I don't feel the same."

James said nothing, but he was a comforting presence at her back. He seemed to believe she was strong.

She worried her thumbs, searching for the strength to speak up. "I'm not so sure I want my abilities, either. You were right. Thomas is the one with the real Famine abilities. Not me." It ached to admit it finally.

James smoothed a hand down her back.

The War horsewoman tugged on her long braid, and worried her lip between her teeth, before she finally looked up again. "Yes, but…I think the part I didn't make clear was why I didn't want you gain your abilities. Ginny, it's never been because I didn't think you weren't capable. Unfortunately, I've seen too much of the suffering and pain our abilities can cause. I didn't want that for you. I may have…overreacted whenever you have tried to exercise your abilities. Such as when I found you cooking over at Lou's Place."

"Ginny cooked at Lou's Place?" Nia said.

"Yes, but only during free period's between classes. So Anna and her parents didn't find out," Piper explained.

Anna continued to meet Ginny's gaze steadily. "I don't think I realized how important your cooking was to you back then. Truthfully, I was probably jealous of your fearlessness."

"Fearlessness?" Ginny said, eyes wide. She shook her head. "I have been terrified of everything my entire life. Unlike you, who's taken on every bully from the age of five on. I wanted to tell you about the cooking. But then—"

"I completely overreacted when I saw you heading into Lou's place," Anna said. "I just—" She bit her lip. "I was afraid of how your parents would react. I didn't know why you were going over there."

"Yes, she was probably afraid of my corrupting influence. Dear Hadrianna gave me quite the lecture about how I wasn't to interfere with any of you." Lou-ki said, striding in and unwrapping the plaid scarf from around his neck and his jacket. "In fact, I was to have no contact whatsoever."

He wore the large plaid clothes of Lou, but was in his smaller, hotter Loki form, with the killer cheekbones, amazing eyes, and fuck-me smile. Ginny could taste the sensation of Pop Rocks on her tongue, even from the other side of the room.

James's hand stilled against her hip.

Anna snapped her mouth closed, and everyone in the room visibly stiffened. "I told you we weren't your chess pieces," she said stiffly.

Lou-ki met the War clanswoman's gaze across the room, his gaze a startling swirling silver. "Oh, I remember every word you said," he said, his voice rumbling with that hint of accent.

Anna snapped her lips closed, and heat rose on her cheeks.

Even Ginny had to catch her breath. *Frosting.*

"What about him? Can I ask him he fancies a sausage roll?" Roger asked.

The same skinny man in the suit who'd let them in the house came in with another man, a chair between them. They placed it between the two club chairs, facing

286

the fireplace.

"Thank you," Lou-ki said with a polite smile before removing his jacket and folding it over the chair's arm. He sat, hands on his knees, a gleam in his eyes. "First, though: the agents are quite happily chasing their own tails." He nodded to James. "Thanks in large part to the proficiency of your friends. The media has found that, alas, Beckwell has regrettably lost all reliable network access and their electronics are failing by the droves. It should slow the story down somewhat. But it won't be long before everyone in the world is aware of what Beckwell is. Along with the kind of people who live here."

"Isn't there anything we can do?" Piper said, then glanced at the others. "The locals are frightened. I saw their fear today."

Ginny nodded, and cleared her throat, reluctantly gaining everyone's attention including the demigod's. *Gingersnaps.* Had she remembered to apply extra-strength antiperspirant today? "Without the barrier, there's nothing to stop Normals from coming to town. From seeing the truth about all of us."

"Indeed," Lou-ki said. "This newest attention, clamoring to uncover the elusive James Short—" here he cast a dark look in James's direction, "—has only added to the furor Beckwell didn't need. With all this attention, someone is going to realize eventually that what they see in Beckwell isn't mere stage effects. Then we'll really be in trouble," Lou-ki agreed with a nod.

He turned to each of the others. "Now, shall we continue our discussion about Ginny and her unusual abilities, or would you first like to partake in the recriminations and attack we paused back in the library? Anyone? Petunia, I'm sure you have comments. Hadrianna, please, don't fear speaking in this company. Ginny? James? Daniel?"

"Nice house. Why are you really helping us?" Nia said.

Lou-ki steepled his fingers and rewarded her with a small smile like a pleased teacher. "No foul language this time?"

"I've heard if you use them too much, they just don't mean as much," Nia said. "Jackass."

He quirked a brow.

"I have a question," Ginny said, daring to raise her hand, and making her the focus of everyone's stare. Again.

James squeezed her fingers.

She licked her lips, and forced herself to meet Lou-ki's gaze. "*Why* are you trying help us? You're Loki. Maker of mischief, powerful Norse god. You don't need us."

"*Help* us?" Piper practically shrieked. "He's the leader of the League of Assholes."

"Extraordinary Assholes," Nia added.

Piper glared the death horsewoman into submission, before aiming her fury at Loki. "He brainwashed Daniel. He threatened my life and Mal's."

"Well, Mal is definitely an asshole," Nia added.

"Nia," Piper growled.

The Death horsewoman rolled her eyes and pulled up the hood on her sweatshirt.

Piper blew out a breath, but some of the heat was gone from her voice. She directed her accusations straight at Lou-ki. "You brainwashed Daniel into strangling me. You helped start a plague."

"You've lied to all of us for years about who you are," Daniel said, his face a tad bronze, which was a sign he might grow horns and go full Fomorian—practically a demon. Of course, he was pissed. He'd considered Lou-ki his best friend…until Daniel had figured out the truth. Then he frowned and turned slowly to Anna. "You've known who he was. All these years."

Anna's eyes widened and her lips fell open. "I... Well..."

"I swore her to secrecy with threats and the like," Lou-ki interrupted, drawing everyone's attention away from Anna.

Lou-ki's Pop Rock flavor gained the subtle bitter taint of a lie.

His silvery gaze fell on her. "Genevieve asked why I've been helping you. Perhaps I haven't. Perhaps I've manipulated you all along."

More bitter tang. Ginny's eyes narrowed. She shook her head. "No. You have helped us. You invited me back into the kitchens and first taught me about my abilities." She gestured toward Piper. "I think you even taunted her intentionally into attacking you at the bachelorette party to help her fully gain her abilities. Just as you spoke to me telepathically today and taunted me into using my abilities to save myself from that crowd." She frowned, and cocked her head. "Your arrival at the library...you were coming to try and help me, weren't you?"

Lou-ki suddenly found the cuff of his plaid shirt fascinating. "You would have figured it out. You're a smart woman. All of you are." His gaze passed to each of them, but seemed to linger particularly on Anna.

Ginny stored that under "she and Anna needed a long discussion about Lou-ki later," because there was a lot to deal with right now.

Lou-ki continued, his gaze this time landing on James. "I was fairly well assured either Genevieve would either fight off her assailant, or that Petunia—"

Nia shot him a singing glare for using her full name.

He held up a hand. "Apologies. That *Nia* would come to her assistance, as I gather she did. Just as I'm sure you'd all have realized soon that the spirit attached to Ginny isn't a spirit at all. He's a tulpa. A thought being."

Ginny's fingers sought out James and he squeezed her hand, turning so his thigh bumped hers.

"Thought being? Tulpa? I don't follow," Nia said. "You're totally trying to change the subject, aren't you?"

"A tulpa. Why didn't I think of that," Anna murmured.

"'Tulpa,'" Bina read off her screen. "'A sentient and relatively autonomous being or object created through spiritual or mental powers.'" She blinked up at all of them. "I'm not sure why that would have occurred to you. They're usually benign."

"Usually, but once mature enough, they often want to free themselves of their creator. If that creator were powerful enough—" Anna, along with everyone else in the room, glanced significantly at Ginny, "—there's a very good chance they might wish to assume their creator's life."

Tulpa. Even the term was strange.

"You mean Thomas," Ginny said, her voice flat. "But he's my brother."

Nia made a grumbling sound of disagreement, somewhere between a wince and a groan. "I'm sorry, sweetie, but if he were your brother, he'd be a spirit, a ghost. I know those. He's not one."

"My team has been following your League, or what's left of it. They overheard the Fates speaking to someone they couldn't see. Someone they believe was close to Ginny," James said, speaking up for the first time since they'd entered the room. His gaze found hers. "Who would be closer to you than Thomas?"

"Oh, you're going down, dead guy," Roger muttered.

Ginny massaged her forehead, her brain not working quickly enough, as though it were all gummed up with batter. First Thomas wanted to attack her. Now they thought he wasn't Thomas her brother…but a thought being? "But…I don't remember creating him. Shouldn't I know if I'd done that?"

"Your spirit and your twin's were connected from conception," Nia said gently. "After his death, when he passed on, your loss—as well as your parents' grief—probably contributed to the tulpa's creation. We know you didn't create him on purpose, and that you definitely didn't mean for him to become dangerous."

"With all your ability, you somehow imbued him with some of it. Half of your rightful abilities," Anna finished. "But that means, Ginny, you're also the only one who can stop him."

Ginny stood and walked to the window, avoiding everyone's sympathetic gaze.

James stood as well, coming and standing beside her, a gentle hand at her back. "This is good news, Ginny. It means we can stop him," he said.

She rubbed her collarbone, as though that would somehow diminish the ache in her chest. Thomas had always said she'd killed him in the womb. Well, looked like she hadn't killed him, not the Thomas she knew.

But she may well have accidentally killed her real brother, somehow stunting his development. Before creating a being who would go on to haunt her life in his place. Her hands trembled and her heartrate sped. This day got better and better.

Roger bumped her leg. *"You were a baby. Missing your brother. This isn't your fault, luv."*

"Maybe not intentionally, but it is my fault."

Lou-ki cleared his throat. "There's more bad news, I'm afraid. We also seem to have developed something of a media frenzy in town, specifically in front of my bar. It would appear our not-so-friendly League tipped off the media that James Derth, aka millionaire and philanthropist James Short, has taken up residence in Beckwell. The two USELESS agents in my bar were listening close and about two minutes from figuring out you, Genevieve, and the rest of their targets were across the street in the library. Hence my directive to get moving very quickly."

James stilled beside her. So completely, Ginny turned and stared a moment to make sure he was still breathing.

"James? What's he talking about?" She vaguely recalled something about the media asking questions of a Mr. Short before she'd blacked out. The first time today— that had been the first time, hadn't it? Hmm. Better schedule a check-up with Daniel. You know, at some point when there were less people hunting for her.

Her husband, the man she'd trusted today to pull her back from the brink and save her from complete possession, whom she'd confided her most terrible secret about what Jimmy had done to her, wouldn't meet her eyes. He frowned down instead at his feet.

She tugged her hand free of his, and he let her.

Anna cleared her throat. "He means the alias James sometimes uses for his business ventures, and to keep his two identities separate, I imagine. The outside world knows next to nothing about James Derth, Famine clansmen and aid worker. They have, however, heard of James Short, one of the most reclusive millionaires in Europe known for attending occasional charity balls and for his invention of a food supplement bar that can feed an entire family in famine-struck areas for nearly a week."

Ginny's gaze ping-ponged from Anna back to James, who still stared down at the carpet. Since Anna would meet her eyes, Ginny started there. "You knew this?"

"I told you, I wouldn't let my sister marry just anyone. I was thorough." The War clanswoman frowned. "I gave you my report. Didn't you read that part?"

Ginny flushed. "I didn't get to that part. And you didn't think to mention it?" Her voice steadily rose.

Anna pulled her braid back around and tugged on it, her gaze skittering away. "That was…probably wrong, in retrospect. It just seemed rather…insignificant in the wake of the other things you were dealing with. I'm sorry."

Heat gathered in Ginny's face. "And to think—"

"Yeah, I can't believe I'm about to take Anna's side on this," Nia said, making her a good target for Anna's glare. Of course, Nia being Nia, she didn't give a *sugar cookie*. "Going back to that whole 'bigger problems' topic? James being a kazillionaire hardly seems like a bad thing. More like 'Yay you!' The douches trying to kill us with the dumb agency name I reserve judgment on. But loads of money? Definitely a good thing."

James grimaced and stepped toward her. "Ginny, I can—"

"Dinner is served," a black-attired male servant said, coming into the room.

Lou-ki rubbed his hands together and stood. "Come. It's not good to fight on an empty stomach. It will have to wait until after dinner."

CHAPTER 29

The interminable dinner over, James and Ginny followed one of Loki's servants through the maze of hallways over carpet so soft their footsteps were silent. All he could hear was the pounding of the blood through his veins. The damned demigod seemed to see through him like Yoda could read Luke. Every comment throughout dinner had seemed pointed, accusing James of bringing this danger down on Ginny's head. It had made the expensive champagne taste like salt water, the meal like saw dust.

He needed to tell her the truth, and it wasn't the white lie about his wealth he was worried about. He'd planned to tell her about it and just hadn't had a chance. The money had never mattered all that much to him, and he'd be happy if she did whatever she wished with it.

No, it was about why the USELESS agents were here for her that was the concern. His throat thickened, and he grimaced. Considering her reaction to finding out his smaller secret, he could well imagine how much worse her reaction would be to finding out the danger he'd caused to her and her friends.

The servant led them down another wood-paneled hall that looked about the same as the last, finally stopping in front of a set of double doors and pushing them open.

Ginny's eyes were glassy as she stood beside him, her lips a trembling line. She'd hardly looked at him and hadn't spoken a work throughout the entire meal. She still wouldn't look at him, her arms wrapped around herself, the lovely eggplant of her dress only accentuating her pallor.

"The house is covered in protective carvings. My master wishes to assure you that your stay here will be safe," the servant said, then bowed. "Enjoy your night." He strode off down through the hall.

"Shall we?" James said, offering his wife his most charming smile.

She walked past him without noticing.

He rubbed the back of his neck and followed her in, barely noticing the luxurious room, lush with deep burgundies, dark wood, and welcoming furniture. Time was up. He had to tell her the truth. He closed the doors behind them.

"Ginny, I should have told you about James Short," he said, starting with the easy truth. "Whatever you want, it's yours."

She turned to him, her expression almost blank, arms still crossed over her chest.

He swallowed and continued, hating the distance between them, the way she held herself apart from him. He'd done that. He and his damned lies. "Most of the profits are dedicated to charity, but I set aside a small portion for the team's expenses and a safety net for Mom. I haven't paid enough attention to it, I suppose, judging from this latest scandal."

He was rambling, but she still showed so little reaction. "I suppose Roger would like a bigger house. One like this maybe?" He took a step toward her. "Would you?" Another step closer. Still no reaction. Frankly, he liked their little cottage. The coziness of it. The fact that it kept them close with no place to hide from each other.

"Should we go find him and ask? I think he passed out after dinner in front of the fire." Another step closer. She was so strong, he hated to see her like this. He'd been wrong about so many things, and thinking he could ever remain objective around this woman was one of those things.

Ginny shifted, dropping her arms and holding one with the other. Still, she said nothing.

He'd rather she go to spare at him. Give him a right bollocking. Anything rather than this hurt silence.

The way Mom always reacted to Dad's lies when he stayed the night with one of his mistresses instead of coming home again. James would never do that to his wife—the mistresses or the lies.

At least, he hadn't meant to. Until the lies had started to add up.

"Ginny, please, talk to me," he said, taking another step closer. Two more steps to close the distance, but it wasn't clear whether she'd want him to touch her. "The money—"

"I don't care about the money," she said, her voice breaking the silence.

He froze, his chest aching. Did she know, somehow? Maybe Loki had told her the truth. Her friends might have figured it out. He needed to be a man and tell her everything before someone else did. The complete truth.

That because of him, because he'd started investigating her, it had raised red flags for USELESS. Before he abandoned his team, his work, and any hope for a different future to try and stop the incarnation of Famine, he'd wanted to know if the rumors were true. If a woman who was considered somewhere around two-hundredth in line to gain the full powers of Famine had somehow skipped ahead. The damned investigations never had shown him anything important about Ginny, anything about the woman she really was that would have told him she'd never been a threat in the first place.

But in his quest to prove he wasn't like Dad and the rest of the family, he'd inadvertently put her under a death sentence.

&

James stood across from her looking so damned delicious in his slate button-down, the top three buttons revealing just a hint of that strong neck. His eyes were more gray than blue in the dim light, a hint of whiskers shadowing his upper lip and jawline. And he thought she was upset because he was a rich.

Frosting, she'd grown up with Mom and Dad's money. Jimmy had married her to try and get it. All she'd wanted to do was prove she could earn her own keep and not need any of that. Money had never given her what she wanted, other than possibly a few extra muffin tins and baking supplies.

"Ginny, please. I can explain," he said, taking another step toward her.

"What's to explain? I wish you'd have told me earlier. But…I guess we don't always get what we wish for, do we?" She felt battered down, weary on a soul-deep level.

Had it only been this morning she'd woken up beside James after a night of incredible lovemaking and thought, gee, maybe things could work out?

Except then she'd been attacked by that crowd, yet learned to control her abilities. Only to be attacked by the one person she'd always believed she could trust. Thomas. Attacked not once, but twice. Brutally, stealing control of her body, her limbs, her tongue. He wasn't even her brother. He was a strange creature she'd somehow created.

A nightmare of her own creation. Who left her feeling sullied and ashamed. Used.

It would be too easy to be sucked down into that whirling vortex of misery she'd been in after the first time Thomas had attacked her. But it made her weaker. She couldn't be weak. He'd attack her again, and she couldn't let that happen. She shuddered, her fingernails daggering into her arm.

James watched her like he was worried she'd shatter. That felt possible.

She didn't want any more revelations, any more explanations. The world was too complicated right now as it was. She couldn't make sense of it. If she'd created Thomas, had she created him to be this dangerous? Whatever the case, she'd given him some of her abilities. She'd made him a threat. Now somehow, she was supposed to stop him. When all of her friends and Loki, a *freaking god* didn't know how?

James closed the distance between them, lifted his hands, but then lowered them without touching her. His hands fisted, his gaze was intense, bluer this close. But he didn't touch her.

His touch was the only thing she did understand. It was his touch that made her feel maybe she was enough for at least one person in this world. His touch that had saved her from the darkness Thomas would have trapped her in. His touch that made her feel alive and warm and like all the shattered pieces could hold together for just a little longer.

Yet now, he didn't want to touch her. Was afraid of touching her maybe.

"I'm so sorry," he said, his voice deep and rough. "For all of this. I promise, I'll find a way to make this better. The USELESS agents—"

She swayed forward, grabbed his shoulders, and

pressed her lips to his. Pressed all her fears, all the fear that Thomas or whatever he was would come for her again and that this time she wouldn't be able to stop him. Hot tears leaked from her eyes, and she squeezed them shut. All she wanted to feel was James's warm lips beneath hers. His hard chest under her fingertips, the tightening of his muscles, the way his hands came up to cup her back.

At first his lips didn't move beneath hers. Then he softened, opened, began kissing her back. His hands slid down to cup her ass, lifting her against him, against his growing hardness.

She lifted her legs, the softness of her skirt riding up as he carried her and she slid against his erection.

Maybe there was desperation in his kiss, too. They were running out of time. The agents, Thomas, the League, everything was coming after them. She'd fallen for him so fast and so hard, she had no idea how she'd bear it when he left, because surely he'd want to leave with his team after this. If they survived. If there was anything left of her, since she couldn't hide here at Loki's from Thomas forever. She had no idea how to stop him, or the agents, or the rise of Famine. Maybe James didn't, either.

Maybe he didn't feel the same about her as she did about him. But last night, when they'd moved against each other, they'd been in perfect harmony, found a rhythm with each other that brought them both closer to the stars. Both free of all the fear and famine and other things they couldn't control down here.

He pulled back just enough to brush the hair from her face, the muscles in his chest bunching against her.

"I should explain," he said, his breathing rough, his voice raspy.

She shook her head. "Tomorrow maybe. I don't want any more revelations, any more explanations tonight. Please. There've been too many already."

He stroked her cheek, his dark gaze sympathetic. "We can talk tomorrow. All I want to do is keep you safe."

"Then take me to bed and make love to me. Let's pretend that tonight, we really could be safe." That there was no tomorrow, with more revelations, more pain sure to come.

He pressed a soft kiss to her lips, and then took her to the huge four-poster bed that looked like it could have been used for the Hulk's honeymoon. And they both pretended that everything was all right for a few hours.

CHAPTER 30

Ginny awoke sometime in the night, chilled to the bone despite the heat of James's body. She slipped out of bed and into the ensuite shower. She scrubbed until she was pink under the near-scalding water and tried to smother her sobs so she wouldn't wake James. When she emerged from the bathroom in a fluffy robe, only the bedside lamp cast light in the large room. James was sprawled across the bed, an arm flung over his face.

It was tempting to touch him, wake him up. But there was the chance he'd still want to talk, and she wasn't ready yet.

She tied the robe more tightly around herself, standing beside the bed but not ready to sleep. Lou-ki said his house was safe for her, but maybe he was wrong and whatever charms he had protected against ghosts, but not tulpas. Thomas, or the being who claimed to be Thomas, had attacked her when she'd slept at least once before, during the tree-melting incident. Roger had told her about other times he'd been afraid he'd "disappeared."

Suggesting Thomas had probably possessed her other times, too, and she just hadn't been aware of it. Nia had said he needed a physical form to use most of his abilities, so he had to have used her before when he'd spread all the famine James's team had found.

Ginny shivered, the chill settling over her again. Maybe she should try and find the kitchens and some strong coffee. Or maybe Nia, who could give her some lessons in Thomas-repelling.

No, he wasn't really Thomas, the twin who should have lived. At least, he wasn't her brother, not biologically. Still, he *had* grown up with her. Maybe that made him partially her brother.

No. He wasn't her brother. He was—

"Ginny?"

—Dangerous.

"Thomas?" She clutched the robe around her, and spun, searching for him in the shadows. She glanced back toward the bed. Maybe she should wake up James. But there was a chance she'd just put James in more danger. James might not even be able to see or hear Thomas to defend himself.

Her fingers closed into trembling fists and she waited for Thomas to make himself visible. He was a thought being. She'd somehow created him. She needed to stop him. And Lou-ki had promised her she'd be safe here.

Although shouldn't that have meant Thomas couldn't show up here?

Her brother slowly materialized some distance from the bed, just within the pool of light from the lamp. His black pig stood quietly at his feet, sans the spectacles. Thomas's hair was a darker shade of red than her own. It was strange, she'd never thought of it before, but he'd have been a good-looking man…if he were alive.

Her knees quaked and her stomach roiled. He wasn't her brother. He'd attacked her. True, right now he was fuzzier than usual, less distinct than when he'd appeared to her before. He flickered in and out of visibility. But that didn't make him less of a threat.

"Ginny, please, I'm so sorry." He took a step toward her.

"No. Stay back." She stumbled toward the bed and James. He was definitely less solid than usual. Did that mean he couldn't hurt her here? He shouldn't have been able to materialize in the first place.

Frantic scratching started at the door. *"Ginny? Luv, if you're in there, you're going to have to open the door for me,"* Roger said.

Thomas was between her and the door.

He stopped and lowered his head, and spread his hands, still flickering. *"I... You have to believe me, Ginny. I'd never want to hurt you. I've always wanted the best for you."*

Funny, it didn't really seem like that anymore. He'd always talked about what was best for "them," not her. A twinge of heat stole through her. For what he'd done to her. For how he'd used her.

"Is that why you've been working with the League? Those three Fates?" She spoke aloud, hoping someone, anyone, might overhear her and come to help. Lou-ki had promised Thomas couldn't come in here. She was supposed to have been safe.

He grimaced. *"The Fates promised to help us gain our abilities. To help me be more than the shadow I was."*

"You just decided to steal my body instead?"

"It's not like that."

Her jaw hardened, and she took a step closer to him. "Then what is it like? Because I remember, especially the second time, how you didn't want me to wake up. You and Barnabas."

"Where's pretty boy? Pretty boy, wake up! Luv, just say no to dead guys. Keep your head in your head." Roger

303

said, banging against the door and making loud squealing sounds in the hall.

Ginny was too focused on Thomas. At least if she could see him, he wasn't trying to attack her. "You wanted me to stay quiet, to just let you…to let you…" She wrapped her arms around herself, and shook her head quickly. The horrible invasive memory crept out from the tiny dark corner of her mind where she'd squashed it. The violation of her trust and her body.

"I'm so sorry. I felt…desperate. I made a mistake. A terrible mistake," Thomas said, his gaze downcast, hands palm up at his sides. His voice cracked. *"You have to forgive me. Please."*

"You attacked me. You stole into my head and tried to possess me. What would you have done if I hadn't woken up? If Nia or James hadn't been there?"

"Nothing. I swear, nothing. I just…Ginny, you don't know what it's like. To have grown up beside you, year after year, decade after decade, and only be able to imagine the kiss of the wind against my face, the touch of a lover's hand, the cold of the snow beneath my feet. All I had were your descriptions, the stories you'd tell me."

Her arms wrapped tightly around her chest. There was no way she wanted to feel sorry for Thomas. He'd attacked her. What her friends had said, about him being dangerous, they'd been right.

Yet a part of him, no matter if he wasn't her biological brother, part of him *was* still the friend and protective brother he'd always been all these years. He had grown up with her. He had stood at her side. He'd told her to believe her dreams, he'd encouraged her belief that she could be stronger and more powerful than they'd ever imagined. Even if it was for both of their sakes.

As though sensing some softening, Thomas continued in earnest, taking a cautious step closer, but then flickering so badly, he retreated with a frown.

"I...I was weak. The League manipulated me, threatened you if I didn't do what they wanted. The first time, with the trees? I barely knew what I was doing, and suddenly we were outside together, and it was so wonderful. Then today? I just...it was like I couldn't help myself. It was wrong. So very wrong. I was weak."

She massaged her eyes. *Cupcake*, what was wrong with her? He claimed the first time he'd possessed her had been with the trees, but Roger said it had happened before that. It must have, if Thomas had been able to spread so much damage. She couldn't possibly believe him. Like she'd believed all of Jimmy's lies, all those excuses about why she couldn't reach him and the late-night phone calls, all of it a thin cover for the lovers he'd taken early on in their marriage.

"But I'm not like Jimmy. I'm your brother. I've always been there for you. I've protected you. It was me who got you away from him. It's because of me you realized what a swine he was."

"Are you taking a piss? The only swine that counts around here is me." Roger said, a low growl emanating from his round little body. *"Shove off, dead guy. Oy! Pretty boy."*

"Ginny? Are you coming to bed?" James called sleepily from the bed.

"Oy! Pretty boy? Dead guy is here. Now."

Ginny's massaged her aching temples.

James scrambled up from the bed in only his boxers, coming to her side and standing in front of her. "Where is he? Your brother." He glanced blindly around the room. "Your name is Thomas, isn't it? If you did care for her, you'd leave her be. You're hurting her."

Thomas moved so he stood directly in front of James, the two men of similar height and glaring into each other's eyes. *"Ginny, you have to know I wouldn't hurt you. But are so sure of this little man's intentions?"*

"Little man, is it?" James said, his voice a low growl…and confirming with his words that somehow, he could hear Thomas even if he couldn't see him.

No one other than Nia and Roger had ever seen or possibly heard Thomas. And at least Nia hadn't fought with him. Ginny's pulse picked up and the hair lifted on the back of her neck and arms. She stepped around James, a hand on his arm.

"Thomas, just go. Please," she begged.

James's tone hardened, and he put his arm around her. "It seems to me it's a much smaller man who would use his sister, take over her body, and make her cause harm, make her dangerous with no thought for her safety."

"Yeah, take that, dead guy," Roger said, James's wingman, even from the other side of the door.

Thomas stepped closer until he was almost standing on James's shoes.

James visibly shivered. His grip on her tightened.

"This is my world, and she was my sister far longer than she's been your wife. If you want to play this game, we'll see who comes out the winner," her brother said. Then he turned to her. *"Perhaps this match was a mistake, Ginny. I'm sure you could do better, especially with the power we'll have soon with the League's help."* Thomas vanished from sight to wherever it was when he wasn't around.

"Good riddance," Roger snorted.

James still glared a few moments longer, then turned Ginny in his arms. "Is he gone? Are you all right?"

She nodded, the pounding behind her temples enough to force her eyes closed. The tremble sliding through her refused to go away. "He's gone."

She went to the door and let Roger in, who danced around her feet.

"Where is the chilly blighter? Let me at 'im," Roger said, darting around the room.

"He's gone. But…maybe you could stay in the room. Keep watch?"

Roger snorted, and walked to the side of the bed. *"At your service, luv. I'll wake you guys up quick as anything if I hear even a twiddle of his thumbs."* He frowned. *"Does he have thumbs? Being dead and all."*

James wrapped his arms around her, tugging her toward the bed. There was a shake in his hands. "Bloody hell, I'm supposed to be protecting you, and I was asleep. If I'd thought Loki's runes wouldn't work, or that there was any chance that bastard Thomas could reach you in here…" James swallowed, his chin on her head. "I'm sorry. So sorry."

Maybe the runes explained Thomas's strange flickering. And possibly why he hadn't attacked her. He was dangerous. She had to remember that. She didn't dare forget it. "We had no idea Lou-ki's protections wouldn't work. Maybe they did in part. Thomas was definitely weaker than he usually is."

"Since we're both awake, maybe we should talk," James said, sitting on the bed.

She sat beside him, and dropped her gaze to her hands. "We're not alone. And I…I'm not ready to talk. There's just been too much today." Her smile trembled as she raised it toward him. "Unless you have some stories about your team's adventures. Or anything else that has nothing to do with what's happening in Beckwell or what we might have to face tomorrow."

His brows squeezed together and his lips compressed. He propped up his pillow and crossed his feet at the ankles, then pulled her toward him. "We do need to talk. First thing tomorrow?"

She massaged her forehead, and curled against him, against the heat of his chest. Her eyelids already drooped. "First thing tomorrow."

Surely with both of them on watch she could get just

a tiny bit of sleep, and tomorrow would be better.

CHAPTER 31

The loud bang on the bedroom door jerked he and Ginny out of sleep. Roger squealed from the side of the bed. He blinked at the large unfamiliar bed, the heavy furnishings.

Bang! Bang! Bang!

"James? You must come quickly. Bring Lady Famine," Maddox growled from the other side of the door. "Perhaps the sausage, too. He might know something."

"Who's he calling sausage?" Roger grumbled.

James tossed back the blankets and groped around on the floor until he found his trousers and jerked them on.

He turned and froze a moment as he caught sight of Ginny's gorgeous backside and the curve of her back as she wiggled into panties and tossed her eggplant dress back on over her head. She turned to find him watching, desire stirring in him. Her lips parted.

Maddox battered the door again. "Are you coming?" He growled, and a hint of smoke curled through the door. "It's Charlie," he said gruffly.

"Charlie?" Ginny squeaked.

James's throat had tightened too much for words. He, Ginny, and Roger burst out the door, almost bowling over Maddox.

The big man led them on a race through the rambling hallways of Loki's house, emerging downstairs in the parlor where they'd begun. Everyone, from his team, her three friends, even Loki were clustered around one of the loveseats. They backed away as James strode in, his heart pounding in his throat. He felt Ginny, her hand touching his back as the crowd parted for him.

He'd been prepared for blood, for his brother pale and bleeding out his last. Because of James. Because James had asked him to stay.

There was no blood. But Charlie was pale and panting, sweating profusely. His eyes rolled back and his body arched. His once expensive shirt was torn to ribbons, revealing Charlie must have spent some time in the gym.

"Hold him still," Nia said through gritted teeth, the tiny Death horsewoman trying to lay both hands on Charlie's thrashing body while he almost threw her off.

James and Maddox leaned over and helped try to hold down his brother. Charlie groaned, the sound low and pained.

"What's happening to him?" he demanded.

"We were out on patrol, helping the townspeople send the USELESS agents on the run. One of them is definitely an experienced agent and gave us quite the run. Then the tulpa attacked Charlie, taking advantage of his exhaustion," Maddox said, then frowned. "It was faster than any demon I've ever seen."

"The tulpa was looking for another body to possess evidently, since Ginny was here and protected by the ruins," Loki clarified, helping to retrain Charlie's thrashing legs. "But your brother is fighting back. Charlie should have been safe once he was brought inside the house. I have wards against things like this."

"It's not a spirit, remember? And if it's inside of him, it doesn't have to follow the same rules, dumbass," Nia said. She gave Charlie's face a light smack. "Get the hell out of him," she commanded. It was her other voice, the dark one that sent chills chasing down James's neck.

His brother continued to thrash. Charlie swore. Another voice cut in, one that wasn't Charlie's but that came from his throat. "I will make all of you pay when I rise," it growled.

The back of James's throat ached. "Come on, Charlie. Fight. Don't let that bastard win." He'd brought Charlie here. Involved him in this mess of his own making.

He looked up at Ginny, standing near the doorway, her eyes wide, face pale. All this time he'd thought she needed to control her abilities or get rid of them. He'd been wrong about everything else. What if he was wrong about that? Maybe she needed to use her abilities, accept them fully if she had any chance of defeating Thomas and the USELESS agents. Hell, her friends all said somehow she'd created Thomas. That meant she could stop him. She had to.

Because all that he'd tried, all the ways he'd tried to differentiate himself from his family, look where he'd ended up? Causing harm to the people he cared about— like Ginny, Charlie, his team—because of his own arrogance and selfishness. Just like Dad.

Nia growled in frustration. "I can't push it out like I did for Ginny. It's stronger. Probably why it could possess someone other than Ginny. Charlie is still a Famine. But if we don't stop the tulpa soon, he'll make his own damned body."

He is still Famine. Nia's words echoed through James's head. Maybe Thomas had gone after Charlie because he'd sensed that hint of corruption. What if

Charlie decided he wanted all that power and agreed to let Thomas borrow his body?

"Where the hell is Ginny? I need her," Nia said.

❧

Ginny fought to keep from hyperventilating. She could see Charlie on the loveseat, and Thomas, almost super-imposed over him. It was like the two of them were in a wrestling match. Charlie was losing. Because of her. Because she hadn't believed her friends. Because she hadn't stopped him. She wanted to, but she had no idea how. She hadn't even known what he was until yesterday. He was like a ghost, so surely that made him Nia's problem. Or Nia could help, tell Ginny what to do.

Someone muscled past her into the room. "Sir, we have trouble at the front door," one of the servants said to Lou-ki, his voice terse.

The demigod swung around with a snarl. "Not now, Mark. Can you not see we're busy here?"

The servant rocked back a step, swallowed. "It's the USELESS agents. They've found us." He cast a significant look in Ginny's direction, and at the other girls. "They're looking for the Famine girl. And her friends."

Lou-ki bit back a curse and signaled to pale-haired Asher to come and take his position. Then he looked up, and his gaze speared her. He strode toward her, her breath quickening with his every step. He stopped right in front of her, his voice rough. "You have to help him. You're the only one who can stop that thing. You can save your husband's brother and stop that thing before it gets loose and uses your abilities to spread endless suffering." He strode out of the room with the servant, his appearance seeming to shimmer and change as he walked, getting bigger and more Lou-like. But no less powerful. "I'll deal with this other…irritation."

Charlie let loose with a long, low growl and struck

out with his arms, landing a blow that whipped James's head to one side. He and Maddox caught Charlie's arms again.

"Where the hell is Ginny?" Nia snapped.

Ginny whispered her response, her throat almost too thick to speak. "I-I'm here."

Somehow, even over the repetitive groans and thrashing, Nia seemed to hear her. She swung around, that silvery-smoky mask shadowing her eyes. "Get onto the other side of him, Gin. You're going to need to help me."

"Me?" Ginny squeaked, all the reasons she shouldn't squirreling through her head. Sure, she might be able to control some of her abilities some of the time. She hadn't practiced anything like this. If she messed up, she could hurt Charlie. Or worse.

"James, make room. She's here to help," Nia said.

"Move!" Anna roared in a commanding voice that sent chills skittering down Ginny's neck, and everyone rushing to her bidding.

Until even Ginny stood beside James, his naked shoulder bumping her as he knelt beside the loveseat and tried to hold down his thrashing brother.

"We're here to help, Charlie. I'm here," James whispered. He cast a quick glance back over his shoulder at her, the stark fear tightening his features. He nodded at her.

"Like I know what I'm doing?" she internally shrieked to Roger.

"You've got this. I am almost eighty-four percent certain," Roger said, nudging her ankle.

"Eighty-four percent!"

Nia grabbed her hands, her grip unbreakable. Her gaze caught and trapped Ginny in its snare, a strange glitter in her dark eyes, and still that strange mask. "I can't do it without you. He's your spirit, remember? You created him, you can control him," she said.

313

Ginny nodded, incapable of speech, her hands clammy.

Nia's strong fingers were icy against hers as together they pressed their hands against Charlie's sweaty flesh. They both flinched back as Charlie bucked again.

"Command him out of there," Nia said.

"What?" She squeaked.

"Tell Thomas to get out. Like I did with you. But with your ability. Push him out."

"I don't know how to do that!"

Charlie bucked again, and slowly lifted and turned his head toward Ginny.

"Do it, Ginny," James urged, half laying over his brother. He turned and shouted up at her. "You have to be stronger. Stronger than Famine. You should be better. Prove it. Prove you're not like them."

"B-but I can't call on my ability that way. I don't work that way. A-and this is a Death thing." Ginny tried to pull her hands free from Nia. James still wanted her to be something other than Famine. He still didn't want her to have her abilities. Maybe he was right. She wasn't strong enough. She'd made so many mistakes. Thomas was a big part of that.

"It's not a Death thing, it's a you thing. You created him. You have to get rid of him," Nia shouted back. "He's fighting, but he's getting weaker all the time. The longer we take, the more of a grip that thing has on him. Ginny, now!"

It was true. She could hardly differentiate Thomas from Charlie now. They occupied the same space. The same body.

"Please, Ginny," James begged. "It's my brother."

"Focus on your ability," Roger urged.

"It's like exorcising a demon. It's one of your abilities," Anna said, which only seemed to make Charlie and the thing in him fight harder.

Ginny squeezed her eyes shut and tried to think of her ability. Of Famine and strength and power and demons and making them go away. Of all the reasons she'd wanted to be Famine, all the good things she was going to do with all that power. Not a spark. The barest of flutters from her ability. Then, nothing. She didn't feel any of it, none of the power she was supposed to have. *Frosting*, her knees felt almost too soft to stand. Her hands trembled. She was cold and tired and weak.

She jerked free of Nia's grip. "I can't!"

Charlie relaxed against the loveseat and began to roar with laughter. Thomas's laughter. "Too weak. I knew you were too weak. I've always been the strong one, haven't I? You've never been enough, and you never will be. You're nothing without me."

"Ginny!" Nia snapped.

"You have to do this, Ginny," James said. "Please. It's my brother."

Ginny backed away, tears coursing down her face.

"Oh for fu— Fine. I'll try something else. I hope your brother doesn't have heart problems," Nia muttered. She hunched her shoulders and closed her eyes. A dark smoke rose around her like a cloak. It grew and grew until it filled the room, started to blot out the light to meager gray.

The air chilled and grew damp. Nia seemed to expand in size, growing into something much bigger than herself. Her fingers tensed against Charlie's flesh.

"OUT," she commanded in a voice that seemed to make the air freeze. She exhaled, her breath a frozen cloud.

Charlie's back bowed upward despite the large men holding him down. He gasped, every tendon and vein straining and distended. Then his breath rushed out, and he sagged back onto the bed. His head lolled to the side. His eyes stared, glassy and blind.

"What the hell have you done?" James whispered, and groped for his brother's throat. "He has no pulse!"

"That's because he's dead. And that's the easy part. Shut up so I can work," Nia said, eyes still closed. She breathed out a puff of frosty air. Her lips started to move in soundless words. Faster and faster. Her fingernails dug into Charlie's pale and unmoving chest.

One moment. Two.

Oh, frosted cupcakes. My friend just killed my husband's brother. Because I was useless. Because I didn't do anything. Because I should have done something. Ginny's thoughts whirled frantically.

The light returned to the room.

Charlie sucked in a deep breath.

Nia stumbled back from the loveseat, holding her head.

Charlie pushed himself upright, the others falling back from him. He blinked and turned his head, taking in everyone. He frowned at all the people staring down at him. His voice was rough when he spoke. "Well. Guess everything went to pot, huh?"

Lou-ki strode back into the room. "I, along with the rest of the town, has bought you some time, but those agents will be back. Should they develop a brain, they'll call in reinforcements soon." He frowned at Charlie. "You're looking better." He turned to Ginny. "You must have stopped the tulpa then. Good. Because the agents aren't going to stop until they have you." Here he glared at James. "I'd hoped we'd have a bit longer before the gods became involved, but I guess we work with what we have."

"I...I didn't stop the tulpa," Ginny whispered. "Nia did."

"No. I didn't stop him, I pushed both of the souls out of Charlie's body." The Death horsewoman nodded at Charlie. "Good thing he's healthy. I wasn't sure for a

316

moment there if I was going to be able to bring you back."

"You didn't know if you could bring him back?" James roared and headed for Nia.

"Hey, I was more concerned about giving that thing a body. It doesn't need much more strength and it can run around all on its own," Nia said, getting in James's face.

Ginny jumped between them. She faced James head-on. Placed a hand on his chest. "It's my fault. I should have stopped him."

His expression turned to stone. "Yes. You should have. But you didn't want to, did you? Still thinking of him as your brother?"

Ginny's blood flared hot then cold. Her hands fisted. She'd spent all night trying to convince herself Thomas wasn't her brother, that all the good things she remembered about their relationship wasn't real. She'd had nightmares of him beside her as a child, crying, asking why she'd want to destroy him. Why he deserved that. James, her friends, none of them could possibly understand.

"You think I wanted anything to happen to Charlie?" She jabbed a finger into her chest. "I don't know how to stop Thomas. It doesn't mean I don't want to."

"You didn't try. What's going to happen when the agents come after you, hmm? If they get you alone? Will you just hope someone will come along and rescue you?"

She could taste his frustration, feel the ache of the pain he'd been in over Charlie's suffering. The bitterness in his flavor.

"No. I'm tired of everyone trying to keep me safe, trying to rescue me, telling me how I should live my life."

James gripped the back of his neck, then wiped a hand down his face and tried to approach her. "Ginny, please."

She backed away from James toward the parlor door, shaking her head. She hurt, too. She was torn to pieces inside, for the brother she was supposed to destroy. For the brother who'd suffered because of her. For the husband who now turned on her. Who'd demanded she show she was stronger than Famine.

"No. You all seem to want me to be something that I'm not. You want me to be better than Famine. Well guess what, James? I *am* Famine. It's in my blood, it's in yours, and if I'm going to stop Thomas, I'm going to have to *become* Famine, not be above it." She shook her head, blinking back tears, then let out a bitter laugh. "Why did you marry me after all that anyway? Sure, the USELESS agents were coming, but you could have seen if I was dangerous and decided if you needed to report back to them without any wedding."

His gaze was steady. And bankrupt of joy.

"Because it's my fault they're after you," he said, his quiet voice seeming to echo in the room.

No one else said a word. No one else seemed to dare to breathe.

Ginny gripped the sides of her head for a moment, then touched her throat and met James's gaze. "But…you said they'd just heard about my friends and I through rumor."

A muscle worked in his jaw. "I lied."

She squeezed her eyes shut a moment. She'd known he'd lied. She'd tasted those lies. But after all this, she'd started to think she could trust him. That they were working on the same team.

That he wasn't just using her like Jimmy had.

That when she was with him, she really was enough.

He took a step toward her. "Please, if you'll let me explain…"

She stumbled back a step or two, and the flavors of anise, spearmint, and lemon balm surrounded her as her sisters flanked her. "You said if USELESS came after you, if they took you to the tribunal, it was a death sentence." She forced herself to look up at James. "You did that to me?"

He took another half step closer, his hands raised. "No. I…was investigating you. To find out if you really would rise as Famine, if you were the one I needed to stop. It raised some red flags. I tried to convince them you weren't dangerous and that I could investigate for them here in Beckwell." He shook his head, jaw tight. "They told me if you gave over your powers willingly, you'd be safe."

"That'd just kill her, too, jackass," Nia growled. "It's not possible to just 'give over' our powers."

"I know that now. They lied. Now, no matter how many times I've begged them to call off the investigation, they won't listen. I've searched for another way to protect you from them. Anything to keep you safe." He looked up at her. "They'll come after me, too, if I don't turn you over. But I don't care. I'll do something, anything to keep you safe."

Ginny searched his flavor for any hint of deception, but there was only dark chocolate. He was literally begging for her understanding. For her forgiveness. Still, if she gave it, as tempting as it was because of how *frosting* much she loved him, this road didn't lead to a happy ending.

She stepped forward and touched her fingertips to his jaw. So she could better read his flavor. Because this might be the last time she got to. The prickle of his whiskers tickled her fingertips, and there were those flecks in his gorgeous eyes.

"That may be, James. But it I succeed, if I survive stopping Thomas, it means I will be Famine. That's what you came here to stop, isn't it? That's the reason you started your investigation that got the gods involved. If I'm Famine, that's never going to be okay with you, is it? Because you hate that part about your family, about

319

yourself. And about me."

Muscle worked in his jaw beneath her fingers. She ached with the need to hear him deny it, to tell her he loved her as much as she loved him, that somehow, this would be okay.

He dropped his gaze away from hers.

But maybe it was better he said nothing. She'd had enough lies to fill a lifetime.

She smoothed her hand up his jaw, that beautiful face cupped in her hand one last time. Then she reached up and pressed a soft, sweet kiss to his lips, the contact over before desire barely had time to begin.

"Goodbye, James," she said, then turned with her friends and Roger, and walked out of the room.

CHAPTER 32

James watched Ginny, the best thing to ever happen to him and the woman he loved, walk out of the room while he stood rooted like a bloody oak in Loki's parlor. Because he refused to lie to her again. Because, no, it would never be okay with him if she exercised the powers of Famine, however unintentionally.

He rubbed his chest, where a physical ache had taken up residence since Ginny had left the room and taken a part of him with her. So be it. He'd still try to protect her, still stop the USELESS agents. No matter what it took.

Loki cleared his throat. "Well. We'll just all give you some privacy then. Let's have a drink in my study," he said, and he and his team filed out from the room.

Too bad they hadn't done that, oh, ten minutes before things had gone tits up between he and Ginny.

Charlie groaned and sank back down onto the loveseat. "Sorry, mate. My knees are knackered. If you want privacy, go somewhere else. I claim this room." He leaned back against the chair.

James choked on a small laugh and ran his hands back through his hair. He walked over and sat down on the opposite loveseat. "Of course. You need anything? I could grab you some water, hell, a scotch even."

Damn Thomas anyway. First, he'd gone after Ginny, then, when that hadn't worked, he'd headed after Charlie. Because, as Nia had said, Charlie was still a Famine, and next to Ginny, the next best thing for Thomas. He seemed to need someone from the Famine bloodline. Hell, he could probably smell the corruption.

Charlie stared at him with narrowed eyes. "I'm fine, just tired. You're the one who looks absolutely wrecked."

James snorted. He broke his gaze from Charlie's. For a moment or two there, he'd wondered if this was it, he'd well and truly failed. Because why wouldn't Charlie let Thomas possess him and revel in all that power?

He'd been convinced his own baby brother would help lead the world to destruction.

"Jamie-boy?"

"It's been a long day." James snorted. "And night. Tomorrow will be worse. We should get some rest." He rose to leave.

"Uh, no? You're going to go find your wife, get down on your knees, grovel, and fix things with her. Not sure if you noticed this or not, but women like her don't come around every day."

James half-turned, an eyebrow cocked. He crossed his arms over his chest. "Women who want the abilities of Famine? No, suppose there aren't too many of those."

Charlie's look was flat. "You know that's not what I meant. I mean, having mostly died and all, I have a new appreciation for all that seize the day shit. You need to be doing some seizing."

"I'm sorry…did you miss the part where she wants Famine ability? And where there are USELESS agents hunting down she and her friends. Because of me. Oh, and that lovely brother of hers, who just possessed you."

"But it's the Famine part that really rubs, isn't it? She was right." Charlie crossed his arms over his mostly bare chest. "Guess that makes her just as bad as the rest of us...and never good enough for you, huh?"

James turned around fully to face his brother. "Are you having a laugh?"

Charlie cocked a brow. "Come off it. You think none of us ever noticed how much better you thought you were than the rest of us?" He made bunny ears with both hands and danced them in front of him. "How much you gloried in the whole 'I'm the family black sheep. Ooh, look at me, saving the world.' Off you went, showing all of us up volunteering in gods forsaken third-world-countries, saving starving babies, while the rest of us are, what? Spoiled, horrible sots not good enough to lick your boots. That's even before you decided to become a secret millionaire and keep that from us, too."

"Where the hell is this coming from? You're the one living it up in London, drinking and fucking yourself into a stupor."

Charlie crossed his arms over his chest. "Let me guess. Your plan was to save me from myself and the horrible corruption of Famine."

James shifted and bit the inside of his lip.

"Just like poor Ginny. Who's either lumped in with the rest of us Famine villains, or a poor victim of her bloodlines and brother. Dammit, James. Open your goddamned eyes. She's not either of those things. She's twisted herself inside out to do what you want, to try and learn about her abilities—but then only use them as *you* see fit most of the time. What the hell is with that?"

That hurt. Especially because it cut too close to the truth. "Like father like son, huh?"

"That is *not* what I'm saying! Bloody hell, man. You're not like that asshole. I mean, besides the inability to see the truth staring you in the face. You've gone around doing good deeds all your life to prove you're not, haven't you?" His eyes narrowed again. "Wait. That's it, isn't it? You think all of us are like him." He snorted not waiting for an answer. "Unfucking believable. If you think I'm like that asshole, when Thomas possessed me you thought, what? That I'd like it?"

"Of course not. You wouldn't want to die."

Charlie looked down for a moment. "He didn't want to kill me. He said he needed me to use his abilities...and if I helped him, he promised me when he was strong enough, he'd let me go and give me whatever I wanted." He paused, meeting James's gaze, his own sparking with fury. "But I turned him down. I fought him. Guess that throws an inconvenient wrench into your all-too-perfect logic, huh? You know what, sod off. I'm tired."

"Charlie—"

"I prefer Chaz. And I'm serious. Get out of here. Either get your head out of your ass and go get Ginny, or...hell, I don't know what else you'll do. Right knackered, remember?"

"Yeah. Of course." He headed once more for the door, though again paused, his hand on the knob, but didn't turn around. His thoughts were racing. "And Char—er, Chaz? I'm sorry. For what it's worth? You're probably a better man than I am."

That thought that chased him back through the labyrinthine halls of Loki's house. Back to the bedroom he'd shared with Ginny, where her scent still clung to the sheets, to the air itself.

Charlie had been offered all that power, and he hadn't taken it. Ginny could have had all that power long ago, and she hadn't taken it, either—to her own detriment as it harmed her and Thomas grew more dangerous.

Both Famine.

Neither were corrupt.

It was Thomas and his brothers and Dad who were corrupt. All these years, he hadn't seen that just maybe, it had more to do with them. Maybe their corruption had nothing to do with Famine ability at all. Famine was no more corrupt than anything else. It was a choice. Meaning it wouldn't corrupt Ginny. It couldn't. Better she rise as Famine than Thomas. If she were strong enough, the gods could send all the agents after her they wanted. She'd be able to protect herself.

He grimaced and massaged his forehead. Well, bollocks.

But family ability or not, in his misguided quest to stop Ginny rather than help her, he'd made it more difficult. And more dangerous—even if Thomas looked like he'd probably have been dangerous long before.

James straightened. But...maybe he could do something about that. About both issues. All this time he'd looked for a way to protect Ginny from USELESS and from Thomas. Maybe he could just take her out of the equation.

He'd worshipped Ginny with his body. Now he'd find a way to protect her with it, too.

He grabbed his phone off the side table, hesitating barely a moment before finding the number, tapping a quick message, and hitting send.

"'The needs of the many outweigh...the needs of the few... Or the one,'" he said softly, climbing to his feet and quoting his favorite movie, *Star Trek II: The Wrath of Khan*.

He strode out of the room, down the stairs, and straight out the front door. Free of any of Loki's runes.

"Thomas?" he shouted into the open air. "Where are you, you cocky bastard? Come and get me. If you think you're man enough."

CHAPTER 33

Ginny's insides still stung, and the feel of James's lips beneath hers was like a brand she'd never forget. She and the girls had retreated upstairs to the room Anna had been given, featuring a similarly large, ornately carved four-poster bed, though this room was done in the same greens and golds as most of the rest of the house. Loki colors. She wanted to just hide somewhere and lick her wounds in private. Or, realistically, cry herself hoarse and dehydrated. Who knew, maybe USELESS would show up and just lop her head off now. She might let them.

She dropped her head into her hands. "Have I just made a horrible mistake? I might talk big, but I have no clue how to destroy a tulpa. He as much as admitted he's been working with the League all this time. He and they seem to be ten steps ahead of us, all the time."

"Then we'll figure it out. All of us. We've been through worse," Roger said, bumping against her leg with a snuffle.

"No. We haven't. I just left James behind with my

heart. He won't come after me because I'm Famine. What a joke, since Thomas is the only one who seems to have all the powers," she said.

"Um, Gin? Can I get you a drink?" Piper suggested. "A couple of drinks even?"

"She can't drink. None of us can. We need to figure out our next move," Anna said, sitting down on the bed next to Ginny and wrapping an arm around her. "We're here for you."

"But there's only so much we—or I—can do to stop Thomas. You need to figure out how to access your abilities when you have to," Nia said, coming to stand in front of Ginny.

There was a soft knock on the door. The girls looked at each other. "Maybe Loki thought you needed a drink, too," Nia said, and padded over to answer it. She pulled it open, then rocked back on her heels and pulled the door open wider so they could all see who stood there.

James.

Ginny's heart flipped over, and she gripped her legs.

Nia cocked her head at him. "I dunno. Do you want to see this asshole?"

"You know, I grow tired of your attitude," James said. He grabbed Nia by the throat and threw her against the wall.

Nia crumpled to the ground with a soft cry.

Ginny froze. No. He wouldn't do that.

Piper screamed and ran to Nia's side.

Anna jumped off the bed and grabbed a nearby chair. She raised it above her head and roared toward James.

He grabbed the chair and ripped it out of her hand, swinging it at her.

It hit Anna in the middle, and she doubled over with an oomph.

Roger raced at James as fast as he could on his little legs. He rammed into James's legs.

James wobbled. Then grabbed the pig.

Roger squealed in terror.

Ginny jumped up from the bed. "No!"

But the words had barely left her lips when James flung Roger, hard, at the wall. There was a sickening crack, and the pig slid slowly down to the floor.

James swung his gaze toward her. She slid off the bed, her heart thundering as he came toward her.

A slow smile broke across his handsome face.

But there was no dimple.

Her breath seized in her chest, and her hands turned icy.

"Thomas," she wheezed.

It wasn't James, but Thomas who smiled out at her from behind James's eyes. Thomas, who slowly, lacking James's smooth grace, walked toward her.

Ginny's skin turned to ice. "Get out of him," she whispered.

Thomas tsked. "Now why would I do that?" His voice was something between his voice and James's, the words flat with no charming British accent. He swaggered toward her. "This was the body I selected for myself. All those dossiers we looked through, all those bodies, this was the one I wanted. Granted, it was a bit less agreeable than I'd imagined for a bleeding-heart do-gooder. But he came around to see the rightness of my position. After I rise as Famine, I may even let him live. For a little while."

She was supposed to be able to stop him. How? Her knees shook, but she couldn't run, couldn't leave her friends alone in the room with him, especially with both Anna and Nia down. And Roger... She couldn't think about Roger. She backed away from him, but bumped into the bed. "Leave them be. We can work this out on our own."

"Oh, but I've worked this out already." He lunged toward her and grabbed her hand before she could scramble back. "You've got something I want," he said. Then closed his eyes and inhaled.

His icy fingers—James's fingers—dug into her forearm. She pushed at his hand, tried to break his grip, but it was like a child trying to break the grip of an adult. He grabbed her free hand.

"Thomas, get out of him," she sobbed. Was James even in there now? Maybe he was experiencing that same terrible darkness she had. "Leave James alone. You told me you didn't want to hurt anyone. You told me that wasn't the real you. We can figure this out. We can find another way."

He cocked his head, the movement so unlike James, yet in James's body it made it even more horrifying. "You really are that stupid, aren't you?" Then he dug his fingers into her skin even more.

Ginny cried out.

Her ability flowed up through her, like water from a well. Only this was faster than usual, hotter than usual. Hot water. Boiling. Steaming. Burning through her veins and out through Thomas's icy connection. Ginny screamed, her knees giving out beneath her.

Thomas's smile grew.

Anna climbed to her feet. Tried to drag Thomas/James away. "Piper, make him sick!" she shouted.

"I'm trying," Piper said from near Nia by the door, her hands outstretched. "But—"

Thomas laughed. "But it doesn't work against one of your own, does it?"

James's team and Loki rushed in through the door. They tried to pull him off her, but it just pulled on her arms between them. They couldn't break his grip.

Faster and faster the heat poured through her. There was only pain and heat burning through her. It was harder and harder to catch her breath. Her friends' hands at her back grew fainter, as though she was losing feeling.

Maddox cold-cocked him in the face. Thomas/James collapsed into a heap on the floor. "No, but fortunately a well-aimed punch still does," he said, contemplating the body at his feet.

Ginny's arms slipped free, and her knees buckled. Her head felt floaty. Her friends' hands felt…well, they didn't really feel like anything. Nia crawled over from near the door, blood dripping from her nose, and she and the girls all had their arms around Ginny. Only Nia seemed to be able to touch her at all, her dark brows lowered, jaw clenched. Anna was tight-lipped, whereas Piper covered her mouth with her hands.

"Uh, Ginny," Roger said, nudging against her side.

"Oh, thank gods. You're okay," she said, wrapping her arms around the pig.

"Er, I wouldn't be so quick, luv. I—and you—are definitely not okay," Roger said. He shuffled to show her his back. *"My spots are gone, for starters."*

She looked down at him, really looked. Indeed, he was now a plain pink pig. A plain pink, slightly transparent pig. She could see the intricate floral pattern of the carpet through him. "Why are you see-through, Roger?" She turned back to Nia. Maybe this was because of what Thomas had done to him, when he'd hit the wall. "What's wrong with Roger?"

Nia swallowed. "Well, I have some good news and bad news for you."

Ginny's insides squeezed. "I thought we agreed you weren't very good at those?"

Her friend's small was tight and grim. "The good news is you and I have the opportunity to get really close again since we need to stay physically close enough that I can touch you at all times."

A sick feeling started to slide through Ginny, pushing aside the floaty this-can't-be-real feeling.

"What's the bad news?"

"The bad news is, you're one half-step up from a ghost."

❦

An hour or so later, and Ginny still wasn't couldn't fully accept the "you're a ghost" statement. Who would? After Nia's pronouncement, though, while inside Ginny had frozen at the words and couldn't seem to move past them, everyone else couldn't seem to stop moving. There'd been bustling to move and secure James/Thomas elsewhere, to get Charlie up and moving, to get Ginny downstairs to Loki's parlor, because surely a warm fire would help. It was back to just the four of them in Loki's parlor. Ginny held up her hand to examine it, watching the light of the fire sometimes flickering through her palm.

"It's as I feared. Our abilities are connected to our life force. And he's stolen a lot of Ginny's," Anna was saying, her voice a soft murmur.

Yes, because now it mattered if they spoke softly around her. After the whole "you're a ghost" thing. Besides Nia, who said that kind of crap? It could have gone more like "your husband is possessed by your dead brother—who may or may not actually be your brother, maybe just a malevolent spirit—and he's rising as Famine, and oh, by the way, you've been turned into a ghost."

"I don't think that's better. Are you taking this seriously? Because transparent is not a good look for me, those spots were the only fashion statement I got to make, and just how long do I have before I go 'poof' and don't come back? At least you almost have color. I look like...fog!" Roger said, pacing back and forth in front of the fireplace.

"Then what do we do to make her better?" Piper said, her voice high.

"Right now, I'm a bit too busy keeping her mostly-not-dead to develop a plan," Nia said tightly. "Ginny? You still with us?"

"You mean is it time to break out the séance candles? Nope. Not yet."

Roger stopped dead in his pacing. *"Is that...sarcasm I detect?"*

"She sounds practically like you," Piper said, her eyes wide as she stared at Nia. "Is that a death thing?"

Is that a... Ginny rolled her eyes and pinched her lips tight. Of course, how could any of them understand? They weren't being turned into a ghost. They hadn't lost their physical forms, or whatever exactly had happened to her. They hadn't just watched the end of their second marriage, this time with a man who was worth her heart, who was worth...everything. Moisture pinched her eyes. A man who'd now been possessed by her brother, or the spirit masquerading as her brother, who she hadn't been strong enough to stop.

"We're going to figure this out, Gin. Just hold on," Nia said softly.

"It's like I can barely see her sometimes. Like she's standing in a thick fog," Piper said.

Had they ever actually seen her? She'd spent so many years trying to pretend to be someone else.

"Have you ever actually let them see the real you?" Roger shot back.

She turned to glare at him. *"What, now you're suddenly going to try and be a wise guiding force?"*

"Now you're going to be the voice of sarcasm and whininess? Besides, if there was ever a time to turn over a new leaf, probably best I take it now. While I still am."

Fair enough. Ginny curled her knees up to her chest. "I'm sorry, guys," she said, looking up at her friends. "I-I'm scared. Where's James? Can I see him? Have we figured out how to get Thomas out of him?" Maybe it was like when Thomas had possessed her. Maybe James was in there still, just…asleep, or a facsimile of sleep. *Frosting*, hopefully he was asleep and didn't know Thomas was running around with his body. Or what Thomas had done with that body.

She struggled to swallow. Maybe he wasn't aware enough to know this was all her fault.

"Loki and the others are up with James. They're trying to figure out a way to exorcise him. Except…" Anna hesitated and couldn't meet Ginny's eyes. "They don't know how to separate them, not now that Thomas appears to be rising as Famine."

Ah yes. Her brother was rising as Famine. She sniffed. Well, at least someone got what they wanted.

"Yes, because poor Thomas never gets what he wants," Roger groused.

And James… Oh, *frosting. James, I'm so sorry. I never meant for this to happen. I never wanted you to get hurt.*

Her friends were still discussing possible ways they could somehow expel Thomas, like they had when he was in Ginny or Charlie. Nia rejected every one. "But it's not the same. Thomas isn't the same anymore. And now he has a Famine heir. He has exactly what he's needed from the beginning."

What he'd needed from the beginning. Ginny frowned. If Thomas would have been born, he'd have been a Famine heir. Instead, he, or the thing that had taken his name and identity after her real brother died, hadn't had a physical form. Something he'd complained about daily. All the things he'd missed. All the things she got because he didn't.

But what had he gotten that she didn't? She'd lost track of how many times had she had to play his game, follow his rules. Whether that meant endless games of tag, a game she'd always hated, or marrying who he suggested was the perfect man—twice—because he'd never have a wedding. He always said all he could do was live through her happiness, she owed him. He'd wanted the power of Famine, so she'd foolishly tried to help "them" gain it. She'd compromised her entire life what she wanted so Thomas could get what he wanted. She'd lived her entire life for him. To make up for a defect that had ended the real Thomas's life. More than *two decades ago*. Because Thomas said she had to live for both of them.

To live for him.

Yet, when their situations were reversed, when he had the chance for power, he certainly wasn't living for "them," was he? Her head spun for a moment, and a shock of cold landed in the pit of her stomach. *Frosted cupcakes*. She really was stupid not to have realized it before now. He'd been waiting for this moment, priming her for the day when he could attack her like this.

Her lips tightened and heat flushed through her, washing away the cold. Her heart started to pound. Short of stealing her body, what could be better than bringing a good-looking Famine heir right to Beckwell by making her marry him?

Only, he probably hadn't counted on James being a good person. Someone who saw Ginny for who she could be. Who'd believed in her. Who'd wanted something better for the world. Her insides ached. And who, against all her better sense and promise to keep things professional, she'd fallen for completely. Worst of all, now he was suffering for her stupidity, while Thomas would get out and unleash all the cruelty, all the destruction he could.

Unless she stopped him.

Unless she *destroyed* him.

She had spent too much of her life not believing she was enough. Now she had to be. Because she had to save James, and stop Thomas.

"Anna," she said, her voice stopping the others and getting their full attention. Or maybe it was just her tone, a curious sharpness to it she'd never used before. "Has Thomas risen as Famine…or is he still rising as Famine? Don't sugarcoat it, please. The truth. Just as it is."

This time, Anna's steel-blue eyes met hers. "I don't think he's fully Famine yet. Because you're still here."

"Even though I have almost none of my ability left?" Ginny looked at Roger. "Thomas seemed to suggest Roger's color—pink or green, anything that wasn't black—had something to do with my remaining ability. No spots mean we don't have much left."

"Your ability and you are the same thing, parts of the whole. So long as you still have essence, he doesn't have all the power yet."

Ginny nodded, and turned to Nia. "You said he's a tulpa, that I created him. Right?"

"Yes," Nia affirmed, then narrowed her eyes. "Why? What are you thinking?"

"I'm thinking maybe I can reverse what he did to me. I can get him and all that he is—all my abilities—out of my husband. I can rise as Famine for once and for all, and let my brother go back to being a memory."

CHAPTER 34

Wind rattled through the trees, and Ginny wrapped her arms around herself to contemplate her parents' graveled backyard. Her chosen battlefield. Hope that didn't make it her Alamo.

Nia stood quietly behind her, the smaller woman's hand light on Ginny's elbow, keeping Ginny tethered to her body. Anna and Piper would be there soon, but were her emissaries to Thomas to tell him where to meet her and that she was willing to trade—her abilities for James. When Thomas was strong enough with her life force and abilities, he wouldn't need James's body anymore. James would be safe.

And she would be...well, dead if the plan with the girls didn't work and Thomas stole all her life force.

The yard was lightly dusted with snow, and all evidence of the wedding down to the last plastic bell had been scrubbed away. Probably before Mom and Dad had left on that holiday they'd been talking about forever, but never seemed to book. Until last week. Just after the wedding. *Frosting*. How could it be that it was only nine days ago? Ten since the stepladder incident and she'd fallen into a handsome Brit's arms, and maybe from that moment started the tumble into love.

Roger bumped into her leg. *"I dunno, luv. Let's try for something a bit less maudlin, shall we? What about 'huzzah! We aren't going to end up erased and dead.'"*

The whole yard was full of memories. Chasing Thomas through the sunshine even though she was the only one who could see him...and no matter how many times she caught him, she always had to be "it." Her first hint of true safety and warmth, curled against James's chest as he carried her across the gravel.

But now he needed her to save him. She blew out a breath and squeezed her hands into fists at her sides. She was enough. She had to be. Maybe nausea was the taste of empowerment.

"That doesn't seem right," Roger said, dancing nervously in the gravel. *"When will he get here? We have a backup plan hope?"*

"He'll get here when he gets here. And..." Another breath. *"We've got this. I'm 75 percent sure."*

"Ha-ha," Roger groused. He snuffled next to her, and his voice grew soft. *"If you'd had a horse like Barnabas, he would have given you better advice. You might have been evil and all, but you'd probably already have risen as Famine. Not hanging around, nearly dead with me."*

Ginny turned to the pig and knelt beside him, shifting Nia's hand to her shoulder. She lifted Roger's snout so his gaze met hers. *"No."*

He snorted. *"No?"*

"No. I wouldn't have been better off with Barnabas. Or any other horse. I have gotten all the 'good advice' I never needed from Thomas and from everyone else. You gave me the right advice. Advice that gave me the courage

to believe I could fall in love with James. And the courage to bring us here, about to stop Thomas or die trying."

"Can we avoid the dying part?"

She wrapped her arms around the little porker, and gave him a hug. *"We're in this together, Roger. You're exactly the partner I'd want at my side."*

Roger leaned into her embrace, snuffling quietly. *"My one regret is that we never watched a porno together. Or went to a strip club. I've always wanted to go to a strip club. The kind with poles."*

Ginny pulled back with a sigh, and patted him on the head. "You are very definitely the horse I deserve."

"Gin, your mom. What's she doing here?" Nia said quietly, nodding her head toward the patio doors.

Mom stepped out onto the patio in her slippers and pulled her sweater more tightly around herself. "Ginny? What are you doing out here? Where's James? You two haven't had a tiff, have you?"

Frosted cupcake. Ginny rose to her feet.

"Come on, we'd better head her off," she said to Nia, and headed for the garden doors.

Three women stepped out from behind Mom. Despite almost being a ghost, Ginny could still taste their essences, even at this distance. The first was tall with steel-gray hair and a matching hardness to her expression—Mrs. Boniface, who tasted of grapes soured beyond wine, well on the way to vinegar. The second was an aging soccer mom with a yellowed complexion from her cancer treatments and declining health—Louise Dole, who tasted of burned muffins. Finally, the perky brunette Daphne Spinner, a spiteful smile twisting her lips, who still tasted like rotting tomato.

The three Fates. And what was left of the League.

Ginny stumbled, but squeezed until her nails bit into her palms, and continued her march forward.

"Well, shit," Nia said, right on Ginny's heels.

"I second that," Roger added.

The Fates stood behind Mom ominously. What remained of the League, it was their machinations that had led, in all probability, to Ginny and her friends rising in the first place. Followed by her current almost-a-ghost problem. And James being possessed.

Now they thought they'd threaten her Mom? Ginny clenched her jaw. Nope. That wasn't happening.

"Mom, what are you doing here? What happened to the holiday?" Ginny said, settling her glare on the three women. She and Nia stopped just short of the patio.

Mom turned, as though noticing the other women had followed her out onto the patio for the first time. The wind ruffled her hair, and the lines bracketing her lips were deeper. She rubbed her arms, her brow furrowing, but focused back on Ginny. "You know your father. A job came up, and he changed his mind. A combination of bad luck and timing, I suppose."

"Oh, I'm betting it was more than that," Ginny said, settling her glare on the most senior of the Fates, Mrs. Boniface. Beckwell's school principal was a control freak of epic proportions, had been since she'd just been the history teacher when Ginny was in school. She was definitely the one in charge. "Let her go. Whatever's happening here doesn't involve Mom."

"Um, you have a new plan, right, luv?" Roger said, bumping her leg. *"What can we do to them? Worse, Thomas is going to be here any minute."*

"I'm well aware of that. But this is my mom, Roger. I'm not leaving her with them."

"Ginny, what's going on?" Mom said, glancing again at the other women. "You look…odd. Louise just brought her friends for tea. To chat about fundraising to build a new community hall."

"I believe Genevieve is aware why we're here," Mrs. Boniface said, her lips curving in a chilly barracuda smile.

"You received our message faster than I expected."

"Careful, Gin. If Anna's right, that makes old Boney-face Atropos. The eldest of the Fates...and the one who can cut the threads of life. I'm not sure how many people I can hold on life-support at once with you and your pig," Nia said softly, her voice for Ginny's ears only.

"What is your obsession with ending the world anyway?" Ginny demanded, buying time. *Cupcakes, applesauce,* and *frosting.* How did she get rid of all of them and keep Mom safe? "What gives you the right to make that decision?" Telepathically to Roger, *"Any ideas how we get rid of them, save Mom, and don't all die?"*

"Luv, I've been telling you we needed a better plan from the start! I wasn't expecting the three hags to show up. I'm thinking, all right?" Roger said back, shifting against her leg.

Mrs. Boniface's thin lips curled upward, more Grinch-like than friendly. "If not us, who? We are the Fates. We see what has been, what is, what will be. There is nothing but irresponsible, hateful humanity from one end of that spectrum to the next. We have a chance to correct the course. To stop this path and force another. We've offered you and your friends a chance to help lead humanity into that better future. What right have *you* to refuse us?"

Nia stuck her spare hand in the air. "Um, pretty sure that's because none of us are psycho-bitches like you are. Just sayin'."

"That's it. The girls. All of you. Let's scare these hags off," Roger suggested.

Daphne closed her eyes and rocked from side to side for a moment, like a cobra before attack. Her eyes popped open and narrowed. "She didn't receive our invitation. She and the four...they're plotting." Her smile widened, and she stepped closer to Mom. Slid a hand down Mom's shoulder, making Mom flinch. "But perhaps our intervention was unnecessary. Why, Ginny, you're looking rather…ghostly. Thomas almost has you, hasn't he?"

"Thomas? What Thomas do you mean?" Mom looked from one woman to the next, her gaze finally landing on Ginny. "They can't mean…" Her shoulders rose and fell faster as her breath sped, she took a step toward Ginny. "What's happened to you? What is everyone talking about?"

Mrs. Boniface settled a firm hand on Mom's shoulder. "That's far enough."

"You leave her alone." Ginny moved to lunge forward, but Nia held her back.

Mrs. Boniface pulled a pair of slim gold scissors from a pocket. Barely as long as her hand, they didn't look especially threatening. But the spicy taste of magic they emitted was so strong, it filled Ginny's mouth until she wanted to gag, and she couldn't look away.

"That's quite close enough. One snip is all it would take," Mrs. Boniface said, holding the scissors near the top of Mom's head. She nodded toward Nia. "You see it, don't you? Her life thread. Tell your friend you see it."

"Please tell me she's lying," Ginny whispered to Nia.

Nia shook her head, her jaw tight. "She's not. When those scissors get close to it, I can see her life thread, too. But they'd be breaking natural order if its cut it too early."

"They've already tried ending the world. Don't think they care," Roger squealed.

"Ginny, for gods' sake, would you please just tell me what's going on? I lost one child, and I will not lose you, too, dammit," Mom said, her voice cracking. She shook off Mrs. Boniface's grip, and straightened her shoulders, regal as a queen. "You listen to me. I can see you're in trouble. How do I fix this?"

"It's not going to work that way this time, Mom," Ginny said, her muscles aching. She might lose James tonight, probably her own life. Not Mom, too.

"If you hurt either of them, you'll discover just what I'm capable of," Nia growled, the dark mask settling over her eyes. The temperature in the air dipped, and her spearmint flavor sharpened.

Louise Dole laughed. "Really, sweetie, as if you can threaten us? We know about you, too. The secrets you keep. You dare accuse us of breaking the rules?" She tsked, her gaze darkening as she stared straight ahead, as though at something only she could see. "My, what a case USELESS will build against you when they discover the truth," she crooned. Her lips curled upward. "We're nothing compared to the trouble on the horizon for you."

"Shut up," Nia snarled. "I can read the stains on your soul, and while reckoning comes for us all, that bitch is a hell of a lot closer to you than me."

"Time's running out, luv," Roger said. He danced nervously, and Ginny followed his gaze toward the rear of the garden.

James's tall frame broke through the distant trees edging the yard. His long stride was quick and determined. He was headed straight for her.

Cupcakes.

"Ginny, *please*. Talk to me," Mom pleaded.

Forget not being able to touch Mom, especially if this was the last time. Ginny lunged toward Mom, dragging Nia with her. Until she was close enough to touch Mom, wrap her in a hug. "Mom, whatever they say, it's not really Thomas. Not our Thomas."

Mom's eyes widened. "B-but he's dead. How can he be involved?"

"It's…complicated." Another glance toward James. She needed more time. "Our Thomas is somewhere better. He's happy." She had to force the words past the thickness in her throat. If this was her last chance to say it, she had to take it. For Mom's sake. And her own. "I just wanted to say I love you. And how sorry I am. I can't imagine how much losing Thomas must have hurt. I probably made it worse, all those times I used his name. I never wanted to hurt you. I just…" *I wanted to be the one you wanted.* "I wondered sometimes. If you'd rather have had a boy." *If you'd rather he'd have lived.*

Mom's eyes widened and her mouth opened, then shut. Her voice, when she spoke, was a bare whisper. "You mean…would I have preferred Thomas had lived over you?"

Ginny dropped her gaze, all those birthday memories of Mom after bedtime with a glass of wine and Thomas's photo album.

"Ginny, what about that plan?" Roger said urgently.

"Genevieve Lack, we require your attention," Mrs. Boniface snapped, just like she'd caught Ginny napping in the back of history class.

Mom grasped Ginny's shoulders and pulled back enough until their gazes met. "Oh, sweetheart. Have I made you think that? Never mind. I…" She straightened, looked Ginny in the eye. "Genevieve Cordelia Lack, I would have rather you'd both survived, of course. But I have never, *ever*, in all my life regretted you, my darling. Or wanted a different son or daughter. You are the daughter I have, the daughter I love, and I couldn't be prouder."

"Oh. My. Gods. Do we really have to keep listening to all this saccharine bullshit?" Daphne moaned loudly. "Let's kill the woman, then hold the girl captive so Thomas can rise."

"We wouldn't have to interfere if Thomas had listened to us," Louise groused.

"As I've already explained, it won't work if she doesn't give the last of her abilities—and her life—willingly," Mrs. Boniface snapped at the two younger Fates, jerking Mom away. She turned to Ginny. "Your mother's life for your abilities. Let Thomas have them. I might even be inclined to throw in your husband, if you act quickly."

"Oh, I have plans for James," Daphne said, licking her lips.

Ginny and Mrs. Boniface ignored the other woman, their gazes locked.

"And I have plans for you," Piper said, as she and Anna rounded the corner of the house. She gave Ginny a quick look. "You okay? Did you invite them?" Piper raised her hands, a cold wind whipping up around her and a strange brightness entering her gaze. Her skunk stood at her feet, its golden eyes filled with hatred as it glared at the Fates. The intensity of Piper's lemon-balm flavor increased as ability stirred inside her.

Nia smiled, a dark glittering mask seeming to descend over her eyes, the sharpness of spearmint crackling in the air.

Anna tossed her braid behind her shoulder, the sweet heaviness of anise heavy in the air.

Calm descended over Ginny. Her friends were here. This was going to be okay.

She faced Mrs. Boniface and the others calmly, all of them looking a good deal less calm.

"We're the Fates, you idiot. We decide what we do, what happens. For everyone," Daphne sputtered.

"We're the four horsewomen of the apocalypse, dummy. If anyone gets to end the world, it's us," Ginny said.

She, Roger, and Nia advanced on the Fates from the front, while Anna and Piper came in from the left.

Mrs. Boniface, clearly the smartest of the group, had already backed against the patio doors. "Girls, let's be reasonable about this," she said, fumbling for the door handle, then retreating back through the door.

"Yes! We've only wanted to help you," Louise Dole

said, almost tripping over her own feet as she backed toward escape and Mrs. Boniface.

"Oh, yeah, totally see that. The whole threatening us, trying to get Ginny's brother to kill her, that was all for our own good, right?" Nia snarled.

"Why are you running? We could take these bitches," Daphne said, shouting at the others. Seeing she was alone, even she showed some sign of intelligence and began backing toward the doors herself.

"We could finish this," Anna said, her voice a low growl that sent shivers down Ginny's neck.

"Um, yeah, about that. Remember the whole James-is-possessed-by-Thomas thing? He's almost here!" Roger squeaked.

Ginny turned. *Frosting.* James/Thomas was only a dozen feet away and closing fast. Prickles danced up and down her neck at his approach.

"Guys? He's here," she said to her friends.

They turned to see James's approach.

The patio door clicked shut, and by the time Ginny turned back, the three women had slipped into the house and disappeared.

Anna growled.

"It's okay, Anna. We'll kick their asses another day," Nia said, her smile small and tight.

Mom jumped forward and wrapped her arms around Ginny. "Oh, thank gods. You're okay. You're safe."

Ginny brought her arms up almost in reflex. *Cupcake*, if only she could really feel the hug, rather than the hollow memory of one, her body barely solid enough to feel Mom's arms. The battle had yet to begin, and she needed to get Mom out of here before it did. Still, she enjoyed the squeeze as long as she could before she pulled back and straightened Mom's hair.

"Mom, listen. You've always taken care of me. This time, it's my turn. I can't do what I need to if I'm worried about you. Please. Go."

Mom kept shaking her head, her eyes shiny with unshed tears.

Ginny leaned in closer. "This once, do what I want. I need you to do this. Take Dad, get out of here as fast as you go. Go somewhere safe and public. Lou's Place or Loki's house would be good options."

Mom's lower lips trembled, but then she nodded. "All right. But we're going to talk more about this. About all of this after. You understand? You be safe." One more hug, and she backed toward the house, the Fates still shadowing her.

If I survive, sure thing. Ginny nodded. "Of course. Just, please. Go."

Mom nodded, and turned. She shouted Dad's name, and he barely emerged from one of the rooms before Mom grabbed his hand and they both dashed for the front door.

Ginny closed the patio door, paused a moment, then slowly turned. To face Thomas in James's body, where they stood near the edge of the patio. He stood in the same spot she'd left James in the dark, that first night they'd met.

She swallowed, then took a step toward him. "Okay, Thomas, let's do this. Time for you to move on and leave the man I love alone."

CHAPTER 35

He'd never considered what being possessed would actually feel like, James mused as he and Thomas marched into Ginny's parents' garden. But it wasn't unlike two men trying to peddle a unicycle.

Thomas was in charge right now, and had stormed them through the fields and trees, spreading destruction as wildly and far as he could. Swathes of farm land lay in salted ruin. Trees had blackened and disintegrated. There were rising shouts coming from the town itself, car horns honking, none of which could be good, but James couldn't investigate now. Especially as he wasn't currently in charge of his legs.

But he was aware and watching and able to throw in his two cents when necessary. Like suggest they go through the fields and see what they were capable of—rather than directly through town, where they were more likely to run into people and potentially cause further harm. He could hear and communicate with Thomas, but their minds were separate. Hopefully that meant come the crucial moment, he could take control and do what was necessary: make sure Thomas went down so Ginny would be safe. Then she could rise and the USELESS agents would be no match for she and her friends.

Nia stood at Ginny's side, the other two horsewomen stepping up and taking their places at Ginny's side, where she faced into the house.

Then Ginny turned, and James's breath caught. Or it would have, if he'd been in control of his lungs. Her red curls tumbled around her shoulders, and she wore a short jacket around her shoulders over a polka-dot blouse and slender slacks that hugged her hips in all the right places. She reminded him of that war-era Rosie the Riveter poster…except redheaded, more kickass, and freaking amazing. Yet, she looked pale and translucent. A literal shadow of herself.

He should have found a way to stop Thomas from hurting her. But when Thomas went after Ginny and the girls, James hadn't been able to exert any control himself yet. Thank gods Nia appeared to be okay, Roger and Anna, too.

Thomas chuckled. "Will you look at that. What is she wearing, a costume?"

James bit back his irritation, and said nothing. He was supposed to be pretending to go along with all this. Agreeing that he wanted to help destroy Ginny over their fight was how he'd convinced Thomas he was sincere in wanting to lend his body for a while.

Ginny straightened and lifted her chin, even if there was a tremble in her fisted hands and she was even paler than usual. "Okay, Thomas, let's do this. Time for you to move on and leave the man I love alone."

James mentally blinked, not sure which part to react to first. Surely, she wasn't going to give Thomas her powers. Surely she and the girls had a better plan than that—because that could kill Ginny.

She'd said she loved him.

Even after what he'd done to her. Even after his lies. Even after he hadn't been able to protect her.

He should have told her how he felt when he'd had the chance. How desperately he loved her, too.

Thomas swaggered forward in a move that made James roll his eyes. What a cocky bastard.

"Then come closer," Thomas said.

No, don't do that. "Roger, make her back off," James tried to communicate to the pig.

The pig flicked his head in confusion.

Ginny and her friends all advanced as a unit. Hopefully the sign of a plan.

"Freeze! Hands where we can see them," a woman shouted, her voice husky and cold. She and another dark-clad man raced around the corner of the house, their footsteps crunching in the gravel. Their matching dark suits labeling them as agents. The weapon they both held in their hands—something between a wand and a revolver, and twice as deadly as either—marked them as USELESS agents. About damned time.

The smaller of the two agents, a male, looked like a kid who'd borrowed his father's oversized suit, his Adam's apple sticking out prominently, face pale. His weapon shook in his hand.

The other agent, a woman, held the situation in her steady dark gaze, her brown hair peppered with gray and her grip on her weapon rock-solid. USELESS had figured out long ago that while their agents were capable of using magic when necessary, a well-placed bullet—silver or otherwise—tended to kill most beings. Or at least slow them the hell down. This female agent looked very comfortable with that weapon of hers. The barrel trained on him.

For once, James was grateful for their efficiency. It would be over quickly. He closed his eyes, and reached for control of his own voice. "Shoot!" he shouted.

There was a loud bang.

"No!" the female agent cried.

Thomas leaped forward and grabbed Ginny's hands, his hands squeezing hard enough Ginny flinched.

A sharp pain tore through James at the same time as the ability ripped through them. Ginny cried out. Power flowed through them. Hot as blood, scalding as steam, it burned beneath the skin.

Thomas groaned in pleasure.

It wasn't pleasure for James, especially when he could see Ginny's agony. Then he spotted it. The minute division between he and Thomas, like a sticker peeling back from the paper. As though he and Thomas leaned away from each other. The power and ability went to Thomas, leaving only the echo of it in James.

Ginny. Dear gods, Ginny! She still stood, but was pale and completely translucent. Her face contorted in agony as much as Thomas's essence twisted with pleasure.

No. Wait. He couldn't hold Thomas. Thomas leaned out farther. Farther and farther. Out of the same space. Out of him. No! James had meant to hold on. He might have been shot, but Thomas was getting away. Bloody USELESS agents hadn't shot in time. They were supposed to kill Thomas while he was still in James's body.

"Now," Nia snarled.

He wanted to shout at them. To tell them to stop Thomas from hurting Ginny, to protect her. To leave him be. He had a plan, dammit. A plan that required Thomas in his body.

Anna and Piper placed their hands on Ginny's shoulders. A shock of electricity jolted through them all. Everything was lit up with piercing light, and he floated for a moment. A second later, the earth roared up to greet him with the friendliness of an oncoming train and slammed into him.

James eyes popped open, and he bolted upright, his breath caught in his throat. He was on the ground. In his body. His head was clear, his body his own. His right shoulder was on fire with white-hot pain, tingles spreading down his arm. Thomas was gone. Ginny. Where was Ginny? He rolled to his knees, his head and stomach roiling, his body sluggish.

"By the gods, we said freeze, dammit," the female USELESS agent shouted again. "So freeze. All of you. That includes you, L. If you fire that weapon again without my say so, I swear I will shoot you myself," she growled, presumably to her partner.

James heard them distantly. He had to find Ginny.

He spotted Thomas first, next to him. Naked and pale, but a physical and whole man, on his hands and knees in the gravel. A hoarse laugh came from the other man's throat, then grew in volume as he rocked back on his heels and stared at his hands. A large black pig held itself stiffly beside him. It watched as Thomas picked up handfuls of gravel and let it trickle out through his fingers. He laughed again. "Oh, Ginny, thank you. Thank you!"

James scrambled to turn. To find her. He almost missed her the first time.

Barely more than a shadow, she was a vague echo of a humanoid shape kneeling beside Nia. Ginny panted, trying to catch her breath.

He crawled over next to her, his head too dizzy to stand. He'd cocked this all up. "Oh, love. What have you done?"

She reached out a hand. "Pretty sure I saved you." Her eyes widened. "Your shoulder…"

He waved off her concern and reached to squeeze her hand.

His fingers passed through hers.

He stared at his hand a minute, horror churning his stomach more than the possession or getting shot had. No. She couldn't be gone. They couldn't have lost. He couldn't have lost her.

She gave him a sad smile. "Roger is gone. But you were supposed to be free. Not get shot." A tingle of cold touched his jaw as she reached out a hand to touch him. "I love you."

"And I love you. We're going to find a way to fix this. To save you," he insisted. There had to be a way. Losing Ginny had never been the plan. She was a horsewoman. This couldn't be possible.

"We said freeze!" the young agent, "L," said, his voice rising on the end with nervousness.

James slowly looked up at the weapon pointed almost directly in his face. Usually, a weapon aimed at his head would have given James some pause.

Not today.

His glare gave the skinny kid a dismissive once over before he turned to the more senior agent. "You're late. Unless you have a way to save her, piss off."

"Late? As in you invited them?" Ginny said, her tone sharp-ish. "That wasn't very clever, James."

He turned toward her again, heat stinging his face. "You weren't supposed to get hurt. I wanted to save you. Besides, you have a better plan?"

"Actually, yes. I do," she whispered, leaning closer and sending chills chasing through him.

"Mrs. Derth, stay where you are. Mr. Derth, we are not here at your convenience," the female agent barked, her dark gaze flicking to Ginny, then over Ginny's three silent friends. "We're here to follow up on reports of a level nine infraction. If you and all of your friends would calm the hell down, I'd like to sort everything out before anyone else gets shot."

"We should kill them all now. While they're still

human," the skinny kid said, his weapon waggling between James, Thomas, and the other three horsewomen.

"Wait for my signal," Ginny whispered. "When I give it to you, I need you to hold Thomas down."

James made the smallest nod and hoped she saw it. Hopefully he'd still be able to act on it, too. Hot sticky warmth trickled down his arm and chest in alarming fashion.

"L, killing them is not procedure," the older agent said tightly, her gaze and her weapon never wavering from somewhere between James and Ginny. Hell, she might have had all four horsewomen and him in her sights. She seemed capable of it. "Now. Hands. Where I can see them."

There was movement behind James as Thomas climbed to his feet. Pale and most definitely naked, he grinned at the agents. "Oh, good. More playmates."

"Thomas, be careful, or you're going to get shot," James said warningly. He glanced toward Ginny. Frankly, he'd be more than happy if Thomas was shot…but if he'd stolen Ginny's life force and she had some plan, Thomas was also the only chance they had to fix Ginny. What the hell was Ginny's plan? And when exactly was it going to happen? She seemed to be getting more see-through by the second.

"If we bring the four in, dead or alive, we're guaranteed a promotion. Dead sounds easier to me," the skinny agent said, his eyes too wild for James's taste. He aimed his weapon at Thomas.

"You might want to reconsider that," Nia said, shifting to one side, and splitting up the group that the woman made so they weren't one large target. "The dead are a lot more trouble than you'd imagine. I plan to be the biggest pain in your ass ever."

A small shot of gravel erupted at Nia's feet.

Nia froze.

The female agent growled, literally growled. "Do any of you understand the meaning of 'freeze' or 'hands in the air'? Because I'm trying to possibly save your asses, but you're not making it easy."

The other agent looked at her. "Save them? That isn't our mission."

"Kid, we're on an investigative mission right now, and you're too young and stupid to understand the ramifications of some of the shit that's going down. Now shut up and listen," she snapped.

Piper raised her hands in the air, and the wind rose around them. "This isn't a good idea," she said, a hint of threat to her soft voice. She stepped slightly in front of Ginny.

"Fine," the female agent said with a snap. "You all want to meet the gods? Great. We'll all go and meet the gods. Then they can kill you and I can go home and get some rest. Hands the fuck up in the air."

Metal slid against metal. James's team, led by Maddox with a two and a half foot broadsword in his massive arms, strode around the corner. The sound of that sword got even the senior agent's attention. She half-turned, her attention wavering.

"Now!" Ginny said.

James twisted and dove toward Thomas's legs. They both went down in a tangle of limbs into the gravel.

There was the sound of weapons firing. The USELESS agents, maybe his team firing back. The clang of steel.

James couldn't afford to find out. All he could do was try and get Thomas pinned to the ground. Thomas was strong and wiry, even caught off guard. But he hadn't been trained to fight by three bullying older brothers like James had. Thomas's pig squealed and rammed its head into James's side as the two men wrestled on the ground, James fighting to get the taller man pinned to the ground.

"Whatever your plan is, Ginny, do it now!"

ɞ

Ginny leaped toward Thomas. The girls were right at her side.

Her fingers closed over Thomas's hand, and she squeezed. He tried to jerk away. Turned his head, his eyes wide as he stared at her. She could taste him. The flavor a hint of spiced pumpkin pie and cream... But there was no sweetness, just raw pumpkin and the bitterness of heavy cloves.

She stared into his eyes, the same shade of green as hers. The same gaze she'd grown up with. Always there for her. So often in this yard, full of happy memories. It was why she'd chosen this place. To remember what he was to her, but that it was time for her to live her life. And time for her brother to rest in peace.

"Ginny, you don't know what you're doing. I'm the one who should be powerful. You can't be Famine. You've never even wanted to be Famine. That was always my dream," Thomas snarled furiously.

"I know," she said. She closed her eyes. And felt...*frosting*, how could she find her abilities now? There was so little of them left. So little of her left.

"See? You're not made for this. Let go," Thomas said.

Heat burned through her, emptying her. It was taking the last of her abilities, the last of her life essence. He was right. She'd never really wanted Famine abilities, all that power. She'd just wanted to make her cupcakes, that feeling of being exactly where she was meant to be when she cooked or baked. She turned to catch one last glimpse of James. With him she'd always been enough. At least she'd had that, right?

"Don't you do this to me, Ginny. Fight!" Roger shouted. Or perhaps more accurately, squeaked, his only presence in her head.

355

"Ginny, you can do this. You have to do this," James said, shoving Thomas down again. "You know how. Find your abilities. Feel them. They're in you. And you are amazing. You can do this. It's just like cooking, right? The same steps."

Thomas clutched a thin black set of scales. "They're wrong. The scales can see who truly deserves the ability. They judge you unfit."

"It's your power. It was always supposed to be your power," Nia said.

"You can't give up, Ginny. Come on, sweetie, please. Fight," Anna begged, practically in tears.

"Feel it deep inside you. Reach in and grab it," Piper urged.

She tasted them all then. Dark chocolate. Sharp spearmint. Anise. Lemon balm. Tears stung her eyes.

"Get the bowls out first," Maddox roared above the sound of metal clanging and weapons firing.

Just like he'd been there when she'd practiced calling on her abilities. Never easier to call on than when she was in the kitchen. Triggered by just the act of getting out the measuring cups and bowls before she baked.

"Then measure and pour the ingredients, one at a time, before you start to stir," Bina piped up.

At her words, Ginny imagined her kitchen. The bowls on the countertop. The ingredients and her measuring cup beside her.

Her abilities stirred.

"Feel it rise up through you. Become part of you," James said.

"The kitchen is steamy and warm, because you've been baking all day," Charlie shouted. "Can't you smell those cranberry muffins?" A gun fired, then Charlie groaned. "Oh, blimey, and is that your banana bread?"

James and his team were reminding her of her lessons. When she was most able to call on her abilities.

Helping her do the same today.

She slipped off her shoes and felt the cold gravel, and beneath that, the earth. The pulse thrummed through her. Ginny closed her eyes. She pictured herself in the kitchen. The feeling that welled up inside her when she was there, mixing the ingredients. The feeling she'd had all those times she'd practiced with James and his team. Getting ready for dinner at the end of the day.

There it was. Just a fluttering spark at first, a tiny bit deep down inside her, beyond the pain and heat of the flow outward from her, toward Thomas.

But she reached for that spark. She grabbed it. Clung to it. Let it grow.

The heat dimmed, grew less painful.

She opened her eyes.

Thomas stared at her, his brow lowered in puzzlement. The scales dipped in his hands. "What are you doing?"

She felt that little spark grow to a flame, then a long line of fire. She reached forward and grabbed the scales, ripping them out of Thomas's hand. She pulled the ability toward her, too, like digging her hands deep into the warm spring soil.

"Ginny, stop!" Thomas cried. He moaned. "No. You don't want to do this. I'm your brother. You love me. I've been there for you. You'd be nothing without me."

It was easier all the time now, to keep reeling it in, drawing the thread of power toward her. Digging deeper and deeper, pulling more and more, faster and faster. It spiraled toward her. The scales trembled in her hands, the metal warm to the touch.

Roger stood once more at Ginny's side, leaned his warm body against her leg. *"You've got this, luv."*

She shook her head sadly, and reached for Thomas's cheek, pressed down into the gravel. "The scales have passed judgment. No, Thomas. You're not my brother.

357

Not the twin who grew and developed next to me. You're what happened out of my missing him. Of my parents' grief. You became my brother, sometimes my savior. But so often you were also the voice that told me I wasn't enough."

"But I love you. And you love me." He was almost translucent now. As she'd been. He looked around, tried to reach for James.

James leaned back. "Nope. No free rides here anymore, mate."

"Ginny, don't do this. Please. I won't hurt anyone. I won't hurt you." He was back to his almost translucent self as she'd often known him, but becoming ever more faded. Her hand could no longer touch his face. His voice was just a soft echo in her head.

"I love you, too, Thomas. But I am enough without you. It's time for me to live my own life. Time for you to rest in peace. Goodbye."

The last of the ability spiraled up and out through him like a lone piece of spaghetti, its tail whipping against her lip. The scales trembled in her hand, light enough to be tossed in the wind.

Thomas was gone. Barnabas was gone.

Only a large, black pig named Roger sat back on its haunches. He looked down at himself, and grinned. *"I do look good in black."*

All that ability rippled inside her, like rich earth without bottom, without end. Complete potential. She could hear the thoughts and flavors of the agents, of James's team around her. Then of the entire town. Then so much farther. She let out a shuddering breath and quieted the rush of thoughts, voices, and flavors. Her heart ached for the end of Thomas, for all the times he had been her brother. But finally, she knew exactly where she belonged, and what she wanted.

"I told you my plan was better," she said.

James climbed to his feet, and he reached for her. "Have I told you recently how incredible you are? Or how much I love you?"

She cocked her head, her lips turning up. "I don't think I could ever—"

The gunshot cracking through the air cut off her words.

CHAPTER 36

James twisted her to the side. Ginny spun to see where the sound had come from. The large heavy bulk of Maddox blocked them both. He fell with a soft oomph. A splash of warm blood splattered Ginny's face.

"Maddox!" She dropped to her knees and cradled the big man's head half in her lap, half on James's.

He smiled, his teeth gleaming. "I have…paid my debt," he said. Then coughed and choked. He tried to see James. "But…I have decided…not…to….kill…you." He closed his eyes.

"L, dammit, what have you done?" the female USELESS agent cried.

James's team closed in on her. Her hand trembled on her weapon. She was outnumbered, bleeding from wounds to her scalp, her side, and her leg, and the odds weren't on her side. Wavering on her feet, she dropped her weapon, raised both hands in the air, and fell onto her knees. James's team swarmed toward her and relieved her of her weapon before clipping her own cuffs on her wrists.

Her partner wasn't smart enough to see it all play out. He wavered the aim of his weapon between James's team and Ginny and her friends. "The others are coming, you know. I called all of this in. They'll be here, they'll kill all of you. Every single one of you."

Piper raised her hand, and Ginny felt her friend's ability stir, as it tickled her own.

She reached out a hand, and touched Piper. Shook her head.

"You think you're all powerful? That you'll be stronger than the gods? You are nothing compared to them. They will crush you with a thought. The agents they have coming will kill you before you ever see them coming. They will kill you and everyone who ever knew you. This town? It will be nothing but a smoking crater by the time they're done," the kid said, spittle gathering at the edges of his lips.

Ginny slowly lowered Maddox into Piper's arms. James reached for her, but she gently waved him off. The kid was her focus now. Her abilities whirled within her, up through the earth through the soles of her feet. She could feel the exact place where the sputtering agent stood, his weight on the planet. He tasted of fizzy sugar and stale cheezies. All he'd ever wanted was to be the star, to be the one the women flocked to and everyone wanted to meet. His sorcery genes hadn't panned out, so he'd joined USELESS, determined to make a name for himself, but hadn't been able to cut it. Then he got partnered with an agent with a reputation for not always following orders as the gods wanted. He thought everything would turn around when one of the gods had told him to kill her and the four. That he'd have everything he wanted.

Ginny paid no attention to the words spewing from the kid's mouth as she stepped toward him. He aimed his weapon at her. The earth jumped up and ripped the weapon from his hand, swallowing it back in its depths. He tried to step toward her. She opened the earth to swallow his feet and hold him in place, writhing. Then she gently touched his face.

The kid stilled, his skin waxen, his eyes huge and focused on her.

"You're going to go back, and you're going to tell them you were wrong. My friends and I, this town, we're not a threat," she said, both aloud and inside the kid's head. "Nod if you understand me."

The kid nodded like a bobble-head doll.

She slimmed out the anger inside him. "You want to be a good person. You will be a good person. You want to treat people fairly, as you'd like to be treated, and you will make a positive name for yourself because of the good things you do. That's what you want, isn't it?"

Another nod, his eyes a little glassy.

"But you're tired now. You want to sleep."

The kid was barely done nodding before he went limp, and Charlie caught him, lowering him to the ground. The kid softly snored.

The other agent, still on her knees, snorted. "They're right then. You are dangerous." Her gaze flicked over the other three horsewomen. "All of you."

Ginny shook her head, and came to stand before the other woman before she knelt. "No. I don't want to end the world. None of us do." At least, so far as she knew. "The group who wants to do that is a group of Fates in town: Deirdre Boniface, Louise Dole, and Daphne Spinner. If you want to stop someone dangerous, go after them." She nodded to James's team. "You can uncuff her." Then Ginny turned back to the older woman. "You and your partner are going to leave Beckwell, and you aren't going to come back. You're going to deliver our message—that we intend no harm, but we want to be left alone—and then you're going to go after the real threat.

362

Those three Fates."

The female agent's smile was thin as Nahla uncuffed her, and she climbed stiffly to her feet, refusing Ginny's offer of a hand. "You're not going to mess with my mind like you did his?"

Ginny offered back a similarly starved smile. "I think you're smart enough to do what's right."

Then, while James's team helped the agent gather up her snoring partner, Ginny turned back to her friends. To poor Maddox in the midst of them.

She met Nia's eyes. "This isn't the way I want this story to end."

Nia nodded, and held out a hand. "Then let's see if we can do something about it."

Ginny and her friends knelt, Ginny and Nia on one side, Anna and Piper on the other side of Maddox's prone body.

"It's worth a try," Piper side, closing her eyes and laying her hands lightly on the big man's hands.

The rush of ability raced through Ginny's bloodstream, the taste of lemon balm growing stronger on her tongue, twining with fresh spearmint. She closed her eyes, and added her own rush of power. Anna put her hand on Piper's other shoulder.

Eyes closed, it was like a symphony of flavors and colors in Ginny's head as their abilities mingled and solidified together. Then coursed through Maddox. First came spearmint, peeling back the veil of death. Anise and War fought back any resistance. Then came lemon balm, healing his wounds. Finally, Ginny was the batter between all of them, calling Maddox back. Making him remember his love of life, his unending hunger for it.

His eyes opened. He sat bolt upright, and the four women fell back. He looked at them, his eyes narrowed.

"I...owe you all my life?" He lifted his shirt, and while the shirt was wet with blood, his skin was smooth and dark, like it had never been damaged. And very muscly.

"Stop ogling my friend," James said jokingly.

She turned and stepped into his arms, wrapped her arms around him, and pressed her lips to his. "Why would I have to ogle him when you're right here?" she said, her voice husky, and her body thrumming with heat that had nothing to do with her abilities and everything to do with James. "I love you, James Derth."

"And I love you, Ginny Derth." He pressed his lips to hers, and she was drenched in the flavor of dark chocolate and James. All he wanted right now was her. Good. They were on the same page.

Someone cleared their throat.

James pulled back slowly, his blue gaze still locked with hers.

Reluctantly, they turned together to find the female agent again, her partner slung over Caspian's shoulder. "They won't listen to me. You are dangerous."

Ginny sighed and cocked her head, her ability whirling inside her again. She stepped closer to them. "I have a better idea," she said. She leaned down to whisper between the two of them, the weight of her ability in her words, the repetition of the words and the idea behind them in her thoughts and theirs, echoing her words. "You, the other agents, and the gods are going to leave me, my friends, my family, and my town alone." She turned and looked back at James with a small wink. "We are not the danger you're looking for."

"You're not the danger we're looking for," the agent echoed.

"You are so sexy when you talk geek," he said, his voice husky with desire.

She smiled, and looked at James's friends. "I don't suppose you could help see them out of town, hmm?"

"It would be our pleasure," Charlie said with a smile,

somehow speaking for the group. Clearly there'd been some bonding while they're been out playing tag with the agents before.

Then she turned back to James. "I need to undo the damage Thomas caused." Her insides still ached at what she'd had to do, even if it wasn't with regret. It was her fault Thomas existed in the first place, and she'd had to stop him. She still had her memories of him.

She dug her feet into the gravel. With the good memories of him, she'd repair the damage he'd caused.

She closed her eyes, and her feet touching the ground, she could feel the damage. The aching blemishes nearby in the soil and to the natural ecosystem. She let the power uncoil within her and flow outward. Blowing away the salt in the soil and instead replenishing it with nutrients deep within the earth and her ability. The trees regrew, taller and faster than any ever had in nature. The citizens of Beckwell and around the world who'd suddenly felt the panic that there wasn't enough, that they'd have to fight each other for what little there was, knew they had enough. They would be okay. She felt all of their thoughts, their fears, their desires, their flavors. She was connected to the entire planet and all the earth. She was connected to her sisters.

Ginny opened her eyes. Surrounded by her friends, old and new, and with her husband at her side who looked at her with love in his eyes. And she knew she had and was just enough, too.

CHAPTER 37

James surveyed his work. Brilliant. It had turned out quite well. Even if it was surrounded by a soft blanket of fresh snow. He couldn't wait until spring for this. He owed Ginny so much more.

"She's coming!" Bina shouted. She and the rest of his team scrambled to finish up their respective jobs.

They joined him in the driveway of the small white cottage with cherry-red trim just as the loud tinkles of the ice cream truck grew louder, and Roger turned into the driveway. A huge, black ice cream truck with paintings of smiling pigs and grasshoppers eating ice cream on the sides, and a penchant for playing show tunes on the loud-speaker. There were no serving doors or windows, and the license plate read "2HUNGRY." Roger had discovered his ability to transform into this, his most powerful form, shortly after Thomas had been dealt with, and he'd driven Ginny and James home. Modern horses evidently knew how to fit into the modern world.

The children of Beckwell, meanwhile, were going to

develop complexes and a very confused association with sweet treats when they ran out begging for ices and met Roger instead. Especially because Roger seemed to enjoy his show tunes at full volume.

Roger pulled to a stop in front of the cottage. The music stopped, and Ginny stepped out.

"Did I keep her out long enough?" Roger communicated to James eagerly. It was like he and Ginny had a child...of the dirty-minded teenage variety. He transformed back into a black pig in a flicker of the air around him to trot happily after Ginny.

"Just," James communicated back. Somehow, the ability to communicate with the pig hadn't diminished after Ginny had risen as Famine, though perhaps that had more to do with Roger than her.

She, meanwhile, was wearing a purple dress with white polka dots that cinched in at the waist, her black wool coat similarly flaring at the hips, and highlighting her bright pink shoes. And her lipstick, as she cocked her head and gave his team and James a puzzled smile. "What's going on?" she said slowly.

James stepped forward, took her hand, and brought her fingers to his lips for a kiss. "Happy two-week anniversary."

Ginny's breath shuddered out, the look they shared could have singed the cottage's siding. "James?"

"Come inside first. I—or rather we—" he indicated his team, "—have a surprise for you." He gently tugged her inside the cottage.

They walked past his team, which now included Charlie, or rather, Chaz, and who all stood in various states of nervous anticipation near the front stoop. Even Maddox's lips twitched into what could have been mistaken for a smile. Ginny stared so hard she almost tripped over the first step onto the back porch.

James caught her and held the door open for her as

she stepped inside.

The smell of fresh paint still permeated the air, and Ginny, her green eyes sparkling, turned to him with a quizzical smile as she toed off her shoes.

"Go on. I'm not going to ruin the surprise," he said.

She crept cautiously down the hallway while he followed not far behind, though his gaze was firmly on her. On the way she held herself now, shoulders high, accentuating all those delicious curves, the bounce of her red curls on her shoulders. They needed another worship session when their friends left. She approached the corner to the kitchen, then let out a soft gasp. Her hand went to her lips, then her wide-eyed stare pivoted from him, back to the kitchen.

He stepped forward enough that he could see the freshly renovated kitchen. The walls were a cheerful sunshine yellow, cupboards all given a fresh coat of white paint, the size of the kitchen nearly doubled, with the back wall removed and allowing for an extension. It was the two double-oven range cookers in gleaming stainless steel, the double-wide industrial fridge, and deep porcelain farm house sink that really stole the show. That, and the stacks of professional quality cupcake trays with a big red bow.

Ginny turned back to him. "How? When? What?"

He came forward, and pressed a kiss to her nose. "Notice how you've only been allowed back to the house at night the past three days? Only for us to spend the time exclusively in the bedroom. Roger, the girls, and your mum all wanted to help. The team and I have been working around the clock. This is only part one, Ginny." He picked up a large white envelope that lay on the countertop, and held it out to her. "The lease to officially rent the Senior Center kitchen for as long as you like, though you probably have enough room here for most of your operations, at least until expansion. That's up to you.

I just want you to know I fully support your venture into the world of cupcakes and muffins, as does anyone who's ever had the pleasure of tasting one."

She just blinked, stared back at the kitchen, then turned back to him. She wrapped her arms around him, and leaned up to press her lips to his. "*Frosting*, I…I barely know what to say. But I think I do know how to start to thank you," she said huskily.

They shared a lingering kiss, and he regretfully pulled back before they got too carried away. "But that's just part one. Let me show you the rest first."

"The rest? James, you didn't have to do this. Any of it, let alone more. I love you, and you love me. You know that's enough."

He caught both her hands, and squeezed, drawing her close. "A fact for which I am forever grateful, because I love you to distraction. Yes, I did have to do this. This is our two-week anniversary, and I intend for there to be many, many more years of anniversaries ahead for us." His voice grew rough as he considered just how he intended to worship her tonight, and he cleared his throat. That would have to wait. "Come on. Back outside."

They slipped back on their shoes and headed back outside, his team still waiting for them, grinning like idiots. Hell, he wanted to do the same.

The team followed them a distance back as he led Ginny back around the corner of the house. The bright multi-colored flowers of every hue and description formed a cheerful rainbow of color against the snow.

A startled laugh burst from her lips, and she slapped her hand over her lips.

He chuckled, wrapping his arm around her shoulders. "And this is your garden."

"They're plastic."

"Some are silk. But yes, mostly plastic."

"In the snow."

"They don't mind the weather."

She laughed again. "They're lovely, but…why?"

He turned her and took both her hands in his. "Because I wanted to show you that even if you are Famine, if you want a garden, I'll find a way to give you a garden. If you want a cupcake business, I'll help you build it." His voice grew raspier. "Because I don't care who or what anyone else thinks you are, *I* know you're Ginny. The sweetest, sexiest, most remarkable woman I've ever met. My wife. The woman I love."

"Oh," she said, mouth rounding.

"Just 'oh'?" he teased, brushing her lips with his and trying to ignore the tiny tremble of unease. She did like it, didn't she? "Flowers are the more traditional gift."

She pulled back with a smile that lit up her face, and warmed his soul. "Yes. But probably only if you don't already give your wife a new kitchen first. Besides, now my two-week anniversary gift isn't going to seem as impressive."

"Why? What were you planning?" he said, pressing soft kisses along her neck then scooping her up into his arms and heading for the house.

"Well, I wanted a symbol of my mended ways," she said, wrapping her arms around his neck. "No more secrets. No more spying. I was going to give you my stepladder."

James laughed, stepping into the house and kicking the door closed behind him. "Gods, you are perfect."

"No. I'm Famine. And me. And damn proud of it."

COMING SOON...

Must Love Death, Late 2018
Must Love War, Early 2019

In the meanwhile, read the first story in the Sisters of the Apocalypse series,

Must Love Plague

ABOUT THE AUTHOR

Shelly Chalmers' first favorite book was Cinderella, so once she could form letters, naturally she turned to romance where everyone "loved" each other—though mostly because she didn't yet know how to spell "like."

A 2014 Golden Heart® finalist, she has a bachelor's degree in English and French, and has never lost her love of romances and their happily-ever-afters. Her stories run the gamut from Regency shifters to space opera. All include a touch of magic, a sense of humor, and a dab of geek. She makes her home in Western Canada, where when not reading, writing, crafting, or hunting unusual treasures and teapots, she wrangles a husband, two daughters, and two nutball cats.

She loves hearing from readers and chatting! You can find her at:

Website: shellychalmers.com
Email: shellychalmers@scchalmers.com
Twitter: @scchalmers
Facebook:
https://www.facebook.com/ShellyC.Chalmers

Check out her Facebook readers group: The Brazen Librarians. Chat about books, have some fun, and get the inside scoop on works in progress.

Plus, if you'd like to be the first to know about Shelly's new releases, giveaways, and other goings-on, sign up for her newsletter, and get Five Magical Things in your inbox once a month. shellychalmers.com